GHOST MOUNTAIN RANCH

JAN SCARBROUGH

Copyright © 2020 Jan Scarbrough
Scarbrough, Jan
Ghost Mountain Ranch
Media > Books > Fiction > Romance Novels
Category/Tags: romance, contemporary, western, cowboys, mystery, ghost of the
past, radical resistance group

Print ISBN: 978-0-9992474-8-8
1st Print release: July, 2020
2nd Print release: March, 2021

Edited By: Karen Block
Cover Design By: The Killion Group, Inc.

This edition is published by agreement with Saddle Horse Press, LLC, PO Box
221543, Louisville, KY 40252.

GHOST MOUNTAIN RANCH

The Secrets Of The Past Still Haunt The Living...

HANK:
On Christmas Eve, Hank accepts the job of ranch foreman over the mountains in the Gallatin Canyon, Montana. But something dark is happening at the Ghost Mountain Ranch, where the past is reaching out in dangerous ways to haunt the living.

DARBY:
Thirty years ago, Darby Heston fled her family's Montana dude ranch. Now she must return to help her father. Would the boyfriend she'd abandoned still be there? Hank Slade has never stopped loving Darby, but is he willing to risk his heart again? Secrets tore them apart once. Given a second chance at love, will more shocking secrets from the past destroy their hopes for the future?

SLADE:
Slade Heston is spending the summer as a hired hand at his grand-father's dude ranch, trying to figure out life, not fall in love. Laurie Chastain is supposed to write promotions for the ranch, but she has a secret goal. What did a 1970s radical resistance group have to do with her grandfather? Laurie's only clue leads her to Ghost Mountain Ranch. Will their growing attraction be enough to protect Slade and Laurie from the ghosts of the past?

KELSEY:
Kelsey Heston's using the skills learned at her family's Kentucky horse farm to improve tourism at her grandfather's dude ranch.

But what is her old college sweetheart doing here? Max Lee has come to Ghost Mountain Ranch searching for a missing woman. Instead, he finds Kelsey. But old secrets are stirring, secrets someone might be willing to kill to keep. Can they finally lay the old ghosts to rest, or will the echoes of a decades-old murder destroy their second chance at love?

HANK

CHAPTER ONE

Six Buckles Guest Ranch
December 2018

HANK SLADE RESTED a forearm on his saddle horn and leaned against it. He peered through the ears of his horse across the valley shrouded in a mantle of snow that stretched out below him. Sagebrush, still smelling pungent and sweet despite the weather, poked through the otherwise unbroken, white landscape. Warmer air from the creek-fed lake generated a ghostly haze in the valley so that the ranch cabins, lodge, and outbuildings appeared cloaked, as if hiding from the world.

Just like Hank wanted to do—hide—or, better yet, run away.

That morning, after plowing the snow from the gravel road to the county highway, he'd ridden up the cleared road behind the lodge on his favorite horse simply to get away. He was a cowboy and wrangler, a stock man who had tended the Dawson cattle and then dude ranch horses for almost twenty-five years. Trouble was, he had nowhere else to go. No real place of his own. No living family. The ranch was his only home and the Dawsons his only family ever since the patriarch Jim Dawson had given him a job when he was thirty and fresh out of the army.

The first Mrs. Dawson had been alive then. Bonnie was the mother of the oldest child Ben. She'd embodied everything a good wife and mother should be, but, as in many things beautiful and perfect, death took her early, throwing the ranch—its real family and extended family—into a tailspin of grief and despair.

But it wasn't long before Liz came into everyone's lives. Poor Jim had not known what had hit him, falling hard for a divorced mother with baggage—a ten-year-old son named Brody Caldera. Jim had been riddled with guilt at first, and probably for years after their wedding. Ben had resented a new stepmother, particularly one as young and beautiful as Liz, so soon after his mother's death. But things have a way of happening for a reason. Baby Mercer was the unexpected cause of a happy marriage that lasted until Jim's untimely death from a riding accident almost two years earlier.

But if things happen for a reason, why do bad things happen to good people?

That was a question Hank could not answer. He was merely a wrangler, not a philosopher or theologian. He dealt with the everyday care of living creatures. He handled routine. Day in and day out, he fed and watered stock, tended hooves and fresh cuts, brushed manes and tails, cleaned and fixed saddles and bridles, mucked stalls, and in the summer saddled horses for city dudes and guided them into the mountains so they could enjoy the beauty of Montana.

His life was simple. His only pleasure, his guitar and a few songs around the summer campfire. He enjoyed the accolades of the ranch guests. He enjoyed helping them mount a steady quarter horse and laughed with them when they dismounted, sore from using muscles never exercised when sitting behind a computer screen. And he loved the Dawsons—from watching the older children grow, to teaching Mercer to ride and rope, to showing Livy— Brody and Stef's daughter—how to care for her new pony. He'd lived through the tragedy of Bonnie's and then Jim's deaths. The Dawsons' happiness was his happiness. Their sadness, his.

He just didn't know how he could live through Liz's remarriage.

Earlier in September

HANK HAD BEEN at the corral when the new dude arrived. Livy had told him his name— Charles Kingston, nicknamed Chaz, some sort of Hollywood mogul. Stef and her friend Leigh had something up their sleeves where this guy was concerned. Something about Stef's novel *Under Montana Stars* and making the eBook into a TV movie. They'd invited the guy to the ranch for two weeks, and because it was the end of the season, he was the only guest.

Hank had glanced up when the dude approached the corral. "Can I help you?"

The guy had nodded. "Liz will be down in a minute. She's taking me on another trail ride."

"I bet." Hank couldn't avoid giving a sarcastic laugh. He'd seen the two of them together earlier that morning, and he didn't like it one bit.

"Excuse me?"

Hank's anger had spiked. He strode over to the fence and glared at the man, wanting to punch the guy so badly his own jaws ached. But this Chaz guy was a guest and Hank was simply an employee. He knew his place in the grand scheme of things. And his place didn't call for him to be rude.

But it'd been damn hard to restrain himself.

"I said, 'I bet.'"

Chaz suddenly looked alarmed. "What do you mean by that?"

"I mean I saw you and Liz coming out of her cabin early this morning."

"Oh?" The man had the nerve to look innocent.

"Don't you go hurting Liz."

"I don't plan to."

"Coming out of her cabin tells me you have other plans."

Chaz shook his head. *Now* he looked angry. "You have no idea about my plans, which, even if you did know, are none of your damn business."

Hank had grasped the railing with a white-knuckle grip. Hell! If this guy gave him the smallest opening, he *would* pop him right in the mouth. "You're on our turf now, mister. There are a lot of people on this ranch who watch out for Liz, especially since she lost her husband. We don't take kindly to folks who disrespect her."

"Trust me. I respect Liz."

"Then keep the hell away from her."

"Or...?"

Hank had lowered his challenging stare. He was close to crossing a barrier by threatening a guest. "Just do it, if you know what's good for you."

Spinning on his heel, Hank had tramped toward the barn. He should have slugged the guy right then and there. Instead, his common sense got the better of him. He'd retreated as he'd done most of his life.

HANK PULLED the brim of his hat farther down to shade his eyes from the sun. God, how he loved this country. Last night's snow and cloudy sky had given way to a cloudless blue one. Even the haze veiling the lake couldn't interfere with the glory of the day—a brilliant Big Sky Country sort of day. Hank settled himself in the saddle, turned his horse's head, and moved back down the road at a leisurely walk. No hurry. Chores weren't going anywhere.

Not like Liz. Chaz had swept her off her feet so fast as to be almost indecent. Their engagement had shocked everyone. Most of all him. But what had made Hank think things would be different?

Liz was the boss lady. He was the hired help. He was too proud to cross those boundaries.

Liz and Chaz had gone to Las Vegas at the end of November to get one of those quickie weddings. Then they'd honeymooned in Hawaii, because Liz had never been there. They were still honeymooning, for all Hank knew. He tried to avoid the lodge and the big house. Just wasn't the same with Liz gone.

"Cowboy up!" he told himself in an angry huff. It's not as if losing a woman hadn't happened to him before.

He'd loved Darby York once just like he loved Liz Dawson now. From afar. Silently. He'd been younger then. Too young to know his mind. Too thickheaded to admit Darby turned his gut into mush. She'd been the ranch owner's daughter. He, the orphaned son of the ranch wrangler. They'd been friends in high school. Hung out together. Even went out for a while. But after her mom died, Darby wanted to get away from home. She'd argued with her dad and run off. Later, he heard she'd married a guy from Kentucky. That's when Hank had joined the army, a pretty unsatisfactory way to nurse a broken heart. He'd never gone back to the Ghost Mountain Ranch in the Gallatin River canyon.

So, Hank shouldn't be surprised by his track record with women, or lack thereof. He shouldn't feel sorry for himself either. He'd keep on as always, doing what he loved to do. Wasn't that the way life worked?

Kicking the horse into a lope, Hank headed toward the barn. The chilly wind against his face felt good, as if its sting could clear his mind and drive away his perpetual sadness.

CHAPTER TWO

NEW TO THE DAWSON RANCH, Ashleigh Kingston still delighted in the frigid weather as she crunched through the snow. She was a California girl, daughter of Charles Kingston and Adrianne Wade, celebrated TV reality star. Her two half-sisters, twins Alena and Amalee, shared their mother's show. They were famous, their opinions sought after, their fashion sense copied, and their every action blogged and Tweeted about.

At fifteen, Ashleigh had made the decision to leave that world behind. Oh, her mother had been furious. Still was. Adrianne had wanted to promote Ashleigh as part of the show when she turned sixteen. She wanted her daughter to become the next big fashion and reality star. But thank goodness, Stef and Brody's daughter Livy had reached out to Ashleigh via her Internet blog and dared her to take the *No Makeup Challenge*. Intrigued after discovering Livy's mom had written the eBook she'd just read, Ashleigh had connected with Livy through email, forming a long-distance friendship until that day in September when Ashleigh had seen the Six Buckles Guest Ranch for the first time.

Her dad had been visiting the ranch. Ashleigh never saw enough of her dad and had been anxious to reconnect with him. By that time, Mrs. Dawson and her dad *had* connected—literally. They'd become a couple. And now they were married. Long story short, Ashleigh had turned sixteen in October and resolved she wanted nothing to do with her mother's reality show but wanted everything to do with being a normal American teenager.

However, it had been hard—harder than Ashleigh had realized it would be.

Oh, she'd given the family a brave speech back in September.

"So many times, we lose sight of who we really are," she had said. "At least I did. I've been hiding behind a mask of makeup since I was twelve. We become comfortable showing only the face we believe society thinks is acceptable or says is beautiful, and we forget to be our own person."

And she'd believed it then. But now, she wasn't so sure.

Who was she really? Without the trappings of glamor and makeup, who was Ashleigh Kingston?

The kids at her new county high school surely weren't impressed by her almost stardom. The few girls in her small class were downright mean, ignoring her on purpose because they were probably jealous. The boys, for the most part, had no clue who she was—or had almost been. Their attention was on rodeo sports or football or working on a ranch. Except for Livy Caldera, who went to the middle school, not the high school, Ashleigh had found herself without friends and certainly without boyfriends.

Livy was twelve, but wise for her age—an old soul. She'd encouraged Ashleigh to make a clean break with the past and her mother's dreams for her future. At the time when she'd moved to Montana, Ashleigh had deleted her blog. She'd limited her online presence with a new Twitter account where she merely followed people, never Tweeted. Her Snapchat and Instagram accounts were the same way—restricted to information gathering, not broadcasting her latest actions, fashions, or opinions.

In a way it was refreshing not being out there. Not airing her life to the curious masses. But it was weird in a way. A big way.

What was left of her life then? How did she get along without the trappings of popularity and success?

With a horse. Livy had said a horse solved every problem. A horse could be your best friend or your worst enemy. He was a challenge and a pleasure. When all else failed, a horse was there to listen to your problems. He didn't care what they were as long as you gave him a few peppermints or carrots and brushed his coat and picked his hooves.

Funny how life turned out. Ashleigh was beginning to understand what Livy meant.

Entering the big barn, she adjusted her eyes to the shadows. The enclosure smelled like horses—earthy and basic. But it was cold. Almost as cold as the outdoors even with the body heat from the horses. Ashleigh didn't mind. She was dressed for the weather, all decked out in her new winter gear, so layered that she felt like the little brother in *A Christmas Story*.

Hank was there, in the gloom, taking a saddle off a horse. She liked the old wrangler. He was kind and always helpful. He never laughed at her awkwardness around Champ, the spotted horse her new stepmother Liz had given her.

"Hey, Hank."

"Hey, kid." He turned to give her a smile. "Don't you have school today?"

"It's winter break, and it's Saturday anyway," she said with a laugh. "I'm on my own. Stef took Livy up to Bozeman for some last-minute Christmas shopping."

"You *are* on your own. I'm sorry."

Ashleigh shrugged. "I'm used to it."

And she was. Back in her former life, her mom and sisters left her all the time. She'd seen more of her dad since she'd been living at the ranch.

Hank gave her a look—one of pity and understanding. He was a loner. She'd noticed that about him. In a way, she felt like the old cowboy. She was happier alone. Her world had been blogs and social media, nothing but an electronic connection to her *friends*. Now she was learning to live with herself without electronics. Or trying to.

"I thought I'd groom Champ," she said.

Hank grinned. "He'll love the attention." He turned and went into the small barn office, never offering to help.

Ashleigh watched him a moment, realizing he was showing confidence in her and her newfound horsemanship abilities. She hid a smile and got to work. Ashleigh found the bucket of grooming supplies Livy kept in the tack room and carried it to Champ's stall, putting it down outside the stall door.

Ashleigh didn't know how most of the ranch horses, left to graze in outdoor pastures, survived during the winter. There were over one hundred of them, kept for summer guests to ride. She'd been told Ben and Hank checked on the horses and left them big mounds of hay, but mostly the Dawson's riding herd lived outside free as the wind.

"Like horses should live," Livy had said. "Keeps them healthy and sound."

A few of the personal riding horses, like Champ and Livy's Duke, were kept in the barn. Ashleigh was glad. She didn't want Champ left out in the snow, no matter how good it was supposed to be for him.

After hooking Champ's halter into the cross-ties as Hank had shown her how to do, Ashleigh stroked the gelding's thick neck. He blew a frosty breath and nuzzled her for a treat.

"When I'm finished brushing," she told the spoiled horse.

Today she'd brought an apple, cut into pieces so the juice wouldn't drip onto her gloves when Champ ate it. She'd learned that lesson the first time she'd given the horse a whole, juicy apple. He had bitten into it, dropping gooey juice on her gloves.

Concentrating on the first step in the grooming process, Ashleigh moved the currycomb around and around the horse's brown and white spotted hide. How could Champ gather so much dirt simply standing in a stall?

A few moments later, a truck pulled up outside. Doors opened and slammed shut. She glanced up to see Hank come out of the office to meet the newcomers. Because it had nothing to do with her, she continued her task. The circular motion of the currying process soothed her.

"Hello, beautiful."

Ashleigh's head jerked up. A young cowboy standing outside the stall winked at her. He had appeared like a ghost from an old-time Western movie. He was tall and muscular with dimples that made his smile seem charming. When he tipped his hat to her, Ashleigh squared her shoulders and turned back to the horse. "Do I know you?"

"Nelson Blake at your service, ma'am."

His voice had an *aw-shucks* quality that she didn't trust. She glanced at him again and recognized him as a boy she'd seen around school.

"As I said, do I know you, Mr. Blake?"

He removed his hat and held it loosely between his fingers. "We're in the same English class. And third period calculus."

Ashleigh couldn't help but grimace. She hated math. It was her worst subject and made absolutely no sense to her.

"And what are you doing here, Mr. Blake?"

"Mr. Blake is my dad," he corrected her in a now low and suddenly seductive voice. "My name is Nelson."

"Well, Nelson, what are you doing here?"

"My dad has business with Brody. Hank went along with him to find Brody while I came to look for you."

Ashleigh gave the boy a skeptical look as if to ask *whatever for?* He stepped forward, almost entering the stall. There was a compelling presence about him. He had an all-male aura—strong and athletic.

Ashleigh connected with the sultry gaze he gave her—with the invitation in his eyes. She'd seen such come-on looks in the past and knew enough to ignore them. But this blatant request threw her. It was so unexpected, especially here. What's more, she didn't anticipate the spark of excitement that shot through her.

She lowered her eyelashes in hopes of covering her confusion. "Why do you want to see me?"

"Everyone at school is talking about you."

"Can't convince me of that." Was he was simply flirting? "Most everyone has been pretty standoffish."

He hung his hat on a convenient nail, freeing his hands, and took another step forward. He caught the halter, moving nearer to the horse and where she stood beside its shoulder.

"That's the way we are out here," he said. "Newcomers, who aren't dudes, are rare. It takes us a while to warm up to people. Besides, everyone says you're famous."

Oh, that. It wasn't about her. It was about her mother and half-sisters.

She turned away from him in disgust. "I suppose you think I'm famous too."

"I don't know. I'm just a cowboy, ma'am. All I know is you're downright pretty."

Out of the corner of her eye, she saw him grin. "I bet you say that to all the girls."

"Only when it's the honest truth."

Was this guy for real? His shy, self-effacing, seemingly simple manner, didn't mix well with the other vibes he gave off. She glanced at him again. He smiled. She smiled.

"I've never met a girl like you." He stepped nearer. "You're sophisticated, classy, not like the local girls."

Ashleigh licked her lower lip. This guy was making her nervous. But in a good way. A strangely flattering way. Suddenly, he touched her left hand that held the currycomb. He took it from her and dropped it into the straw at their feet. Capturing her gloved hands, he pulled her toward him.

What was going on? Her pulse jumped. His actions were surprising, but not unwelcome. His blue eyes sparkled, announcing his intentions, and she didn't fight him.

Slowly, he lowered his mouth to hers and kissed her softly, parting her lips and then deepening the kiss. Her whole world spun in a cavalcade of colors. Oddly, she'd never been kissed—sweet sixteen and never been kissed. Alena and Amalee would be appalled if they knew the truth.

And not so oddly, she found she enjoyed it. It was a dream come true in the most unlikely place—the stall of a horse barn—for Adrianne Wade's youngest daughter to experience her first kiss from a true Western cowboy.

After a few heart-stopping seconds, Nelson lifted his head and then focused on her. She blinked up at him and licked her lower lip once again.

"Come with me to a Christmas dance," he whispered. "Monday night. In town. Say you'll come."

She was breathless. "Yes!"

"Great! I'll show you a good time."

She nodded.

"Pick you up at eight."

Nelson backed away and picked up his hat, setting it firmly on his head. He gave her a wink, spun on his booted heel, and strode out of the barn.

Truly and utterly amazed, Ashleigh stared after him.

CHAPTER THREE

"I wouldn't trust Nelson Blake."

Ashleigh was startled by a low, husky male voice directly behind her. She whirled around from grooming Champ to see another teenage boy taking the place Nelson had just vacated by the stall door. Bundled in a Sherpa-lined jacket that had seen better days, he wasn't ruggedly handsome like Nelson and didn't wear a cowboy hat. His jaw was covered in a light stubble, but Ashleigh noticed traces of acne blemishes scaring his complexion.

What was this? Her day to be waylaid by mysterious boys?

She used her best haughty manner as a comeback. "I beg your pardon?"

"Nelson has a reputation for playing fast and loose with his words *and* his women."

"You make it sound as if I'm one of his women." Ashleigh didn't like this new guy and his presumptive accusation. It was as if he'd glimpsed her inner thoughts. And that bothered her. She'd hardly had time to admit to herself the twinge of attraction she'd felt for Nelson Blake.

"Most girls fall for him." The boy brushed a lock of black hair from his eyes. "He's a smooth operator."

"I'm not most girls," she said in her own defense.

"I saw what I saw."

Now she was really affronted. He'd seen them kiss. "You seem to know a lot about him."

The new guy shrugged. "I understand he's trying to get into your pants."

A sharp stab of guilt rocked Ashleigh. She'd known what Nelson wanted, but to hear the words spoken made it sound ugly.

"Now that is rude."

"Sorry," he said with another shrug. "I call them as I see them."

"Why are you here? Who are you anyway?"

"My name is Josh Adams, and I live here in the bunk house with Hank."

"Really? I've never seen you."

"I like to keep a low profile."

Ashleigh looked askance. "You must." She turned her back on him. She picked up a hard brush from the bucket and ran it down Champ's back.

A minute ticked by. She'd given him a cold shoulder, but the boy didn't get the message and leave. Instead, he stood at the door to the stall staring at her.

She tucked a strand of hair under her slouched hat out of her eyes and turned back to glare at him. "What?"

"I heard you singing to Champ. You have a pretty voice."

Now she was really creeped out. She hadn't realized she'd sung as she worked. How long had he been spying on her?

"Champ is the first horse Hank lets people ride," Josh said, continuing to talk as if in a conversation. "He's an old gelding and knows how to take care of beginners. Like you."

Another reminder she was out of her element even though she'd chosen to live in Montana. Is that why she had knots in her stomach much of the time? Was she that scared of her new environment? She would never admit it to her dad and she'd never tell Livy who'd grown up on the ranch. They'd both laugh at her. Her dad would tell her new experiences were good for her. Livy would just admonish her to *cowboy up*. Even girls needed to *cowboy up*, to gather what pluck and nerve they possessed to make it today's world, Livy always said.

That's why Nelson's kiss had been flattering. Even though Ashleigh hadn't realized it earlier, she'd been anxious about how kids treated her at school. The kiss meant she was making headway. And that was a good thing. What wasn't so good was this Josh guy's off-handed praise of her singing. She kept that part of herself to herself, because music had been her only comfort during the hard times of her life.

"So, if you live here at the Dawson Ranch, why haven't I ever seen you here?" Ashleigh asked. "Or seen you at school?"

"Maybe because your head is in the clouds?"

Ashleigh scowled at him. That was downright cruel.

"I don't mean it in a bad way," John hurried to explain. "You're different from most kids around here. You don't think you're better than anyone else. In fact, you're nicer than most of the stuck-up county girls, and you have a wide-ranging view of life that they don't have."

"Thanks, I guess."

"It's true," he said. "I've watched you in school. We have classes together. You try to be friendly, but most of the girls snub you."

They surveyed each other for a beat.

"You didn't tell me how you heard me singing."

Josh jerked his chin upward toward the hay loft. "When I finish my chores, I sit up there and read books."

Now this was new. A guy who read books. "You don't play computer games?"

"Nope. I don't own electronic stuff."

"A purist? That's strange these days."

He grinned at her then. "Yep. I'm old-school, partially because my mom never had the money for stuff like that and my dad was always away."

Ashleigh was interested in people. The fact this guy didn't come onto her was fascinating in itself, but his honesty was something else out of the ordinary. He didn't seem like a guy who played games, and after coming from a life of constant game-playing, Ashleigh could appreciate that.

"You don't mean to tell me you actually read real books?"

"Yep." He nodded, now looking bashful. "I pick them up at the library."

"You're a throwback," she said and gave Champ a pat. Dropping the hard brush in the bucket, she prepared to leave the stall.

"You're not done until you pick his hooves," Josh reminded. "It's the single most important thing you can do for his hooves."

She'd forgotten. "Oh, yeah."

"Let me help with that."

Josh came into the stall, crowding her like Nelson had done earlier but didn't make a move on her. Ashleigh stepped back to watch him work. He chose a hoof pick from the bucket and moved to the rear of the horse. With quick efficiency, he ran his hand down the inside of the hind leg, causing Champ to lift it. Then resting the hoof on his knee, Josh scraped out the dirt, cleaning around the area were the hoof sole met the hoof wall.

After three more hooves, he stood up and turned around. "All done."

"You look like you know what you're doing."

"Should." He came out of the stall, dropped the hoof pick into the bucket, and shut the door.

"It's all new to me."

"You'll learn." His smile said he had confidence in her.

More confidence than she often had in herself, Ashleigh figured. Watching him from under her eyelashes, she returned his smile shyly.

Blushing, Josh looked away. He was a strange kid, this Josh Adams, truly a throwback as she'd said. Ashleigh was used to guys like Nelson. They were familiar. She knew how to handle them, in a way. She'd seen her sisters do it, and if she hadn't wanted to be kissed, she was pretty sure she could have stopped him.

Josh carried the grooming tools for her. They walked together toward the tack room.

"You haven't told me why you live with Hank," she said, making conversation. "I didn't think he was married."

"He isn't. It's just a place to stay until I graduate high school."

"Okay." That really didn't explain much.

He seemed to know he hadn't satisfied her curiosity. Turning, he faced her. "Story isn't pretty. My mom remarried and didn't want me hanging around. I'm eighteen already—my birthday's in late November—but I don't graduate until June."

"Happy birthday," Ashleigh said, finding herself able to relate to his situation. There were times when both her mother and her father hadn't wanted her around. "Where's your dad?"

"He's in the army. He's deployed. I don't need a guardian anymore, but I do need a place to stay before I can enter the service. Brody and Stef were nice enough to let me stay here."

"Seems like the Dawson family takes everyone in," she said. "Look at the way they accepted me and my dad."

Josh nodded. "The Dawsons are good people." He paused, surveying her thoughtfully. "Care for hot chocolate? Hank keeps a one-cup coffee maker in the office. He has some hot chocolate cups to put in it."

"I'd welcome some, actually."

Josh grinned. He had a nice, friendly grin. He seemed incredibly young and vulnerable. And that's how she felt much of the time.

CHAPTER FOUR

AFTER GROOMING Champ and encountering two boys in two different ways, Ashleigh trudged back to the big house, her head spinning as she relived the afternoon's events. Was Josh right? Should she be cautious around Nelson Blake? But she'd been flattered by the older boy's kiss, by the attention he'd paid to her, and by the prospect of going to a dance with him. It was all very thrilling and grown up.

Something within compelled her to seek out the excitement of going to a dance with Nelson. There was a bit of danger in it. Adventure. Maybe she was her mother's daughter after all.

The Dawsons called the huge log cabin by the lake the *big house* to distinguish it from the original ranch house built by Jim for his first wife Bonnie. After her death and Jim's remarriage to Liz, he had built a five-bedroom house that Brody now lived in with his family. Brody was Liz's son and a champion bull rider. Their daughter Livy was Ashleigh's best friend. Her only friend.

Ironic, wasn't it? She had plenty of friends back in California— or people who claimed to be her friends. Ashleigh wasn't so sure anymore if that were true. Most of her life had been spent being lonely. The pseudo friends had never been there for her, not like

Livy, a twelve-year-old who understood her better than she understood herself.

When she had arrived in Montana, Livy had asked her to live in the big house. After all, the two-bedroom cabin where Liz now lived and shared with Ashleigh's father Chaz would be crowded. And who wanted to live that near to a pair of newlyweds anyway? Livy had made a face. Too much kissing and handholding and other things going on. Ashleigh had agreed—and quickly too. The thought of her dad as a sexual being was a bit too gross and way too much information.

But Livy had also seemed to understand her loneliness. Sometimes Ashleigh thought that was the real reason Livy wanted her to be nearby—just down the hall in Brody's old room.

Ashleigh quickened her steps as she neared the cabin. Livy and her mother were already home.

"Hey, Ash!" Livy called as she pulled packages from the back seat of a SUV marked with a *Six Buckles Guest Ranch* sign.

"Hey, yourself." Ashleigh stepped up behind her friend. "Need help?"

"Yep, but don't peek! Your present is in there somewhere."

Ashleigh hid a smile. "I wouldn't think of looking." Livy took Christmas so seriously. Her new cousin had so much fun with it.

Once she and Livy had tried to figure out their relationship now that Livy's grandmother had married Ashleigh's father. Although they were related *by marriage*, they had thought it would be fun to officially find out how. After using a search engine, they'd discovered a *Table of Consanguinity*, but that information had only confused them more. Finally, they'd agreed to simply call themselves *cousins* and forget anything formal.

"Mom has taken the baby into the house." Livy pulled a frown. "Charlotte was grumpy the whole day. Mom told me to get all the packages."

"Well, I can help."

And there were a lot of store bags. Had Livy and her mother

bought out the whole town of Bozeman? Ashleigh couldn't figure out the allure of shopping. Her mom and sisters loved it. They were used to going into shops on Rodeo Drive in Beverly Hills and being recognized for their celebrity. She hated that. Shopping online was fine with her. Once she discovered the Six Buckles Ranch was not the end of the world and UPS and FedEx still delivered, Ashleigh had done her Christmas shopping on Amazon.

Ranger, Livy's black and white border collie, met them at the front door. He was getting on in years and liked to stay indoors. As Livy and Ashleigh carried bags down the hallway to Livy's room, Ranger trailed behind them, his toenails clicking on the wooden floors.

"Dump these on my bed and get out," Livy ordered. "You can't see what I bought."

"Geez." Ashleigh rolled her eyes. "You're not like my mom. Adrianne would be spreading everything out on the bed for me to see, and then she'd parade all her new clothes around the room asking for my opinion."

"Well, these things are *not* for me," Livy said. "They're Christmas surprises. Some of them are Mom's."

Ashleigh shrugged. "Okay, then. If I have to leave, I guess you won't get to hear about my date tomorrow night."

That got Livy's attention.

"Date?" Her voice elevated with surprise and delight. "What date?"

Ashleigh shrugged again, giving off the appearance of nonchalance. "Oh, some boy from school. His dad was here to see Brody. He stopped by the barn where I was grooming Champ and talked to me."

"Tell me!" Livy shoved aside the pile of packages from where she'd dropped them on her bed and plopped down in the empty space, sitting crisscross. "Don't keep this from me!"

Livy's enthusiasm was exactly what Ashleigh loved about her friend. If Livy was ever angry or unhappy, her emotions didn't last long. And Livy didn't seem to second guess herself. Not like Ashleigh. Maybe it was Ashleigh's upbringing, or lack thereof. Maybe it was because she'd basically raised herself. Whatever it was, Ashleigh often found herself moody. Introspective. Too serious by half. That's why Livy was good for her. Her Yin to Livy's Yang.

"It's quite simple, actually," Ashleigh said. "Nelson rode to the ranch with his father and then came into the barn just to see me."

Livy blew out a breath that sounded like a whistle. "Whew! Nelson Blake? The high school quarterback?"

"I don't know. He says we have classes together, but I sit up front and have never met him."

"Wow, you go, girl!" Livy bobbed with excitement. "He's a knockout. Every girl in high school wants to date Nelson Blake."

That bit of information thrilled Ashleigh. Maybe she was finally making a breakthrough with the kids at school. Then she recalled Josh's dire warning and narrowed her eyes.

"Do you know Josh Adams?"

"Sure." Livy cocked her head, questioning. "He lives on the ranch and stays with Hank."

Ashleigh lifted her chin in disdain. "Well, Mr. Adams doesn't think much of Nelson."

"Figures," Livy concurred. "I hear the two had a run-in over a girl last year."

Livy was a fabulous source of information, and her comment gave Ashleigh the confidence to go forward with the date. Josh could simply be a sore loser. She need not fret about Nelson.

Livy looked suddenly worried. "Do you think Brody will let you go?"

"He's not my parent," Ashleigh stated flatly. "I can do what I want."

Ashleigh could tell her answer troubled Livy, but she didn't care. She was determined to go on this date.

"Shouldn't you ask your dad?"

Shifting her weight to another foot, Ashleigh scowled. "Chaz is on his honeymoon. I don't want to bother him with this. Besides, he doesn't care what I do."

"Oh." Livy rubbed her nose with the back of her hand and looked thoughtfully at her. "I suppose you'll need to figure out what you're going to wear."

Ashleigh panicked at the thought. "Crap! I don't have anything new and maybe nothing suitable."

Where were her shopaholic sisters when she needed them?

"When I finish hiding my gifts, I'll help you look through your closet," Livy offered.

"You're the best!" Ashleigh fled next door to begin the search process for the perfect outfit.

CHAPTER FIVE

LATE MONDAY AFTERNOON, Hank sat behind the office desk in the barn. Over the last year, Brody had given more responsibility to Hank. It was now his job to keep track of the feed and vet bills and any other expense incurred by the horses on the dude ranch. Not that Hank didn't appreciate Brody's vote of confidence but sometimes he'd rather be out doing the physical work of tending horses instead of hunkered over a bunch of paperwork.

Josh found him there. Hank liked the Adams kid. Reminded him of the boy he used to be, except for the reading thing. School work had never been Hank's gift. It had been a no-brainer for him to go into the army after what happened with Darby, losing her like he did. He'd needed to get away from ranch life and home—or his lack of home. His parents had been gone a few years. He had no family. Leo York, Darby's father, had been kind enough to take him in at his ranch over in Gallatin Canyon. Maybe that's why Hank didn't mind giving Josh a break. He'd been given one himself years ago.

The kid shrugged off his coat, placing it on an empty chair, and tossed his battered cowboy hat on top of it. He made himself a hot chocolate and stood by the window drinking it, staring out into the approaching dusk of the December day.

Hank looked up from the row of figures and furrowed his brow. Something about the tension in Josh's stance told him the boy was troubled.

"Something eatin' on you, kid?" Hank asked.

Josh glanced back quickly, almost as if he couldn't believe Hank's perception. Hank lay down his pencil and pushed back from the desk, rocking back in the office chair. He must have hit the spot. The boy wasn't much of a talker. His head was too much in the clouds—or his books. Hank had his doubts Josh would make a good soldier, but the kid wanted to follow in his father's foot-steps. Who was he to deny him that opportunity?

Josh let out a deep breath. "I'm worried about Ashleigh."

Now there was an admission. Hank wasn't aware the two teens had much contact. He'd never seen them together around the place.

"Ashleigh Kingston?"

Of course, it was Ashleigh Kingston. There weren't many Ashleigh's around. She was Liz's new stepdaughter. A cute girl. Livy's friend.

"Yup." Josh looked down at his boots.

"Out with it then. I've got this damn paperwork to finish."

Josh glanced up. "She's going on a date."

"So?"

"With Nelson Blake."

Hank blew a concerned whistle. He had even heard about Nelson Blake's reputation. The information made him sit up straighter.

"When is this date?" Hank asked.

"Tonight. In an hour." Josh moved his coat and hat and sat on the edge of the chair. "Livy says they're going to a dance in town. Livy's all excited about it."

"Does Brody know?"

"Livy says yes but won't stop her. Ashleigh told him her father wouldn't mind." Josh ran his fingers through his already tousled hair. "Livy says Brody doesn't think it's his place to interfere since he doesn't know what Chaz would say or do."

Hank chewed his lower lip thoughtfully. "Everyone around here is intimidated by that Hollywood guy," he grumbled. "If she were my daughter, I wouldn't let her go to a school dance with that boy."

"But that's just it. There aren't any school dances this time of year," Josh pointed out.

"Where are they going then?"

Josh shook his head. "I don't know. Maybe to a bar in town. That's my best guess."

Hank studied his young bunkmate. From the fervor on Josh's face, it seemed he had a plan. "What do you think we should do?"

"If I had a car and a driver's license, I'd follow them to make sure she gets home okay."

Hank gave an imperceptible smile. A boy after his own heart. "I have a truck. You can ride with me."

"You'd do this for me, Hank?"

"Of course, kid. Keeping the girl out of trouble is a no-brainer."

But it was more than that. Hank would do anything for Liz, including protecting her new stepdaughter.

THE NIGGLING REGRET began to eat at Ashleigh the moment she climbed into Nelson's Ford pickup, and he slammed the door behind her. Her concern grew as they drove under the Six Buckles Guest Ranch sign and left ranch property. The road to the main highway was winding and dark. The Absaroka mountain range on the east and the Gallatin Range on the west flanked the road. Somewhere in the darkness, the Yellowstone River flowed through the Paradise Valley, working its way north and then eastward out of Montana and into North Dakota, where it eventually joined the Missouri River.

Ashleigh had smiled shyly across the seat at Nelson, who kept up a string of aimless conversation. The console lights reflected the animation on his face. He seemed older than she remembered from their short conversation. Maybe knowing he was a football player, a big man on campus, had changed her impression of their first meeting.

Or maybe being alone with a strange boy, almost man, was doing the trick.

The road to Livingston had seemed long, as if they'd never make it to town. She should have asked for more information, because they were more than half way there when she found out this wasn't a school dance as she had assumed. They were going to meet Nelson's friends at a bar. She was only sixteen, and as far as she knew, so was Nelson. Maybe he was seventeen, but that didn't mean he could get into a bar legally. He'd laughed when she'd mentioned it.

"We do this all the time," he'd said. "They don't care."

Ashleigh slapped herself mentally, remembering her older sisters had never been bothered by the inconvenience of being a minor. From the time they were her age, they'd been in bars and places where grownups wined and dined. But the excitement of Saturday afternoon and Livy's contagious enthusiasm dissipated along that long, dark highway. She knew her dad Chaz would never allow this escapade. If he found out, she'd be in big trouble.

The Wild Horse Saloon was more of a honky-tonk than any reputable dining place Ashleigh had ever been. It had seen better days, that's for sure. The jukebox music was loud, the floors dark and sticky with spilt beer or whatever, and the lights dim. Thank goodness political correctness didn't allow for smoking inside. She envisioned old-time cowboy movies with a layer of cigarette smoke hanging low over the card sharks and skimpy-clad dancing girls. At least, she didn't have to deal with that.

What she had to deal with was being ogled by two of Nelson's male friends. Their girlfriends gave her an evil-eye stare too, as if she were some sort of rival. That was a joke, but at the moment

Ashleigh wasn't laughing, even to herself. Her nervous stomach made her physically sick. She smiled at the four others, but with the blaring country music so loud, she couldn't hear anything they said. It was almost as if she was wrapped in her own private cocoon, insulated from what was actually going on around her.

"Want something to drink?" Nelson shouted in her ear.

"Sure. How about a soft drink? A Coke, maybe."

"C'mon, Ashleigh, how about a beer?"

"I don't like beer," she replied.

"C'mon, girl. We're out to have fun."

"Nelson, I just want a Coke." She said it as firmly as she could.

"Okay, okay. Suit yourself."

Nelson left her sitting at the table with the two other girls as the three guys went up to the bar for drinks. She felt overdressed next to them with her tight blue jeans, denim shirt, and boots. The other girls wore denim short-shorts, frayed and cut up to their crotches, and skin-showing tank tops. Ashleigh gave them a weak smile. They glanced at each other, almost laughing at some sort of inside joke between them.

"Do you know where the bathroom is?" she hollered at the girls.

"Over there." One of them indicated its location with a toss of her head toward a side door marked "Restrooms."

"Excuse me, please?"

They stifled their laughter as Ashleigh left the table. She was so out of her element. So alone. That shouldn't bother her, she told herself, as she shut and locked the bathroom door. It had one toilet and a white sink with a mirror over it. Washing her hands, Ashleigh stared at herself in the foggy, cracked mirror. Her carefully applied makeup looked false. Livy had agreed using cosmetics wouldn't hurt for something as special as a first date. But after taking the *No Makeup Challenge*, it had seemed strange to cover her face with it again.

This wasn't her—trying to act older than sixteen, her face plastered with foundation, mascara, blush, and lipstick. Coming out to this bar with a boy she didn't know wasn't her either. She may not know who she was, or who or what she wanted to be or do, but Ashleigh knew this date was not her.

Her sisters would laugh at her if they discovered how she felt. They always seemed on a roll—a high of shopping, parties, and men. She'd given up that life by moving to Montana with her father. What in the hell was she doing tonight trying to capture something she'd already rejected? Did her sisters' lives affect her so much subconsciously?

Whatever. She was here with Nelson. She'd make the best of it and move on. She didn't have to go on a date with him ever again.

Ashleigh freshened her lipstick and puffed up her hair. Then she rejoined Nelson and his friends.

He kissed her cheek when she sat down. "Here's your Coke," he said, and the others laughed.

"Thanks." She took a sip and smiled at the group. It was hot, so she drank a few more sips, noting everyone else chugged down bottles of beer avoiding her eyes. The soft drink tasted good and it was cold. She gulped it down.

The music cranked up even louder. "Dance with me!" Nelson yelled.

Great. That was something she could do. More in her element.

Ashleigh let him grab her hand and pull her to her feet. They joined a small group of older-looking cowboys and cowgirls gyrating on the dancefloor. The hard-rocking country beat poured through her as she threw herself into the fast-paced moves. It was exhilarating. Liberating. Ashleigh forgot her troubles and laughed. She was finally having a good time.

After two more fast dances, the music switched to a slow one. Nelson wouldn't let her go back to the table. He caught her up in an embrace, swaying with her. He kissed her hard on the lips, cupping a hand on her butt. Ashleigh tried hard to protest but couldn't seem to get the words out. She felt sick to her stomach. Dizzy. Confused.

The only reason she continued to stand was because Nelson held her in his arms.

What was wrong with her? Why was she suddenly so sick?

The music ended. Nelson let her go. She stood on wobbly legs as the floor cleared. Everything seemed to move in slow motion. Her brain was fuzzy. Ashleigh took a deep breath trying to get her bearings. All she knew was that she didn't want to be here any longer. She wanted to go home.

More laughter. Lights spinning. She couldn't move her legs. She swallowed more quick breaths.

"Ashleigh!"

Someone called her name. Who? She twisted her head but saw only Nelson and his friends surrounding her. The girls held cell phones pointed at her.

"Ashleigh!"

She tried to take a step toward the person calling her name but crumpled instead to the hard, stinking floor. Eyes wide open, her vision blurred, and she couldn't move. Paralyzed. Alone. Helpless.

Then a man came to her rescue. He wore a cowboy hat like everyone else. But she thought she knew him. She should know him. But she couldn't remember his name. Or anything. It was easier to fold into herself. To slip away. To forget and let go.

CHAPTER SIX

THE WAITING room of Livingston's hospital emergency room was an impersonal, scary place for someone with a loved one behind its closed doors. Hank and Josh sat on hard chairs, their hats dangling between tense fingers.

"How's Ashleigh?" Stef cried as she and Brody pushed through the doors and rushed into the waiting room.

"I don't know how she is," Hank admitted. "They won't tell me anything because I'm not her parent."

"Let me see if I can fix that," Stef said. "I have Chaz's cell number. They might need to talk to him to get permission for treatment."

She left the trio to go to the admission desk, and Brody took a seat beside Hank.

"Good God, man, what happened?" Brody asked.

"We have Josh to thank nothing *more* happened," Hank reported.

"Livy too," Josh added. "She told me about the so-called date with Nelson Blake."

"When I heard about it, I didn't think it was a good thing for Ashleigh to go." Brody's face looked chockfull of guilt. Hank couldn't blame him. He felt guilty too, for Liz's sake.

"We followed Nelson's truck to the Wild Horse Saloon."

"That place has turned into a dump."

Hank nodded. "A dump that serves underage kids."

Brody sat back in his chair. "That's something I plan to speak to the sheriff about. Go on."

"Josh followed them into the bar while I waited in the pickup," Hank continued. "I figured the kid would be less obvious going inside than an old cowpoke like me."

Josh joined the narrative. "I watched Ashleigh dance a few dances with Nelson Blake. I didn't like the way he touched her during the slow dance. It wasn't right."

"Oh, boy." Brody rolled his eyes. "Chaz is going to be pissed."

"After the music ended, Nelson left her and Ashleigh stood in the middle of the floor as if she couldn't move. Like she was in a trance. Nelson and his friends gathered around laughing and making fun of her. I started toward her, calling her name, when she collapsed."

"Whatever happened?"

Josh's face was a mask of despair. "I don't know."

"A date rape drug. That's what happened." Stef came back to join them. "I know the nurse. She told me they think Ashleigh was slipped Rohypnol."

Angry heat flashed through Hank's body. Damn those kids! Brody and Josh expressed the same sentiments by cursing aloud.

"I've given the nurse Chaz's cell phone number," she told them. "The staff will try to get in touch with him."

"I suspect they're still in Hawaii," Brody said.

Stef nodded. "Due home in a couple of days."

Josh stood up and faced them. "Can we see Ashleigh?"

"Not yet. They want to keep her a few hours to see how she sleeps it off." Stef sighed a mother's worried sigh. "If you two take Brody home, I'll stay here with Ashleigh."

Brody climbed to his feet. "We have a stop to make before going home," he said.

Hank stood up too. "The sheriff?"

"Yup," Brody said. "C'mon, boys. Let's go get us some justice."

~

THURSDAY AFTERNOON. Somehow Ashleigh had lost two days of her life. She'd spent one day in the hospital and yesterday in her bed at the big house sleeping it off some more. Whatever *it* was.

Stef had told her it was a date rape drug. Nelson and his friends had slipped her a roofie. She didn't remember. Didn't want to remember.

Ashleigh remained in bed—too embarrassed to get up and face her new family. Only Stef and Livy had been into her room to see her. Even then she'd experienced a tsunami of shame that had washed over her. How could she have let this happen? Adrianne's daughter? Supposedly a sophisticated, hip, Hollywood chick, she'd been slipped a roofie in a small-town bar in Montana, of all places. It was humiliating she'd been so naïve.

Josh and Hank had saved her. She'd not been raped.

"You need to get out of bed and go tell them thank you," Stef had told her. "It's not the end of the world. Trust me. It may seem like it at your age, but nothing terrible happened."

But it seemed like the end of the world. Ashleigh couldn't let Stef convince her otherwise.

So, she remained hidden in her bedroom, sitting up in bed and slowly eating the chicken noodle soup and grilled cheese sandwich Stef had delivered. Without an appetite, nothing tasted good, but she nibbled at the food anyway. She didn't want to be rude to Stef. It wasn't often she had a real mother's attention.

"Hey." Livy cracked open the door and stuck her head into the room.

"Hey," Ashleigh answered.

"Your mom is on your phone."

Phone? Ashleigh glanced around the bed covers and the nightstand. She didn't remember seeing her cell phone. Not lately, anyway.

"Ah." Livy looked uncomfortable. "Hank had to go back to the bar to pick it up. You didn't need it, so Dad kept it for you."

"Oh, okay." Strange she hadn't missed her usual lifeline.

Livy came into the room. "Do you want to talk to her?" She extended her hand with the phone in it.

"Sure." Ashleigh took it from her. "Does she know what happened?"

"Ah, yes."

The moment Ashleigh said "hello," a string of expletives filled her ear. References to *going viral* rang through the device. Ashleigh swallowed hard.

"Hello to you, too, Adrianne. Yes, your youngest daughter is fine." Ashleigh's tone was mocking, because her mother had not asked about her welfare. Instead, the reality TV star had exploded in anger.

"What do you mean getting yourself plastered all over YouTube? In a dump in a backwoods Montana town, no less?"

"Hold it, Mom. I don't know what you're talking about."

"You don't?"

"No, I don't. I didn't put anything on YouTube."

"Oh, that's right. Little Goody Two-shoes no longer goes on social media. She's turned her back on her mother and sisters. Too virtuous to join them in their world."

Eyes wide in alarm, Ashleigh gazed at Livy, who shrugged and nodded self-consciously. What her mother was blabbering was true. She had left her mother's world. But what had happened to make her so mad?

"You told me you were going to stay off the internet," Adrianne snapped. "Instead a video of you goes viral with my name smeared all over the tabloids because of it. If you've changed your mind, then for God's sake let our PR staff control your content. Our brand does not need these disgusting videos of you popping up everywhere."

The brand. Of course. Adrianne Wade cared nothing about her wellbeing. Only so far as it affected her *brand* did she care what Ashleigh did or said.

Although she knew this truth about her mother, hearing it said aloud caused a sharp pain to hack into Ashleigh's heart. Suddenly, she was tired. Physically from her ordeal, but more so emotionally, from the actuality of her mother's lack of love.

"Thanks, Mom, for your concern," Ashleigh said letting her words drip with sarcasm. "Yes, I'll take care of myself. Merry Christmas to you too."

Then she tapped the disconnect button and let the phone drop from her hand.

Livy stood by her bed, biting her lower lip, unable to speak.

Without looking at her friend, Ashleigh held out her hand. "Let me see it."

Livy pulled her phone from her pocket and sat on the side of the bed. "Those creeps at the bar took videos of you standing in the middle of the floor looking drunk."

Livy gave Ashleigh the phone. Licking her lips, Ashleigh tapped the play button and gaped at the phone in her hands. Quickly, the nightmare from Monday night became reality. That drunken girl didn't look like her, standing there in the gloom of the bar with music blaring. Ashleigh heard laughter in the background, giggles from the person taking the video. Someone called her name, and she turned. Wobbled. Swayed. Then she fell. Next, there was a shot of her face with her eyes staring up at nothing. Vacant. Sad.

"Look at Ashleigh Wade, daughter of Adrianne Wade," the person taking the video said. "Can't hold her liquor."

Fear. Anger. Shame. A mass of emotions surged through Ashleigh. "I don't remember any of this," she said in a hushed voice.

"Of course, you don't."

"I feel so ashamed."

"Don't," Livy admonished. "It's not your fault."

"But I feel like it is."

They sat together a few moments. Just having Livy nearby was a comfort.

"How can I face everyone at school?" Ashleigh moaned.

"Mom says by the time our break is over, everyone will have forgotten the video," Livy said. "Besides, my dad got the authorities to investigate that bar and talk to the parents of those kids. We don't know what will happen to them yet. But my dad canceled business with Nelson Blake's dad. He told him that he wouldn't do business with a man whose son disrespected his stepsister."

"But that video is bad for my mom's business. How many views did it have?"

"Over three million."

Ashleigh rolled her eyes. "Geez."

"My mom says that bad publicity won't last long. She said the president would Tweet something, and the conversation would change. No one will care about your video in a week."

That was probably true. Ashleigh let out a big sigh and rotated her shoulders to relieve the tension there. No. People wouldn't care in the long run. However, once something was placed on the internet, it didn't go away. It was left in some cloud somewhere, a testament to her lapse of good judgment when she was sixteen-years-old.

CHAPTER SEVEN

THE NEXT DAY IT SNOWED—MAYBE only two inches but enough to cover the ground in powdery white. The cold air felt bracing, invigorating. Ashleigh trekked from the big house to the barn in the silence of midday. She almost felt alive again. Herself. Her mother's displeasure didn't bother her anymore. She'd lived with Adrianne's anger most of her life.

The barn was gloomy. The quiet movement of the horses in their stalls and the horsey smell was comforting. She noticed the light in Hank's office. She wanted to thank him, but her first goal was to find Josh. Would he be reading in his hayloft hideaway?

She topped the ladder and peered over the edge. "Hey."

Josh sat under the steeply pitched roof hunched over a book lying in his lap. A frosty window gave scant light. He looked up and smiled. "Hey, yourself."

Ashleigh got to her feet in the hayloft and wrapped her arms around herself, shivering. "Aren't you freezing?"

"I'm used to it," he said.

Ashleigh trembled and came over to sit down across from him on a bale of hay. "I'd freeze my butt off up here."

He smiled at her, ignoring the remark. Instead, he said, "I'm glad to see you up and around."

It was her turn to take a big breath. His kindness made her shy. "I came to thank you for saving my life."

He grinned. His own shyness caused his gaze to drop to the pages of the open book. "Oh, I wouldn't be that dramatic."

"But no telling what would have happened to me if you hadn't arrived."

Josh looked up, his eyes sincere and full of concern. "I knew Nelson, and you didn't. I knew not to trust him."

"But I didn't listen."

"As Hank tells me, sometimes we have to learn our lessons the hard way."

Ashleigh rolled her eyes and sighed. "Well, that sucks."

"*C'est la vie.*"

How many cowboys knew the French for *that's life*? Or maybe her head was filled with Hollywood stereotypes. The modern cowboy wasn't like the old-time movie ones.

"You're philosophical about it," she said.

"I've learned to be." Josh shrugged. "Besides, I think those kids got most of what they wanted—YouTube exposure, a way to humiliate you."

"But I haven't done anything to them."

"You're you. You're beautiful and new. Your mother and sisters are famous."

"That pretty much sums it up," Ashleigh agreed. "Except for the beautiful part."

"Don't sell yourself short, Ashleigh."

Their gazes locked and held until they both became embarrassed and looked away. The silence was uncomfortable for a few beats.

Ashleigh changed the subject. "What are you reading?"

Josh flipped the book shut to show the cover: *Bonhoeffer: Pastor,*

Martyr, Prophet, Spy by Eric Metaxas. "It's the story of a Lutheran pastor in Germany who stood up to the Nazis."

Ashleigh searched his face, noting the passion in it, the awe. That Josh admired this man from the past was an insight into the boy, who wasn't simply a hired hand or a stupid teenager.

"You've got to respect a man who was willing to die for his beliefs," Josh said.

"Yeah," Ashleigh agreed, seeing the connection. "Or a friend who comes to the aid of a naïve girl."

Josh had the grace to blush. "It wasn't much."

Ashleigh laid a gloved hand over his. "Thank you all the same."

HANK CAME to the bottom of the ladder and called up to Ashleigh. He'd seen her come in and realized where she was headed. When she peered down over the edge of the hayloft, she grinned and said *hi*, appearing shy.

"Brody asked me to pick up your dad and Liz in Bozeman," Hank said. "He said you can come with me if you want."

She looked unsure of herself, as if she was reluctant to go, as if fearing a confrontation with her father. Hank knew where she came from. He wanted to avoid the trip too. Seeing Liz all properly married, was not his idea of a good time. Still, his boss had given him a task, and Hank would follow through, no matter what he personally felt about it.

Ashleigh looked over her shoulder. Josh said something, but Hank couldn't pick it up.

"Please," Hank said. "I can use the company."

That was an understatement.

"Okay." She turned and descended the ladder.

It was approximately a forty-five-mile trip to the Bozeman Yellowstone International Airport via US-89 N and I-90 W. The main roads were cleared from the recent snow. This was Montana, after all. Snow was a winter event. If you lived here, you got used to traveling in it, and the main roads were essentially kept clean after minor snowfalls.

Once on the main highway and the Six Buckles Guest Ranch van warmed up, Ashleigh broke the ice between them. "I thanked Josh for saving me, and I want to thank you too, Hank."

"Hey, kid, it was a no-brainer. We couldn't let anything happen to you."

"But it could have turned out so differently."

"It didn't."

Ashleigh glanced at him from the passenger side. "It was stupid of me to trust someone I didn't even know."

"We all do stupid things."

"I guess."

She was beating herself up. Hank felt sorry for her. He knew what it was like to have parents so distracted by their own lives that they couldn't pay attention to their child. Crap, even at his age, the remoteness of his parents so long ago still bothered him. It was one reason he'd envied Darby and her close relationship with her mother. It also had helped him understand Darby's reaction to the tragedy of her mother's death.

"We learn by the mistakes we make," Hank said.

She smiled and studied her hands. "Josh said you said that." Ashleigh then examined him again. "It doesn't seem fair, though, learning from mistakes. Why don't we listen? Josh warned me about Nelson. I didn't listen."

"Human arrogance," Hank ventured. "We like to think we know what's best."

"I guess."

A few more miles of silence.

"I can't believe you've made mistakes, Hank," Ashleigh said. "You seem so settled. Like you have your head on straight."

Hank gave a snort. "I'm far from settled, kid. I've made my share of mistakes, believe me."

She glanced out the window and let his words settle in. Then she looked back. "I've wondered why you don't have any family. You seem okay not being married. My dad never was. When he and my mom divorced, he was a different guy for a long time. That's why I'm glad he found Liz."

Hank gripped the steering wheel, fighting with his emotions that were as bitter as the snow-capped mountains flanking the valley road. He didn't answer her. Couldn't.

Eventually, Ashleigh put two and two together. She wasn't a dumb kid. In fact, she was observant and intuitive, much to Hank's dismay.

"You were in love with Liz too," she stated flatly.

His mouth was dry. All he could do was nod and concentrate on driving.

"Geez," Ashleigh uttered in surprise. "And my dad shows up and marries her. I bet you were sad."

"That's an understatement," Hank replied keeping his eyes on the road.

Ashleigh angled in the seat to view him better. "Why didn't you marry her when you had the chance? After Jim died?"

He didn't want to talk about this. He kept his feelings bottled up. Expressing feelings wasn't what a wrangler did. Emotion was something a woman did.

Ashleigh must have recognized his hesitancy. "I'm sorry. It's none of my business."

"She's the boss lady," Hank said slowly. "I respected her grief. It wasn't my place. Besides, what could I offer her?"

Saying it aloud should have made him feel better, but it didn't. The truth made him sad, sadder than he'd been in a long, long time.

Ashleigh digested his words. "Does she even know you loved her?"

Hank shook his head. Liz didn't know. And neither had Darby York so many years ago. His feelings weren't something he revealed. Too personal. Too intense. Too scary.

So why was he telling Chaz Kingston's daughter? Liz was now her stepmother. It didn't make sense to reveal something so intimate to this young girl.

But Ashleigh understood. Quietly, she said, "Don't worry. I won't tell anyone."

He nodded. "Thanks. I appreciate that."

She sat back in the seat. "Geez, this must be hard for you, seeing my dad and Liz together. Picking them up at the airport like you are."

"It's not a piece of cake."

More miles traveled in silence. They turned onto I-90 heading toward the Bozeman Pass at an elevation of 5,702 feet.

Finally, Ashleigh stated, "You should have told her, Hank. I know it's none of my business, but you should have told her."

"No, it's not your business."

She chewed her lower lip a moment. "You didn't give Liz a choice. If she didn't know about your feelings, she didn't know she had an option."

His insides quaked. He didn't want to talk about this.

But the teenager wasn't finished. "I understand you couldn't say anything to Liz when she was married to Jim."

"It wasn't right." He had fought his feelings for years. Just as he'd fought what he'd felt for Darby when he was a kid.

"I get that." She let out a breath. "It is what it is, but you need to learn from this, Hank."

"What?"

"You say we learn from our mistakes. Well, I say you need to learn from this too. The next time you're in love with someone, tell her. Don't be afraid. It can't turn out any worse."

Wisdom from the mouth of a babe. "There won't be a next time. I doubt I'll fall in love again."

"Well, that's sad."

And that was the biggest understatement of all.

CHAPTER EIGHT

Christmas Eve 2018

Liz Mercer Caldera Dawson Kingston settled down in the leather sofa facing a blazing fire. Her stomach was full of her daughter-in-law Stef's wonderful Christmas Eve dinner—turkey, dressing, all the trimmings. It was nice to have a younger woman in the family in charge for a change. Nice being the pampered matriarch.

In the corner of the lodge great room, a Fraser fir was lit and decorated and surrounded by so many presents Liz could hardly see its base. For the first time in years, she had not participated in the tree decorating, a Dawson family tradition. She'd not wrapped a single gift either, bringing all of hers back from her honeymoon in Hawaii already wrapped.

Her husband Chaz sat down beside her and handed her a glass of merlot. How different it was to think of him as *her husband.* But it was a good thing. And comforting. She basked in his love and approval. That she should be so lucky for a second time was truly amazing.

"Have a seat," she said with a smile to her daughter who

approached the sofa. Mercer, her husband Drake, and their adopted daughter Gracie had arrived in Bozeman yesterday from Tennessee via an Atlanta flight.

Liz scooted closer to Chaz, and Mercer took the end space. Her daughter was pregnant and wore the first blush of motherhood well.

"It's fun having children around again," Liz said.

"Jim would have loved so many new faces," Mercer reminisced, then looked at her mother in alarm.

"It's okay." Liz patted her daughter's knee. "I'm sure Jim is watching. His spirit and Bonnie's are all around us."

It was true. Jim's eldest had returned home. Ben had left his job at the *real* ranch north of Livingston in the spring to keep tabs on the ranch. He'd never liked the *guest* part of the ranch and remained at loose ends, hoping eventually to talk her into converting the ranch back to cattle. Still, he was home, and Jim would have liked that.

Brody fussed over the fire as it crackled and popped filling the room with a radiant warmth and rustic smell. He and Stef were happy together. Jim would have loved the family they'd created.

Stef had brought a chair from the dining room near the tree. Baby Charlotte sat on her lap, looking sleepy, while Livy and Ashleigh examined the presents, hardly able to contain their excitement. Jim might have been happy with her remarriage. He certainly would have liked how Ashleigh had taken to the ranch and its independent lifestyle.

"Can we open the gifts now, Dad?" Livy asked.

"In a minute," Brody answered. "You know we always sing a few Christmas carols first."

Livy looked less than pleased. But it was a family tradition, one Jim had cherished.

"Come on over, Hank," Brody said, pulling up a chair. "Sit near the fire."

Hank Slade. Liz watched the wrangler saunter up to the fire and sit down. He'd brought his guitar and strummed a few notes, tuning the strings. She and Hank were of a similar age. He'd been at the ranch when she'd arrived as a young, married woman. They'd seen a lot together. She liked to think of him as her friend.

"Here comes Santa Claus, here comes Santa Claus, right down Santa Claus lane," Hank sang, and everyone joined in.

"Ashleigh has a good voice," Liz whispered to Chaz.

Her husband nodded, beaming with pride for his daughter. "She didn't get the talent from me."

Carols followed in swift order from *Jingle Bells* to *O Come All Ye Faithful*. Liz sipped her wine and reveled in the moment. This could have been a different celebration if it hadn't been for Hank and Josh Adams. If they hadn't intervened and saved Ashleigh from that horrible group at the bar, this night might have been spent in a hospital or someplace worse.

Josh felt like part of the family. He sat beside Ashleigh and Livy, laughing and joining in the carols. Liz didn't mind letting the boy stay on the ranch. He needed a home until the end of the school year, and he'd done a great service for her stepdaughter.

Even though Hank sat near the fire and sang, he seemed unsettled. When she'd seen him at the airport two days ago, she'd thrown her arms around his neck in gratitude for his help with Ashleigh and kissed his cheek.

"Thank you so much for what you did for my stepdaughter," she'd whispered into his ear.

Hank had stood stiffly, never moving while she hugged him. Then he stepped back, disengaging. "I didn't do much."

"You've always done so much for my family," she'd protested. "All these years, Jim and I couldn't have gotten along without you." She didn't catch his response, because she'd turned to give Ashleigh a hug.

She had spoken the truth to Hank that evening at the airport. He was part of the Dawson clan as surely as any one of her children. They were all one big family, after all. Blended by kinship and friendship. And love.

~

TIME TO OPEN GIFTS. Hank couldn't take it. How was he supposed to? There sat Liz, all lovey-dovey beside that Hollywood guy. It ate at his craw, maybe because it could have been him. Like Ashleigh said, he should have spoken up. But that went against the grain. He'd never done it in all his years and wasn't about to start with his employee's widow.

So now he sat on the edge of the Christmas gathering, taking it all in. He wasn't even a part of the group like Josh was, surrounded by Livy and Ashleigh, handing out gifts to be opened one at a time, then oo-ed and ah-ed over. Showing off presents and exclaiming over them was a Dawson tradition. He'd seen it over the years since Liz had joined the family. She didn't like the chaos of tearing up carefully wrapped gifts as if the family were wild animals. No, it was one at a time for Liz. Show and tell. But as a result, the gift-opening process took hours to complete.

These people were his friends. But they weren't his family, no matter what they liked to think. He had no family. No one to call his own. He wore that sadness on his sleeve as if it were part of his clothing, his overall being.

In the end, Hank Slade was a nobody. He had nothing but his guitar, his saddle, and the clothes on his back. Hell, even the horses he rode and loved belonged to the Dawson Ranch. No, after fifty years of living, he had nothing. No roots. No family. Nothing.

Ate up with feeling sorry for himself, Hank climbed to his feet. This mood was no good. Not on a happy night like this.

Brody noticed his movement. "You okay?"

Hank jerked his head toward the kitchen. "Getting more coffee," he said.

Brody turned back to the festivities, and Hank walked into the kitchen. The Dawsons always kept a pot brewing and a plate of cookies ready for their guests. He couldn't eat one more bite at the moment. Stef sure was a wonderful cook.

Hank poured a cup and sipped the steaming black coffee. He returned to the kitchen door, leaned against it, his cup in his hand. Ashleigh had just given Josh a gift from the whole family, she'd told him. The boy opened the shiny red package to uncover an expensive iPad.

"Complete with an app so you can download any book you want," Ashleigh said, the delight obvious in her voice.

The boy looked pleased. And grateful. That had been Hank at one time. Newly come from the army, thankful for any work, and more than happy to have a family atmosphere around him. He'd been like Josh. Still was, come to think of it...after all these years.

That's when he realized he needed to leave. He couldn't stay any longer at the Dawson ranch.

Lost in the anguish of knowing he'd never see Liz again once he left, he startled when the kitchen phone rang. The Dawsons maintained a landline because cell reception was a spotty thing in the mountains.

Hank answered it. "Six Buckles Guest Ranch. May I help you?"

A gravelly voice replied, "I'm looking for Hank Slade. Do you know where he is?"

Like a blast from the past, Hank recognized the voice. A myriad of emotions tumbled through him. "This is Hank. Leo, is that you?"

"Thank God," the old man said. "Hank, I need you. I need you to come home. I want you to run my ranch."

And just like that, his prayers were answered, as if his decision to leave had been heard by an overarching power. Leo York, Darby's father, had to be in his eighties. That he wanted Hank was some sort of miracle. That Hank was ready to go home to the only home he knew, was another kind of wonder.

~

Ashleigh kept one eye on Hank throughout the lengthy gift opening. That the wrangler played a good game impressed her. She didn't know how he did it, watching her dad cuddling up to Liz. She was happy for her dad but sad for Hank. He was an enigma. He had a past he kept hidden from everyone, but he'd opened up to her. That made their bond special. That made Hank special.

When the party broke up and the family members collected gifts and coats and loaded trucks and SUVs to return to the various houses and cabins on the ranch, Ashleigh saw Hank put on his coat and leave by himself.

"I've got to give Hank his gift," she told Brody. "I'll be home in a few minutes."

Brody nodded his approval. "You know Hank just told me he's got another job and will be leaving the first of the year?"

Surprise sailed through her. "No. I didn't know."

"Yup. Seems to be a spur of the moment offer. But sounds like a good deal for Hank."

Ashleigh couldn't blame Hank. She'd run away from her troubles herself by coming to the ranch and leaving the pressure of her mother back in California.

She found him standing next to the lake, looking out over it. Buffeted by the wind, he had his hands in his pockets and the collar of his jacket turned up.

"Whatcha' doing?" she asked coming up beside him. "It's too cold to be out here long."

"Sayin' goodbye." His voice was gruff as if full of emotion.

"I heard."

Hank glanced down at her. "A job just fell into my lap."

"Well, that's a good thing," she said. "I don't know how you can stick around here."

"I can't."

The silence of the frigid Montana night engulfed them. They stood quietly a few moments, each wrapped in their own thoughts.

Finally, Ashleigh said, "I wanted to give you a Christmas gift."

"Ah, you didn't have to do that. Your dad and Liz already gave me a new iPhone."

"That was from them. This is from me." She reached into her pocket and pulled out a small, wrapped box. "Here. I didn't know what to get you, but this seemed appropriate."

Hank accepted the gift and unfolded the paper. When it was unwrapped, he held a sterling silver pendant in his hand.

"It's a Saint Francis of Assisi medal," Ashleigh said. "He's the patron saint of animals. See how he has birds in his hands and a dog at his feet?"

"Thanks." Hank stared at the oval medallion sitting in the open palm of his gloved hand. "It's the nicest gift I've ever received."

Ashleigh rolled her eyes. "I don't know about that. But I thought it was appropriate because you care for animals."

"It is appropriate. Thanks, kid."

Awkward silence. Ashleigh scuffed her boot against the snow. "Maybe you and I can text each other sometimes," she said. "Since you have a new iPhone and since you're leaving."

"Maybe an old dog can learn new tricks," he said with a laugh.

"I'll miss you, Hank." Ashleigh stood on her tiptoes and kissed him on the cheek.

"I'll miss you too, kid."

"Merry Christmas, Hank."

"Merry Christmas."

Before she started to cry, Ashleigh dodged away, back up the incline toward the log lodge. When she reached the porch, she turned around.

Hank Slade walked alone in the distance toward the bunk house and to whatever future awaited him.

DARBY

CHAPTER ONE

February 1971

HE WAS DEAD.

She ran her index-finger over the black ink newsprint, reading slowly. The police officer had been on duty near the window. When the bomb blew, inch-long, industrial fence staples shattered the window and pierced the man's neck. He was dead by the time the ambulance arrived.

It had been raining that night. Steady and cold. She'd huddled in the driver's seat parked down the street. Placing one hand on her pregnant belly and the other clutching the pendant around her neck, she had told herself she was still good for something—smart enough and courageous enough to drive the getaway car.

"Let's go, honey," he'd said when he jumped in the passenger side.

She'd driven away slowly so not to draw attention.

Over the past month, she'd made Molotov cocktails for them. She'd filled glass bottles with gasoline, inserted a cloth into each mouth to be lit by a firecracker. The members who were not hampered by the extra weight of pregnancy had tossed the fire bombs setting an army recruitment office on fire and torching a tree in the police chief's front lawn. They'd called it a success, but last night, they'd upped the game.

And now a man was dead.

But they had wanted to kill more of them. The bomb detonated fifteen minutes early. If not, it would have exploded during shift change. More would have died. As it was, they'd made an important statement. They were revolutionaries.

Last night's action had showed the others, the intellectual snobs who had purged them from the original group. They weren't good enough for the main faction—too undependable, not brave enough, too weak. But they had showed them. They would read about their success in the newspaper and hear about it on the radio. Those snobs would know they hadn't been the ones to strike first for the Movement. *They had.* The People, the outcasts, the ones who didn't count. Power to the People!

They called themselves The People because they were a family —men and women—held together by love and sex, a commitment not only to the revolution, but to themselves. Some of them already had children. Just like she would have soon, a new life to grow up in a new country. They had gone underground, living under assumed identities. Who would question a man walking down the street with his pregnant wife? Who would think a family with children was out to change the world?

That's what set them apart from the others—being a family. Loving each other. They were loyal to themselves first and then to the cause. They'd all been screwed by society. When they succeeded, things would change. The streets would run with blood like it had in Cuba. No longer would America be a place for the rich. The little man would have his say and his woman would be right by his side.

If it took the death of a policeman, so be it.

CHAPTER TWO

February 2019
The Heston Breeding Farm
Near Lexington, Kentucky

THE FEMALE REPORTER was too near, peering over Darby's left shoulder, judging each brush stroke. "You're quite good."

Darby York angled her body, subconsciously to shield her work from prying eyes. An oil painting of a mare and foal took shape on the canvas in front of her. She clutched a collection of long brushes in her left hand, each tipped with its separate color combination, and with her right hand, she stroked the canvas with a dab of burnt sienna.

"What is your name again?" Darby had age on this young woman. She wasn't going to let herself be intimidated.

"Laurel Chastain. Most people call me Laurie."

"Well, Laurie, oddly enough, I've had quite a bit of success here in Kentucky and among a certain horsey-set nationwide."

"You must so love what you do," Laurie said, "especially in this beautiful place."

"It's my passion." A solitary passion between her and the subject on canvas—an oil painting of a Thoroughbred or an American Saddlebred horse that comprised most of her commissions. In fact, the whole creative process was relaxing, meditative. Yet, it was more than a passion. It was Darby's life. "I always sketched. My husband encouraged me to do more. Col sent me to art classes. He supported me. In fact, he built this studio for me almost twenty years ago when my small children got on my nerves so badly, I couldn't concentrate in the house. Now I regret separating myself from the children, but at the time I needed the quiet, the space."

In fact, Colton Heston always had more faith in Darby's ability than she did. "You've got a gift, darling," he'd say. "You should be proud of it. Exhibit your work."

But Darby had always demurred. She didn't quite believe in her talent. Even now. Even after agreeing to this interview with a magazine reporter.

Laurie turned away from the easel and canvas to survey the framed oils and watercolors hanging on the walls of the one-room studio. "And I understand your husband was twenty years your senior."

Although winter sunshine streamed through the studio window, throwing points of light across the hardwood floor, and a cheery fire blazed in the stone fireplace, Darby felt cold. Her sanctuary had been violated. Her life. She swallowed hard and studied the reporter.

"Twenty-four years my senior to be exact," Darby said using a sarcastic inflection. Col had understood her. Her husband had loved her more deeply than she'd deserved. For that Darby was thankful—for that and so much more.

Laurie glanced over her shoulder with a smile. "That's right."

Why did Darby feel the woman had done her research a little too well? Maybe some sixth sense told her. Or maybe she was too sensitive about criticism as her daughter Kelsey often pointed out.

"Why horses?" The questions continued. "Aside from the fact

your husband has owned winning race horses and you live on a horse farm in Kentucky."

"I grew up with horses, back in Montana." Darby removed her glasses from the bridge of her nose and twisted to get a better view of the reporter. "I never get tired of painting them. There's something about the touch, the smell, the feel of a horse that tells me I belong with them. Almost like my lifeline. I was so lucky to marry a man who had the same horse enthusiasm."

"A man who made it possible for you to follow your dream." Laurie's words seemed an indictment more than a statement.

"Well, yes." That was a funny way of putting things. Strange funny. Darby had never thought of her life in that way. It didn't seem to her as if her dreams had come true. Far from it, she felt she had only coped in the best way she could.

"So, do you paint from photos all the time? You have perfect subjects outside your back door."

Darby's tension eased a bit. Maybe Laurie really *was* interested in her art, not her life. "Sketching live subjects and then balancing the sketches with a photograph or two seems to work well for me. I draw with pencil, then do preliminary paintings in watercolor to get to know my subject before I even put oil paint on canvas."

Laurie nodded and wandered to the back of the studio. Ten paintings of various sizes stood propped on easels. These were the painting for Darby's upcoming show called "Women with Horses."

The reporter studied the oils for a moment, then asked the obvious, "Why women and horses?"

"Why not?" The answer was flippant, but the subject seemed a no-brainer to Darby. "For centuries, women have loved horses. It seems a natural combination for a woman painter to explore."

Laurie examined each one. "Some of these must have been commissioned."

Darby put down her brushes and joined the reporter. "Yes, the two with women on American Saddlebred horses were commissioned. The riders live here in Kentucky and take part in local shows. They've loaned their paintings to me for a few months."

Laurie had stopped in front of two separate paintings of women garbed in nineteenth century dress. Each woman stood at the head of a horse. The paintings were subdued, blurred, and dreamy with muted tones of grays and blacks. "I like these. Where did you get your idea for these?"

"My imagination."

"They're beautiful."

"Thank you."

"You really need to be proud your talent. You're better than you believe," she said.

Unable to meet the reporter's eyes, Darby felt her face and neck grow hot. She moved on to the next set of canvases. They were different from the previous ones—rugged, painted in browns and yellows, with western horses ridden by cowgirls holding lariats in their hands.

"Where did these come from?"

"I grew up on a dude ranch. These are paintings from my memory."

A memory filled with regret. Darby turned from the collection. It had taken her twenty years before she could paint cowgirls and quarter horses. She had hoped exploring the western subjects would diminish those mostly bitter recollections. The dreams. It hadn't. The demons she'd dwelt with for so many years still gnawed at her gut, affecting her days and nights as they had since she'd left home thirty years ago.

In fact, Darby York Heston had run for far too long. She'd hidden away as Col's wife and mother of his children. But she was tired of running. Not that change was a snap-the-finger kind of thing. She couldn't transform herself overnight. Change happened in baby steps.

The ringtone for Darby's cell phone sounded. She pulled it from her pocket and read the screen. "This is my daughter. I need to take it."

"Go ahead."

Crossing over to the fireplace for privacy, Darby answered the call. "Hello?"

"Mom? Sorry to interrupt."

"That's okay, Kelsey." More than okay. Darby regretted agreeing to the irksome interview. Col had told her she was too damn private. She needed to believe in herself. He always urged her to have more confidence—get out there, show off her talent, and be proud. Step one of her resolve to change was the art show. Step two, the interview.

"A man called the office looking for you. He said he was from the Ghost Mountain Ranch in Montana. I gave him your cell phone number. He said it was something about your father. I hope that was okay."

Darby's heart raced, nearly exploding. Okay? How could it be? But Kelsey didn't know it wasn't all right. In fact, for many years she'd pestered Darby about her mother's past. About the grandfather she and her twin brother Slade had never met.

"Yes. Thank you." Darby took a deep breath, holding back the urge to cry. "It may be your grandfather."

"No, he said his name was Hank Slade."

Darby's past rushed headlong into the present.

"I thought it odd his last name was 'Slade' like our Slade," Kelsey said. "But he did tell me it was about my grandfather."

Darby didn't answer for a moment. Couldn't. Finally, she said, "Yes, Leo, my father, is getting to be quite old."

The desire to flee washed over Darby, but there was nowhere to go. Kelsey had no way of knowing what had kept her mother away from Montana for thirty years. All her daughter knew was the state and the ranch were sore spots. With her own father gone, Kelsey had grown curious. Now this one phone call would open a huge can of worms.

"I need to get back to my guest," Darby said, hoping to cut off any questions.

"Sure. I just wanted to warn you."

"Thanks. I appreciate the heads-up."

Darby pressed the off button and pocketed the phone. She had turned toward the reporter, when the phone's ringtone played again. Swallowing her fear, Darby pulled out the phone to read an unfamiliar number on the screen.

Col had implored her to face her past. To find out what had really happened to her mother. Maybe then the dreams would stop. The nightmares.

Darby had been good at avoidance during his lifetime. Now after his death, her husband might get his wish. Her history had come calling.

HANK SLADE PLACED the receiver back on the cradle, hauled a lung full of air, and faced Leo's I-can-take-it expression. "She won't come."

"I didn't think she'd come." Leo's voice was flat. His old, rheumy eyes followed Hank across the office floor.

Hank sank into his desk chair. His shoulders slumped. "She said she was busy."

"But you sure did shame her good."

Hank tilted back in his chair. "Tried to."

"Well." Leo pushed himself out of the arm chair across from Hank's desk. "I thank you for doing what you could do."

"For as much good as it did." Hank rummaged through the stack of papers on his desktop shifting an invoice into another pile on the right. When he came on at the Ghost Mountain Ranch back in January, he hadn't realized the extent of Leo's estrangement from his only child Darby. "Thirty years is a long time to hold a grudge."

Leo hefted on a Carhartt coat over his down vest and picked up his cowboy hat from a side table. "Girl ran away, and she's just not coming home."

Hank's gut snarled into a knot like the one he'd felt that Friday night when he and Darby were eighteen. He'd been worried then about the first kiss he wanted. Now he worried about the man he'd known most of his life. Leo was no longer the energetic cowboy he remembered. Bad heart, plus a fall from a horse had taken its toll on the eighty-five-year-old. "I hope I didn't have anything to do with it."

"Nope." The old man grasped the office doorknob with a gnarled hand. "Her mother dying like she did caused Darby to leave."

"But why would she leave you?"

"She had her reasons."

His answer made no sense, but that was all the taciturn man would give. Leo set his cowboy hat on his head, opened the office door, and stepped out onto the porch.

Montana cold blew into the cabin, and Hank felt the chill more keenly than normal. It seeped inside him, turning the concern he felt into an icy shard in his stomach. Hank tapped a finger on the desk. He'd left the ranch at eighteen, after he and Darby had broken up, and he'd never been back. But if his dad had been alive and he knew he might be dying, he'd have come home straight away.

"Damn, Darby, this isn't right."

He stood, snatched up the phone, and dialed the office number back in Kentucky where a woman who said she was Darby's daughter might answer again.

"THAT MR. SLADE called the farm office again, Mom."

Darby tightened her grip on the assortment of brushes. Her hand trembled as she turned to gape at her daughter. Why hadn't Hank taken no for an answer?

Kelsey came into the room and hesitated a moment. After the call from Montana had interrupted Darby's interview, the reporter had wrapped up her questions and left. Now her daughter tipped up her chin and looked her mother straight in the eye.

"I just lost my daddy a year ago," she said, "but it feels like yesterday. I can't believe you haven't seen your father in forever. I can't believe you haven't wanted to see him."

Darby's world spun crazily around her. She put down her brushes and took a step forward. Her footstep faltered, and with a sweaty hand, she clutched the back of an empty chair. "I had my life here in Kentucky. With your father and you kids. My art. Your dad needed me."

Darby shifted her weight, unable once again to believe she'd produced such a pretty child. Kelsey took a deep breath and, for a moment, forced her gaze away as if not buying what her mother said.

Kelsey was a beautiful girl. Model beautiful. With her long blond hair, perfect face and blue eyes. But she was smart, too. More than book smart. She had an innate intelligence most kids her age didn't have. Kelsey ran Heston Farm's accounting department and kept track of their breeding schedules. Heaven knows, Slade had had no aptitude that way.

Seconds ticked by with agonizing slowness until Kelsey turned back her passionate gaze. "Mr. Slade said my grandfather might be dying. He's old. Your father needs you now. You should go, Mom."

A chill crawled across Darby's skin. "I'll think about it."

"No. You should go."

Darby shook her head, her heart drumming in her ears. "I can't pick up and leave this farm, especially not now with my art show planned."

Kelsey stared at her as if aghast by her words. "I've always known you to do pretty much whatever the hell you wanted to do. Daddy indulged you maybe too much, and maybe it's time you paid back your own father for being there when you grew up. Just like Daddy was there for Slade and me." She turned on her heel, and with a slam of the studio door, she was gone.

Sagging into the chair, Darby tried to slow her racing heart. She'd never been the butt of one of Kelsey's crusades until now. When her daughter thought something was right, she stood up for it, made herself its champion. She wouldn't rest until Darby got on that plane to Bozeman. Until, in her mind, Darby did what was right.

But could she do it? Wispy memories teased Darby's thoughts. She went back in her mind to the innocence she left so long ago. The horses, the city guests, her beautiful mother singing in the kitchen. Oh, how her mother would have loved Darby's twins. She'd have been so proud of them. Spoiled them. Her father Leo would have loved them, too.

But all was not sweet innocence in Montana.

Her thoughts reverted to that last terrible day, and icy tendrils twisted around her heart. After that day, the dreams had started. And the guilt.

Then there was Hank. For whatever reason, he had returned to the ranch. She'd have to face him as well as Leo. She couldn't do it. She couldn't go back.

But with Kelsey up in arms, Darby knew she couldn't *not* go back. Besides, she'd told herself she was taking baby steps to change. So far, those small steps had been nothing. Had cost her nothing. If she did go back to the Ghost Mountain Ranch, it would be the biggest baby step of them all.

CHAPTER FOUR

Early March
Ghost Mountain Ranch
Gallatin Canyon, Montana

"What the hell is going on in here?"

Darby's pulse jumped. She swung around, an unwanted lump in her throat, to find Hank lurking at the barn door and silhouetted by one overhead light.

She forced herself to breathe. It frosted in the cold air smelling of a mix of horses, hay, and leather.

"Hello, Hank."

Once she had believed in the dreams this man had created for her until she'd discovered dreams were only fairy tales.

Hank sauntered toward her between the stalls with that long ambling gait she recalled. Even with his coat on, Darby could tell his shoulders were broad and his hips still trim in his long, denim-clad legs. But there were differences—the gray in his hair, the weathered lines around his eyes. He was no longer the lanky kid she remembered, but a grown man—big-framed and rugged.

"I heard you came back."

His voice remained beautiful and luscious, deep and strangely compelling. She'd reacted to his voice from the moment he'd come to the ranch with his dad. How old had he been then? Fifteen? Old for his age. An old soul, she'd thought.

"Thanks to you." She gave a disgusted shake of her head. It was Hank's fault she'd come home. Hank and her daughter Kelsey, who'd shamed her into checking on her father.

But ultimately, she had come home because she'd run too long. Because after Col's death, she'd vowed to change, and part of that change was learning the truth about her mother, if she could. She had turned her "women with horses" art show over to her friend Carol at the local studio and packed her bags.

Hank stopped in front of a stall near where Darby stood. "What are you doing in the barn?" He stroked the nose of the paint cow pony hanging his head over the old, wooden poles.

"I couldn't sleep. Time change."

He nodded. She saw something softer in his steely expression, but before she could figure out what it was, it was gone.

"I thought you were a burglar," he said.

"In Montana? In the dark of night?"

"Different day and age. You can't be too careful."

She stared down at the dirt beneath her boots. They were dancing around the real issues—the time between them, the way she'd disappeared from his life never to return until now. But those were issues she wasn't ready to confront, let alone explore with a man who'd once been the love of her life.

Yet, she suddenly found she wasn't as impervious to him as she'd expected. Simply standing beside him caused her heart to give a sharp kick against her ribs. A delightful awareness flooded her, leaving her feeling lightheaded.

Hiding her reaction to him, Darby turned to the bay mare in the stall beside her. She looked very pregnant. "How's Leo?"

"Physically, well enough." Hank's answer was terse. "Not sure about mentally."

She fought a sharp stab of guilt. That was unexpected, too. "What do you mean?"

"He's tired. That fall took the fight out of him."

Fight. Yes, her dad had always been a fighter. Those were the things she remembered most from living with him and her mom. They'd fought like cats and dogs, as the cliché went. She never knew them *not* to argue. But they had seemed to make up some-how. After she'd gone to bed, Darby heard them next door in their bedroom laughing. The other noises coming from that end of the cabin had told her, after she was old enough to understand, that they enjoyed making up.

SILENCE HUNG between them like the quiet of a starry Montana night. Hank didn't know what to say. How to react to the girl, now woman, he'd once loved. The woman who'd neglected her own father and seemed not to care. Darby York had matured over the years, much as he had done, he supposed. She wasn't the same slim school girl, quick to bound onto the back of her mare and gallop with him along the creeks and valleys they called home. That impetuous, fun-loving spirit seemed to be gone.

He kept his hand against the neck of the paint, letting its warmth ground him, its reality help him cope with Darby's arrival. She was slender enough even in her heavy coat to still tempt him and swirl his blood. Her red hair was flecked with gray at the temples, and she wore it in a long braid down her back as if to keep it out of her way. The natural, unsophisticated look about her remained—something familiar, warm, and cozy.

The skin on her face looked soft and youthful, unwrinkled, with a rosy flush on her cheeks. He remembered her mouth, those kiss-able lips.

How long had it been since he'd kissed a woman?

Yet, in the gloom of the barn aisleway, her green eyes were sad.

That's what struck Hank the most. It was almost as if the light had dimmed from them. When had that happened? When her husband died? Or had it been earlier? Back in the day when they explored each other's sexuality and been so very much in love? Or had it been when her mother died?

"I'm glad you came home," he said in a gruff voice.

She didn't look at him. "I didn't have much choice after all your phone calls."

Blamed him, did she? His hackles rose. "When I got back to the ranch in January, I couldn't believe you hadn't been home in thirty years."

"Things got in the way." She evaded his eyes as well as his criticism.

"Leo didn't want me to call you, but I couldn't let it rest. It made no sense to me."

Darby turned with a flash of anger in her eyes. "It wasn't your business."

"No." He let out a slow breath, knowing she basically had a point. "But this ranch *is* my business. Leo gave me the job of keeping it going, running it at least one more season, helping to get it back in the black. It's my job as long as he's alive and wants to keep it going."

What was left of the anger on her face flattened into a scowl, and she turned back to the horse. Running her gloved hand down the mare's neck, she acted as if Hank had vanished.

He tried to control the sudden resentment roiling inside him. She had vanished on him when he was eighteen. He'd said nothing then. Let her go. Went his own way. That wouldn't happen today.

"I don't understand why you ignored Leo all these years. If I had a father, a family, I wouldn't turn my back on them."

She twisted around to face him, her face distorted in fury. "I *have* a family. In Kentucky."

His body tensed. He ignored her anger. "I know your mother's death hurt you, but Leo was hurt, too. You should have stuck around to help your dad run through all that."

"Well, I didn't." She stepped away from the stall with a toss of her head. "And as you said, Hank Slade, it's really none of your business. I'm back now, thanks to you. Give everything else a rest."

"Duly noted," he said, getting a grip on his own feverish temper.

She pushed past him and strode out of the barn, running again as was her habit.

"That went well," Hank said to the paint horse. The animal tossed his head, much as Darby had done, but it was more as if in agreement, not anger. The bay mare snorted steam at being left alone.

Hank didn't care so much about whatever bothered Darby. He only cared that Leo York was hurting. Leo was his boss, and he'd given him a chance at a new life. Hank was determined not to let the man down as his daughter had.

CHAPTER FIVE

A HARD KNOCK sounded on the cabin door, a gloved fist pounding against the wood. "Breakfast in the crew dining hall in ten minutes!"

Leo. Darby groaned and rolled over in bed. Her father had always been adamant about being on time for breakfast. If you were late, you didn't eat.

It was six-thirty; the sun had yet to rise. Darby quickly threw off the Hudson Bay blanket and down comforter that had kept her toasty all night. When her sock-covered feet touched the squeaky cabin floor, she cringed and remembered just how cold a Montana winter could be. In the one-room space, a hand-hewn, log bed frame and dresser, probably made by Leo's grandfather, gave the cabin rustic charm. Dudes from the East would love its quaintness, for sure. She was not as thrilled. Summer guests didn't see the harsh reality of winter weather.

Fortunately, when she'd returned from the barn last night, Darby had taken a long, soaking bath in the claw foot tub. This morning she didn't require much more than a splash of chilly water on her face to awaken her before she dressed for the winter weather in thermal underwear, jeans, wool socks, flannel shirt, down vest, and a pair of weather-proof, insulated pac boots.

She felt ready to tackle the day. And her father. She wasn't so sure about Hank. The thought of facing him again after last night's skirmish gave her a peculiar feeling, half apprehension, half uneasy anticipation.

Darby pulled on her parka, went outside, and stood for a moment on the porch, taking stock of the ranch as the light of sunrise illuminated the valley. She took a deep breath of icy air. Leo's grandparents had bought a homestead here along the Saga Creek during the 1930s. They built the ranch, one cabin at a time, eventually offering overnight and weekly stays for Eastern guests because they paid better than the uncertain income from ranching at this elevation.

When she arrived in the rental car from the airport in Bozeman last night, Leo had hardly said a word and installed her in a guest cabin next to his own. The other guest cabins stretched down the valley past the lodgepole dining hall, so by settling her in the one next to his, Leo made sure he could keep an eye on her—almost as if she were still a girl of fifteen.

Darby pulled on her gloves and tugged her knit beanie over her ears. It felt like sub-zero. She stepped down the stairs onto a cleared, gravel path. Wind sliced across the lawns where sagebrush poked above a layer of snow. In the distance, a horse's sharp neigh split the frosty silence.

Buffeted by the wind, she hiked toward the dining hall. Smoke rose from the chimney, an indication someone lived in this otherwise remote ranch. Usually during the summer months, a crew of twenty-four worked the place. Darby wasn't sure who stuck around after the season ended.

She clomped up the steps to the dining hall. Under the covered porch, she stamped her feet to clear her boots of snow and opened the heavy wooden door. Inside a real fire crackled in a stone fireplace. At the long dining table, two men sat savoring mugs of steaming coffee. One was Leo. He gazed at her through thick glasses. In the light of day, he looked old like the cracked leather on the sofa and his face sagged at the jowls. His gray hair had thinned to almost nothing.

The other man was an elderly wrangler who looked as ancient as her father. He had ruddy cheeks and a Santa Claus beard. She remembered his name was Pete…Pete Harden.

Darby crossed the floor to join them. "Nice to see you again, Pete," she said, addressing the hired hand as she pulled off her hat and removed her gloves, stuffing them into her pockets.

"Howdy, there, Miss Darby. You sure have grown up."

"It's been a few years." Darby stripped off her parka, dropped it on the worn sofa facing the fireplace, and sat next to her father who remained seated at the head of the table.

"Dad." She nodded toward Leo, but he ignored her in favor of his coffee mug. Not an auspicious start.

"Still have that pretty red hair." Pete stirred sugar into his coffee. "And you're pretty just like your mama."

Memories flooded back, and Darby gave Pete a weak smile. Her mother had been beautiful and tall, so much like Kelsey. "Not too much gray in it yet."

"No, ma'am. 'N' you sure do look pretty."

Darby bent her head, glancing askance at her father to gauge his reaction. None, of course. The steaming coffee held all his interest.

At that moment, the kitchen door swung open, and a stout woman with ample hips backed into the room. She carried a large tray filled with steaming platters of food. Like everyone else, she wore blue jeans, pac boots, and a flannel shirt. She set the tray on a sideboard and from there placed plates of scrambled eggs, bacon, biscuits, and fried potatoes on the table. Pete reached for the eggs, served himself, then passed them to her father. The woman intercepted the plate and gave Leo a scoop of eggs. She then shoved the plate toward Darby.

Darby served herself and, narrowing her eyes, watched the

woman bending over her father. She assisted Leo with each dish, even buttering his biscuits as if he was a child and couldn't do it for himself.

"We can't do much on this ranch without Ellie's help," Pete said with a wink when he noticed Darby's interest in the woman. "She's a damn good cook."

Darby offered a faint smile, then turned her attention to placing fried potatoes on her plate. What was it with that woman? The father she remembered never needed or wanted anyone's help.

Ellie suddenly stood up and surveyed the table, a dismayed look on her face. "Oh, Leo, I've forgotten your fried apples."

Leo patted her hand. "That's all right, Ellie. You sure don't need to worry about it. Sit down and eat."

Darby pushed back from the table and stood. "I'll get the apples. Are they in the kitchen?"

"Setting in a bowl next to the stove. Thank you, honey."

Darby didn't miss the smile that appeared obligatory or the term "honey" that grated on her like sharp nails on the proverbial chalkboard.

The kitchen was situated between two dining halls. The one designated only for guests was closed off until the season started in early June. Darby found the bowl of fried apples on the countertop as noted. She hesitated a moment and took a fortifying breath. The room smelled delightful, filled with wood smoke and the warm aroma of breakfast fixings. When had her dad taken a liking to fried apples? Her mother had not been a cook, so Leo had always seemed satisfied in the morning with a cup of coffee and toast until a cook came to work for the season.

Times had changed certainly. But then, it *had* been thirty years.

Darby caught her lower lip between her teeth and shoved her shoulder into the swinging door leading to the dining room. She could back into a room as easily as the treasured cook.

Yet, when she turned around, her boot caught on an uneven piece of planking, and Darby stumbled, losing her balance. The bowl of apples flew from her hands and sailed through the air. The stoneware dish crashed onto the floor, breaking into big chunks, and the apples sloshed into a sticky glob on the floor.

"Hell's bells!" Darby couldn't help the expletive. It shot from her mouth as quickly as mortification overwhelmed her. Leo glanced her way and frowned. Curse words had always been frowned upon.

"That's all right." Ellie stood up, pushing her chair back from the table. "I'll get it."

"No, I made the mess, I'll clean it up," Darby insisted.

"Whatever you say, honey."

Darby knelt on her hands and knees and picked up the pieces of stoneware. Just then, the door opened, and Hank strolled into the room, tossing his cowboy hat onto the antler of a trophy buck hanging on the wall. He shrugged off his Carhartt work coat.

"Mornin'," he said to her looking down.

She glanced at his boots and then up his tight jean-clad legs to the hint of stubble along the chiseled line of his jaw. What was that silly grin? That chortle deep in his throat that he tried to suppress.

A strong flush of annoyance rushed through Darby. *This can't be happening*! She scrambled awkwardly to her feet. "Good morning, Mr. Slade. Did you sleep well?"

He slid a gaze over her body, and she bristled at his all too obvious scrutiny, because it thrust instant warmth through her body.

"Slept fine as always. What about you, Mrs. Heston? Is it too cold here for your Eastern blood?"

Irritating man. "We have cold weather in Kentucky." She turned from him in a dismissive huff and headed toward the kitchen.

Did she actually hear him snicker? Darby returned with paper towels to gather the apples. Then she made a second trip with a wet, soapy rag to scrub the stickiness off the floor. By the time she sat down beside Hank, she knew her breakfast was stone cold.

Pete pushed a pot of coffee across the table toward her. "I hear you have some damn fancy horses in Kentucky."

Hank picked up the pot, poured her a cup without asking, then refilled his own mug.

Darby shot him a glance of exasperation. What if she didn't want coffee?

The cowboy ignored her glare, cradled his own mug, and took a big gulp.

Pete laughed. "Hank has a mouth of cast iron. He can drink anything hot."

"Better with a little whisky in it," Hank muttered into the mug.

"To answer your question, Pete, my husband owned a thorough-bred breeding farm." Darby tilted her head to concentrate on Pete and ignore Hank. "Now my daughter and son run it. Yes, we have some very fine horses in Kentucky. As they say, fast horses and beautiful women."

Her jest fell on deaf ears.

Digging a fork into the eggs on her plate, Darby brought the food to her lips. Cold, as she expected. She swallowed down a mouthful. The atmosphere around the table remained quiet and strained, as chilly as the eggs. Everyone threw uncomfortable glances at each other and ate as if there would be no hot meal tomorrow. For the hundredth time since she'd packed her bags in Kentucky, Darby wished she hadn't left home.

"I suppose these so-called gentlemen expect me to introduce myself," the cook finally said with a glance of displeasure at her colleagues. "My name is Ellie Montgomery. I'm the breakfast and lunch cook during the season; full-time cook the rest of the time."

"Nice to meet you, Ellie," Darby said with a polite nod. "From the little I've tasted, you're an excellent cook."

"It's nice having another woman around here. Gets a bit lonely during the winter."

"I'm sure."

"Your daddy took me in a couple years ago." Ellie tapped a finger on the tabletop. She must have felt she needed to explain. "Didn't have no place to go, and Leo gave me room and board and a job. Been loyal to him ever since. Been almost like a father to me."

Throat suddenly tight, Darby forced a smile. "That's nice."

Ellie sat across the table and next to Pete, allowing Darby to have a good look at her. The cook had a generous bust. Her long blond hair had a touch of gray at the temples like Darby. Could she be about Darby's age? Not beautiful, but not bad looking either, no matter the extra weight. Typical salt-of-the-earth kind of woman, Darby supposed.

Yet, what was her relationship with Leo? Was it as platonic as Ellie made it sound?

Darby's tight throat seemed to close up. She briefly shut her eyes. When she opened them, Hank studied her over the rim of his coffee mug, observing her with a curious warm approval, and something more…that something more she'd been unable to put her finger on last night. Suddenly, she lost her appetite but then forced herself to take another bite.

Ellie had no problem eating and talking, carrying on a one-sided discussion about the weather, road conditions, the ranch resident moose, and the need to get to town for more groceries before any more bad weather set in. The men kept on eating and nodded without comment as if they were used to Ellie's one-way conversations.

Finally, his plate clean, Hank pushed back from the table. "I need to check the herd today at the winter pasture."

Horses used during the summer season for the paying guests were turned outside during the winter.

Leo spoke for the first time. "Taking Pete with you?"

"Nope," Pete said. "I'm taking the paint into town for the vet to look at his leg. Ellie's going with me to get supplies."

"Then Darby will go with you, Hank," Leo directed.

Darby fought to stop her mouth from dropping open in surprise. She tilted her chin up instead. "What if I don't want to go?" She wasn't used to being ordered around. "Don't you still keep the herd over the mountain in the next valley. You seriously don't expect me to ride across the mountain on horseback? In this weather?"

"We *are* in the twenty-first century," Hank said. "We have a truck, and we take the highway, Darby."

The way Hank said her name made her head feel fuzzy. The world unexpectedly spun in a crazy fashion. She was a widow, for heaven's sakes, and Hank Slade was the guy from her past. He shouldn't make her name sound sexy, and her heart shouldn't skitter in her chest.

"No matter," she said, recovering and glancing at her father. "I'll pass."

Abruptly Leo slapped his hand down on the table with a resounding crack. "You ain't no royalty, Darby. Do what you're told. Get up and go with Hank."

Her chest knotted with anger. This was her daddy of old—the gruff man she'd once obeyed without question. The father she'd once loved. Darby pushed back from the table, refusing to be provoked into a hostile response.

She was no longer a child. Why did she suddenly feel like one?

CHAPTER SIX

DARBY STRUGGLED to calm the shivering of her chilled body, aware that more than the Montana cold affected her. She'd already made a fool of herself in the dining hall by dropping the bowl of gooey apples. Could she survive the trip with Hank without making another fool of herself?

Stepping out on the porch, Darby saw Hank pull up to the dining hall steps in a battered and muddy pickup truck. He leaned across the front bench seat and opened the passenger-side door for her. "Hop in."

She climbed inside. The cab was already warm. Buckling up as Hank put the truck in gear, Darby settled in for the ride to the winter pasture. Her companion had put quilted coveralls over his jeans and now wore a knit cap pulled over his ears with a *Made in America* flag on it. Not wearing a cowboy hat, he didn't look a bit like a cowboy. And he seemed all business, keeping his eyes on the snow-packed, gravel ranch road that meandered through the grounds and under the log entrance gate with its sign reading *Ghost Mountain Ranch*.

The ranch road met the main highway at the end of the valley. Hank glanced at her as he turned right. She looked away from him toward the passenger-side window. The main two-lane highway, a thin ribbon of civilization, wound its way southward along the Gallatin River. In summer, sport fly-fishermen stood in the shallows flicking their lines, but today the whitewater looked icy and uninviting.

Rock escarpments and forests of aspen, Douglas fir, and lodgepole pine made this part of Montana so different from the rolling bluegrass fields of Kentucky. The whitewater of the Gallatin River split the mountain ranges with their ten- and eleven-thousand-foot peaks. It was rugged country. Starkly beautiful in the winter. But damn cold.

In the frosty light of morning, Ghost Mountain loomed over the valley casting a long menacing shadow. Darby suppressed a shiver. The ranch was one step away from wilderness—dangerous and unpredictable. She much preferred the gentler hills of the bluegrass.

Darby cast a furtive peek at Hank. She especially liked the stubble on his chin and the way his long hair, curling around the back of his ears, poked out from under his knit cap.

"Gonna be a nice day," Hank said, his voice low and rich. He looked at her quickly, as if sizing her up as she did him. "But we're in for some weather tonight."

Darby grunted in response. Why did the man throw her off balance with his deep silences and pointed glances? Waves of testosterone emanated from him even at his age. She was too old to react to its lure.

Col had never been rough and rugged like Hank. No, Colton Heston had been a refined, Southern gentleman, but not what she'd call handsome or manly. Col's kindness had been the reason she'd married him so long ago. His money hadn't hurt either. Whatever both their motivations, they'd made a successful union and raised their twins to adulthood, but she'd never felt sexually attracted to her husband. Not like the simmering attraction she felt for the man in the cab beside her.

Darby's heart gave a little kick. Years ago, hers had been a passionate, first-time love. She'd thought she'd marry Hank and make a life with him. But it hadn't worked out that way.

"We were so incredibly young," she said in a quiet, reflective voice.

It was Hank's turn to grunt at her comment, not moving his eyes from the roadway.

"What did you do afterwards?" She was unable to say the words "after I left home," but she figured he'd know what she meant.

"Joined the Army."

That was all he offered. Darby surmised he'd never married. Had she broken his heart that badly? Darby tried not to be curious, but memories, good and bad, overwhelmed her, pummeling her at every angle. Like the day her mother died. Her guilt after that day was omnipresent, as if she were at fault. If only she'd been home...

Darby wet her lips, stunned by her continued self-reproach and her unexpected reaction to Hank. She felt that old pull drawing her toward him. Maybe it was better he kept quiet. Maybe it was better not learning any more about the man her former boyfriend had become.

Thankfully, the road was well-plowed, and they made good time.

"Why doesn't Leo live at winter pasture?" she asked after a while, unable to quell her curiosity. They reached the intersection where the road turned west to skirt the mountain range and join the next valley where the winter pasture was located. "If I remember, it's at a lower elevation, not as snowy as the dude ranch in the mountains. There was once a cabin near the property, I think."

"Asked Leo that when I came back." Hank chanced a look her way, his eyes hooded. "He said because he didn't want to leave the ranch. Didn't give me a good reason."

"He was always a stubborn man."

"Like his daughter?"

Hank's observation cut into her, burning her gut. She clamped her mouth shut and turned to the window again letting the scenery take her breath away instead of Hank's criticism.

Thirty minutes later, they arrived at the winter pasture, a fenced two thousand acres of Montana bottom land that Leo leased. Just back from the main highway stood the old cabin Darby remembered. A big metal out-building occupied the area behind and to the left of the cabin. Hank parked on the side where the snow wasn't so deep.

"We pay someone local to feed the horses every other day. I come on weekends to check on the herd and make sure everything is okay," Hank said. "Jump out. We gotta switch trucks."

Darby stepped out of the pickup into a drift of snow. Thankfully, it didn't cover the tops of her boots. She stood with her arms crossed against the cold as Hank opened the wide barn doors. Inside were big rolls of hay and a white flatbed truck backed inside. It already carried two rolls.

"Climb in."

Darby clambered into the cab of the hay truck. Hank started the engine and cold air blasted them. Darby shivered, hugging herself more closely, and Hank turned down the fan.

"Needs to warm up."

You think? Darby didn't voice her thoughts, still unsure of herself in a place where she'd once been so comfortable.

Hank drove out of the barn, shifted gears and turned onto the highway for about a mile. Then he turned once more into a side road where a gate halted them. He left the cab, leaving the door ajar and letting more cold air rush in. After opening the gate, he climbed back in, drove through the fence, and reversed the process to shut the gate.

There wasn't a horse in sight.

As they jounced along a road invisible under the snow, Hank honked the horn, its shrillness sounding out of place in the silence of the meadow. The truck topped a small ridge, and Hank stopped again.

"We keep about eighty horses out here."

Darby surveyed the vast valley of unbroken white flanked by distant mountains. Sunshine glared off the snow. The sky was bright blue without a cloud, truly Big Sky Country.

"This is so different from my husband's Thoroughbred farm in Kentucky."

"Yup. I bet you have some pampered horses."

Darby thought of the blankets and heated stables back home. "Our horses wouldn't know how to survive out here."

"We usually don't have this much snow. Plenty of good grazing last year. Pete said they didn't need to feed as much hay then. Each one of these rolls weighs eight hundred pounds."

Hank put the truck in gear and drove down the other side of the ridge honking the horn. At the bottom, he opened his window and with a wireless remote, lowered the hydraulic arm on the back of the truck. It held the first roll of hay. As he drove, maneuvering in a long oval, he pushed another button, and the hay spun freely, dropping big clumps behind the truck.

Hank nodded in the direction of a second ridge. "Look over there."

Darby glanced to her right in time to spot the first horse top the rim and trot down the other side. One after another, the herd emerged following the leader. Bays, paints, chestnuts, appaloosas— every color of sturdy, Western horse showed up and dropped their heads to feed on the hay.

Hank got out, switched the arm to the second roll of hay, and distributed it along the farther end of the meadow. More horses appeared.

"How do you keep their water from freezing?" Darby asked. Thawing frozen water buckets was always a problem on the farm.

"Got a spring that doesn't freeze. We're lucky that way." Hank stopped the truck. "Come on. Let's check on 'em."

Darby exited the truck, pulled on her knit beanie, then joined Hank, her boots crunching on the snow. She wanted to be a trooper, but it was damn cold. Even for March. In Kentucky, the first forsythia and daffodils would be blooming.

As they walked among the horses, a few came to greet them, snorting their happiness for the newly distributed hay and the human's attention. Hank called each one by name. "Hey, Scout. How ya' doin' Mickey? Looking good there, Daisy." Here and there, he rubbed the blaze on a face or patted a furry brown neck.

"Be glad the wind's not blowing," he said over his shoulder to Darby. "Wind chill gets brutal out here."

"I know." Darby stroked the muzzle of a small, inquisitive geld-ing. She could see her own breath and that of the horse. She'd grown up with the Western way but had become accustomed to living a different, softer lifestyle.

Hank surveyed the herd. "All look good, considering."

"That's splendid." Darby shivered and stamped her feet. She wanted to go back to the truck, but kept her mouth shut.

"Dammit. Two are missing."

How did he know that with so many horses milling around? She could barely count them, but Hank seemed to know each one.

"C'mon, let's hike to the top of that ridge and see if we can spot the fugitives."

GIVEN THE CIRCUMSTANCES, Darby was a real trooper. Hank heard her breathing hard behind them as they hiked through the snow to the crest of the next rise. Once at the top, he sucked in the cold air and surveyed the vastness of the valley stretching in front of him.

Joining him, Darby grabbed her knees and doubled over to catch her breath.

"Out of shape, huh?" Why did he like to pester her? He'd teased her back in the day, but it was different this time. An underlying anger stirred in his gut. It was one thing to leave him, but Leo?

She gulped in air. "I'm not usually climbing mountains back in Kentucky."

"This is not what I call a mountain."

"You know what I mean."

She stood up. The consternation on Darby's face was priceless.

Hank suppressed a grin and turned from her to scan the valley. It was odd having her here, as if a specter had materialized from the past. But she wasn't a dream. Darby York Heston was very vital and very much alive. He'd loved two women in his lifetime. Liz McKenna had ultimately married another man, but the other woman, his first love, had disappeared on him.

Trouble was, loving these women had always been one-sided. All on his part. Sadly, he'd kept his feelings to himself. He couldn't see much changing even though Darby was now single and free. Not unless he had enough nerve to open up, which was something very hard for him to do and something he'd never done.

"What did *you* do after you left the ranch?" he probed without glancing back. She'd given him the opening by asking him the same question earlier.

Silence for a moment, then she responded, "I went to Kentucky and got a job taking care of horses. That's where I met my husband."

Hank removed his hat by the brim, wiped his forehead with the back of his hand, and let her answer sink in. Shouldn't there be more to the story than that?

"Seems you married a very rich man."

More hesitation. "Colton was the heir to a Kentucky bourbon dynasty. He worked in the business with his brother for years, but when I met him, he was ready to make a change. We soon bought a farm, and using his inheritance, he invested heavily in a Thoroughbred breeding operation."

Damn. How could he compete with anything like that? A damn bourbon heir of all things? Might as well be a damn prince. He was only the heir of his father's guitar and a pretty damn good saddle.

"I suppose you were happy." His question was more of a statement. Who wouldn't be happy in a setup like that?

Another pause and a soft sigh. Then a tentative laugh. "Yes, I was happy enough. We had two wonderful children."

Strange answer, but this Darby had become foreign to him. Reserved, but strangely despondent—as if an underpinning of despair plagued her life. With a rich husband and children, she should be head-over-heels in happiness.

Yet, everything about Darby was disconcertingly familiar even after all this time—the way she turned her head, her womanly scent in the truck cab, the way she laughed, her natural reticence, and the glint of her red hair against the brilliant sunshine.

The wind was brutal on the ridge. They needed to get back. Movement on the horizon caught his eye, and he chuckled. "There they are! Those guys!"

She perked up. "Where?"

Hank pointed. "Down there. In the valley. About two miles from the rest of the herd. Must be running with the elk."

"Oh, I see them." The tension between them eased briefly. "What will happen to the horses?"

"I suppose they will eventually find the hay, foolish critters."

"Aren't you concerned?"

"Nope, not after spotting them. They look fine."

"Great." Darby spun on her heels. "We can go back to the truck where it's warm. My face feels about to fall off."

Hank caught up with her as she marched down the ridge and fell into step beside her. The crunch of their boots was magnified by the quiet around them.

Unsatisfied by her answers so far, Hank's gut gnawed with curiosity and anger. He didn't understand her. Why hadn't she come home sooner? What had happened between her and her father?

"I don't get it, Darby," he said. "Why didn't you come home even once? I get it you were married and had kids and a pretty good life.

I get it your mom had died. But Leo was still here. Pete told me your father has been pretty damn lonely all these years."

Darby stopped in her tracks. He noted the spark of fury in her eyes and the tightness in her lips. She blew out a frosty air of disgust and answered quietly, "I told you before, Hank Slade, it's none of your business. I don't want to talk about it."

She walked away from him, but he caught her arm to stop her. "Answer me, will you?"

The sunshine showed her beauty even though she was bundled up to her neck against the cold with a scarf and a knit cap pulled over her ears. The tip of her nose was red. He wanted to take his gloved hands and warm her face and nose. He wanted to kiss those lips drawn tight with anger.

Whoa, easy son. Darby was still one fabulous filly, and he was still man enough to want her.

Hank swallowed hard, searching her eyes. "The girl I once knew wouldn't neglect her father."

Darby answered him by lifting her chin, setting it at an obstinate angle, then she shook her arm free. He let her go, supposing she'd not answer him.

But she did. She looked him right in the eyes, and for the first time, he saw tears pooling there.

"That's just it, Hank," she said. "Leo's not my father. I was adopted."

CHAPTER SEVEN

Why had she revealed her deepest secret to Hank?

Darby had never told anyone, not even Col, about what she'd learned the last night she'd been home at the ranch. Her mother had died tragically the previous day. Her father's surprising disclosure had only added to Darby's confusion and anger. The truth had hurt like hell.

If she was adopted by Leo, why had they never told her before then?

Now it all came careening back to her—especially the guilt of her mother's death. If she and Hank had not been together on that very romantic campout in the mountains, maybe her mother would still be alive. Maybe if she'd been a better daughter, Darby could have stopped what happened. Those thoughts had haunted her all these years, coloring her past and now her present.

Making the decision to leave, to sever all her ties with her father, had been spur of the moment, but ultimately a deliberate decision. She could never go home. At the time she ran away, she'd surrendered to her heavy feeling of remorse. Coming back had been because Kelsey had shamed her into it. Guilt was a heavy taskmaster. It wasn't a good way to live. It wasn't productive, but she was used to its weighty burden.

Acutely aware of Hank's shock and sudden sympathy, Darby sat stiff and silent on the drive home, her gloved fists folded in her lap. The atmosphere in the truck was strained, to say the least. When they arrived at the ranch, she declined to eat with the crew and hid out in her cabin for the rest of the afternoon.

As she always did when troubled, Darby picked up the sketchpad and charcoal pencil she'd brought with her and sat down at the small desk shoved against the window where winter light pooled on the desktop. She drew. It soothed her. She lost herself in her imagination, putting her dreams on paper.

Shadows had fallen across the room by the time someone rapped on her door. It was five-thirty, and the sun had almost set. Darby rose, stretched her cramped muscles, and answered the knock. It was Hank, of course.

He stood there on the threshold, cowboy perfect, with his arms full of wood. They gazed at each other through the gathering darkness, then he grinned sheepishly, this time without any judgment or ridicule. "You'll need this tonight."

"Oh, thanks." She stepped aside. Already the room had grown uncomfortably cold. She'd forgotten to tend the stove.

Hank did it for her. He clomped into the room, bringing in with him a trace of wood smoke and cold air. She caught his personal scent too—leather and soap—and a sudden longing flooded her, leaving her shaky.

He poked the fire into a blaze. Then he turned on a lamp. "Too damn dark in here."

"I was too busy to notice." Darby watched him move around her room, filling its space with his rugged masculinity. He went into her bathroom, and she heard him test the flow of water in the sink.

"Still good," he said coming out. "Not frozen." Then he noticed her sketchpad, studying the charcoal drawings for a long moment.

When he lifted his head, his gaze lingered on her for an unsettling moment. "You used to do that when we were kids."

Her mood lifted. She nodded. "I'm a professional artist now. I sell my paintings on commission."

Until that moment, Darby hadn't realized how important that distinction had become to her. Being a professional set her apart from others who simply drew for a hobby. It made her unique. Col had understood its importance to her, and something inside her was glad she'd admitted it to Hank as well.

He picked up the pad of paper. From memory, she'd drawn two ranch horses in the winter pasture—their shaggy coats and tousled manes, their gentle eyes, and sturdy legs. A few simple lines represented the mountains in the distance.

Hank surveyed her work. "This is damn good."

The room seemed suddenly ablaze with something more than the heat from the wood stove. Hank seemed to sense it, too.

Moistening her lips, Darby removed the paper from his hands. Goosebumps spread across her skin. "It's nothing. Needs more work. Maybe I'll paint it when I get home."

He wore a cowboy hat now and had taken it off, dangling it loosely between his fingers. "Okay."

"I have my own studio," she said, abruptly aware of the tightening in her chest and the need to explain. "At the farm. Col built it for me. I'm supposed to have my own showing this month. 'Women and horses,' I call it." Why was she telling him this? He didn't care about her home. Her real home. He only cared about this ranch and his duty to Leo.

"Well, that's great," Hank said, as if he didn't know how to react to her sudden enthusiasm and her nearness. She sensed his restless uneasiness. He shifted his stance. "Best come along to the dining hall if you want to eat supper. You know Leo's rules."

Darby's heart gave a hard thud. She dropped her gaze, a flush of embarrassment warming her face. "Sure. Be right along."

How quickly Hank put her in her place by reminding her of the significant things in life…like Leo's expectations and showing up to dinner on time.

~

SNOWFLAKES CLUNG to her eyelashes and knit cap, making it white and wet by the time Darby completed the short trek to the dining hall. Snow fell hard and stung her face. The temperature must have already plummeted twenty degrees. After clearing her boots, she entered to find the same scene as the morning meal. Everyone was at their place at the crew table.

Her father didn't look up to greet her. His behavior was off-putting, and her irritation with him increased.

"Gonna get another damn snowstorm," Pete complained from his seat at the table.

She removed her coat and hung it on the rack. "In March? Are we going to be snowed in?"

"Likely," Leo growled into his coffee mug. "You won't be able to take off for a few days."

Darby drew in a slow, steady breath and then blew it out. How did he know she already wanted to leave? She approached the table, her eyes on the man who had been her father when she was growing up. He glared at her, daring her to speak. The tension coiled inside her as she stared at him.

"I have questions for you," she said. "Stuff I need to know about my mother."

Leo grunted as if dismissing her.

Before she could react to his disdain, the door burst open behind them, and Hank blew in with the wind. He stomped his feet and, like he'd done in the morning, tossed his hat onto the rack of antlers hanging on the wall.

"Going to be a rough night," he said to the room. He hung his coat on a corner rack.

Darby hesitated. Now was not the time to quiz Leo. Not with

Hank barreling toward the table and pulling out the chair for her to sit down.

"Ma'am," he said with a polite nod.

His gaze warmed her, touched her like a caress. She glanced away. "Hank."

Sitting next to Hank was a challenge to her equilibrium. She marveled at him. How he'd changed. He was a man now, not the kid from her past, and she was a woman whose husband had been dead over a year. She technically was single. Just like Hank.

Darby smiled to herself. She liked the man he'd become. There was something loyal and kind about him, like a family dog. That was an awful way to think about him. One she'd never say aloud. But who didn't love the faithful family dog? She ducked her head and listened to the banter of the men around her.

"Got the paint's leg tended," Pete told the group at the table. "Doc says he'll be okay with stall rest."

"Horses at winter pasture look fine. None the worse for our snowy winter," Hank reported.

Leo mumbled thanks for the update. "Ordered more hay to be delivered next week," he said. "We need to get ads placed in the dude ranch news for summer help."

"Summer can't get here soon enough," Pete grumbled. "Damn tired of this weather."

Ellie chose that moment to back into the room carrying a huge tray. "You gentlemen can help me by getting our guest something to drink," she said and set the tray on the sideboard.

Hank turned to Darby. "What will it be?"

Their eyes connected. Once again, she felt that strange tingling sensation. Self-conscious, she muttered a reply. Something about she'd have what he drank. He grinned at her and poured hot, black coffee into her mug.

"Do you have cream?"

"Sissy Eastern way to drink coffee." Hank went to the sideboard to pick up a cream pitcher. He brought it back to the table and handed it to her. There was a gleam in his eyes like the Hank of old.

He was kidding her. Col had never joked with her. Never made fun. Maybe that had been because of the disparity of their ages. Or maybe because their marriage was more one of convenience and respect rather than passionate love and friendship.

"You can stop making goo-goo eyes at Hank and help Ellie get food on the table," Leo said to her in his crotchety voice.

Darby bit her lip to control an angry response and stood, gripping the edge of the table. Why did he treat her like that? She wasn't his child. "I'll be glad to help Ellie." Her voice was icy. Pete and Hank stared at her.

"Oh, don't bother, Darby, honey." Ellie bustled from the sideboard to the table. She served a helping of what looked to be beef stew onto Leo's plate. "I've got this under control. You sit down, dear."

Ellie handed the bowl to Pete, who waited on himself. Darby sat down hard and scooted up to the table. Her gut curled with resentment. Leo wasn't the only one to treat her like a child. Ellie's sing-song voice calling her "dear" and "honey" was another irritant. As far as she could figure, that woman was several years her junior.

Tension hung in the air over the table. Gazes shifted back and forth, making for an uncomfortable silence. After everyone was served beef stew, green salad, and cornbread, the men put their heads down and dug into the food as if they hadn't eaten in three weeks.

Ellie rolled her eyes and looked over at Darby. "If I didn't feed them some salad, these cowpokes would never eat anything healthy," she said, lowering her voice to speak confidentially, woman-to-woman. "Meat and potatoes. That's all they want."

She glanced at Ellie and forced a weak smile. "My son is like that."

"Then you know, don't you? Men! That's why God created

women. We have to civilize them. They don't know what's best for themselves."

Grunts came from the three men at the table, but they didn't complain about Ellie's good cooking or her bright conversation. She didn't mean it, after all, and they seemed to know it and take her criticism in stride. After they'd all finished and devoured Ellie's peach cobbler for dessert, Darby offered to help wash dishes. She didn't give Leo time to dictate.

In the kitchen, Ellie plunged her hands into the hot, sudsy water in the sink. "Mighty glad for the help."

"No problem." Darby picked up a towel. It had been a long time since she'd dried dishes with a dishtowel.

Suddenly, flashbacks riveted her to the spot, shadowy memories of warm cocoa and hugs, the smell of roaring fires and sagebrush, the laughter of Eastern guests in the summer, and horses...always horses. Darby swallowed hard and held the towel immobile. Often, in her childhood innocence, feeling safe and loved, she had stood at this very spot helping her mother dry dishes. Once she'd been a happy-go-lucky teenager without a care in the world. Her horse and her boyfriend were her top priorities. The Ghost Mountain Ranch had been her world. Her life.

The flashbacks were better than the dreams.

"I bet it's hard coming home," Ellie said as if probing for more.

Drawn out of her reverie, Darby averted her gaze and picked up a clean plate to towel off. "Yes."

"I lost my mother, too."

Darby didn't want to talk about it. Why was this woman trying to befriend her? She didn't need her sympathy. Or her friendship.

"I couldn't talk about my mom for a long time," Ellie went on.

Was she implying Darby should have gotten over her mother's death by now?

"She died of cirrhosis of the liver," Ellie said. "It was long and hard."

"I'm sorry."

"The reason I'm bringing this up," Ellie peered at her from under her lashes, "is that Leo wants you to go through your bedroom. Sort out your things. Take what you want. I believe he's put your mother's personal belongings in the room, too."

"You mean my old bedroom in his cabin?"

"Yes. He never goes in there. Just shut the door years ago. Left it like it was. Your leaving has been hard on him, honey. Now that you've come home, he says you need to get rid of what you don't want. We can donate anything worth giving away."

What the...? A chill crept across Darby's skin. Leo had kept her room closed since that day? And why was Ellie interfering? Sure, she seemed to take care of Leo, but still she wasn't his wife. Couldn't Leo speak for himself?

Being here, back at the ranch where there were so many good memories, as well as the bad ones, Darby suddenly wanted answers —about her adoption, about her mother's death. If she couldn't talk to Leo in a civilized way, could she get these answers by sorting through her old stuff? Maybe that's what she needed to do to find the closure Col had urged her for years to discover.

CHAPTER EIGHT

IT WAS hard to be finished with the past when so much in the valley remained the same, as if ghosts haunted the ranch and its inhabitants.

After doing dishes, Darby came out of the kitchen and found Hank sitting on the edge of the leather sofa, guitar in hand, strumming a few cords. A cozy fire flamed in the fireplace. With a bent pipe clenched between his teeth, Leo rocked in the wooden rocking chair near the hearth. It was a relaxed scene. The aromatic cherry smell of tobacco filling the room was warm, comforting, and nostalgic. Leo was as she remembered him—never in a hurry when he smoked his pipe, filling the bowl with pinches of tobacco, tamping it down with arthritis-gnarled hands, and lighting the tobacco with a wooden match. He drew the smoke into his mouth and rocked, his movements deliberate, masculine...and fatherly.

She sat down on the stone hearth simply to separate herself from Hank and give herself space from Leo.

Ellie sat beside Hank, her cheery attitude such a contrast to the pain tumbling through Darby's heart. "Play for us, Hank," Ellie urged.

And Hank played, singing softly, a wide variety of old-fashioned, cowboy songs: "Back in the Saddle Again," "Home on The Range," and "Happy Trails."

Darby shut her eyes. Hank's voice was deep and soothing, just as it had been during those long-ago summer months when he'd serenaded only her. When they'd camped in the foothills, just the two of them, under the big Montana sky, millions of stars overhead as cover and their love their only blanket.

"I always sang 'Happy Trails' at the end of our nightly campfires at the McKenna Ranch," Hank said, as if he too had fond memories of another time. "It was a song most of the older guests knew, and it sent them off to bed in good spirits. Liz, the owner, always loved it when I sang."

"I can't wait for bonfires this summer," Ellie said. "We need an extra touch like your singing for the guests. Don't we, Leo?"

Leo grunted his approval. And rocked. His eyes were shadowed by his bushy eyebrows, making him look as if he disapproved of life. Darby felt his keen gaze rest on her the longest—judging her, assessing her—until her guilt for leaving him so long curdled in her stomach. He was old. Infirm. He had taken care of her and loved her when she was a child. He had been the only father she'd known.

And then when Hank thrummed the cords of another song, ripples of recognition jolted her. It sounded so familiar. The lyrics were from songwriter Ian Tyson's "Four Strong Winds" written in the early nineteen-sixties and sung by many popular folk groups then. Hank had sung this and other Tyson songs to her back in the day.

Now he sang in his poignant, baritone voice and looked straight at her. The song was about failed love.

The good times *were* gone. Darby leaned forward and hugged herself, seeking protection from the overwhelming sense of nostalgia, of unrequited love, of guilt and shame. She was swamped by all the useless feelings she'd suppressed or thought she'd conquered. She shut her eyes and breathed deeply. This was pathetic. She was as stuck as she'd been at eighteen. Filled with guilt. Scared. Sorrowful.

At the last chord and as Hank's final note died away, she sprang to her feet. "Best head to bed now. Thanks for the dinner, Ellie. I can see why you're an asset to the ranch."

Ellie beamed a smile. "It's my calling. What I love to do."

"Leo." She nodded her farewell to the old man.

He snorted. "Go with her, Hank."

"That's not necessary." Darby put on her coat, zipped it up, and quickly went to the door.

"Go with her, Hank."

Before Darby shut the door, Hank had followed her out, jerking on his jacket. He closed the door behind them.

"This isn't necessary." She strode down the steps into the now blinding snowstorm. The wind was brutal.

"When are you going to quit running away?"

"I'm not running away."

He seemed unconvinced. "Been doing that a long time."

"You're a fine one to offer advice."

Her words were blown away. Pellets of snow pummeled her face with ice as she tramped toward her cabin. She stumbled and struggled to stay upright. Hank grabbed her arm. He held on to it all the way to her front door. They stamped up the steps together.

Darby turned trying to shake off his grasp. Although a down jacket shielded her, his gloved fingertips seemed to burn through the thick fabric. Staring at him, she noticed his eyes. They advertised his emotions, but anger wasn't what she read in them.

"I stopped running in December when I came home." His voice was low and firm.

"Good for you." She sounded childish. Spiteful. Afraid.

"Stop running, Darby. Make your peace with Leo."

She shook off his hand and stepped back, her heart slammed with sudden anger. "You know nothing about all this. Leave it, Hank."

"Tell me, sweetheart. Let me help."

He reached for her again, clutching her upper arms, and held her immobile. She shot him a warning look that had no effect on him. Instead, he dropped his head and covered her lips with his. His body shielded her from the wind. He was warm, even though his kiss suddenly spiked cold, raw desire racing through her body. Hank made her feel safe. And that scared her even more.

Darby stepped back, throwing up her arms and shaking herself free. He let her go. She wiped her mouth with the back of her gloved hand, saying more with that action than words could ever say. Turning on her heel, she fled through the unlocked cabin door, slammed it shut, threw the bolt to lock it, and rested her back against it, her breath coming in heavy gasps.

"Good night, Darby," Hank said through the wooden barrier.

He was gone. And she was alone.

DARBY WAS DETERMINED NOT to let Leo wake her up in the morning. Heck. There was no point. She had never fallen asleep. She'd not wanted to dream—to relive her mother's horrible death as she'd done for so many years.

More than that, Hank's kiss had aroused her, a predicament she hardly expected at her age. In fact, much of this visit was unexpected. She'd not counted on the myriad of over-the-top emotions, the resentment, and guilt. She'd not anticipated feelings for Hank that had sprung so naturally from within the hiding place of her heart.

Stepping outside the cabin, Darby pulled the door firmly shut. Doors weren't usually locked at the ranch. A cowboy tradition. She paused a moment to inhale the cold mountain air. Overnight, the ranch had been enveloped in another big snowfall. The path to the dining hall trampled down the day before, was covered and hidden. Walking was difficult. Darby's breath came in frosty puffs as she trudged the distance from her cabin to the dining hall with its welcoming ribbon of smoke rising in the bright, cloudless, blue sky.

"Good morning, Ellie," she greeted the ranch cook, whom she found in the kitchen.

Ellie glanced up from an iron skillet where she scrambled eggs and smiled. "Good morning, honey. You look mighty chipper today."

Right. Darby smiled to cover the truth. She was far from chipper but planned to put on a good show. "Can I help?"

"Will you set the table? I'm running a bit behind this morning."

"Be glad to." Setting the table—another memory of childhood—gave Darby a chance to keep herself busy even though her mind whirled with too many unanswered questions. What was going on between her and Hank? Did Leo have anything to do with her mother's death? Had they argued before it happened?

She had already placed the plates and utensils on the table when Leo arrived and hung his jacket on the coatrack. He crossed to his seat at the head of the table, ignoring her until he sat down.

"You talk to Ellie yesterday?" His voice was coarse and cranky.

"About what?" She'd spoken to Ellie more than she'd talked to her father, but she wasn't going to give the elderly man the satisfaction of letting him know she knew what he meant.

"Your old room."

Darby arranged a fork, knife, and spoon around the last plate. She let him wait, her insides churning with anger. Then she looked him in the eyes. "Yes, sir, I got the message."

"Good." He avoided her gaze. "Now bring me the coffee."

Clamping her mouth shut, Darby retrieved the coffee pot from the kitchen and poured him a cup.

She stood behind him with the pot in hand wanting to ask the questions she'd suppressed for years. But she couldn't. Old habits die hard. Even at her age, she remained a child in Leo's eyes, and in her own eyes when she was around him. That was another reason she'd left and never returned. She'd wanted to grow up. And she'd found a man who'd treated her like an adult. She and Colton had been equals in many ways.

Pulling herself up to her full height, Darby tilted her head and glared at the Leo. More than anything, her inability to change—to grow up around her father—infuriated her.

"You can stop frowning at me," Leo ordered, "and sit down."

How did he know? Darby pivoted on her heel and took the coffee pot back to the sideboard. "Why are you so cantankerous?" she asked more to herself than to him.

Turning back toward the table, Darby struggled to slow the tempo of her breathing. Leo acted as if he hadn't heard her, but she knew he had. He may be old, but there was nothing wrong with his hearing.

As he brought his cup up to his lips, he said, "You had a phone message on the office answering machine this morning."

"I did?"

He took a sip and lowered the cup. "From my granddaughter Kelsey."

Darby's heart hurtled into her throat. "Is everything all right?"

"Said nothing was wrong. Just wanted to talk," he said. "Sweet sounding girl. She needs to come out to the ranch."

Darby pressed a palm to her heart. Thank heavens nothing was wrong, but she had no intention of letting Kelsey come out West. She'd never known any of her grandparents. Her daughter wouldn't miss a thing.

"There's a landline on the table in the corner," Leo said. "By the window."

"Thanks."

Two hours ahead in time, Kelsey was already in the farm office and picked up right away when Darby dialed. She smiled when she heard Kelsey's voice. Talking to her daughter brought sanity back into Darby's life.

"Mom! I was worried about you. The national weather mentioned a big storm out there."

Darby looked out the dining room window at the frozen, white landscape. "It was big all right," she told her daughter. "But folks here are used to it. They take it in stride, although the main roads may not be plowed today."

"Well, you stay safe, okay?"

"I plan to. What's going on at home."

"Lady Dreamer foaled last night. She was bred to Tap Dancer. Remember? Daddy planned the breeding. It was one of the last major decisions he made."

Darby let out a long breath. Yes, she recalled how Col had fretted over the decision to breed that mare to that stallion. Spring was a busy time in the Bluegrass with so many foals arriving.

"And Slade broke up with Katherine."

"He did? Whatever for?" Her son Slade and his girlfriend Katherine had seemed a perfect match for each other. But how would Darby know? She'd only met the girl a few times.

"Slade said she was only interested in him for his money," Kelsey said. "He was pretty adamant about calling it quits."

Darby bit her lip. When she married Col, people had gossiped about the same thing. She'd been a lowly stable groom, his employee. She was a gold-digger, they'd said. The Heston family would be ruined with her becoming part of it.

But it wasn't that way. She hadn't married Col for his money, more for the security he provided. And the affection. She'd been in such bad shape after her mother's death that she'd automatically turned to the man who provided refuge. Giving Colton two children—his heirs—had been part of their bargain, but one she gladly accepted. She'd wanted children to love. She'd wanted to be a good mother, as hers had been to her.

Back in the day, Sarah York had been Darby's life, her steady rock, allowing her to grow her wings and fly. Horses and barrel racing, her sketches, and loving Hank—she'd been free to be herself with all her varied interests, but that's because Sarah was always there. Loving her. Caring for her. Darby couldn't imagine the

Ghost Mountain Ranch without her mother. Even now, not having her here crushed Darby's soul.

Pete and Hank appeared in the distance heading toward the dining room. Darby turned from the window, suddenly feeling powerless.

"I wish I was home," she told Kelsey. "Slade probably doesn't need a mother's help, but I feel strange being so far away."

"You know Slade, Mom. He acts as if he doesn't need anyone's help."

"I'd be a bad mother if I didn't try to offer it."

"You're a great mother," Kelsey said. "Slade just thinks he can handle things by himself."

She'd once been that way. "I understand. I'm just glad I had your father all those years to help me."

Kelsey was quiet for a beat as if agreeing. "We miss him, don't we?"

"Yes." Darby found her throat tightening with sadness. "Hey, I'd better go. Don't worry about me. The wranglers here will see I'm well cared for."

At that moment, the door opened, and Pete and Hank tramped in, stomping their feet, bringing with them fresh air, wet snow, and a hearty morning cheer. Darby ended the call and replaced the handset on the cradle.

"Morning all!" Pete pushed up to his place at the table. "I can use a swig of that coffee, Miss Darby. It's as cold as hell out there!"

Glad for the distraction, Darby served Pete, then turned to Hank. She caught him watching her across the table, and then his face flushed from his cheeks to his scalp. Immediately, she was propelled back to her current reality.

Last night's kiss.

What had it meant to Hank? Had he tested her to measure her response? Had he been as aroused as she?

"Good morning, Hank," she said, adding coffee to his cup.

He brushed away a lock of hair from his forehead as if he could sweep away his evident discomfiture and nodded. "Darby."

"I hope you slept well," she provoked him.

He responded with a cocky grin that twisted Darby's heart. "Like a babe."

Her eyes narrowing, she poured herself a cup and returned the pot to the sideboard. "That's strange. So did I."

CHAPTER NINE

SHE'D TOLD herself she wanted answers. Maybe now she would get them.

Leo's small cabin—her home growing up—was unchanged. Darby entered the front door of the three-bedroom cabin and stood silently in the living room. Cozy with scuffed wooden floors, it retained its same cabin shabbiness along with the familiar pipe tobacco and fireplace aroma. But gone was the strong, sweet, floral scent of her mother's Giorgio perfume. It had permeated the house and everywhere her mother went, making it her overt calling card.

But that had been thirty years ago, for heaven's sakes. Darby couldn't expect things to be exactly the same.

Her footsteps faltered as she approached the closed door to her bedroom.

Giving herself a mental shake, she grasped the handle and opened the door. She could do this.

Her past rushed headlong to smack her in the face. The air smelled stale, laden with dirt and disuse. However, her tiny bedroom was weirdly the same although layered with inches of dust. The same pink flowered comforter she'd used as a teenager covered the four-posted twin bed. The matching curtains, now faded and threadbare, remained at the window to obstruct the winter sun. A pink stuffed rabbit and a Cabbage Patch doll still sat on a bookcase amid a jumble of teenage girl mementos, childhood school papers, and old text books.

Darby's heart drummed loudly in her ears as she pulled open the closet door. Everything she'd left that day remained like a misplaced specter of her teens. Her clothes from the nineteen eighties hung inside—the fringed cowgirl shirts, a denim jacket, a pair of acid washed jeans, a gray sweater dress and a couple of miniskirts that looked as if a skinny model had worn them—or Kelsey. For sure *she* couldn't fit into them any longer.

Darby sat down hard on the bed and fought back the ghosts. Why on earth had Leo kept all this stuff? Had he hoped she'd come back? As years passed, why didn't he bite the bullet and get rid of everything?

Sadly, in the same way, she had kept the memory of her mother alive.

Maybe she and her father weren't that different after all.

No. She didn't lie to her children.

She wasn't like her father. Not at all.

Pressing her lips together as a wave of determination swept her, Darby jumped to her feet and stripped the bed. She folded the bedding and left the sheets and blanket on the bare mattress. She yanked the clothes from the closet and stacked the vintage outfits on the only chair in the room. She'd donate them or something. Maybe Ellie would do it for her when the weather broke. Then Darby yanked open each drawer and filled the wastebasket full of trash. She wanted nothing from this room. Nothing from her old life. It was over and done with. She'd moved on a long time ago.

But had she?

Her skin grew cold and clammy, and once more Darby sat down on the mattress. Deep in her heart she knew she wasn't over everything that had happened when she was eighteen. The dreams kept it alive. Hadn't she suffered enough?

She let out a long breath of resolve. Thirty years. That was too damn long. Col had tried to help her, get her counseling. But she'd resisted. She'd hid herself in being a good mother, in her art, in her cushy lifestyle married to a millionaire. All the while, she'd covered up her remorse and heartache.

Her mother had been everything to her. From the time Darby was little they'd had the best relationship, almost like sisters. She'd idolized her beautiful mother. Her perfect mother. If she'd been a better daughter, if things had been different that day, maybe her mother would still be here.

Darby briefly shut her eyes to process all she'd uncovered in her room. Somehow, she had to get over her mother's death, to shed light on that horrible event. She really did need answers.

Long moments passed as her heart hammered and she sat surrounded by things that had once been her life.

Then she remembered. Ellie had said her mother's personal belongings were stored in the room. Where were they? Darby got to her feet and searched again.

On the top of the closet shelf, under a bunch of folded sweaters she'd missed, Darby found a wooden chest about the size of a shoe box. She didn't recognize it. The box was locked and there was no key.

If this had belonged to Sarah, if it contained answers, then Darby needed to find the key. And that, as the old saying said, would be like finding a needle in a haystack.

Was this all that was left of Sarah York's personal belongings? Good heavens, what a legacy? At least Darby had a few paintings to be remembered by. And her children. In them, she'd leave her mark. Much as Sarah had left hers in her daughter.

That thought was a bit of comfort.

But this dusty room was too much gloom and doom. Suddenly, the cabin walls seemed to close in on her. The scent of sweet pipe tobacco in the living room became overpowering. Darby grabbed her coat and the wooden box. She left the musty bedroom and her childhood home, escaping outside into the crisp mountain air.

In the distance, Pete plowed the road to the highway, the noise of the tractor a distraction in the quiet, pristine surroundings. Darby trudged through the drifting snow, squinting against the brightness of its reflection. She'd once loved this ranch—the summer dudes, the horses, the thin air, and freedom. She gathered her emotions and struggled to control them once more as she had throughout the years.

When she found Hank in the office, he glanced up from the paper on his desk, surprised to see her.

"Hank," she said, then paused for a deep breath. "I need your help."

HANK LOOKED UP AND SMILED. Darby's interruption was very welcome. He didn't like paperwork, but here he was, stuck in the ranch office going over the summer reservations and trying to account for the advanced payments.

Damn if she didn't look as pretty in middle age as she'd looked in high school. He should have been sorry he'd kissed her last night, but he wasn't. Not one bit.

He sucked in a quick, ragged breath. "What can I do for you?"

She extended a small, wooden chest toward him. "It's locked. I don't know where to find the key."

He took the box from her hands. It didn't appear to be well-made or expensive. The initials C.C. were etched on the top. Hank turned it over to look underneath. "Where did you get this?"

"In my old room." Darby pulled off her knit cap and held it loosely in her gloved hands. "Leo wanted me to clean out my belongings. Ellie told me there were personal items in the room from my mother. This is all I found. I don't recognize it."

Hank placed the box on his desk and leaned back in his chair, his eyes hooded. Darby grew antsy and shifted from foot-to-foot, never turning away from him. What was up with her, anyway? He didn't understand her behavior—now or back then.

He forced a weak smile, then turned his attention to the problem at hand. "I may have to damage the box to get it open."

"I don't care." She shook her head. "If it holds something of my mother's I want to see it."

She paused, their gazes connecting, her uneasiness obvious. Then she licked her lips and focused on the floor.

"I have nothing belonging to my mother." She hesitated. "Only my memories."

"I'll do it," he said. "But take off your coat and stay awhile. I don't bite, and don't worry." He offered a grin. "I won't jump over the desk and kiss you."

Her breath left in a rush, and her face flamed. She raised her chin a notch. "Okay."

Darby removed her gloves and coat while he rummaged through a desk drawer. She stuffed the gloves in the pockets and hung the coat on the rack. Then she sat down in the chair across the desk from him. Hank smiled to himself. He'd always enjoyed teasing her, disturbing her goody-goody behavior. He'd once got the best of her prissiness. During that camping trip, she'd let her guard down, opened up to him. He'd always wondered if she regretted their lovemaking. Had that been the reason she'd disappeared?

Hank held up an envelope opener for her to see. "I may have to force the top open and break the lock."

"Do it."

She was nervous, in a hurry. He was not. He enjoyed being there with her. And he wanted answers as much as she.

"When we were kids, I don't remember you ever telling me you were adopted," he said and poked tentatively at the space between the lid and base of the box.

"I didn't know." She paused as if choosing her words. Her jaw was set and her eyes glassy. She sat with her hands balled in her lap. "I found out that night."

"What night?"

"The night after my mother died."

Hank probed the edge of the box with the letter opener, focusing mostly on Darby. "That was weird how she died."

He'd never understood it. What had her mother been doing hiking the trail to Ghost Mountain alone? He guessed it had been easy for her to lose her footing and fall from the overlook, but most locals knew that trail. And they knew better than to be on it when it was growing dark.

"Remember that morning when we drove home from the campout and found the sheriff and county rescue at the ranch?" Darby's eyes grew pensive. "Remember how we were told my mother had died, falling from the cliff? How they'd found her broken body near the lookout, maybe a hundred yards down on the rocks?"

Hank nodded, but he didn't think Darby noticed. She'd directed her gaze over his head at some unseen shadow, at the past that still haunted her.

"I went crazy," she said.

"You were very close to your mother. No one could comfort you." And Hank had tired, but she'd pushed him away—screaming, crying, out of control.

She shivered and clasped her hands in her lap. "After her body was brought down the trail and taken away and everyone left, Leo drew me aside and told me the truth." Her voice broke. "He said we wanted to protect my mother's reputation. He said we'd let everyone think my mother fell while hiking."

Hank longed to reach out to her, touch her and ease her struggle. Her heartache.

But he'd never been able to tell Darby his feelings. It wasn't something a guy like him revealed. Not the cowboy way. Too personal. Too intense. Too scary.

"My mother didn't fall, Hank," Darby whispered. "She jumped. Leo told me my mother committed suicide."

~

"Good god, Darby," Hank said. "Are you sure?"

Darby had unburdened herself, and it felt good. All those years, she couldn't make herself tell Col. What would he have thought about her? Her family? She'd kept the secret festering inside her. But there was something about Hank, the taciturn, no-nonsense cowboy. He could always be counted on. And he'd known her back then. He'd understood how she'd grown up. He'd understood how much she loved her mother.

And there was something more. An instant attraction springing up between them—a feeling she needed to curb and run away from. She didn't want any more complications in her life, for it was already too complicated. Too unsettled.

"Why didn't you tell me then? Is that why you ran away? I don't understand."

"Do you think I understand myself? Even now." Darby needed space. She stood and turning her back on Hank, looking out the window. "I was staggered by her passing. By Leo's revelation. How could she kill herself, Hank? How could she have left me like that?"

"I'm at a loss for words. I can't pretend to guess why she'd do something like that."

"Neither can I, but all I can think about, then and now, was that if I'd been there at the ranch, if I hadn't been with you, I might have stopped her."

She didn't voice the deeper-seeded fear that ate at her gut daily. That plagued her dreams. It was silly, looking at her anxieties through adult eyes, but the child within still believed if she'd been better, somehow, her mother would not have taken her own life.

He stood, pushing back his chair, and came up behind her, holding her upper arms. She felt his breath on the back of her neck.

She heard the compassion in his voice. "You can't blame yourself for something your mother did."

"But I did blame myself. Then Leo slipped and admitted he wasn't my real father. I don't even remember how the subject came up. Just that I suddenly knew my parents had lied to me all those years. I wasn't their child. Who was my real father? No one knew. That's when I really lost it, Hank. I packed a bag and took money from the petty cash in this very office. I left and didn't come back."

She was shivering. Hank turned her around and gathered her to his chest, welcoming her in his caring embrace. He felt so warm. So safe.

"Why didn't you tell me, Darby? I never knew what happened to you. To us. I thought it was something I'd done."

She pressed her cheek against the rough flannel of his shirt. Darby heard the steady beat of his heart and inhaled his clean, male scent. It would be so easy to succumb to the temptation of Hank. Just like she'd surrendered to Col all those years ago—had let him care for her, sustain her. She'd not had to face her fears then. Her anger. She had let her sweet husband protect her with his money, his lifestyle, his children.

No more. There'd be no more running.

Placing her hands against his chest, Darby pushed back. The tender expression in his eyes almost killed her. Firmly, she stepped back, away from his embrace.

"I don't know why I did what I did back then, Hank. You weren't at fault. All I can think is the shock made me a little desperate. Crazy." Lifting her chin, standing her ground, she asked, "Now will you please help me open that box?"

CHAPTER TEN

SHE DIDN'T WANT his support. Okay. He could understand that. He'd lived with rejection for many years. He was so used to that small stone of sadness in his heart that this moment was simply part of his reality.

Hank moved back behind his desk and sat down again. Concentrating on the task at hand, he continued to be well aware of Darby —her agitation, her angst. If he had lived without the love of a woman all these years, she'd lived with something uglier. Guilt. Blaming herself for the death of her mother was a heavy cross to bear.

"I don't understand how Leo knew your mother committed suicide," Hank voiced his curiosity, trying to grasp that missing piece of the puzzle. "Did she leave a suicide note?"

"No." Darby shut her eyes as if trying to grapple with his question. She slowly shook her head. When she opened her eyes, they glistened with tears. "I don't know. He never said. I simply took it at face value that he knew it. I wasn't in the habit of questioning my parents."

"At the time, I thought you and Leo had argued. I can see now you were too upset to think straight."

She nodded in agreement. "I'm guessing the trauma of every-thing that happened that morning when we returned from the camping trip blew my mind. I wasn't thinking. Only running..."

Her voice trailed off. The overwhelming wretchedness of the moment hit Hank hard. She'd run, and he'd run. He hadn't stopped avoiding his past, nursing a broken heart, until Leo gave him this job. Until he'd come home to the ranch after Christmas from the McKenna Ranch.

Hank let out a long breath. His jimmying worked. The top of the box suddenly popped open, and the contents spilled onto the paperwork on the desk.

Darby stood transfixed and stared at the desktop. "You did it."

"Not much here of value."

"But this." Darby leaned over and lifted an orange pendant by its black satin cord. "It's beautiful. I remember my mother wearing it."

The stone dangled from its cord catching the light from the window. Hank watched Darby's almost reverent touching of the necklace. She held it up to the window and then turned it over in her hands.

"What is it?"

"Citrine," she said. "It's a variety of quartz. Look how it's wrapped in sterling silver and copper. My mother used to say the stone was her guardian angel. For love and protection. I guess she wasn't wearing it that night."

"Or maybe Leo took it from her when she was buried," Hank offered.

With a sigh, Darby put the necklace around her neck and hid it under her flannel shirt. An awkward silence fell. What else could he say? He only knew this guilty obsession of hers had to end. It wasn't healthy.

"There's more." He broke the silence and picked up a faded china mermaid with a blue tail and a white seashell, items of signif-icance known only to Sarah York. He placed them on the desk for Darby to examine. Then lifted out a handful of old snapshots, the kind of photographs people used to develop at drugstores. They were yellowed and grainy with age.

Darby extended her hand toward him. "Let me see."

Hank gave her half and continued to sort through the other half. He couldn't place the era, but most of the people in the pictures looked like hippies—long hair, bare feet, tie-dyed T-shirts and blue jeans with wide legs. In most, the people were smoking, and if he wasn't far off the mark, they were smoking weed.

"Do you know these people?"

Darby tilted her head to the side and focused on the images. "I've never seen them or these pictures."

At least this mystery had changed the subject away from her mother's death. He handed Darby the rest of the snapshots.

After a moment, she said, "I believe that's my mother."

She shared the photo, letting Hank have a look. He had to agree. The blond woman sitting on the lap of a long-haired hippie with her arm around his neck appeared to be a very skinny and younger version of Sarah York. There was a baby sitting on a blanket near the duo sucking her thumb. She had bright red hair.

"I guess if you needed proof Leo adopted you, you have it now," Hank said as the thought occurred to him.

Darby accepted the photo back from him, staring at it sadly. "Yes, I guess you're right. That child looks like me. I wonder if this is my father. And who are these other people?"

"There are a couple names on the back," Hank said. "Chelsea Clemons. Tim Krebs."

"But my mother was Sarah."

"What was her maiden name?" Hank asked.

Darby released a long breath. "I never knew. She never told me. It was as if she'd arrived at the ranch from another world." She shook her head in bewilderment. "I never knew my grandparents. It was if my mother had no history."

"Do you think Leo would know?"

She caught his gaze with a look of determination. "I don't know, but I think it's time to ask him, don't you?"

$\sim$

HIS BLUE EYES flashed as they sought hers. Heat flooded Darby's cheeks. They surveyed each other, neither speaking. What was it about Hank? Sometimes she felt as if she'd never been away from him, as if they still had that teenage bond.

"It's almost dinnertime," Hank said. "You go on. I'll follow along in a few minutes."

Darby quickly scooped up the snapshots and put them into her pocket. She slipped on her coat, pulled the knit cap down over her ears and the gloves on her hands. It was cold outside. She couldn't simply run from cabin to cabin without a coat like she often did at home when going from the house to her art studio. Cold didn't seep into your bones in Kentucky like it did here.

At the office door, she paused and forced herself to look back at Hank. "Thanks for the help."

He nodded, his gaze bathing her with more than common regard. It was the look she'd seen in his eyes many times since she'd returned. A look she remembered.

Darby stepped out into the frigid air, deeply aware of the sexual undercurrent between them. But it had to pass. She couldn't act on anything. Not with their history.

It took a good ten minutes to slog through the snow drifts to the dining hall. She stomped up the stairs to the porch, cleared the snow from her boots, and stepped inside. The blazing fire was a welcome sight. After pulling the photos out of her pocket, she put them on the coffee table, then shrugged off her coat.

As usual, Leo sat at the head of the table. She felt his scrutiny warming her back as she thawed her hands near the fire. He was the first to speak in his gravelly voice. "I see you've gone through your room."

Darby waited to gather her thoughts before responding. She beat down the sudden rise of anger. But it was still there, bubbling below the surface. Bending down, she took the snapshots, clutching them in her hands. She faced Leo and walked slowly toward the dining table.

"Why didn't you get rid of that stuff in my room a long time ago?"

"Sorta thought you'd come back for them things someday." His eyes shifted evasively. "'Sides, weren't my place."

"Well, I did come back, and I'm here now." She dragged in a shaky breath. "And I don't want anything. It's all junk."

"Suit yourself."

"But I want to know who these people are." Darby dropped the pictures onto the empty plate in front of him. "Do you know them?"

Silence—except for the pop and crackle of the fire. Darby stared at her father, her heart drumming loudly in her ears. Time ticked by with agonizing slowness. He moved the photos around on the plate with a gnarled finger but didn't pick them up.

When Darby heard the voices of Pete and Hank coming up on the porch, Leo glanced up. "Best help Ellie get food on the table," he said, ending their soundless standoff.

Her mind rooted in the past, Darby followed instructions as she'd always done—angry at herself, angry at Leo, but glad for a moment of respite from the heavy tension.

"Can you use some help?" she asked Ellie, who was ladling tomato soup into a porcelain tureen decorated with painted daisies. Darby's mother had used that same bowl. Ellie placed the tureen on a tray along with slices of crusty white bread.

"Sure. Can you finish cutting up those carrots and cucumbers? If I didn't feed 'em some salad, those guys would never eat anything healthy," Ellie said.

Did Ellie think those guys couldn't get along without her? "Will do."

"Good. I'll get 'em started on the soup." The other woman left the kitchen carrying the tray.

A cold chill of regret rippled through Darby. Something wasn't right. Leo was keeping secrets, and the knowledge of a real mystery surrounding her mother's death hit her hard. Why hadn't she been curious all these years? She'd never been particularly inquisitive as a child. She'd taken everything at face value. After all, life on the ranch had been good—secure. She'd trusted her parents.

Silently, Darby completed peeling the carrots and cucumber. She sliced them into the salad and tossed them with the lettuce.

When Ellie came back, she shot Darby a knowing look. "That Hank sure is sweet on you."

Darby grunted a noncommittal reply and turned away. Why would Ellie think she'd want to discuss anything with her, especially something as private as her love life?

"If I had a hunky guy sweet on me, I sure wouldn't ignore him." She gave a quick snort, almost as if she was disgusted by Darby's behavior. "Some folks sure don't know when they have it good."

Darby forced herself to control her irritation. Her relationship with Hank, or lack thereof, was none of Ellie's damn business.

"This is ready." Darby picked up the salad bowl. "I'll take it out. I guess you put dressing on the table."

With that, she left the kitchen, glad to escape. In the dining room, the men were slurping hot soup from deep bowls and chatting about the snowy day. Darby placed the salad bowl in the middle of the table and sat down next to Leo. Ellie joined them, sitting across the table. A bland smile was pasted on her face.

"Salad again?" Pete complained. "Ellie, you'll turn me into a rabbit."

"Do you good, Pete Harden. You ain't no spring chicken. Got to get your vitamins somehow."

Darby caught Hank watching her from his place beside her. She turned to Leo. He had moved the photographs to a pile beside his plate as if they were no value.

"Well, do you know those people?" she asked.

His spoon paused on the way to his mouth. "Nope."

Hank passed the soup tureen toward her. Darby ignored him and pointed at the photograph on top of the stack. "Is that my mother?"

Leo downed a mouthful of soup and looked askance at the pile of snapshots. He wiped his mouth with a napkin and favored her with a look of resignation. "Yup, that's your mother. Don't know them other folks."

A lump formed in Darby's throat. Briefly she glanced at Hank, then back at Leo. "Safe to say, that baby is me."

"Yup. That's you before you came to the ranch."

"I always thought Darby was your daughter, Leo." Ellie's eyes gleamed with curiosity. "May I see the pictures?"

Leo shoved the stack toward Ellie. She picked them up, and sorted through them one at a time, studying each photograph.

"I adopted Darby when I married her mother." Leo's voice stayed soft. "Sarah wanted me to give Darby my last name."

Darby laid down her spoon. Her stomach burned. Her appetite gone. Leo was the only father she knew. Her biological father, the man who had slept with her mother, the man who'd fathered her, had not wanted her, but Leo did.

Yet, overcoming their thirty years of estrangement proved difficult.

"That was a mighty kind of you, Leo." Ellie's tone was syrupy. "I always knew you were a good man."

Darby didn't know what to say. She couldn't respond. Her mouth was dry. Her tongue felt like cotton.

"We never knew Darby was adopted, Leo," Hank said. "Why didn't you tell anyone?"

Leo rubbed the back of his neck and winced as if he'd committed a mistake but wasn't going to apologize for it. "Sarah didn't want me to tell anyone. Said Darby's father was no good. That I was a better man. Said I could be the daddy Darby needed."

"But you *did* tell me." Darby pushed back from the table and stood. "The day after Mom died. You spilled your guts to me then. Of all times, when I needed you the most. When I needed my father, you told me I didn't have one."

"You were talking crazy." Leo rubbed his hands together. "You blamed yourself for your mother's death. It wasn't your fault."

"But why did you tell me I was adopted? Why then?"

Leo looked around the table the way a person might who was cornered with no way out. "Don't know. It happened. I was a bit crazy myself then. Just lost my wife. But you ran away before I could explain things." He paused and looked up at her with eyes full of sorrow. "You never came home."

The tension in the room popped like the crackling of the fire.

Hank and Pete stared at their bowls as if wanting to slip away. Ellie had crossed her arms and regarded Darby with cold look.

Darby tightened her fists and leaned against the table. "Nothing to come back for."

"That's why I decided to make a change." Leo suddenly regained control at the table, lifted his head and drew back his shoulders, seeming to grow in inches. "I've changed my will."

Every eye in the room focused on the eighty-five-year-old.

He cleared his throat. "You've made it clear you don't want this ranch. I'm leaving it to Pete and Ellie and Hank."

"But why?" The question shot out of Darby's mouth as quickly as the shock of her father's announcement ripped through her heart.

"They have no family, and they're dependable. I count on 'em. Ranch won't run without 'em."

By implication, Leo meant she wasn't loyal. He could never rely on her. She'd run away, hadn't she?

Darby's breath hitched. She had always trusted this ranch would be hers someday. It was a strange contradiction. Knowing she was adopted from the time of her mother's death, that she wasn't really a "York," she'd continue to view the ranch as being her one, true inheritance. Slade and Kelsey had inherited the bulk of Colton's estate. His millions. In the back of her mind, there'd always been the Ghost Mountain Ranch.

"Fine." Tears welled in her eyes. "You all can have it."

Turning on her heel, Darby grabbed her coat and fled the dining hall.

CHAPTER ELEVEN

DARBY ALWAYS RAN. Had it done her any good? An hour after the incident in the dining hall, Hank followed her to her cabin with an armful of firewood. It was a good way to buy entrance. His knock produced a terse, "Come in."

Hank stacked the wood beside the cast iron stove. "I thought you might need something to keep you warm tonight."

The flames had gone out, and the room was bitterly cold. He removed his coat anyway, then added wood to the stove and poked the ashes, bringing the fire back to life. When he stood from his kneeling position, he turned back to Darby. She sat in the room's only easy chair with her parka on and a blanket wrapped around her legs staring at nothing. Her mother's pendant was still around her neck, and Darby held the gem in her hand. Hank sat down on the edge of the bed, the mattress sinking under his weight.

"You'll never find out about your mom if you keep running away like that," he said. "That's no way to get Leo to tell you the truth."

"What else will he know?" Darby's tone was bitter. "He said he didn't know any of those people in the pictures—just my mother."

"He's old. Maybe he can recall details if you talk to him normally, not shout at him."

She took a deep breath and chewed on her lip, taking his criticism in the spirit he'd offered it, he hoped.

"I just get so angry." She looked away, unable to meet his eyes. "My mother never liked confrontation, and I guess I'm the same way. It's always easier to dodge the problem than to meet it head-on."

"Seems to me you've got no choice." He hated to see the suffering in Darby's eyes. Was there anything he could do to comfort her? To make her see she needed to stop running?

"You're right." She turned her head to look at him. "I get so scared of my own anger. Col used to roll his eyes at me and wait for it to subside. He knew how to handle me. How to let the anger play itself out."

How could he forget? Darby had her own family. A life. Children. She'd had a happy relationship with a man for many years. But he'd had nothing. Just a hard bunk, a few good horses to ride, and freedom to do his own thing.

His vision blurred. But what he really wanted was a woman to love. And to be loved in return.

He turned away, feeling suddenly numb. Would he ever have that intimate connection with another human being?

"I don't know why Leo upset me so much." She took a shallow but audible breath and shook her head slowly. "You deserve this ranch. You and Pete. I don't know Ellie."

"I'm sorry Leo changed his will." He studied Darby with a longing so intense it hurt. "This was your home. You were brought up here."

"Leo's right. The ranch hasn't been my home for years."

"But it seems wrong somehow."

"It would be wrong for me to take it after being gone so long."

They regarded each other, and then Hank looked away unable to meet her eyes. The room grew warm from the woodstove. It grew too quiet. Darby unwrapped her legs and stood up. She removed her coat and put it down on the chair. She moved to her desk and flipped open her sketchpad.

"Have you seen the drawing I did yesterday of the horses and mountains?" she asked without looking back at him.

"No? Why?"

"It's gone. The paper it was on has been ripped from the pad."

"What the...?" Hank stood and looked over her shoulder. She was right. The drawing was missing, torn from the sketchpad. Only a jagged edge remained to prove it had once existed.

Hank was so close he could almost feel the heat radiating from her body. Shutting his eyes, he breathed deeply. She was so near, warm, and vibrant, standing there in front of him, smelling of vanilla. He longed to touch her. He fought the treacherous longing that thrummed through his body.

Then, giving into desire, he caressed her shoulders, rubbing his hands down the flannel fabric of her shirt. She trembled in surprise but didn't turn around or pull away. Hank tightened his grip on her and drew her back against his chest. He softly kissed her hair, then moved it aside to kiss her neck.

"Dear heavens," Darby moaned, leaning back against him.

Hank wrapped his arms around her in a big bear hug. She felt so good. So alive. So perfect. Memories of their time together flooded through him. Why had she run away? They could have had such a beautiful life.

"Hank," she whispered. "Don't."

"Why not?"

"I don't know why not."

She pulled away from him. Taking a step, she turned around. Her eyes brimmed with tears.

"We were once so good together," Hank said.

"That was long ago. Things have changed."

Maybe. But not the way I feel about you. Hank couldn't say what he felt. He'd never been able to express emotional things since he was a kid. Since he'd told his mother he loved her, and then the next day she left him and his dad for another man.

"I know." He turned away. No point in tormenting himself. He picked up his coat. "Get a good night sleep."

"You, too."

He walked to the door and paused with his hand on the handle. There were so many things he wanted to say to Darby. Memories of Chaz Kingston's teenage daughter Ashleigh came back to him. At the McKenna Ranch, she'd warned him he'd face this moment again someday.

"You say we learn from our mistakes," she'd said to him in December. "Well, I say you need to learn from yours, too. The next time you're in love with someone, tell her. Don't be afraid. It can't turn out any worse."

"There won't be a next time," he replied. "I doubt I'll fall in love again."

"Well, that is sad," she told him.

Hank had not been honest with Ashleigh Kingston. The truth was he was already in love...with a memory. Now the memory was a reality—a live, breathing woman with long red hair. And his tongue was still tied. He couldn't admit his love remained as strong today as it had thirty years ago.

It *was* sad. Profoundly, utterly sad.

He hovered in the doorway unable to leave. His heart hammered in his chest. He'd gotten aroused when he hugged her, and now he wanted more than a simple *good night*.

"I didn't know how much I'd miss you," he said in a low voice.

She raised her head and looked at him. Her eyes glittered with unshed tears. Was she as sad as he?

Hank dropped his coat on the chair and came back toward her. "I've learned you can never get over the loss of a loved one." He stood silently in front of her for several heartbeats. "You can only get through it. Your loss always hurts, but you can get through it."

She raised her chin a notch, and he was afraid she'd defy him. "I'm at fault. My mother's dead because of me."

Darby didn't realize he was talking about himself as much as her feelings about her mother. If it had to be that way for her to understand, fine. He'd keep talking about her mother. "You don't know you're at fault. You don't know why she committed suicide. Maybe she waited until you were gone from the ranch before she did it. Maybe that's the only way she had the courage to do it."

Her eyes grew huge. Hadn't she thought of that? She was so used to beating herself up, she couldn't see things rationally.

He couldn't either. Not at the moment. He shouldn't want what he wanted. It shouldn't gnaw on him. Darby didn't love him, but he'd loved her for years. He wasn't willing to wait any longer, not when she needed comfort like he needed it, too.

Hank's gut clenched, and for a whisper of a breath, he took the same risk he'd taken when he was eighteen-years-old. He pulled her into his arms and kissed her.

"Dear heavens," she whispered again, clinging to him, almost begging for more.

He had no business kissing her but couldn't control himself. Didn't want to control himself. "Let me make love to you."

Darby nodded, briefly, as if she fleetingly gave into her impulses. "It's been a long time for me, Hank."

"Me too," he admitted.

Squeezing his eyes shut a moment, Hank took a deep breath. Making love was not the same as saying *I love you*. Maybe in the next hours, she'd learn he didn't have sex without commitment or love. Maybe he could show her the truth that sang in his heart.

DARBY AWOKE as the dawn sun split the crack in the curtains to find Hank gone. He must have slipped out during the night, leaving her snug and warm in bed. But she still smelled like him—all musky and male. Like sex.

Stretching out her legs, she turned on her back to stare at the log ceiling. Last night, this comfy bed had been a much better experience than the bedroll on the rocky Montana soil so many years ago. She was older now. Dare she think more experienced? She'd been married after all and had given birth to twins.

But there was something else that made it better. Making love with Hank had felt like that—making love. Not the obligatory sex she'd had at first with Col that had gotten better with age. Had Hank meant it to feel like making love? Had she?

And there'd been no nightmares.

For the first time since her arrival, Darby's pulse quickened with anticipation as she thought about facing the day. And Leo. No matter what happened now, Hank was with her. He didn't say it, but she knew it, deep down.

Crawling out from under the covers, she brought the fire to life and then dressed in front of its warmth. She was tired, even after the deep sleep. It wasn't because of the energetic sex, but a mental exhaustion stemming from her years of avoiding the guilt that also haunted her.

Seems to me you've got no choice.

Hank was right when he said that last night. Col had tried to make her see her problem. Begged her to get help. Therapy was no longer considered a sign of weakness, he said. Only after his death had she decided to change. Yet the change had not come in big ways. She'd addressed the need to move on with her life by doing the small steps. Not the big one. Not tackling the two-thousand-pound elephant in the room—her guilt.

In the chilled bathroom, staring at herself in the mirror, Darby brushed her long hair until the curls crackled. With experienced hands, she twisted the strands into a single plait that dropped down her back out of the way.

She didn't want to live with guilt any longer. In her head, she knew she was not responsible for her mother's death. Col had drummed it into her throughout the years. But she'd chosen to ignore the reasonableness of his argument. Darby hadn't pushed her mother off the cliff. Her mother was an adult. Darby had been the child. Her mother's mental state and her decision to take her own life wasn't a child's fault.

Could Darby believe her innocence? Was it possible for her heart to trust what her head knew?

She closed her eyes and pinched the bridge of her nose. Her chest felt heavy, weighted down by years of regret. Now was the time to act. She must stop stewing in the anxiety she'd carried for so many years. The only way to atone for her guilt was to understand the past. Why had her mother been so unhappy with Leo and her daughter? Why had she committed suicide?

Darby took a long breath. Yes, Hank was right. She needed to talk to her father.

CHAPTER TWELVE

SHE WAS LATE TO BREAKFAST. Darby opened the dining room door and snowflakes twirled into the room. She stepped inside and removed her coat. The scene at breakfast was the same as it had been during all of her visit. Leo sat in state at the head of the table. The two wranglers were already chowing down, and Ellie had recently come into the room from the kitchen carrying biscuits. Steeling herself, Darby crossed the floor.

"A little late this morning, aren't you, honey?" Ellie took her seat. Her smile was designed to win favor. Yet Darby couldn't help but think the look Ellie gave her was filled with speculation. Did she know Hank had spent the night?

Darby felt warmth rising in her cheeks. "Yes, well, I overslept."

"Don't worry," Leo said gruffly. "None of us are going anywhere today."

Surprised, Darby glanced at her father. He met her gaze, his eyes naked with sadness. Then he turned his head away, shutting her out once more.

But it was a start. Somehow Darby's heart lifted. She was odd man out here—the only one without a monetary stake in Ghost

Mountain Ranch. But today she felt different. Like it didn't matter. Was it because of Hank?

She went to the sideboard and filled her plate. When she turned, plate in hand, she caught Hank's gaze so intent she could hardly drag her eyes away. Visions of their night of lovemaking flashed through her mind, and her heartbeat quickened. He grinned and ducked his head to hide a smile, appearing to concentrate on his half-eaten breakfast.

"I need more coffee, Darby," Leo said, but there was a softer tone to his voice. Had he watched the interplay between her and Hank? Could he see that their old chemistry was back big time?

Ellie jumped to her feet, her chair scraping on the hardwood floor. "Leo, I'll get it."

Darby had already set down her plate and picked up the coffee pot. "No. I'll get it."

Ellie raised a shoulder as if she didn't care. "Oh, okay, honey." She sat down.

The hint of anger transmitted in Ellie's tone startled Darby. What was *that* about?

Leaning across her father's left arm, she poured steaming coffee into his mug. He smelled of pine soap and smoke. He smelled like her daddy.

She stood up and released a sigh, surveying the people at the table. "Anyone else?"

Heads shook no. Darby returned the coffee pot to the sideboard. She picked up her plate and came around the table to take her seat next to Hank.

As she approached, he climbed to his feet and drew back her chair. "Ma'am," he said in his deep drawl and, when she sat down, pushed Darby up to the table.

Ellie winked at him with a mischievous grin. "My, aren't *we* the gentleman."

Grunting in response, Hank took his seat. There was visible

tension in his neck and shoulders, his posture rigid. Maybe he didn't care for Ellie either.

But she made herself play nice and favored Ellie with a forced a smile. "Your breakfast looks delicious, as always."

"Just doing my job." Ellie hadn't caught the light sarcasm in Darby's voice. Irony seemed to sail completely over her head. She turned to Leo and patted his arm. "That's why I love it here. My work is so important. Must keep my boy here in good health."

Not a man of many words, Leo absently touched Ellie's hand without looking at her and gave it a squeeze. When Darby was young, her father had not cared for ingratiating, smarmy people. Why then did he put up with Ellie? Maybe in his old age when he couldn't care so well for himself, someone solicitous was too hard to resist.

Times had changed. Everyone was older, for sure. Growing up, Leo had never told Darby he loved her. It was simply something she understood. Like breathing, it was as much a part of her father as his love for her mother. Sarah had been more of an extrovert, always quick with a hug and a verbal endearment. Sometimes Darby had seen the small smile on her father's face when her mom hugged his neck and said *I love you*.

They'd been a happy family. Or so Darby had thought. She'd always wanted a marriage like her parents. A love like Leo and Sarah's.

Unable to eat, Darby glanced at her father again. No wonder that terrible night so many years ago had been such a shock. Leo had loved her mother as much as Darby. What had they done to cause her mother to take such a drastic step? Why had Sarah taken her own life?

A chair scraped on the floor, and Pete stood up. "Good breakfast as usual, Ellie." He nodded to the group. "Best be getting on the plow. More snow fell overnight, so better keep up with it."

"Leave your dishes," Ellie said. "I'll clear the table."

"No, ma'am, I'll take my own and go out through the kitchen."

Ellie followed him carrying her dirty dishes.

As she left the room, Hank climbed to his feet. "More coffee, anyone?"

Darby met his steady gaze. She saw his blush. Was she blushing too? Doggone it. She wasn't a silly teenager with a crush, but she felt like one again.

"You can warm up mine," she said.

Hank topped off her coffee and handed her the creamer. He sat down once more and studied her over the rim of his mug. *Do it*, he seemed to urge with his silent stare.

Darby pushed her plate away and turned to her father. "What do you remember about the day my mother died?"

Leo snorted and pulled a frown. "Nothin' subtle about you now, is there, Darby girl?"

She drew a deep breath. "I wasn't here. I was away that day, if you remember. I don't know what happened. It's a question that has bothered me for thirty years."

Ellie returned from the kitchen. She picked up an empty serving dish from the sideboard but remained there holding it, not moving, watching them. What was with her? Was she suspecting more family drama to play out?

Leo leaned his chair back and rubbed his chin with a gnarled finger. He was silent for a long moment. "Thinkin' back, seems as if we were booked full that summer," he finally said. "With a bunch of young, summer employees wanting to play cowboy."

"My dad was already head wrangler here," Hank recalled. "But I can't remember anything different about that summer or that day."

"Head too full of my daughter, don't ya' think?"

"Perceptive as always, Leo." Hank laid a hand on Darby's shoulder. It was warm with his support.

She leaned forward, focusing on her father. "Was my mother depressed? Was she sick? I've often wondered if she had cancer."

"Nope." Leo shook his head. "Nothing like that. Least not that I know of."

Darby was close to tears. A lump rose in her throat, and she swallowed hard. "Then I don't understand."

Leo's eyes were grim. "It was a bad time. Finding her body. Nobody knew what had happened. Why she'd hiked the trail alone." Words tumbled from his lips, grief rushing out. "Then I had to tell you. It was bad. I didn't know how to tell you. Didn't know what to say. Then you left."

His words held a finality to them. For the first time, Darby saw the scene from Leo's point of view. She was a parent now herself. She often didn't know what to say to Kelsey and Slade. How to help.

"I'm sorry, Dad." Her voice was gentle. Yet, there was a hollowness in her chest. She fought the urge to stand and run, to indulge her emotions alone, away from prying eyes. But she'd promised herself baby steps. Staying, feeling the pain, was part of her journey.

Hank's grip tightened on her shoulder.

"I'm not feeling so good," Leo said. "I have a headache. I need to rest."

Ellie hurried toward Leo and, gripping his elbow, helped him stand up. "I'll take you back to your cabin so you can lie down. This mess can wait."

"Thank you."

"We'll clean up, Ellie," Hank said.

Her throat dry, Darby watched Ellie assist Leo with his coat. Then Ellie put on her own coat and ushered him across the room, Leo leaning against her arm. Wind blew and rattled the windows as she shut the door behind them.

In the silence that followed, Darby heard her unsteady breathing. She turned and met Hank's somber gaze. "I'm glad I came. He's frailer than I thought."

"It's hard to see him like this."

They both rose. Hank picked up his dishes. Darby followed his lead and collected her half-empty plate.

"Yes." She gave a rueful laugh. "It's hell getting old."

But it seemed like something more—like the memories of her mother were too hurtful for her father and brought him great pain.

Darby released a sigh. "I'll clean up the kitchen. I need something to do to keep myself busy."

CHAPTER THIRTEEN

Since Hank wouldn't let her tackle the kitchen duties alone, Darby took Ellie's place at the sink, hot water up to her elbows, giving him the job of dryer.

"Doing this always reminds me of my mother," she said, a warm memory curling through her heart.

"Yep."

"She was a wonderful mother, Hank. In fact, almost perfect. Hardworking. Sweet. Loving. I've tried to be like her with my own children but can't quite live up to her standard."

"I bet you're a good mother."

Darby closed her eyes, trying to center herself as the previous, aching regret came back full force. No, she wasn't like Sarah. She'd always been too much of an introvert, too tied up in her artwork, her own world, unable to outwardly show her love with hugs and kisses.

She opened her eyes, turning toward Hank to see him watching her with a tender look on his face. "Kelsey thinks I'm a good mother."

"There ya' go." He kissed her forehead. "Don't sell yourself short. Your daughter should know."

She winced, embarrassed by his attention and the sudden recollection of last night's lovemaking. After all these years, could this really be happening? This revitalized attraction? The puppy love she'd had for Hank had carried her forward into the first few years of her new life in Kentucky. But that was a long time ago. She'd given up that fantasy as her relationship with Col grew stronger and they married.

What about now? Did she need his love? Did she even want it?

Hell. Did he even love her back? Truly? He'd never said the words, although she remembered saying them to him that night they camped out under the stars.

Turning back to the sink, she pulled up the stopper and water drained from the basin. "My son has never been as verbal as his twin sister." She dried her hands on a towel and turned back to Hank. "Slade's a quiet boy. Too much like me, I'm afraid."

Hank reached for another dish towel to dry his hands. He hung it back on a rack being careful to make it neat, taking his time, as though he needed to gauge his next words.

"Your son's name is Slade?"

Darby jerked her head back, her posture suddenly stiff. She'd never told Hank the name of her son. There was a heavy feeling in her stomach when she met his gaze again.

"Yes," she said in a low voice.

He regarded her perceptively through eyes that sparkled. "Why did you call him Slade?"

She dipped her head, hiding her face and feeling her neck and face grow terribly hot. "Well," she said, then hesitated. "I sort of named him after you."

AN HOUR LATER, Hank sat behind his desk in the ranch office, his eyes blurring, and doodled on a blank pad of lined paper. *Hot damn!* Darby had named her son after him. The honor made Hank burst with pride. Ironically, he never would have known about her son named Slade if Hank hadn't called that day and if she hadn't finally come out to the ranch.

His heart slammed against his ribs. The effect of the revelation of her son's name was something new, something more than plain old sexual attraction. Whatever happened between Darby and him going forward, he'd always have the knowledge she'd once loved him enough to call her son by his last name.

Hank stared at a long list of figures. He hated this part of his job. Ellie had done the accounting books before he signed up. Maybe he should let her handle them again.

It was much more fun to think about Darby and relive his night with her. Never in a million years would he have dreamed Darby York wanted to make love to him. He wasn't a damn heir to a fortune like her husband. Just a simple horse wrangler. She could have anyone, yet last night she'd chosen him.

His musing abruptly ended when the door flew open and Pete stamped into the office. Snowflakes had settled on his hat and clung to his scruffy beard.

"Damn cold outside," the wrangler grumbled.

"I hope this is the last of it," Hank said.

"Humph. You know we can get snow in July."

"Anyhow, let's hope this is the end of the big storms. What's up?"

"We got all the signs of labor. Mare's restlessness and sweating. Keeps circling in her stall."

"Yep. Sounds like it." Hank rubbed his chin. He didn't relish the mare foaling on a night when the vet couldn't make it out. He hoped nothing went wrong.

"I cleaned out her stall and made sure it was bedded with plenty of straw."

"We gotta keep an eye on her." Hank opened his desk drawer and withdrew a pack of batteries, handing them to Pete. "Here. Make sure your radio is charged in case you need to get in touch with me."

"Will do. Plan to spend the night in the barn if she doesn't go before then."

Hank released a long breath. "Thanks, Pete. Don't know what I'd do without you."

Pete shrugged as if it was nothing. The cowboy was a fixture at the ranch. Been there as long as Hank could remember. The man had to be pushing seventy and had the bowlegged gait of a lifelong horseman to prove it. Like the pink bunny in the battery ad, he kept going and going.

Instead of leaving right away, Pete hung around the office, surveying his boots, as if he had something else on his mind.

"Need something else?"

Cowboy hat in hand, Pete sank into the chair across from Hank. "What do you think about this will thing? Leo sure surprised the heck out of me leaving me part of the ranch. I feel sorry for Darby, though, her being the rightful person to get it."

Hank rocked back in the chair, bracing a boot against the bottom desk drawer. "Yep. Shocked me, too. But I suspect she doesn't need the ranch."

"No, but still ain't right."

"You know the history here better than I do."

Pete placed his hat on the desk, removed a glove and rubbed the bottom of his nose with a finger as if satisfying an itch. "Sure do. I even remember when Darby came to the ranch with her mother. She was a pretty little thing with red baby curls."

Hank sat forward, facing Leo across the desk, anxiety suddenly in his shoulders and neck. "So, you always knew Darby was adopted."

"Sure, but it was not something Sarah wanted known. She convinced Leo not to talk about it."

Hank shook his head. "I don't understand why not."

Pete looked uneasy. He cleared his throat, and his gaze skittered away toward the door. "She had her reasons. I respected her wishes."

Did Pete know more than he was letting on? Hank squinted and sat back again, crossing his arms. "It would help if we knew why Sarah committed suicide. Darby's ate up with guilt about it."

Pete abruptly came to his feet. Slowly, he drew the glove back over his right hand, secured his hat on his head, and went to the door. He opened it, letting cold air rush in. Before he stepped out into the snowy weather, he gave a quick glance back at Hank.

"I'm not sure she did."

The wooden door slammed shut. Hank gaped at it. What the hell? Then had Sarah's death been an accident?

He stood and went to the window. In the distance, whirling snow engulfed the old wrangler. Hank stayed there chewing his lower lip and watched him disappear toward the barn.

CHAPTER FOURTEEN

DARBY'S BOOT skidded out from under her on the step to the office, and she barely caught herself. As it was, she tripped up the icy step, grabbing the snow-covered railing for support. So much for a graceful entrance. She was aware that her heart pounded, and her hands sweated inside her gloves.

Sucking in a breath, the cold air stinging all the way down into her lungs, Darby knocked once, then opened the office door. Hank stood as she entered. She felt her face grow warm, and it was not from the fire in the wood stove.

"I checked on Leo," she said without any preliminaries.

Hank sat down. "How is he?"

Darby removed her outer garments, hanging up her coat. She smoothed back her hair with the palm of her hand. "I didn't see him. Ellie was sitting in his living room knitting. She said he was asleep in his room."

"I suppose that's good." Hank looked up and captured her gaze. "He doesn't seem the same after that accident."

"That's what you said." And what had gotten her out to the ranch. Had Hank had other motives? Or was this thing between them simply the byproduct of their unexpected nearness?

She studied her boots, aware of his rapt perusal. There were always choices, and she'd made hers long ago. She couldn't expect Hank to forgive and forget, knowing full well what a hard time she always had doing just that.

Raising her head, Darby forced herself to look at Hank, once more intrigued by the rough planes of his face, his day's growth of beard that gave him such a manly look. He was a full-on cowboy, that was for sure.

She fingered Sarah's pendant. "I looked for my mother's pictures in the dining room after checking on Leo. That's where I left them. They were gone. Have you seen them?"

"Nope. I still have the wooden box." He leaned back in his chair, rocking back and balancing with a booted foot on the desk drawer. "Last time I saw the photos, Leo had them at the table."

Darby sighed. "That's what I thought. I went back to his cabin and asked Ellie. She hasn't seen them."

"I guess Leo took them."

"I suppose so." She shrugged and turned away, glancing at the wall phone. "Can I use the phone?" Looking back, she gave him a smile. "I'd like to call my daughter."

"Sure. Have at it."

The wall phone was the rotary type. "I haven't seen one like this in years."

"Yep. You know Leo. He's a sucker for the old ways."

Memories of her mother nagging Leo swirled in Darby's head. Sarah had always wanted to do things the modern way. Not her father. He was old school. Their differences had started plenty of arguments. Darby grinned at the recollection and caught Hank's gaze again. It touched her, warming her, making her body tingle in an unfamiliar and wicked way. She cleared her throat and dialed the number.

Kelsey was as usual in the farm office. "Mom," she said, "I've been wondering about you and meaning to call."

It was good to hear her daughter's voice. "We had more snow, but I'm safe and sound."

"The article by Laurel Chastain came out yesterday," Kelsey said. "I have the actual magazine here, but it's also online if you want to see it."

Darby had forgotten about the interview. It seemed like such a lifetime ago. "Give me the web address, and Hank will help me look it up on the internet."

"Hank?"

"You remember. The guy who called you from the ranch."

"Oh, that's right." Kelsey's voice had a perceptive tone to it as if she'd heard something different in her mother's voice. "You'll have to tell me about this Hank."

Darby grunted and changed the subject. "How's your brother after the breakup?"

"He seems okay. Disinterested as always in running the farm."

With a sigh, Darby looked out of the window at the snowy fields beyond. What was she going to do with Slade? Even before his father's death, he seemed aimless, not a bit serious about his responsibilities.

"Carol from the art gallery called yesterday," Kelsey said. "She wants to go ahead with the show next week and thinks you should be here."

Darby pressed her lips together and once more looked down at her boots. She felt a sinking feeling in her stomach. How could she leave the ranch? And Hank? He held a bigger attraction for her at the moment than her artwork.

At the same time, how could she *not* go to her own show? She'd worked so hard on it.

She scuffed her toe against the hardwood floor. "I'll have to let you know." She glanced up to meet Hank's gaze. "It depends upon how my father is doing."

"I understand." Kelsey hesitated. "Do you want me to tell Carol anything?"

Darby pulled in a gulp of air, then released a deep breath. "Tell her I hope to be there. If not, will you stand in for me?"

"Sure, but I know nothing about art."

"I know, baby, but you're prettier than me. You'll attract plenty attention to the show."

"Oh, Mom."

They rung off soon after, and Darby hung up. She turned around to see Hank concentrating on his accounts. He wouldn't look up.

"So, you're going home."

"Eventually." She took the chair across from him. "Kentucky *is* my home, Hank."

"Yep," he drawled and lifted his eyes. "With Leo's will changed, there's nothing to keep you here."

"That's right."

She could scarcely breathe under the spell of his gaze. She saw that his mouth tightened. Their night together sat between them like a thousand-pound bull moose. *What makes you think you can step back into my life?*

Darby's cheeks burned, and she looked at her hands, trembling with shame. She'd left him. She'd run scared, making a totally new life for herself, leaving this one behind. Suddenly chilled, she boosted her chin. Hank was right. There was nothing to keep her here. Even Hank.

She switched subjects, back to the other problem troubling her. "My son seems at loose ends since his father died. I don't know what to do with him."

Hank studied her with a small smile on his lips, his eyes growing thoughtful. "Send him out here. We'll make a cowboy out of him."

Her eyebrows shot up in surprise. "Oh, Slade wouldn't want to do that." And she wouldn't want it either. It would be another tie to this place, one that might force her to change her mind.

The base radio on Hank's desk suddenly crackled, interrupting further discussion.

"Pete to base."

Hank picked up his device. "Go ahead."

"We're a go down here."

"I'll be right there."

"Okay. Clear."

Darby scooted forward in her chair. "What's going on?"

Hank stood and reached for his outerwear. "Mare's in foal. I need to get down there to help Pete."

Darby swallowed hard and climbed to her feet. Waves of nostalgia filled her stomach. This was like home. She'd been with Col and the foaling staff during many births. It had been something she and her husband had enjoyed watching together, bringing them closer, like a real team.

"Can I come with you?"

Hank zipped up his coat and searched her eyes. "Sure. If you want."

"I do want. The birth of a foal is an amazing experience."

"Come along then. You know the way."

He left her to bundle up for the cold weather and then follow his boot tracks in the drifts of snow.

CHAPTER FIFTEEN

THE MARE'S water had broken by the time Darby arrived at the barn. Leo was there standing outside the stall, watching quietly with Pete and Hank.

"What are you doing here, Leo?"

"Where else would I be?"

Ellie stepped forward out of the shadows. "I couldn't keep him away."

Darby shook her head. "It's not your fault, Ellie. I learned a long time ago he has a mind of his own."

"That's the pot calling the kettle black," Leo said with a snort.

Same old Dad.

Darby pushed in between Leo and Hank to stand against the rough wood railing of the square box stall where she could observe the birth. Hank welcomed her by shoving his arm against her shoulder, leaning into her, and grinning at her. Her heart gave a hard kick and her mouth suddenly went dry. She pushed against him too, savoring his warmth, smelling his leather and musk scent that mixed so well with the horsey aroma of the barn.

Could this interaction really be serious between them? How

long before something gave—her need for the security of home or his need for freedom?

Darby sighed and returned her focus to the mare. The foaling stall was bedded with straw and was small compared with the spacious brick and metal stalls where Heston Farm thousand-dollar newborns saw life. Here, there wasn't the big crew of farm personnel or an on-staff veterinarian. This birth was going to be a basic procedure. Mother Nature at her best.

The bay mare was a quarter horse, and unlike Col's thoroughbreds, a much smaller, stockier horse. She had a muscular body and a broad chest, perfect for her work on the ranch. Like other births Darby had seen, the mare's tail had been wrapped to keep it out of the way. She only hoped the foal was in its proper position in the birth canal with its nose resting on its forelimbs and its two front hooves presenting first. If not, the foal would be in jeopardy. And so might the mother.

With a grunt, the mare went down onto the straw.

"Shouldn't be long now," Hank said.

Beside her Leo gasped. Darby turned to look at him. For a split second, his face, neck and arm muscles jerked rhythmically. Then his body went limp, and he crumpled onto the dirt of the barn floor.

"Dad!" Darby dropped to her knees over Leo's prone body. Her father's eyes rolled back into his head. "He's dying!"

Hank elbowed her aside. "Pete, call 911!"

As Pete sprinted from the barn toward the landline at the office, Darby felt Ellie's grip on her arms, pulling her to her feet and holding her back from Hank and her father's body.

"Let go of me!"

"Hank will take care of him," Ellie said, her voice soothing in Darby's ear.

Darby shook herself free and took a step forward. Hank placed Leo on his side to help keep her airway clear.

"Is he having a stroke?"

Hank glanced over his shoulder at her, fear written on his face. "I don't know."

"Oh, my god," she cried out and shoved a gloved fist up to her mouth.

Her chest tightened with terror, and she relived the moment she'd seen her mother's mangled body on a stretcher. Leo had stopped her from running forward, from seeing the actual horror of her mother's death. She'd lived it, though. From that moment on, the scene of the rescuers carrying her mother down the mountain had haunted her and her dreams.

Now this.

Paramedics from the Big Sky Fire Department arrived in what seemed like hours, but fortunately was about twenty minutes. Thank goodness Pete had plowed the ranch road.

"He's unconscious," the uniformed officer said looking up from his examination. "Has he fallen recently? Hurt himself in any way?"

"He fell from a horse three months ago," Hank said.

"Didn't go to the doctor like I told him he should," Ellie mumbled. "Pig-headed old man."

"I think it's best we summon the air ambulance and get him to Bozeman."

"He's my father," Darby said. "Do what you must."

"We've got room for one person," the paramedic said.

Darby had no qualms, making her decision quickly. "Let Ellie go with him."

Ellie looked surprised. "Me?"

"Yes. You've been taking care of him. Not me. He'd want you."

Hank grasped Darby's arm, offering her support. She stepped nearer to him, seeking his comfort, his validation she'd done the right thing for once by letting Ellie go along in the helicopter.

"We'll follow in our truck," Hank told the first responders as they loaded Leo onto a stretcher and pushed it out the barn door followed by Ellie.

Then Hank turned to Darby and drew her into his arms. She

sank into his embrace, tears stinging her eyes. Over his shoulder, she noticed the mare standing in her stall and beside her, a wobbly foal struggled to gain his feet on long, spindly legs.

Leo was in the ICU and breathing with the aid of a ventilator. Hank held Darby's hand as they looked down at her father's comatose body. Doctors had diagnosed him with a chronic subdural hematoma, probably caused by a head injury from the fall. Bleeding had occurred over weeks with blood slowly collecting just under the brain's surface. In an attempt to save his life, surgeons had drilled a burr hole into Leo's brain and suctioned out the blood to relieve the pressure.

The healing was now up to the eighty-five-year-old man. Would he have amnesia from the injury? Would he be able to talk? Walk? Horseback riding was absolutely out the doctors had told them.

"I just want him to get well," Darby said through a cascade of tears. She pulled her hand away from Hank's and wiped her eyes with a tissue.

Hank silently agreed. He wasn't convinced Leo would live.

"Let's go." He slipped his hand under her elbow to usher out of the room. "Nothing we can do here."

In the ICU waiting room, Ellie sat on a two-seat sofa with her knitting. Pete sat nearby. They had commandeered a corner of the room near a window, pulling chairs together in a conversational semi-circle. Hank showed Darby to one of the empty seats in the circle. She sat down and took a deep breath, her face pale and eyes dark from crying.

Hank stood a moment, collecting himself. From the view outside the window, the weather remained gray, but snow chances were fading. Night was falling. It had been a rough day with the birth of the foal and then the rush to Bozeman. Hank figured the difficult times weren't over, not until Leo was out of the woods.

He sat down next to Ellie. She was silently chewing a wad of gum and knitting, seeming absorbed in her task, but probably biding time like they all were. She smelled of lavender and peppermint.

"Well?" Pete had lately come from the ranch with Ellie's bag of yarn and needles. "How's it goin'?"

Hank shook his head. "The same."

Pete let out a long breath. "Sure am sorry about this."

"We all are." Hank let his words fade into the silence of the room. They were the only ones there at the moment, the only ones waiting for news of a sick loved one.

Hank clenched his jaw. There was nothing he could have done for Leo, not after that fall. No one could have anticipated this turn of events, although he supposed he should have known something more was terribly wrong. Leo was old. As Darby said, he'd gotten frail. Perhaps Leo had recognized as much before Christmas. That's why he'd called Hank to come back to the Gallatin Canyon and run his ranch.

Hank rubbed his chin. "You said something earlier to me, Pete, about Darby's mother."

Pete shifted his eyes and swallowed. Both Darby and Ellie lifted their heads, eyes wide with curiosity.

The old wrangler looked nervous. "I just said I knew when she was brought to the ranch. I was there."

Hank offered a half-smile. Would Darby like to hear about it? Pete's story might be something to pass the time. "Go ahead and tell us about it."

Pete scanned the small group and shrugged his shoulders. "Even if he makes it, I 'spect Leo won't mind. I know you won't hear this from him. I know he promised Sarah long ago to keep quiet. Seems as if he's kept that promise all these years. He's an honest and good man."

Darby leaned forward, resting her elbow on her knees. "If you know something about my mother, Pete, I'd like to hear it."

161

Pete's face flushed. "You may decide otherwise after you hear what I have to say."

CHAPTER SIXTEEN

EVERY NERVE in her body seemed to hum, turning her anxiety into nausea. Darby let out a breath and clasped the pendant around her neck.

"I know you're going to find it painful. But it's water over the dam now. Not sure it's worth tellin'."

Why did Pete keep saying she wouldn't want to hear the truth? What was the problem?

"Why would my mother keep a secret from me?"

His gaze darted away, delaying. Then Pete cleared his throat. "She was ashamed. She hadn't had the best life until she came to the ranch. Until she met Leo.

It was if a vast chasm had opened up, and Darby balanced on the edge afraid to topple in. Now that she thought about it, she knew nothing of her mother's history. Not a word. Leo's had been an open book with the ranch and all the history that went with it, but then, Leo wasn't her real father.

"I don't care. I want to know. Need to know." She heard the desperation in her voice and sat back in her chair, rubbing her sweaty palms against her jeans, trying to calm her nerves.

"Okay." Pete chewed his lower lip and leaned forward, looking her in the eye. "You want the truth, then I'll give you the truth."

The moment was surreal. Hank and Ellie stared at Pete, seeming to hold their breaths as well. For Darby, the world was suddenly quiet, all the hospital noises fading into the background. She bit her lip and searched Pete's blue eyes, seeing discomfort in them and a deep resignation.

"Probably do me good to come clean," he said. "Fess up to my part in everything."

"In what?" Hank's tone was sharp. He scowled at the old wrangler as if to say *get on with it.*

"When Darby was only one, her father brought her and Sarah to the ranch. He wanted me to take them in, get Sarah a job if I could. Then he left them."

"Why would he do that?"

"He was my half-brother."

Across from her, Ellie gasped. Darby felt herself slipping into that ever-widening crater as the implication hit her. "That makes you my uncle."

Pete nodded, his gaze skittering away, then back again. "Yep."

"So, Darby's father was named Harden, unless that's not your real name." Hank had sense enough to ask. Darby couldn't form the questions that pointlessly racketed in her mind.

"Nope," Pete said again. "Tim and I had different fathers. His name was Krebs."

A wave of panic rushed over Darby, pushing her farther toward the open void she'd felt since her mother's death. *Krebs.* That's the name she'd seen on the back of the missing photo. Her father was Tim Krebs, not Leo York. Did it matter now? That man had not wanted her, but Leo had. Leo had married her mother and given Darby a new last name, an identity, a home, a life.

"Where is this guy now?"

Darby raised her head at Hank's query. Unlike her, he was not overcome by the emotion of the unexpected revelation. He seemed skeptical and wanted more details.

"He's dead."

Ellie gasped again.

"Oh." Darby released a pent-up breath. "Why didn't Leo tell me all this? Why was he keeping it from me?"

"Don't get sentimental about Tim," Pete said. "My brother wasn't worth it. He wasn't a good man. Spent time in jail. Died of a drug overdose, they say. As for Leo, he was trying to protect you. Sarah, too. He was keeping his promise to her. They didn't want you to have anything to do with Tim or the life Sarah led before coming to the ranch."

Darby couldn't form the words.

But Hank did. He seemed to read her mind. "What life? What do you mean?"

"Back in the sixties and seventies, Tim and Sarah were in an underground movement. Sarah was known as Chelsea Clemons. They blew up buildings for political reasons. One blast killed a policeman. When Sarah came to the ranch, she'd become a liability to Tim because of the baby—Darby. Besides, like Tim, she was running from the law. The ranch was a safe place to hide."

Darby slid into the abyss. Her mother—sweet, beautiful, loving Sarah—was a criminal. No matter her motives, her mother had lied to her by not telling her the truth. Now Darby's whole life was a falsehood.

In the silence that followed Pete's admission, Darby heard her own frightened breaths, the pounding of her heart. She stood, slung her purse over her shoulder, turned away from the group, and quietly left the waiting room.

DARBY HAD MADE it to the hospital lobby before Hank caught up with her. "Darby, wait!"

He grabbed her arm and stopped her. She wouldn't turn around. She wouldn't face him.

His heartbeat raced, nearly exploding in his chest. "Where are you going?"

She glanced over her shoulder. Her face was ashen. Slowly, he turned her around, and he held her upper arms, trying to draw her close. She was shaking uncontrollably but resisted his attempt at comfort.

Lifting her chin, Darby focused on his face, as if seeing him for the first time. "I'm going home."

"Home? Back to the ranch?"

"Back to Kentucky."

He didn't know what to say. He surveyed her face, seeing the pain. "You can't leave. What about Leo?"

"What about Leo?" She shook off his grip and took a step backward. "He's nothing to me."

"He raised you. Protected your mother. You."

"My mother is nothing to me either."

"What?" Hank couldn't believe her words. Her mother had always been everything to Darby. They'd been so close. That's why her mother's death had traumatized Darby so much. "You're not thinking straight. Stop a moment and think things through."

She squared her shoulders and set her jaw. "There's nothing more to think through. I'm going home to my children. To the home Colton built for me. It's where I belong."

Hank's chest ached. His knees felt week. She couldn't do this. Not after she'd come home. Come back to him. Not after they'd spent the night together making love.

"But what about us?" He heard his words as if from afar. Pleading, desperate words.

"There is no us."

That was more than Darby had given him when they were eighteen. Then she'd simply left. Disappeared. Vanished with no explanation. Now she supplied a reason. She didn't care about him. He was nothing to her, not like her rich, dead husband.

Darby gave him a curt nod and turned. He reached for her, but she'd moved on.

"But I love you," he said.

Darby hesitated a step. Then she walked on. It was only after she'd gone through the hospital doors and disappeared down the street that he realized he'd finally told her he loved her.

It was too little too late.

His vision blurred. He would not cry. He was a man. A cowboy. He'd suck it up as he'd always done. What else could he do?

Hank turned back to the elevator to go to the ICU, knowing his heart was broken. One more time.

Yet, for some reason, it felt worse than ever before.

CHAPTER SEVENTEEN

Lexington, Kentucky, art gallery

DARBY STOOD with a glass of merlot in her hand, holding it like it was the proverbial lifeline. Hushed conversation and soft music from a three-piece, string chamber group filled the crowded room. White-coated waiters circulated with plates of *hors d'oeuvres*. Each of Darby's oil paintings was highlighted by a gentle spotlight that focused on her artistic interpretation of a woman and horse, showing off her hard work, her talent, her passion.

"Congratulations, Mrs. Heston. This artwork is lovely," a woman complimented her. She dripped diamonds and *haute couture*, at odds with the Kentucky twang to her voice.

"Thank you." Darby managed a half-smile and gripped the glass so tightly she feared the stem would break.

Having been back for two weeks, she didn't have much to smile about. Even her long-awaited art exhibit held no enjoyment. Kelsey had masterminded the event. Darby knew her daughter had recognized her depression upon her sudden return home. Without Kelsey's encouragement, Darby doubted she could have arrived at this moment and functioned as well as she did.

Darby hadn't told Kelsey the reason she'd run from the ranch. Her daughter didn't need to know what a screwup her mother actually was, a nobody who'd managed to marry the right man at the right time in her life. Kelsey's father was Kentucky royalty, so to speak, with his old bourbon and thoroughbred connections, but her mother's family was dysfunctional and criminal.

Smiling again at another patron, Darby swallowed the anxiety riding high in her throat. She could perform, but just barely. She could nod and sip her wine and make aimless chitchat. But her heart was devastated for so many reasons. For so many things said and left unsaid.

Had she heard Hank correctly? Had he said he loved her?

It didn't matter. She didn't deserve his love. Darby was broken, a fraud—like her mother who hadn't been the saint she had always thought. Darby's whole life had been predicated on her mother's perfection and love. She'd always known she couldn't live up to her mother's example. That she wasn't good enough. Not like Sarah. No mother was like Sarah. No mother could compare, least of all herself.

What a joke.

Now the rose-colored glasses had been stripped from her eyes. She saw reality, and she struggled to live with it. For so many years she'd lived with horrible dreams and carried guilt because of her mother's death, letting it ruin her life in many ways. Col had been right when he told her she wasn't to blame. She should have listened and trusted his wisdom.

Darby took another sip of red wine, letting is slide smoothly down her throat, hoping it would ease her sorrow or, at least, deaden her memories.

Her son Slade stood in a darkened corner of the room his arms folded across his chest. He didn't need to hold a bourbon glass for security. Darby crisscrossed the room to stand beside him.

"Nice turnout, Mom."

Slade was so good-looking, so all-American male. Darby smiled, unable to hide her pride in him. "Yes. I'm pleased."

"You should be. You've worked hard."

Darby shrugged, a poor attempt at nonchalance. "Painting is my passion. I'm thankful I had your dad's support."

"You've always been my role model, Mom. I wish I had your kind of drive and enthusiasm. I wish I had your talent."

His words settled over her like a comforting blanket. Darby held on to them in her mind, twisting them over and over. How ironic. Life was full of contradictions, and if she wasn't so depressed, Darby might find this one amusing. She couldn't think of herself as a role model.

Kelsey joined them. All blond to Slade's dark coloring, Kelsey was the most strikingly beautiful of Darby's twins.

"Carol is pleased with the turnout." Kelsey surveyed the busy art gallery. "I've heard many praises for your work."

"That's nice." Darby drank her wine and perused the wealthy horsey-set in attendance. Colton would have been proud. She hung onto that thought and swallowed another mouthful of wine. Maybe she could get drunk. Maybe then she could forget.

Ms. Dripping with Diamonds suddenly swooped down upon them, clutching her bejeweled hands together. "I must have one of those western paintings," she said, gushing with delight. "Tell me they're for sale."

"Everything is for sale," Kelsey told her, "except for the two paintings of American Saddlebred horses and riders. They were commissioned and are on loan for this show."

"Then I must have another one. I love the cowgirls! They are so authentic!"

Kelsey glanced at Darby as if to gauge her mother's reaction. "See Carol," she told the woman. "She'll take care of you."

The customer hurried across the floor to seek out the gallery owner, and Darby walked slowly toward the painting in question. It was of a buckskin quarter horse and cowgirl holding a lariat. Darby stood silently, eyes prickling with tears. The painting had been done from memory. Darby let recollections take over, but this time they were current ones—of a recent visit to Montana, of a boy who'd become a man worthy enough to love.

Sniffing, Darby spun and stepped away. It didn't matter. Nothing mattered. She was home now where she belonged.

CHAPTER EIGHTEEN

THE NEXT DAY Darby flicked on the gas logs in her studio and flames whooshed into a blaze. She didn't need the heat—spring was coming to the Bluegrass—but she wanted the comfort the cheerful light produced. In Montana, Hank had brought her wood to warm her cabin. The old stove had gone out so quickly, and he had stoked it, bringing the fire back from ashes. This push-button fire seemed so much more civilized.

Carefully, Darby steadied a blank canvas on an easel, making sure it caught the light from the window. She arranged her assortment of brushes on a nearby table and set out new, unopened tubes of oil paint. If only she had the sketch of ranch horses that she'd done the first day, she would paint them, but her drawing had disappeared from her cabin. Could she recover the moment among the herd from memory?

Did she want to? She fingered her mother's pendant, still hanging around her neck. Montana was a lifetime away. Just like her childhood, her first love, her mother's death. It was so long ago.

The white canvas taunted her. Her mind was as vacant. Darby didn't know what she wanted to paint, what statement she wanted to make. She felt as if she had no direction. No reason for being.

Her husband was dead. Her children were grown. What was left for her? Even the nightmares had ceased. This studio, that had always been her refuge, seemed cold and uninviting. It was almost if she could no longer hide here. It was no longer the place for her to dream her dreams.

Darby turned away from the easel. She sat down on the sofa facing the fireplace and gazed into the flames. If her mother had felt such despair, she could now understand why Sarah had taken her life. Not that Darby would commit suicide. She hadn't the courage. She was much better at running and avoiding the hard stuff.

Trouble was, she no longer had anywhere else to go.

Kentucky was her home. Wasn't it?

The door to the studio opened. Darby turned her head to peer over her shoulder. Kelsey hung up her coat on the rack by the door, then came over and took a seat across from her.

She didn't say a word, just clasped her hands and stared at the floor. Darby didn't know what to say. Kelsey's gaze shifted to the fire. She looked as if she had something on her mind.

Clearing her throat, Kelsey focused her eyes back on Darby. "I heard from Hank just now. He called the office with news of your father."

Darby moved in the seat, the sofa suddenly feeling too soft, too enveloping. She couldn't gather her thoughts to reply.

Kelsey leaned forward, elbows on her knees and suddenly intense. "He told me my grandfather is well enough to go home today. He said someone named Ellie would take care of him 24/7."

"That's good." Darby rushed a breath and braced herself for more recriminations. She knew Kelsey wouldn't hold back.

"He told me you left Montana with your father in the hospital."

The words were damning. Guilt crawled through Darby's gut. "I did."

There was a heavy silence, almost as if Kelsey was figuring how to say what she wanted to say. Darby couldn't bear it. She stood and collected the remote for the fireplace from the mantle, switching off the flames. It was much too hot anyway. She turned around and eyed her daughter.

"When I asked Hank why you'd leave like that, he told me about my grandmother."

"Damn!" Hank had no business interfering. What was he thinking? Her mother's failings were her concern and hers alone.

Kelsey raised her head and met Darby's gaze. She chewed her lower lip, her face softening with compassion. "I'm so sorry for you, Mom. I know how hard it was to lose your mother. For all of my life, you've been sad. Now you learn she wasn't the saint you thought her to be."

"Yeah, it isn't too pleasant to learn after all these years that my mother was a criminal. The truth is pretty much too hard to handle."

Kelsey stood up to face Darby on an equal level. "But what is the truth? Do you believe the word of that old cowboy? Shouldn't you go home and ask your father for the real story?" She hesitated. "Now that he's on the mend. Now that he is going to live."

Darby felt her body begin to tremble. She blinked back tears before Kelsey could see them. "But…"

Kelsey crossed her arms, her gaze unflinching, her voice steady. "No *buts*. You have no excuses now. No reason to remain here. The art show is over."

Her daughter was telling her she wasn't needed in Kentucky, not on Colton Heston's farm. "You're right." Darby took a deep breath. "I'll think about it."

"You'd better." With nothing more to say, Kelsey gathered her coat. She paused at the door. "I don't get you, Mom. You have so many people who love you—Daddy, Slade, and me. If I was loved by so many people, I'd get over what happened long ago, the things I couldn't control."

Kelsey shook her head, sighed, and left the studio, shutting the door forcefully. Darby remained alone with her familiar guilt and regrets. She stared at the door, the studio suddenly feeling empty and colder than ever.

Thank God, Leo was okay. She was glad Ellie was able to care for him. But shouldn't that be Darby's job? Leo was old and frail. He was all that Darby had left of her past.

And Hank. Her thoughts swung back to him, to that look he'd given her. It had been full of hurt. She had abandoned him once. Maybe she should return to the ranch to learn if what she'd thought he'd said was true.

She had to admit her life had changed for her at home. After Montana and Hank, things just weren't the same in Kentucky.

THINKING about returning to the ranch was not the same as making preparations to do so. Lips pressing together, Darby fought the sinking feeling in her stomach. She didn't want to go back to Montana, but she knew she must. She'd left so much unsettled. As Kelsey implied, Darby needed to get her act together.

She could almost hear Leo telling her to *cowboy up!* All her life, until the time she'd left home, he'd order her to quit complaining. When a horse tossed her, he'd tell her to dust off her butt and climb back into the saddle. "It makes you tough," he would say.

But she hadn't been tough. She'd panicked and run. And now with the news about her mother she had even more heartache to get over, to try to comprehend.

Unable to concentrate but needing to do something active, Darby picked up a dust cloth and bottle of wood polish. She cleaned the studio from top to bottom, dusting shelves and buffing wooden furniture. This was her domain, her responsibility. The cleaning lady who came once a week to clean the big house had never set foot in the art studio.

Washing the bathroom was a mind-numbing task but gave her a

sense of accomplishment. Could she clean the dirt out of her life as easily as she'd scrubbed the toilet bowl?

"Mom? You here?"

Darby poked her head out of the bathroom to see Slade enter the studio. "I'm here."

He carried several canvases each wrapped in brown paper. "I've brought these over from the gallery. Where do you want them?"

Darby came out drying her hands. "Just set them along the wall. Thank you."

Slade propped the paintings against the wall as instructed, then paused to offer her a smile, not acting ready to leave.

Why did she often have trouble talking to her son? There was often an awkwardness between them that didn't occur between her and her forthright daughter.

"What's going on?" It was a generic question. If Kelsey had already told him about Leo, it would give him an opening to ask questions, but if not, Darby might find out what seemed to be bothering him.

"I've been offered a job," he said without much enthusiasm. "In Lexington."

"You have?" This was an interesting development.

"Yes." He sat down in the chair recently vacated by Kelsey. "But I don't know if I want to take it."

Darby found her seat on the sofa. "Why not?"

Slade ran a hand through his black hair as if frustrated. "I know I'm supposed to help Kelsey take over at the farm, but she's doing a fine job without me."

"The horse farm is your inheritance, too."

"I know. Dad wanted us both to run it." He slumped in the chair. Then taking a deep breath, he favored her with another smile that also seemed sad. "The thing is, Mom, I don't know what I want to do with my life. I don't know if I want this job I was offered or if I want to help Kelsey. Nothing seems to click."

Darby sat back, breathing deeply, and shut her eyes. Like her,

Slade was at a crossroads. She could stop running, go back home, and make up with Leo. She could find out if she had a future with Hank. Or she could continue hiding here.

Slade, on the other hand, had a world wide open to him, but he didn't know what he wanted. He'd never had the passion for art, like she'd had or the talent for organization and schoolwork like his sister. As a mother of a grown child, she couldn't give him the answers he sought, but maybe she could facilitate them.

She opened her eyes and smiled at him, hoping he felt reassured. "I must go back to Montana. I'd like you to come with me."

He straightened. "Montana?"

"The Ghost Mountain Ranch." She nodded. "You can meet your grandfather." Pausing, Darby searched the darkened fireplace for answers she didn't have. She took another breath for courage. "And you can meet the man I named you after," she said in a soft voice. "His name is Hank Slade."

CHAPTER NINETEEN

Staff dining room, early evening
Three days later

HEAD DOWN over the guitar in his arms, Hank strummed absently, picking out cords but not making a recognizable melody. He'd had a real, paper letter today from Ashleigh Kingston, who lived across the mountain range in Paradise Valley. She'd given him the news of the McKenna Ranch. His old boss Brody and his wife Stef were pregnant again. Their teenage daughter Livy said the two were like rabbits. That had brought a smile to Hank's lips. From the mouths of babes, as the old saying went.

As for Ashleigh, she was doing *good*, busy with schoolwork. She still loved Montana. Her boyfriend Josh would graduate at the end of the year and planned to go into the service, the Marines, if they'd take him. Her dad Charles and new stepmother Liz had spent the months since Christmas holiday in California. She missed her dad but had enough to keep her busy with school and learning to ride. Josh was teaching her.

Liz. Hank now plucked a sad tune, a ballad of unrequited love, which seemed to be the story of his life. He'd loved Liz but had lost her to another man, not that he'd ever tried to win her. His had been more of a one-sided love, all on his part. Recently, he'd lost Darby...again. This time to her own pig-headedness, her fear, and unrelenting guilt. And with Darby, he'd even admitted he loved her. It had taken all his courage to say those words. Sadly, Ashleigh had been wrong. Saying them was no better than holding them in, keeping his feelings to himself.

He glanced up from his place on the hearth, the warmth of the fire roasting his back. Ellie quietly sat on the sofa, her fingers making her knitting needles fly. Leo puffed his pipe, sitting as usual in his rocker. He'd returned from Bozeman a little weaker, but still as cantankerous as ever. Hank pulled a deep breath, thankful for at least this much family. A bachelor like him needed friends and a few good horses to be content. He'd never truly needed a fickle woman.

Without warning, the door to the dining room opened. Looking up, thinking to see Pete, Hank was surprised when a lanky kid took a step inside and looked around. He was bundled in a slick parka and lace-up, snow boots, a tourist probably, more of a summer-type dude. But close behind him, a woman entered. Hank didn't recognize her for a moment, because she stood in the shadow. Then a flush of adrenaline surged through his body.

Darby.

He stood and placed his guitar on the hearth. "What are you doing here?"

"Nice to see you, too." Her tone was sarcastic, but there was a slight grin on her lips.

She showed the young man where to hang his coat on the rack, hung hers up too, and came into the center of the room and into the light.

"Leo." She nodded at her father. "I'm glad you're feeling better."

"Humph! Ain't dead yet. Can't get rid of me that easily."

Smiling now, she turned to the boy and motioned him forward. "Leo York, I want you to meet your grandson Colton Slade Heston."

Hank shuffled a step back, disbelief racing through his body.

Slade stepped forward, offering his hand. "Pleased to meet you, sir. My mother has told me a lot about you and the ranch."

Leo took his hand, held it, and for a moment seemed speechless. Then he grunted. "I'd stand but the damn doctors have me hobbled."

"No, don't bother, sir," Slade said. "I'm so happy to be here."

A moment of awkwardness followed, then Darby turned to face him. "Hank Slade, this is my son Slade."

"Slade." Hank nodded and shook the boy's hand. He had a firm grip, like a man.

"And this is Ellie, chief cook and indispensable caretaker."

Slade dipped his head in acknowledgement. "Ma'am."

Darby sure had raised a polite kid. The boy knew his manners. More than the hired help, as it turned out.

"Are you his father, Hank?" Ellie asked without a blink of shame.

Darby blushed scarlet, and Hank felt his own cheeks heat up.

"No, Ellie," Darby said recovering quickly. "Slade and his twin sister were born in Kentucky several years after I left the ranch."

Put in her place, Ellie frowned. "Well, I didn't know. He seems to be named for Hank."

Darby lifted her chin. "When Slade was born, I wanted a strong name for him. True, I picked the name Slade because of my memories of home."

Hank caught Darby's gaze and held it for a long moment. Her presence was overwhelming. His spine tingled. What did she want? Why had she come back? It took all the willpower he could muster to break their connection and turn his head away.

"How did you get here?" he asked, trying to sound normal as if it was an everyday occurrence that the love of his life would materialize from nowhere.

"We rented a car in Bozeman," Darby said. "A four-wheel-drive.

I must admit I'm surprised the weather is nicer since I was here last."

"Weather's broken," Leo muttered. "Spring's a-coming."

Ellie had finally taken stock of the situation and was getting into gear. "Would you like something to eat? I have some stew left from supper."

"No, thanks, ma'am," Slade said. "We ate before we left the airport."

"Well, here, then." Ellie stood up and motioned toward the sofa. "Have a seat, and I'll go rustle up some coffee and cookies."

"That would be lovely."

Darby and Slade sat together on the sofa in front of the fire. Hank's legs collapsed under him, and he sat down on the stone hearth.

Darby smiled at him, then broke eye contact and rubbed her hand down the leg of her pants.

More silence. More uneasiness. The fire crackled and popped behind Hank. In his own defense, he picked up his guitar. It protected him, sheltered his confused heart.

"Hank plays guitar and sings very well," Darby told her son.

"I'm back in the saddle again," Hank sang the words to the old Gene Autry song. "Out where a friend is a friend."

He glanced up to see her smiling at him again. With a rush of breath, he launched into the chorus.

WITH HER HEART hammering against her ribs, Darby sat back against the sofa cushions and forced herself to remain calm. She could see the tension in Hank's shoulders and in the rigid muscles of his neck. Her return had upset him. She couldn't tell about Leo, but she'd spotted a decided glare of annoyance in Ellie's eyes when she left to gather up the coffee.

Soon, Ellie backed into the dining hall from the kitchen

carrying a tray. Slade jumped to his feet and hurried to lift the tray from her hands. She motioned for him to put it on the coffee table. As Hank continued to sing, Ellie served Leo, leaving Darby and Slade to pour their own coffee.

Darby offered a steaming mug to Hank. "Black, like you like it."

He set down his guitar. "Thanks." His gaze swept over her as he accepted the mug.

"I've missed your cookies, Ellie," Darby said as much to cover her nerves as to compliment the younger woman.

"I make 'em like Leo likes 'em."

"I don't know what we'd do without you," Darby said, meaning every word.

The next few minutes were awkward for Darby. She was acutely aware of Hank, of his eyes that bore into hers—damning, pleading —filled with a myriad of emotions. The old urge to flee was over- whelming. But she bit her lip and hung in there, cowboying up, as Leo would say.

After more moments of difficult silence, Ellie stood up. "Time to get Leo to bed."

"Humph!"

Ellie moved toward the old cowboy. "Now, Leo."

Uncomfortable seeing their interaction, Darby also climbed to her feet. "I'll clean up for you, Ellie."

Ellie flashed her a look of dislike but didn't respond. Darby collected the dirty mugs and empty cookie plate and carried the tray back to the kitchen. When she returned, Leo had his coat on and was leaning against Ellie's arm. They were all standing.

"Where do you want us to stay, Dad?"

Leo shot her glare. "The boy can stay with me in your old room. Ellie's been staying in the third bedroom. She looks after me."

Darby's breath hitched. That was a gibe, for sure.

"You can stay in your cabin or bunk with Hank," Leo mumbled. "I don't really care."

So much for making amends with Leo, but in Darby's mind, her father had his own apologies to make.

Slade helped Leo and Ellie into the rented car and drove them the short distance to Leo's cabin where he assisted them into the house. Darby walked beside Hank down the icy gravel path to the cabin, where he stopped at the car and lifted the tailgate to collect her bags. Then they continued on in silence. There was no suggestion of her bunking with him.

Hank didn't say a word as he set down her bags in the cold cabin and fueled the woodstove. The room was slow to warm. Thankful for her coat, Darby hugged herself and focused on her boots. She sighed softly. To say she was uncomfortable was an understatement.

On his knees in front of the woodstove, Hank looked over his shoulder. His gaze darted up at her. Heat flooded Darby's cheeks. Why was this so hard?

Hank stood up, dusting off his hands. "Why did you come back?"

To find out the truth from Leo. To see you. To stop running.

But she couldn't admit to any of those things. Instead, she deflected, answering with only part of the truth. "I thought Slade needed a change. I also thought he should meet his grandfather before it was too late."

"Mighty strange reason coming from you."

She drew a deep breath, inhaling the clean, male scent of him. His remark should offend her, but he had the right to be bitter. Shame writhed like a snake in her belly. "That's a fair statement."

Seconds ticked by with agonizing slowness. Darby pressed her lips together. They stared at each other like strangers. Had they ever made love? Had they ever been in love? Or were they both simply unable to speak what was in their hearts?

"My art show was a wonderful success," she said, avoiding the dilemma at hand.

A rusty laugh escaped Hank's lips. "You must admit this is a great irony. Darby York returning to Montana without anyone dragging her back."

"It was my home," Darby said faintly.

"I thought your home was in Kentucky." Hank walked to the cabin door. "At least, that's what you told me three weeks ago."

As he left the cabin, Darby opened her mouth to answer him, but she couldn't form the words.

CHAPTER TWENTY

MORNING CAME, but no one knocked on Darby's door demanding she get up. When she finally left the little cabin, the sun was bright, thawing the wet ground, welcoming the day. The snow had retreated to the high country and left a sea of mud. It was still chilly, coat weather, but spring was on its way.

Darby paused on the threshold to the staff dining hall. All was quiet and dark inside. Was she that late? Going into the kitchen, she immediately spotted Ellie cleaning up from breakfast. It wouldn't be long before the summer crew arrived, and she'd have help. Would that be a good or bad thing for the woman? She liked being in control, didn't she?

Fighting the fluttering in her stomach, Darby advanced into the room. "I'm sorry to be late."

The look Ellie gave was decidedly hostile. "You'll have to manage on your own."

"I see you're busy." Darby went over to the coffeepot. "I'll just grab something to start the day."

The coffee was hot and bitter, a wakeup shock to Darby's system. She stood in the shadows, sipping from the mug she cupped in her hands and watching Ellie work.

"Have you seen my son?" she asked after a few moments.

"He's driving Leo around the valley in the old golf cart. Leo wanted to show him the ranch."

With a slight headshake of amazement, Darby turned away and set down her mug. "Thanks."

She left the kitchen, her footsteps echoing in the empty dining hall, and then paused on the porch to get her bearings.

The staff hadn't had the luxury of a golf cart when the snow was knee deep. Now her son was chauffeuring her father around the ranch in it. Leo had taken an interest in Slade, it seemed. Why so suddenly? Did he see something in her son that he'd missed seeing in Darby?

In the distance, she heard a nickering horse. A squealing whinny replied to it. Another mother and son combination enjoyed the beautiful morning in a paddock near the barn. Darby smiled to herself, remembering the birth of the colt. This was why she had loved the ranch as a kid and why she'd loved living with Col at his horse farm. April had arrived with all its newness and the potential of newborn foals.

Striding across the wooden bridge, she tossed her head back loving the day with its crisp air and sunshine. At the paddock, the curious colt stretched his nose through the slats of the fence, and she stroked it. He was already friendly, and his mother didn't seem to mind her presence.

Darby didn't know how long she'd stood at the fence watching the grazing mare and foal. She didn't want to move. Didn't want to go forward to confront what she needed to confront. So, of course, her troubles came toward her.

Slade puttered along the gravel road in the battered, old golf cart. He was alone. Stopping near the paddock, he climbed out and came up beside Darby, dangling his arms over the top of the fence to stroke the foal's tuft of mane.

Her mouth grew dry. How many times had she seen Slade just like this, hanging over a fence? As a kid, he'd climb the bottom rail so he could hang over the top. Now he was tall enough not to need the bottom railing. As a kid, he'd talk with Col about the newborns, their pedigree, and their potential. Why didn't he want to be part of his father's horse farm now? He seemed to love it as a child.

But today he seemed happy. The cold wind had reddened his cheeks and ruffled his hair.

"You need a cowboy hat," Darby said with a wavery smile. "Although a lot of cowboys wear ball caps these days. Less romantic, I guess, but you'd look good in a real hat."

He hesitated, not replying for a few strained seconds. Then he expelled a breath and glanced at her. "Mom, I'm staying here."

Darby's chest suddenly got tight. "What do you mean?"

Slade rested a forearm on the fence and turned to her. "Leo has asked me to stay for the summer. He says the ranch needs more hands. I can ride. He said Hank will teach me the rest."

Darby shifted her stance. He'd caught her off guard. She'd never expected his reaction to the ranch. And Leo. "But what about home?"

"What about it?"

Yes, what about it? Who was Darby to question running away from home?

"Uh, I guess I need more time to think about this."

"What's there to think about it?" Slade asked. "It's a summer job. It's something new. You know I don't have anything waiting for me at home since I turned down that other job offer."

Darby twirled around and wandered a short distance away. What he said made sense. But she couldn't give him her blessing. Not yet. Not before talking to Leo.

"This is a great opportunity for me, Mom, to learn something different. Another way of life. I want to buy the ranch a real four-wheeler, a UTV, to help with work and transportation between buildings. This old golf cart pretty much sucks. They need a new vehicle."

She returned to him with a half-hearted smile. "Slade, you've been making your own decisions for several years now. I'm not telling you no. I just need time myself to process it." She released a breath. "Where did you leave your grandfather?"

DARBY FOUND Leo in his cabin, sitting at his window, his shoulders slumped, staring out the dirty glass with a forlorn look on his face.

"I can't do much more than this," he told her when she came inside. "Doctors' orders."

Darby sat down across from him. "Well, we want you to get better."

"Damn doctors don't know what needs to be done on this ranch. The season don't wait for a sick man to get better."

Darby leaned forward, resting her elbows on her knees. "My son tells me he's staying here for the season."

Leo glanced at her, then let his eyes slide away. "His choice. I told the boy we needed help."

"I'm not objecting."

He snorted as if to indicate she didn't have a choice.

A sudden lethargy gripped her. She was tired of running, of feeling the guilt that had eaten her soul for so many years. Reaching over, she took one of Leo's hands, wrapping his gnarled fingers in her own.

"Why didn't you tell me about my mother? Why did Pete have to do it? Why did you and my mother keep her past a secret?"

For the first time in a long while, he met her gaze. "I know you're angry with me, but I was trying to protect you. You were a baby when it all started. Sarah and I got used to keeping the secret. Only Pete knew, of course. It might sound lame now, but it's the truth."

The journey had ended. "It's okay, Daddy," she said.

Tears formed in the corners of Leo's eyes. Darby reached over with a fingertip of her left hand and wiped them off his cheek. When she sat back and smiled, she realized his gnarled hand grasped her right one, holding it tight. Just as it had when she was a child.

CHAPTER TWENTY-ONE

DARBY FOUND Hank in the office fumbling with his books. She grinned shyly at him when she came in and sat down. They surveyed each other across the desk, each it appeared, afraid to speak.

She finally cleared her throat. "Seems as if you have another wrangler for the summer."

He averted his gaze to straighten the papers on his desk. "Yep."

"Can you make a cowboy out of him?"

Hank lifted his head, meeting her eyes. "You don't care?"

"He's twenty-three years old, Hank." She shrugged. "He pretty much has his own life to live."

"He said you'd be upset because he doesn't want to work with his sister."

Darby scooted back in the chair and pressed her lips together a moment. She cocked her head, letting her feelings settle. Not used to accepting herself, she needed to start accepting her children. "That may come eventually," she acknowledged. "Who knows where Slade will be next year. Where we all will be." Her voice trailed off, and she dropped her head to study her fingers.

"Where do you want to be, Darby?"

She looked up and saw him, really saw him, for the first time. Hank was no longer the lanky kid who'd stolen her heart in high school. He was a middle-aged man. They had much in common, didn't they? His day's growth of beard gave his face a rough appearance. The hair on his head was turning gray, as were the flecks in his beard. His big hands were work-toughened and calloused. But there was a glimmer of affection in his blue eyes. And fear and sadness. Did she see hope too?

Darby licked her lips as she studied the cowboy across from her. Where did she want to be? It was a good question. She didn't know. Kentucky didn't feel like home. The Ghost Mountain Ranch remained haunted by the past. But Hank was here. Was Hank her future?

She drew a breath before speaking. "What did you say to me that night at the hospital?" She paused. "You know, when I left."

Hank ran a hand through his thick head of hair and swallowed hard as if he suddenly grew nervous. "I don't know what you mean."

Grinning, Darby shook her head. "You know very well what you said, but it was so faint, I was afraid I'd heard you wrong."

He offered a bemused smile. "Oh."

Was he sweating? He'd never said he loved her. She'd just gone on the assumption years ago. But as the saying went, assuming something was never wise.

"I think you said the *L* word," she teased.

He blushed, turning as red as his red flannel shirt.

"If you meant it, you need to convince me. It's time to cowboy up, buster."

Hank's jaw clinched. He hesitated a moment, then placed his hands on the desktop and pushed to his feet. There was a new determination in his eyes.

"Darby York, you know damn well I love you."

She tucked her chin, playing coy. "I do?"

He came around the desk and pulled her into his arms, holding her in a great big grizzly bear hug. They stood that way, drawing warmth from each other, feeling each other's heartbeat, until Darby slipped her arms around his neck.

"I always thought you knew," Hank whispered, "but I could never say it."

"I did know, but it's always nice to hear it said."

"Biggest mistake I ever made. Not telling you."

Darby drew back a little to gaze into his eyes. "My biggest mistake was running from the ranch and you."

"No," he said firmly. "There are reasons for things. You've had a good life. You've got your two kids."

Yes, she had her kids, and she'd had a wonderful life. But her life wasn't over. A new chapter was just beginning.

"What if I stayed at the ranch, too," she ventured. "But I won't stay unless you agree to marry me."

His mouth dropped open.

"Because I love you, too, Hank Slade."

Then she stood on tiptoe and kissed his lips so completely that the past was forgotten. Only the present mattered. They would make a new future together.

"THINK ABOUT IT," Darby said over the landline phone to Kelsey. "You can come in June after the breeding shed is shut down. The summer season on the ranch is just getting started by then."

"It sounds tempting, Mom. I'd like to meet my grandfather and Hank since he's going to be my stepfather."

Darby turned around, letting out the length of phone cord, to grin at Hank behind his desk. "Hank wants to meet you, too."

"Tell her to stay for the summer."

"Hank wants you stay for the summer season, help us with the dudes."

"But I'm a dude, too."

"I know, baby, but you're a dude with a skill Hank needs right now." Darby winked at her new fiancé.

"What's that?"

"Hank knows nothing about computers, and he hates paper-work. His books are a mess, and you know I'm not good at math either. We'd like you to automate things. The office at the ranch is still run like it was fifty years ago."

Kelsey hesitated. Darby could almost hear her mind churning. Just for once, she wanted all her family together, in her Montana home, where it all started. When she married Hank, she wanted them all here.

"Say yes, Kelsey," she begged. "Take a leap of faith." Darby looked once more at the new old man in her life. She couldn't get enough of him. That's why she'd moved into his cabin, preferring to let him keep her warm at night rather than the woodstove. She smiled at him again, and he blew her a kiss in return.

"Take a leap of faith, Kelsey," Darby repeated. "I did."

The End

SLADE

CHAPTER ONE

Chicago
April 2019

SHE WAS DEAD.

Laurel Chastain looked up at the doctor standing across the hospital bed with his hand on her grandmother's wrist. He met her eye and nodded.

She placed a cold hand on her mother's shoulder. "Mama Bev is gone, Mom."

"No, Laurie," Debbie said quietly. "No."

"Yes." Laurie firmed her grip, fearing what was to come.

"No!" Always the drama queen, her mother's scream reverberated off the stark white walls and cut into Laurie's heart. *Not now, Mom. I don't need this now.*

"Come along," Laurie drew her mother to her feet from where she sat by Bev's bed. "Let the doctor do what needs to be done."

"Oh, Laurie!" Debbie sobbed against her shoulder. "What will we do now? What will we do?"

Good question. One Laurie didn't know how to answer. Her grandmother was the rock of their little family of three. After they'd moved in with her grandmother, into the two-bedroom, walkup apartment in Roger's Park, Laurie had gained a modicum of freedom she hadn't had since her parents' divorce. Because of Mama Bev, Laurie didn't have to be her mother's mother as she'd done since she was twelve.

"C'mon. Let me get you home. We can talk there about what's to be done."

What was to be done? They depended upon Bev's social security check to pay for the apartment. Debbie cleaned houses in Winnetka during the week, taking the train up and back. Those were steady jobs, but they were cash transactions. Her mother wasn't accumulating Social Security for later in life. And Laurie wasn't either. She didn't make much money writing, working freelance jobs, short-term assignments, and selling them to magazines or blogs. Not the career she'd dreamed of when she'd studied journalism in college.

A nurse handed Laurie a plastic bag containing Bev's clothing and personal items. Laurie had to detach herself from her mother to take it. She knew she'd have to come back and make arrangements for the body, but first her mother needed calming down. They'd been at the hospital since seven o'clock the night before when an ambulance had taken Bev to the hospital. Now it was five in the morning.

"Let's go, okay?" She didn't have time for her own grief. She'd deal with that numb spot in her heart later.

Her mother shuddered. "I can't go."

"You've got to. There's nothing you can do here."

"But she's my mother." Debbie hiccupped her opposition. Her eyes were a mess of tears and her nose red.

Not again. Laurie sucked in a breath trying to calm herself, then forced a slow breath out of her mouth. She needed to take care of her mother, because Mom had never, not once, taken care of anyone. Not her husband. Not Laurie. Not even herself. Why? It was a question that had haunted Laurie's childhood, causing friction between them.

Stepping back into that all too familiar role, she found a clean tissue wadded up in her pocket and thrust it at her mother. "Blow your nose."

Mom did as she was told, then handed the tissue to a nurse. Laurie could see a look of sympathy in the nurse's eyes when she took the tissue from her mom and disposed of it.

That was it. Laurie didn't need anyone's pity. "We're going now."

In her heart, Debbie was a passive person. Her rebellion over, she let Laurie lead her to Bev's Chevy which Laurie had parked near emergency services. The sunrise had just broken the gray Chicago horizon.

At home, Laurie was lucky to find a parking spot on the street. They climbed the steps to the third-floor apartment and went inside. It seemed like a longer distance, the staircase steeper. Already the living area seemed too quiet without Bev. Too empty. Laurie sat her mother down at the kitchen table and put on a pot of coffee.

"Mama Bev always said she saved enough money to bury her," Laurie said more to herself than to Debbie.

If not, they would be in deeper trouble.

The coffee was black and hot. Debbie poured cream into her cup and brought it to her lips, sipped it carefully and watched Laurie over the rim. Laurie sat in the second chair and left her own cup of coffee untouched. Her hands trembled. She clasped them together under the table. The plastic bag from the hospital was in her lap.

Laurie shut her eyes a moment, drawing up strength from within. Her grandmother had been a practical, no-nonsense person. What would she do in a time like this? Finally, she pulled open the bag. Inside was Bev's purse, the same tie-dyed, sling shoulder bag, ragged on the edges, that she's seen her grandmother carry forever.

Had this purse come from her hippie days? Once, when the two of them had had a heart-to-heart talk, Mama Bev had claimed to be a real revolutionary with long, straight, blond hair and free-flowing granny dresses. She'd shown Laurie the photos, yellowed pictures of Bev's friends from the past. She'd seen her mother in one of them, a child of five or six, totally out of place among the long-haired, young people smoking weed and doing whatever they did in their communal living arrangement.

Bev had told her living that kind of life had given her strength, the kind of strength she and Debbie had always counted on.

And now Bev was gone.

"What are you looking for?" Debbie asked.

Laurie glanced up at her mother's red-rimmed eyes. "Her checkbook."

"She keeps it in her bedroom."

Laurie nodded. Her mother had no clue why she wanted Bev's checkbook. But to make sure, she checked the zippered pocket in the purse. There was nothing in it except a faded newspaper clipping folded up into a neat, compact square.

Laurie smoothed it out flat on the table and leaned over the discolored ink print. "Look at this. It's about a bombing in February 1971 when a policeman was killed."

"That's why we left Los Angeles."

Laurie's head jerked up. She stared at her mother. "What do you mean?"

Debbie shrugged and added a packet of sugar to her coffee. Laurie saw her hands shake. "All I remember is we had to leave our house in a hurry. A bunch of us in several cars. I couldn't find my doll in time, and they left it there. I cried."

Laurie sat back. What the hell? Why hadn't she heard about this in all of her twenty-two years? Had her grandparents really been some sort of felons?

Debbie stirred her coffee Her eyes blurred as she drifted back to her childhood. "Mom's friend Tim dropped his girlfriend off in Montana. She couldn't go with us because she had a red-headed baby named Darby. I liked Darby, but Tim said babies were too much trouble. He also said I was too much trouble. I'm glad they didn't make me stay at that ranch. I didn't like the name of the place. It was scary."

"Why is that?"

"Wouldn't you be scared of a place called Ghost Mountain Ranch?"

CHAPTER TWO

Gallatin Canyon, Montana
April 2019

THE VIEW TOOK his breath away. So did the height.

Slade Heston laid a gloved hand on the shoulder of his ranch-raised and trained black horse. The gesture was more to calm his nerves than to settle those of the easy-going, rock-steady Tennessee Walker. In the distance, a snow-capped mountain range rose out of the blue-sky Montana day. In the valley far below, a roadway meandered alongside a ribbon of river. Perpendicular to the road, his grandfather's guest ranch stretched up a draw following Saga Creek as far as the eye could see.

"I'd forgotten how gorgeous Ghost Mountain Ranch is," his mother Darby said from beside him.

She was sandwiched between him and his stepfather-to-be, Hank Slade, and riding a golden-colored buckskin gelding with a black mane and tail. For a mother, she looked young and beautiful with her red hair tied back in a ponytail.

Although Slade had been named for the middle-aged wrangler his mother was engaged to marry, they were not related. Hank was simply part of his mother's life before and now after the death of Slade's father.

On this day saturated with sunshine, the three of them had ridden the trail to Sunset Point, a rock escarpment eight thousand feet above sea level. They'd followed the valley along a clear stream fed by fresh snowmelt and crossed an alpine meadow before taking the rocky path up to the summit. Along the way, he and Hank had dismounted and cleared fallen limbs and logs, prepping the trail for the tourist season to come.

Now they sat relaxing upon their horses, catching their breaths, and taking in the staggering scenery visible between the pines. Even without binoculars, Slade picked out the corrals and dining halls, the guest cabins, and the larger cabin he shared with his grandfather Leo York and Leo's caretaker.

"Which one is Ghost Mountain?" Slade asked, then wished he could bite back the words instead. His family had history with that mountain.

Out of the corner of his eye, he saw Hank reach over and place a gloved hand on top of his mother's hand where she rested it on the saddle horn. Hank's show of support and their love for each other was evident and sometimes a bit embarrassing. Slade had never seen a confirmed bachelor and a middle-aged widow acting like teenage love birds before. Certainly, his mom had never behaved this way with his father. That lack of overt affection between his parents was a curious situation that pricked Slade's heart with grief. And was perhaps the reason he never had connected long-term with any of his girlfriends and was still single.

"The peak, there, to the right of the ranch," Hank said pointing. "It's about a thousand feet lower than Sunset here. There's a walking trail behind the corrals if you want to explore. Always carry bear spray. You never know."

Slade nodded. His head hurt from all he had to learn.

"That mountain is where your grandmother died," Darby said a little too quietly.

"I know." Since coming to the ranch, Slade had finally realized how much his grandmother's suicide continued to affect his mother, and how it had shaped her life for thirty years.

He glanced over at Darby. A person couldn't ignore a family's past. His mother was an instance of trying to do that, having run from the heartache of her mother's death as a teenager. Married to his father, she'd lived in Kentucky, trying to bury her guilt and grief by raising her children and painting horses. A renowned equine artist, she'd never come back to Montana until last month.

"You sure she committed suicide?" he asked. "If she was on a trail at night, it could have been an accident."

Hank scowled at him, and Slade knew when to shut up. No more questions in the presence of Darby.

"Slade, Hank's got you looking like a true cowboy." His mom said, and he was grateful for her deft change of subject.

Yet, when she grinned at him, he had to blush a bit shamefaced. He *did* look the part—boots, Stetson hat, real leather chaps. Instead of the English saddle he was used to riding, he rode a Western one complete with saddlebags and a rolled-up rain slicker attached behind the cantle. He even carried a can of bear spray and a ranch-issued walkie-talkie. All he needed was a rope, a holster, and a six-shooter to complete the picture.

Slade licked his lips. Trouble was, he didn't feel authentic. He only hoped he could hold up his end of his summer commitment. In a short time, Leo and Hank had become important to him. He wanted to do right by them, not be the unsure college graduate he'd been back in Kentucky.

He shrugged to himself. Could he prove himself out West? In the old days, many men had done so.

But many men had also died trying.

~

"It's almost time for supper. Leo is a stickler for being prompt." Slade held the landline against his stomach so his sister could hear it growl. He leaned against a wall of the ranch office where the ancient landline phone hung. One battered desk, two chairs, and an even more battered file cabinet made up the space. "What do you want, Kelsey?"

"Just seeing how you're doing." His twin sister's voice sounded nonchalant. She was holding down the fort at the family horse farm in Kentucky.

Being the underachieving twin was difficult. When he was a kid, he couldn't even play Superman with Kelsey without messing up. One evening when they were nine, they'd been playing in the barn. Kelsey suggested they jump from the loft into a pile of cedar shavings. He wasn't sure about that. It seemed dangerous. But Kelsey had no fear. She jumped, landed on her butt, then stood up and taunted him. "C'mon, you chicken!" Slade couldn't let a girl, especially Kelsey, beat him. So, he'd gathered his courage and jumped. And broke his foot.

Now he set his jaw, fighting the knot in his belly. She wanted something from him.

"I'm okay," he said. "Tired as hell. And I can't get used to this weather. Yesterday, it was only twenty-nine degrees. Today it's a heat wave of fifty-nine. And it's April, for god's sakes."

Pointless bullshit, but he'd been taught politeness—even toward his sister.

Then the other shoe dropped. "I ran into Katherine yesterday."

Slade let out a huff of disgust. "Is that why you called? I don't have time for her drama." But as usual, his sister had her own agenda and would speak her mind before she'd let him go.

"She told me you gave her no warning about the breakup. She didn't know you were unhappy. You broke her heart, Slade."

"And her pocketbook. Katherine's a gold digger, and you know that."

"That may be true, but…"

"No buts about it, and why are you calling me about old news? It's really none of your business."

He heard her sigh. Kelsey Heston had mothered him from the playpen. She'd always bested him too. In school, she was a straight A student and class president. She graduated from the University of Louisville in three years with a degree in equine business, knowing she'd run their father's horse farm. And she was a head-turner, with her long blond hair and long legs. She was a hard act to follow even by seven minutes.

"My point is…"

Yes, what is your point?

"You're too closed-up, Slade. No one knows what you're thinking. You can't expect to succeed in any relationship, if you don't open up to people."

"Is that it?"

"Yes, that's it." A pause. "But I need your help."

Slade tapped an impatient boot on the hardwood. "I figured there was something."

"Mom told me the ranch is only three-fourths full for the summer. That's crazy. There's no way for Leo to make money, if guests don't show up."

"Leo's old," Slade defended him. Kelsey had never been to the ranch. She'd never met their grandfather. "Only one wrangler worked for him until he hired Hank. And that was only in January."

"I know." She drew a breath. "But we need to do something. We're family. I've talked Mom into hiring that reporter, you know, the one who came to the farm and wrote the article about Mom when she had her art show?"

"What the hell for?" Kelsey made no sense. How would a reporter help? He could only guess at her reasoning. But as usual, she orchestrated things and now from a thousand miles away.

"Well, if she works at the ranch during the season, she can write articles about it, how wonderful it is, you know, and people will want to come next summer. Besides, the pieces will improve the ranch's search engine optimization on the internet."

Another dumb idea, but Kelsey's dumb ideas often had a way of working out.

"What do you want me to do?"

"Nothing yet. She hasn't accepted my offer, but if she does come, be nice to her when she gets there."

As if he wouldn't be nice? *Geez*.

"And keep your eyes open for other ways to publicize the ranch," Kelsey said.

Hell, he was too busy fixing fences, clearing trails, and learning to tie a cinch knot. He had no time for Kelsey's little schemes.

"Sure," he said to get her off the phone. "Gotta go. Dinner's waiting."

CHAPTER THREE

HER MOTHER SLEPT. *Finally.*

Laurie carried her coffee into her grandmother's bedroom and pushed back the sadness lodged in her throat. She sat down on the unmade bed, took a sip, then put the mug on the bedside table. It had been a long night and day. She was worn out, but too anxious to sleep. The caffeine certainly wouldn't help with her exhaustion but might keep her awake a while longer until she found her grandmother's checkbook.

The ringtone on her cellphone trilled. Recognizing the number, she answered it. "Yes?"

"Laurel Chastain?"

"This is she."

"This is Kelsey Heston. Do you remember me? You interviewed my mother Darby Heston in March for the article you wrote for Southern Magazine about her first art show."

Darby. "I remember you, and I remember your mother." How could she forget that gorgeous Kentucky horse farm that looked like it should be in a movie with its big, stone house and matching barns, lush grass, and white fenced paddocks? Until now, she'd not associated the passionate artist she'd interviewed with the name her mother had mentioned earlier in the morning. Was this some sort of serendipity?

"I'd like to hire you for at least three months," Kelsey said.

"What do you want me to do?" Surprised, Laurie's voice rose in pitch.

"I want you to work at a guest ranch in Montana. My grandfather owns the Ghost Mountain Ranch."

The coincidence chilled her to the bone. "What did you say?"

"I want you to do what you do so well and write articles about your experiences at the ranch. It needs some positive PR."

Laurie couldn't think straight. "I don't understand. And what do you mean by *work*?"

"The ranch foreman tells me they need a housekeeper to daily clean the guest cabins."

Great. A maid. Like her mother.

Kelsey stopped to draw a breath. Did she sense Laurie's reluctance? "We thought if you actually worked at the ranch as a crew member, you'd have a better feel for it. And there'd be plenty of time off duty to enjoy the area. Yellowstone is nearby. There's horseback riding and fly fishing."

"Things I don't do."

"Well, yes. I understand." A pause. "My point is, I'll pay you well, plus you'll have your crew pay. All I need are positive pieces about your experiences during the summer. We want to promote the ranch. Get word out that it's a great place to visit."

The offer of double pay sounded tempting. "I'm dealing with a lot here," Laurie said, buying herself time to think. "My grandmother died this morning.

"Oh, I'm sorry."

"Can I get back to you?" Kelsey asked.

"Yes." Another pause. "Can you let me know by the end of the week? I'll need to make other arrangements if you can't."

"Sure. I'll call you soon. 'Bye."

Laurie picked up her coffee mug and cupped it in her hands,

then shut her eyes against the afternoon light streaming in the bedroom window. Two salaries would go a long way to ease their financial troubles for a while. Besides, she could sell the articles and make more money that way. But her mother was fragile and dependent. Could she leave Debbie so soon after Mama Bev's death?

Laurie didn't know what to do. She couldn't concentrate. Couldn't make a decision. Today had been too much heartache. Opening her eyes that felt gritty from lack of sleep, she shoved aside her uncertainty. Other things needed doing at the moment.

Like paying for Bev's funeral.

The top drawer of her grandmother's bedside table was jampacked with scraps of paper—old receipts, copies of credit card statements, a laminated bookmark with the Serenity Prayer on it.

God grant us the serenity to accept the things we cannot change.

Like a three-thousand-dollar funeral home estimate for a simple cremation service.

Where was that darn checkbook?

Laurie rolled her shoulders to ease the tension in her neck. Bitterness caused her to purse her lips. Some people had it so easy. Like Darby Heston living on her rich husband's horse farm and painting pictures simply because she wanted to, not because she needed to make a living.

Laurie found the bottom drawer of the table crammed with worn, spiral-bound notebooks—the kind kids used at school for note taking. She pulled them out and scattered them on the bed, opening the cover of each one to find out what was inside. Her grandmother's cramped handwriting filled each page front and back. They had to be Mama Bev's diaries because they contained little bits of everyday information.

The year 1971 was the oldest one.

~

Tim took Chelsea to his brother Pete at a ranch in Montana. Tim was pissed with her about her baby. Thankfully, Glen stood up to Tim about Debbie, or we might have been purged because monogamy is not condoned in the collective.

Glen killed himself. He should have waited for Tim. He's the bomb-maker. Not Glen. I wonder if he was stoned. He must have used too much dynamite. I was so ticked off when I found out. What am I to do now? I have a child to feed. Tim said I should go with them to Chicago and hope my parents take me in. We've been underground a long time. My parents don't even know about Debbie.

Her grandfather was Glen Haven. Laurie had heard his name. No wonder she'd never met him. He'd blown himself up, probably for some godforsaken cause long before she was born.

Curiosity got the best of her, and she leafed through the other diaries finding tidbits of family history. Bev did come back to Chicago. She'd reconciled with her parents and then earned a nursing degree. She never remarried. But nothing Laurie discovered in the diaries was as interesting as the reference to a ranch in Montana and the description of the death of Bev's husband. Why had her grandmother never mentioned him, except for saying his first name occasionally? They had never put flowers on his grave on Memorial Day like they did for Bev's parents.

Laurie shuddered. Maybe he didn't have a grave. If he blew himself up, maybe there was nothing left to bury.

She sat back and chewed her lip. What had the lack of a father done to her mother? Was that the source of her dependence? Her melodrama? Had her own father gotten tired of all that poor-me complaint? Is that why he finally left them?

Her heart hammered and her vision suddenly blurred. Her parents' divorce had been a pivotal part of her childhood, affecting her life in ways she could not even imagine.

But the family tragedy had started long ago. *Glen killed himself. He should have waited for Tim.*

The names *Chelsea*, *Tim*, *Darby*, *Pete*, and *Ghost Mountain Ranch* were too much of a coincidence for them not to mean something.

Was there a story here?

Her own story?

Maybe she'd take up Kelsey Heston's offer and spend the summer in Montana cleaning people's dirty linen and toilets.

Laurie brushed a strand of blond hair away from her eyes, then noticed something she'd overlooked. Right there, almost in the open, as if it was meant to be discovered, she found Bev's checkbook on the top of the bedside table under a box of tissue. The balance was a hefty ten thousand dollars. She could pay for Mama Bev's funeral, and Debbie would have enough to live on for a while.

Maybe it was a sign. Maybe Laurie *was* supposed to investigate the Ghost Mountain Ranch and the story she found there.

CHAPTER FOUR

SLADE SLAMMED down the telephone receiver. He was late for dinner again. Leo would be angry.

Snatching his Carhartt coat from the rack, Slade pulled it over his down vest. As he hurried out the office door, he settled his big felt Stetson on his head. Wearing the cowboy hat took some getting used to, but as his mom said, it made him look the part.

Would his life have been different if he'd known his grandfather in the old man's prime? Spent summers at the ranch and not grown up the pampered son of a wealthy, Kentucky bourbon heir?

Slade strode from the office toward the duo dining halls. Even though it was cold, spring surrounded him—the gentle smell of wet ground, the roar of the rushing snowmelt in the nearby creek, the greening grass between thick sagebrush. He hoped hungry bears waking from hibernation would stick to the high mountain meadows and streams. He'd hate to surprise one.

The log cabin staff dining room and the one for guests were connected by a kitchen. Heavenly smells filled the air as he approached. He dropped a hand over his belly to quiet its rumbling, then sprinted up the steps to the crew hall.

After pushing open the heavy door, he paused on the threshold to adjust his eyes to the bright light. A fire crackled in the stone fireplace. It was April but the warmth felt good. A worn leather sofa, and a couple of upholstered chairs faced the hearth. This room was a getaway for staff as well as a place to dine.

His mom and Hank sat on one side of a long wooden dining table, and staff members Ellie and Pete on the other. The rest of the summer crew had not yet arrived. When that happened, Slade expected there'd not be room for them even though the table was large. Maybe they'd eat in shifts.

"Glad you could join us," his grandfather called from where he sat at the head of the table.

Flushing, Slade removed his coat and laid it on the couch, then tossed the Stetson toward the rack of antlers on the wall like Hank did. But the brim nicked the point of an antler, and his hat toppled to the floor. Heat rushed up Slade's neck. *So much for trying to be cool.*

He snatched up his hat and placed it on top of his coat as if he'd meant to do that all along. Leo scowled at him, and Slade hurried to his seat at his grandfather's right hand.

"Sorry," he said. "I was talking to Kelsey."

Leo grunted. "We didn't wait for you."

"No, sir."

"Don't expect Ellie to serve you, young man. You get your own food."

"Yes, sir."

Slade stood and scooted back his chair. It toppled backwards onto the floor. *This can't be happening!* As he picked up the chair, he heard the wrangler sitting across the table snicker.

"You'll learn, boy." Pete Harden was an honest-to-god Western character with his bowlegged gait and Santa Claus beard. He'd been living the cowboy life for most of his sixty years.

Slade grabbed his plate and hurried to the sideboard to fill it.

"This looks good, Ellie," he said over his shoulder in an effort to ease the embarrassment heating his face.

"Thank you, honey," Ellie answered. "I hope you like it."

Ellie Montgomery was a woman about his mother's age, nearing fifty, but not as slender or pretty as his mom. Her hair was blond but steaked with gray, kind of dirty blond. She was the ranch's only cook until the dinner chef arrived for the season. After Leo's injury and subsequent surgery for a subdural hematoma last month, Ellie had lived in his grandfather's cabin as his caretaker. Of course, his grandfather thought he didn't need a *damn nurse*.

Back at the table, Slade sat down and shoveled beef stew into his mouth. "I didn't realize how hungry I was," he said between mouthfuls.

Pete winked at him and gave Slade a gap-toothed grin. "Doing real work, are you now, boy?"

"Yes, sir."

Pete was right. He wasn't used to all the work of a ranch hand. In fact, he was sore as hell from the unfamiliar physical activity.

Slade buttered a slice of bread and took a bite. It hadn't taken him long to learn relationships were complicated around here. According to his mom, Pete was his uncle, his real uncle, being her biological father's half-brother. Darby had never known her actual father, a man she'd just discovered was named Tim Krebs.

This meant Leo wasn't her real father or his real grandfather. Because Pete was related, Darby's mother Sarah had come to the ranch looking for help. Leo had fallen in love with Sarah and adopted Darby when they married. His mother had been only fourteen months old.

That was the sketchy family history. All Slade understood was Leo York had raised his mom, not the slime ball who'd gotten his grandmother pregnant and dumped her. Rearing a child was hard work, so Slade considered Leo his grandfather, not some irresponsible creep from the past.

After the sharpness of his hunger was satisfied, Slade lifted his head and glanced at his mother. "What's this scheme of Kelsey's?"

"*Which* scheme are you talking about?" Darby asked with a grin. They both knew Kelsey had many of them.

"The one about inviting a reporter to work here during the season."

"A reporter?" Now Leo was interested.

"The one who interviewed me earlier this year, Dad," Darby said. "Kelsey thinks it would be good to have some positive publicity for the ranch. If the woman works here, she'd give her readers a good idea of what we have to offer. That could improve our visits for next year."

Leo snorted and shot Darby a disgusted look. "All reporters are direct descendants of the devil himself."

Darby pooh-pooh his remark by raising her eyebrows. "Now, Dad."

But Slade agreed with his grandfather. He had no love for reporters, not since he'd been hounded by them when his father died a year ago. They stuck their noses into places where they weren't wanted and publicized personal information.

His breath hitched. He now grasped his objection to Kelsey's plan. "Reporters are looking to cash in on someone else's problems," he said.

"The woman wrote a nice article about me."

"Really, Mom?" Slade couldn't believe her. "That article described your paintings and your talent, sure, but it also implied you paint because you have nothing better to do. There was a decided bias against you because you have money."

Darby shook her head, her eyes filled with doubt, and sat back in her chair. "I didn't get that from the article."

Slade shrugged and looked down at his almost empty plate. "You read into it what you wanted to see."

"Maybe you did too, Slade," Hank pointed out.

Slade hesitated. It would do him no good to challenge his mom, not with Hank, her white knight, sitting by her side. He exhaled and nodded. "Yes, maybe you're right."

∾

DARBY PULLED the thistledown comforter up to her chin and snuggled lower among the pillows on the hand-hewn log bed. She wore her flannel nightgown which made her feel cozy and warm and the quartz pendant on its black satin cord that had been her mother's. The woodburning stove in the corner blasted out heat.

She fought her drowsiness. This was the best time of day, waiting for Hank to come in from his nightly rounds. The light by the bedside cast a circular glow on the hardwood floor, and the cabin they shared was quiet.

Would Hank be tired too and crawl into bed wanting sleep? Or would he talk with her while getting undressed? Or want something more?

The corner of her mouth curved upward with her silent questions. She loved Hank. Finding him again after thirty years had been a surprise. She'd never thought she'd find love after her husband's death. For her new love to be a return to her first boyfriend; well, that was something equally surprising.

What she felt for Hank was different from what she'd felt for Col. Not more, really. Simply different. Colton Heston had been older, a true bachelor, who had wanted to marry and have his own family. He'd had an agenda. She'd been a groom for one of his breeding stallions, a job not many women were trusted to handle back then. They'd met at the stable, one of his three stone barns on the Heston country estate. They'd courted there, although Darby had been too immature and naïve to realize that's what Col was doing with his attention. She'd simply been flattered.

After her mother's death, guilt and sorrow had eaten away at her heart until Col showed her how to open up again. How to love.

He had been kind, a true gentleman, a savior. She'd given him his family—twins, a boy and a girl. He'd given her security and respect. Theirs had been a good life.

But somehow, although she never realized it, she'd never gotten over Hank and the young love they'd once shared. They had been torn apart by the circumstances of her mother's death. Somewhere a hard rock of grief had remained in her heart, and because of it, she'd never reconciled herself to her mother's suicide.

Why would Sarah kill herself? For a long time, she'd thought it something she had done.

The front door squeaked when it opened. Darby pushed herself up higher against the pillows. Anticipation tingled in her chest.

As foreman, Hank had a three-room cabin near the barns—a small living room, bathroom, and the bedroom in the back where Darby waited.

Hank tiptoed into the room with his boots in hand. "You awake?"

Her pulse spiked. "You know I am."

"Good." He dropped his boots and started stripping off his jeans and flannel shirt.

"I'm sitting here thinking and worrying about Slade." She watched as he left the room to go into the bathroom. The toilet flushed, and the water in the sink ran.

Hank came out of the bathroom toothbrush stuck in his mouth. "Don't worry about him." As he brushed, he favored her with a gentle regard.

"He's never known what he wants to do." Darby clutched the covers. She loved the tender look in Hank's eyes and the powerful tone of his voice. "He's not good in school, not like Kelsey."

Hank grunted, left the room, and came back naked, wiping his hands on a towel. "Stop worrying. He'll get it together. Slade is right where he needs to be at the moment."

She shrugged, her gaze following Hank as he dropped the towel on a chair and crossed the floor to the bed. He didn't look bad for a man approaching fifty. In fact, he looked pretty damn good.

"I guess I shouldn't compare him to his sister," she said.

"You got that, sweetheart."

Hank lifted the corner of the blanket and slipped under it. Soon Darby had her answer about what he wanted to do tonight, and it had nothing to do with talking. Or going to sleep.

A smile tugged at her lips. What had she done to deserve a second chance at love?

CHAPTER FIVE

A week later

ARRIVING at Bozeman Yellowstone International Airport on the United flight from Chicago-O'Hare, Laurie disembarked and made her way to the baggage claim area. Her rolling bag finally arrived, and she yanked it off the moving belt. When she turned around, a pair of dark gray eyes peered at her, eyes belonging to a tall, broad-shouldered and entirely too-sexy man holding a black felt cowboy hat. Her heart took a curious nosedive.

She squared her shoulders. She hadn't come one thousand miles to ogle a cowboy, no matter how appealing he looked. His black hair curled in waves and touched the collar of his red flannel shirt, which was unbuttoned at the neck revealing dark chest hair. She swallowed once, noting the man's features were classically chiseled with high cheekbones and a square jaw.

"Are you Laurel Chastain?" he asked.

She drew in a deep breath. The man's deep voice irritated her. She shifted her stance and reclaimed some control by extending her hand. "You know *my* name, sir. I feel you have me at a disadvantage."

He took her hand. His palm was callused, but his fingernails were clean and short. He held her hand a little longer than was necessary for a handshake, and a disturbing heat surged through her body.

"Slade Heston."

"Mr. Heston." She removed her hand from his grasp.

"Call me Slade."

"Slade." She fought a surge of anger that had cramped her stomach.

"I'm here to meet you."

That was obvious.

"Can I carry something?"

"No thanks." She had her carry-on bag and the rolling luggage. She was capable of handling it all.

"Suit yourself. The truck is this way." He turned on his heel and led the way to short-term parking.

So, this was Colton Heston's son? For her article earlier in the year, she'd done a little research—the internet was a wealth of information. The elder Heston, now deceased, was heir to a Kentucky bourbon dynasty and owner of a Thoroughbred horse farm. The woman who had hired her, Kelsey Heston, was Slade's twin sister, and Darby, the woman she'd already met and interviewed, was his mother.

Laurie shrugged her bag higher over her shoulder and kept pace with her guide's long strides, dodging tourists and a group of campers loaded down with gear. She had time to glimpse snow-capped mountain ranges outside the large glass windows of the airport terminal.

Was she really in Montana? It seemed surreal.

"I hear the weather was good yesterday for the Derby, unlike the roller-coaster weather here in Montana." Slade said when they reached his pickup truck with a faded *Ghost Mountain Ranch* printed on the front door panels. He loaded her rolling luggage onto the second-row seats. "Today is actually nice though."

"Derby?"

"Kentucky Derby."

"Oh." She climbed into the passenger side. "I've never thought much about horse racing, but I guess it's in your blood."

He scowled and started the truck. "Being a reporter, you probably know all about my family."

What was that prickly tone? Laurie buckled her seatbelt and turned slightly to study his eyes. "I researched your mother for an article in March."

"I read it."

A few heartbeats of silence passed. She surmised his reaction from the set of his jaw. "You didn't like it?"

"It was good enough."

"Just *good enough*?" Irritated, she raised her voice. He was talking about one of her babies. She put herself into everything she wrote.

"The article wasn't fair to my mother." His tone was stony. He kept his eyes on the road.

"How's that?"

"You'd know if you really knew my mother," Slade said. "You made assumptions about her that weren't true. You don't know her history."

Laurie sat back and glanced out the side window taking in the raw new sights of white-capped mountains—a far cry from urban Chicago that was raw in other, less beautiful ways. Getting to know Darby's history was the reason she'd come to this godforsaken land and taken the demeaning job. She wanted to know if the people at Ghost Mountain Ranch had played a part in her grandmother's life, thus influencing her mother's life for the worse and then her own.

She wanted the story.

Why had her grandfather Glen Haven been building a bomb? Was he really a radical?

Doing online research before she left home, Laurie had found a recent DVD documentary about the militant underground movement in the 1960s and 1970s as well as plenty of information about it on other websites. One source said there were nineteen hundred bombings in the United States in those years. It was commonplace. But mostly, these explosions weren't lethal, simply misguided statements of idealistic young Americans who opposed the war in Vietnam. They had wanted to create a better world for themselves and the less fortunate. Only a few extremists on the fringe actually wanted to kill people.

But actions have consequences. Her grandfather wasn't the only one in the underground resistance movement to blow himself up building a bomb. One famous case was in New York City where three people were killed in a single townhouse blast. Yet, none of Laurie's investigation had turned up any reference to her grandfather, or without having a last name, the leader who was called Tim.

Her only clue was at the Ghost Mountain Ranch.

Her nostrils flared as she turned back to gaze at Slade's profile silhouetted against the sunlit driver's side window. What a gorgeous man. It wasn't right for a guy to be so handsome, and for her to be so easily smitten by those good looks. It scared her.

"Well, maybe you can help me understand your mom," she said.

But he didn't respond. So, she looked away out the side window as they entered a mountain canyon.

WHEN HE'D RETURNED from Bozeman with Laurie, Hank had put Slade to work in the tack shed. There, over forty Western saddles rested on wooden racks nailed to both sides of the wall. They were caked with dust and dirt from last season. It was now Slade's sole responsibility to clean and condition each one with liquid saddle soap before the new season started in June.

He rubbed the soapy sheepskin pad into the cracks and crevices of a leather saddle. At least the task kept him out of the reporter's way. No woman had the right to be so drop-dead beautiful. Like his sister, she was a leggy blonde. But Kelsey's eyes were brown like his while Laurie's blue eyes gleamed brightly taking in every one of his flaws and failings.

How could that kind of penetrating stare stir up a guy's lust?

A ranch two-way radio nearby crackled. "Pete to Slade."

The dinner bell had clanged long ago. Slade wiped his sticky fingers on a towel and grabbed the walkie-talkie. "Go ahead."

"You better get your sorry ass to dinner before your grandfather bursts a blood vessel."

"Okay. Out."

Late again. Slade snatched up his hat, and coat and took off to the dining hall. Arriving late was nothing unusual for him. Maybe once more crew members got to the ranch, his grandfather wouldn't care so much. But Slade got the feeling that Leo minded simply because he *was* his grandson.

The dining room was toasty warm and smelled good enough to rumble his stomach. Ellie must have outdone herself. He hung his coat and hat on the coat rack. No tossing the hat toward the antlers tonight. Not with the reporter in attendance and everyone watching his late arrival.

He crossed the floor toward the table and stopped dead. She sat in his place, at the righthand side of his grandfather. *What the hell?* Looks as if Leo had gotten over his hatred for all reporters. Was the old man already a fan of their newest crew member?

Hank motioned toward the chair next to Pete on the other side of the table. Slade clinched his jaw, getting the message. Before sitting down, he picked up a plate from the sideboard and filled it. All the time, he was aware of Laurie's gaze, and when he turned back to the table, she didn't lower her eyes but kept them focused on him. He could feel the mesmerizing spell of their sudden attraction.

He sat down, lowered his head and ate, acutely aware of what she was doing across from him. She sipped from her glass of water. Took a bite of food, all the while gazing at him with a look of interest. Finally, she turned to his grandfather.

"How did the Ghost Mountain Ranch get its name?" She gave Leo a smile that was designed to charm the socks off any man.

Slade glanced at Darby. His mother's mouth drew tight, but she said nothing, continuing to eat as if the question didn't bother her. Those at the table who knew about the tragedy thirty years ago grew quiet. How would Leo answer this one?

"Mighty simple." Leo had the decency to blush. "We're tucked along the Saga Creek right under Ghost Mountain."

"Ghost Mountain is a fascinating name. I'm guessing there's a reason it's called that."

Not cool. Didn't she notice Darby turning pale?

"The old-timers say it's because of an Indian legend. A tribe of the Shoshone called the Sheepeaters lived in the high mountains around here. They say an Indian maid threw herself from the lookout over Saga Creek because her lover did not return from a hunt. Some say they've seen her ghost walking the trail to the overlook."

Darby's chair scraped against the wooden floor as she pushed it back and stood. "Excuse me. I'm not feeling well."

She fled the dining room. Hank excused himself too and was not far behind.

Laurie looked confused. "I'm sorry. Did I say something wrong?"

Leo sniffed and shook his head. "No. My daughter is too damn sensitive. She needs to toughen up."

"Oh."

Slade watched Laurie raise the glass to her lips. Their eyes met. Hell, why was he insanely attracted to her? The intensity of it made his stomach cramp. He set down his fork. Sweat beaded on his forehead.

Ellie's abrupt bark of laughter surprised him, and he turned to look at her.

"You see, honey," Ellie leaned against the edge of the table toward Laurie and said in a confiding voice, "Leo's wife, Darby's mom, committed suicide years ago at that same lookout point. She threw herself off the cliff. It's not something we talk much about because it upsets Darby. Leo, well, he's gotten over it after all these years."

Laurie regarded everyone at the table, then met Slade's gaze without wavering. "I understand. I won't mention it again."

After dishes were done and Ellie had taken Leo back to his cabin, Slade found Laurie standing on the dining room porch. She leaned against one of the wood posts looking toward Ghost Mountain in the distance. He came up beside her and inhaled her wonderful female-and-vanilla scent.

"It is so beautiful and quiet," she said, her voice wrapped in awe. "So peaceful."

"I know."

"It smells so fresh and clean."

"I was blown away when I first saw the mountains and this ranch." Slade caught a quick breath. "Almost like I'd come home."

She glanced up at him as if considering his words. Then she looked away. "The ranch is in its own little world, secluded, cut off from the twenty-first century and all reality."

"Hell, cell phones don't even work here," Slade said with a laugh.

She turned toward him again, examining his face. When she licked her lips, Slade crossed his arms over his chest and took a step back, putting space between them.

"I want to climb that mountain." She paused, turning from him to search the peak across the valley, now shadowed by the coming darkness. "I want to see that lookout."

"You told us you wouldn't mention the mountain," he called her out. "Why do you want to see it?"

"Because there's a story." She sounded so confident.

Suspicion jangled in his gut. He frowned and dropped his arms to his side. "You mean about my grandmother?"

"Maybe." She paused. "But also about that Indian maid whose love drove her to her death. I've never seen a love like that. Never believed in it." Another hesitation and a small sigh. "Will you take me?"

Air whooshed out of his body in surprise. In the growing twilight, Slade felt an uneasiness creep up his neck.

There were many reasons not to humor this woman. Who was she? Where did she come from? She had no business snooping into his family's history, *but* the legend of Ghost Mountain might make an interesting article. Kelsey had asked him to help her promote the ranch *and* be nice.

Oddly enough, Slade found he wanted to do just that—be nice.

CHAPTER SIX

Next morning

SLADE GLANCED up as Pete carried another saddle into the tack shed. He wiped his brow with the back of his hand. "Good god, Pete, not another one?" He'd only made it through ten saddles. His task seemed endless.

Pete moseyed over to him. "Hell, no, Son. This is Jeremiah's saddle."

"Jeremiah?"

"Yep, new wrangler. Came early to help us doctor the herd before round-up."

"Okay." Slade knew he didn't have enough experience for that kind of work. His title was *ranch hand*, which meant he did anything Hank told him to do. Like cleaning these saddles. He cast a grim look at the wall. The task seemed enormous.

Pete caught his gaze and guffawed. "Better you than me. You're younger. Don't like all that standing."

"If you do it right, it takes time," Slade said.

"Yep. And Hank's a perfectionist, so you'd better not miss a speck of dirt."

That was reassuring.

"Head on up to the dining room," Pete said, leaving the shed. "Jeremiah is there grabbing lunch. You can meet him."

"Will do."

Lunchtime. Would Laurie be there too? He couldn't avoid her at every mealtime as he'd done at breakfast. Nope. He'd better get used to seeing her around.

Should he seriously consider her request? Last night, he'd been all into the idea of taking Laurie up Ghost Mountain. Heck, he'd never been there himself. Yet, a sleepless night had tamped down his enthusiasm. She was aware of his background, probably better than most, being a reporter. She knew he had inherited money. His job as a ranch hand was simply for the summer, and she knew that too.

Hell, if he wanted to make something of himself, he needed to get his act together and go back to Kentucky with a plan for his future.

What he didn't need was another gold digger, like his ex-girl-friend Katherine.

CLOUDS HAD HOVERED LOW over the ranch all morning. Laurie spent the time going through each one of the thirteen guest cabins with Darby. She'd taken notes. There was a heck of a lot of work to be done before the first guests arrived in June.

As she hiked along the gravel road back to the dining hall, the soft smell of wet earth filled her nose. What had she gotten herself into? Two months of dusting handmade log furniture, scrubbing porcelain sinks and clawfoot tubs, and changing sheets hung over her like those earlier clouds.

"This trip had better be worth it," she muttered.

There'd better be a story here someplace, more than the puff pieces she'd been hired to write. Was it an ancient legend or the people who lived there? Did they hide secrets?

The clouds had cleared out and the sun was well up, striking green pastures and the rough-railed fences, shimmering off the rocky outcrops and pine vistas of Ghost Mountain. Laurie lifted her head and studied the looming mountain. Was there any truth about its haunting?

At least one woman had died on its cliffs. Darby's mother. But that woman's ghost plagued more than those rocks or this small piece of civilization beneath it. She'd recognized Darby's haunted look in Kentucky and had found it hard not to write about it in her March article.

And also, there was Darby's son. She'd felt the sparks kindle between them. And it wasn't just sexual attraction. She couldn't put her finger on the thing she felt. She hadn't experienced that instant connection to anyone ever before and it felt a little disconcerting.

Laurie's life had taught her not to trust men. She avoided relationships. Better to do things herself. Be independent. She didn't need a man, and she didn't need to feel attracted to one.

But heck, there it was. That stupid attraction igniting between them.

Laurie shook her head to clear her thoughts. She was in Montana for a selfish reason. She wanted to understand Mama Bev's secret life, so she could understand herself. That's all there was too it. Nothing more.

At the dining hall, she opened the door and crossed over the threshold. She'd taken two steps inside the room when she was surprised by a sudden bark.

"What the heck?"

A black and white dog came out of nowhere, charging her and rising on his hind legs to plant his front paws on her chest. The blow of his attack forced her backwards. She fell on her butt, then his furry body pushed her flat onto her back. She stared up at the creature's happy brown eyes and lapping tongue that slathered her face with excited licks.

"Finn!"

The dog slunk away to his master's side, and a rough hand reached down and hauled Laurie to her feet.

"Sorry about that." A tall man looked her up and down in a way that made blood rush through her veins, but not in a good way. He had a ruddy face, a rakish handlebar mustache, and hair as black as Slade's. "Finn gets carried away sometimes," he said.

"No problem," she answered in a short breath and then wiped the slobber off her face.

"Hell! You're muddy. Sorry about that too."

With that blunt exclamation, the newcomer brushed the front of her down jacket with the palm of a gloved hand, then he pulled her toward him so he could reach her back where he swiped at the mud on her jeans with strong, quick strokes.

"What the hell?"

Laurie glanced sideways to find Slade at the door. He held his cowboy hat loosely in his hands and wore a look that advertised his anger.

RAGE RIPPED THROUGH SLADE. What the hell was Laurie doing in the arms of a man? And why was his hand on her butt?

"What's going on?" His father had taught him not to manhandle a woman. And so, had his mother. Women were to be respected. That this guy's hands roamed freely over Laurie made his blood boil.

The cowboy gave Laurie's backside a swat, then turned toward Slade. "Just repairing the damage Finn managed to inflict on this lovely lady."

Laurie shook herself like a dog as if to rid herself of the man's touch, then stood straight lifting her chin. "The lady's name is

Laurie, and I'd thank you to keep your hands and your dog to yourself."

"My pardon, ma'am." The man tipped his hat. "Finn, you see, is a lover most of the time. He just gets carried away when he sees a pretty lady."

Slade shifted his gaze toward the noise of a thumping tail and a faint whine. Finn, a dog, was black and white like a Border Collie, but had the look of a medium-sized Spitz. The dog appeared friendly enough, but he wore a spiked collar that looked as dangerous as hell.

Slade cleared his throat. "Perhaps introductions are in order." He held out his hand, although he really wanted to slug the guy. "My name is Slade Heston. My grandfather owns this ranch."

"Jeremiah." Jeremiah, no last name, returned a hearty handshake. "Wrangler for the season. And you've already met, Finn, my Karelian bear dog."

He'd likely won his huge silver belt buckle riding broncs. With his Western shirt and gleaming, leather boots, he seemed bigger than life, so he didn't need a last name, did he?

"I'm Laurie Chastain." Laurie's tone was smooth with a touch of amusement in it. "May I pet your dog? Is he safe?"

"Go ahead." Jeremiah scratched the dog's ears. "All Karelian bear dogs are uglier than a cuss, but he's a lover—like his owner." He glanced at Laurie in that I'll-love-you-good way.

Slade rolled his eyes. Was this guy for real?

Laurie dropped to her knees and stuck out her hand. Finn came over to her, and she stroked the top of his head. "His fur is so soft, but his undercoat seems coarse. Why the collar?"

Jeremiah stood beside them with his thumbs in his belt, a real cowboy stance. "Finn's been known to stand up to a bear or two in his day." Jeremiah reached out his hand toward Laurie again. "If he ever gets tangled up with one, a grizzly won't be biting him 'round his neck."

Laurie took his hand, and Jeremiah pulled her to her feet.

Slade's breath came faster, and he felt a decided burning sensation in his stomach. "I don't know about you all, but I have work to do." He headed toward the dining table. "Looks as if Ellie's got lunch ready."

Lunch was informal without the attendance of his grandfather and Darby. Hank and Pete moseyed in.

Hank ladled potato soup into a bowl and sat down beside Slade. "I see you met Jeremiah."

"Oh, yes." He stared across the table where the new man sat next to Laurie, who was sitting once again in his spot. "We've met."

Jeremiah returned his pointed gaze with a look that surely called him *greenhorn*. Slade bristled but kept his mouth shut. He did that most of the time when his sister Kelsey called him out too. He had to be really angry before he'd act.

Hank put away soup and sandwich as if starving, then rested his elbows on the table and glanced around. "Darby and Ellie have taken Leo to a doctor's appointment in Bozeman. 'Fraid we're on our own for supper tonight. Ellie said there's fixings in the kitchen. Jeremiah, Pete, and I are going to Bozeman as well. We've got to pick up supplies."

"Sounds good," Slade said.

He soon found himself in the kitchen, holding a dishtowel and standing beside Laurie. They'd been assigned kitchen duty. He didn't miss the little bit of domesticity. Neither did he escape the feel of his heart pounding against his ribs.

She looked at him, then returned to the soapy sink full of dishes. "Well, have you decided?"

"Decided what?"

"To take me up Ghost Mountain."

"There's no *taking* to it," he replied. "I've never hiked the trail. It will be like the blind leading the blind."

"I love your clichés."

"No joke. I don't know my way."

"Maybe Jeremiah will take me."

Slade set his mouth in a grim line. "I've got thirty more saddles to clean."

She shrugged. "Then I'll have to wait until Jeremiah is free."

He silently cursed Jeremiah but also felt an inexplicable need to please Laurie. *When the cat's away, the mice will play.* Another cliché, but the platitude seemed to fit the situation.

"Okay." He released a long breath. "Meet me by the barn at one o'clock dressed for a hike."

She turned to him, grinning. "You're the best, Slade. Simply the best."

CHAPTER SEVEN

SLADE DIDN'T FEEL like the best. In fact, he felt inadequate, especially now that the ranch had an authentic bronc buster. But he couldn't let Laurie go up the mountain alone, and he'd be damned if he let Jeremiah take her.

Always carry bear spray. You never know.

The Ghost Mountain overlook trailhead was behind the barns. The trail was narrow and rocky. He couldn't see horses using it. Slade led the way. He headed straight upward. Soon thick sagebrush from the valley floor gave way to aspen and scrub pine. Pushing himself hard, he had plenty to prove, to himself and to Laurie.

She followed behind him, breathing heavily as the trail ascended. He glanced over his shoulder as they struggled up the incline. Her cheeks were flushed, but her eyes glittered with excitement. She'd changed into cropped pants and a long-sleeve shirt rolled up to her elbows and pulled her blond hair back from her face into a ponytail like his mom often did. On her back, she'd slung a small daypack.

"Do you always get what you want?" Slade turned back around

to keep a cautious eye on the path. The wind blew, smelling wonderfully of pine needles and moss.

"Not so much," she said. "Why?"

"You seem like a very persuasive person."

"I'm like my grandmother. She always maneuvered to get her way."

"*Maneuvered* is an interesting choice of words. *Manipulated* sounds more appropriate."

A snort of laughter surprised him. "You're very perceptive, Mr. Heston. Do you feel as if I manipulated you?"

"Let's just say, I felt well-maneuvered."

She laughed again. "Point taken."

Slade fell quiet to concentrate on a fallen log. He scrambled across, then turned back to offer Laurie his hand. She didn't take it but clambered over herself as if making a statement of independence.

He had a knack for picking women who were all wrong for him. His past girlfriends had been needy creatures, more interested in his money and good looks. Laurie was different. A surge of ill-advised lust erupted, and he cautioned himself to watch his step with her as well as watching the trail.

Taking the lead, Laurie hiked ahead of him. The view of her curvy backside did nothing for his sudden self-awareness and resolve. He blew out a breath, making his cheeks puff out. This might be a long afternoon.

Within fifteen minutes, however, they reached the trail's end, an exposed stony summit cordoned off by a short jack pole fence, the kind of western fence used on rocky terrain where post holes couldn't be set.

"It's breathtaking," Laurie exclaimed going right up to the fence.

They were surrounded by fantastic views of the valley and mountain ranges in every direction. But Slade didn't care for it, getting an eerie feeling. Was it only his fear of heights? Or something more? His grandmother had died at this lookout.

Laurie glanced back at him. "This area is beautiful and certainly doesn't look creepy."

"What did you expect to see? An actual ghost or two?"

She shrugged and sat down, perching on the edge of a nearby boulder. She drew a bottle of water out of the daypack and offered it to him. "I don't know what I expected. I thought there'd be an actual ledge or something where a person would stand to jump. Like a diving board, I guess."

Slade took the bottle from her. Laurie had a second one. He watched as she unscrewed the top and brought it to her lips. Trying to suppress a sudden rush of arousal, he took a drink himself. He didn't need this unexpected complication.

Glancing once more down the rocky cliff, Slade turned away from it and rested against a boulder farther from the drop off, so he didn't need to look down. He understood now why his grandmother had died. No one could survive a fall from this height, especially with all those sharp rocks below.

"My mother doesn't talk about her mother's death," he said, "but Hank said Sarah, her mother, came up here at night. They found her body the next morning."

Laurie capped her bottle and returned it to her daypack. "Your grandmother was named *Sarah*?"

"Yes." Slade handed Laurie his empty bottle. "What I know about her I've learned recently, and most of it from Hank."

"Did she come up here alone?"

"That's what Hank said, but I wouldn't want to hike this trail at night…and alone."

"Yes, it seems odd." She paused as if reflecting. "Have your mother and Hank been a couple a long time?"

"In a way." Slade had to smile. "They knew each other in high school. Then, when Sarah died, Mom ran away from home. That's when she met my dad."

"So now your mom and Hank have renewed their love. It's very sweet, don't you think?"

"I suppose."

"You must not be romantic." She turned to look at him. "You don't sound happy about their relationship. Have you ever been in love?"

"No." He couldn't count his short time with Katherine as true love. "Have you?"

Turning around, Laurie cast her gaze skyward. The wind whipped around them, suddenly chilly. "No. I'm not sure I believe in falling in love."

Interesting. "No boy friends?"

"Not at all." She turned back to him with a quiet regard that delighted his insides like the wind tickled his face. "And I suppose you're footloose and fancy free."

"At the moment."

He usually didn't talk like this with a woman. But there was something about Laurie that made him open up more than usual. Maybe it was the fact she'd admitted she was good at manipulating. But he didn't feel controlled. He simply felt comfortable.

She smiled at him, seeming to stroke him with her gaze. Then she shifted her body back toward the overlook and searched the horizon once more. "I was wondering why your grandmother killed herself."

"No one knows. Hank said Mom blamed herself for years. In fact, she only made peace with it when she came back in March to take care of Leo. But you can see, it still upsets her."

"Fascinating. I'm intrigued by true life stories."

"You know Leo adopted my mom, don't you?"

"I'm not sure I did. So, he's not really your grandfather?"

"No. But he raised my mom, so that's good enough for me."

She grew quiet a moment, as if enjoying the scenery. He dared hope she enjoyed his company as well.

"Was your grandmother always called Sarah?"

"I guess." Why was she so interested in his grandmother? And her name? *Oh, the story.* She was a reporter sniffing out a story.

"Pete told my mom and Hank everything they know about my grandmother's past."

"How would Pete know about that?" she asked.

He glanced around once more Laurie, meeting her eyes. "He and my real grandfather were half-brothers."

"They were? That's intriguing. Did your mother know that?"

"I'm not sure. You should ask Pete.

Laurie thoughtfully rubbed her chin. "I may just do that."

Slade's stomach took this unfortunate moment to growl. He put his hand on his abdomen, feeling the heat of embarrassment flush his cheeks. "I guess it's time to eat. Want to head back?"

"Sure." Laurie climbed to her feet, shouldered her bag, and headed down the trail ahead of him.

Slade cast another quick glance at the overlook. A cold chill swept through him, and it wasn't the breeze. Now that he'd seen this place, he could better appreciate his mother's angst over her mother's death. Then he hurried after Laurie.

They hadn't gone far when he heard rustling in the underbrush. He looked to his left beside the trail and his steps faltered. A brown bear puffed and grunted and stared at him with beady black eyes. Laurie stopped, and he bumped into her, catching her right arm in a fierce grip.

"Oh, dear God!" Her voice was low and crackled with fear.

Frozen with dread, he swallowed the urge to flee. He didn't see any cubs. Maybe this wasn't a sow. So maybe that was a good thing. But if this guy had a fresh kill nearby, Slade knew their lives were in serious danger.

A span of several heartbeats passed with the bear standing his ground, not moving an inch. Neither did they. Heart thudding in a dreadful beat, he tried to recall Hank's words. *Don't run. Always carry bear spray.*

That's it! He fumbled for the can of bear deterrent hooked to his belt. It was the size of a giant canister of aerosol hair spray.

"Get behind me, Laurie," he ordered, but she didn't move.

He jerked her behind him, and at the same time flicked off the plastic safety. His hand shook as he extended his arm with his thumb on the trigger. Fearing to lose his grip, he grabbed the bottle with two hands. At that moment, the mass of angry brown fur charged.

Slade's heart slammed into his throat. He deployed the bear spray, tilting the can downward toward the animal, not straight at it, and whipping the can back and forth. The cloud rose in time to hit the rushing creature in the eyes and nose with an acrid fog of mist. In a split second, the bear veered left away from them and vanished into the underbrush.

"Let's get the hell out of here!"

Trembling, Slade grabbed Laurie's hand and started down the trail at a fast walk—a very fast walk.

LAURIE STUMBLED down the trail holding tightly to Slade's left hand. In the right, he clutched the can of bear spray as if it was a weapon. Visions of long teeth and claws flashed across Laurie's mind. They didn't talk. She couldn't. Her heart was still in her throat, so to speak. It thumped wildly, and she gulped in mountain air with each step.

When they reached the valley floor and saw the back of the barns, she uttered a sigh of relief. The creature hadn't followed them. She'd made sure with quick glances over her shoulder. Now the safety of the wooden structures loomed ahead of them, and they hurried toward them.

Dear God, what had she gotten herself into? Again, she second-guessed her trip to Montana. Chicago was wild, but she was used to an urban wild, not the real thing.

Slade dropped her hand as they approached the barn. "Are you okay?"

"I have a few scratches on my leg." She'd fallen once, tripping over an exposed root. "But I'll survive, thanks to you."

He shook his head. "It worked." He held up the can. Slade seemed dazed, but he had taken control of the situation, saving both their lives.

"I guess the locals know what they're talking about," she said.

"I'm glad I listened to Hank."

The ranch truck parked near the paddock indicated the men had returned from Bozeman. As they entered the cool darkness of the first barn, Finn trotted toward them. No longer afraid of him, Laurie stooped to scratch behind his ear, gathering comfort from the friendly dog. She stood to let out another breath of relief as Hank passed heading out of the barn.

"Where have you two been?" Hank hefted a bag of feed from the truck bed and came back inside. He headed into the feed room. They trailed behind him.

"We hiked Ghost Mountain," Slade said.

Hank turned to look at them, and for the first time noticed the can of bear spray Slade continued to carry in his hand.

"Slade saved my life." Laurie's heart shuddered when she thought how brave Slade had been. "He's my hero."

"What the hell?"

"A bear charged us." Slade's hand trembled. He placed the bear spray on a shelf. "It was brown."

Jeremiah joined them. He must have overheard the conversation. "Could have been a grizzly, but you can't always tell by the color. Did it have a shoulder hump?"

"How should I know what kind of bear it was?" Slade glanced at him. "I just know it was brown. We didn't see any cubs, or anything. Thank God for the bear spray."

She rubbed the back of her neck. "We didn't bother it, but it attacked anyway."

"Could have been a bluff charge," Hank said, "but you did good using the bear spray."

Jeremiah twirled his mustache. "Probably a juvenile sowing its oats. Hank, you thinking what I'm thinking?" he asked in a deep, slow drawl.

Hank nodded as if affirming the two were on the same wavelength. "Whatever kind of bear it is, we don't want it near the ranch."

"I'll take care of it."

Jeremiah left them to collect a saddle from the tack room and other gear, even some sort of rifle. Laurie had been told he'd brought his own horse to the ranch. She didn't understand much about horses. This one appeared short and stocky and was brown with a black mane and tail. Once saddled, the horse looked like other cowboy horses she'd seen in movies and on TV. The way Jeremiah mounted up Laurie knew he'd been riding all his life.

Whistling to Finn, the new man turned the horse in a circle until he faced Hank. "No worries, Boss. Finn will find him. We'll drive that visitor high into the mountains."

Wheeling the horse again, Jeremiah gunned it out of the paddock. Finn caught the excitement of the chase and took off barking. Laurie didn't think a horse could make it up that rough, narrow trail, but the wrangler must have had no doubts about his mount. Her last view of Jeremiah was as the horse picked its way, now at a safer walk, from the trailhead up the mountain path.

"I don't envy that bear," Hank muttered with a laugh. "With those guys on its scent, that critter doesn't stand a chance."

CHAPTER EIGHT

SHE NEEDED to collect her thoughts and a bit of privacy. Laurie left the barn to return to her cabin behind the dining hall. It was only one bedroom with a desk and chair, but luckily it had its own bathroom. She was glad she didn't have to bunk with other staff, but she was expected to eat with them and help serve guests, if needed.

Drawing hot water, she stripped off her clothes and sank into the old-fashioned, claw-foot tub to soak away her jitters.

"What a day" she said aloud. Mama Bev would not believe it. Her curiosity about Ghost Mountain had almost cost her life.

But Slade had saved her with his funky can of bear spray. How in the heck did it stop a raging bear in its tracks? More research needed.

She sank lower, resting her neck against the edge of the tub and letting her relief sink in. This would be her first article. She'd write about the importance of being prepared in the wild. Maybe she'd add Slade's heroics. That should please his sister.

Warmth spread through her that had nothing to do with the steaming bathwater. What was it about Slade? For a rich kid, he was surprisingly humble. He was easy to talk to, as if they possessed a strange bond. She didn't get it—this feeling that seemed to envelop her whole being.

She rubbed her eyebrow, the water dripping down her face. *No.* Her heart feeling full had nothing to do with Slade. She was simply glad to be alive.

~

SLADE HAD TOLD her Darby had insisted on installing Wi-Fi in the staff and the guest dining rooms. Modern guests would demand better communication, she'd told her father. Hank didn't care. Leo grumbled a bit but gave in. Laurie certainly appreciated the modern convenience. So, after cleaning up, she carried her laptop to the dining room and set it down on the big table.

Opening it, she logged in. Then she Googled bear spray, Karelian bear dogs, and for good measure, she threw in the name *Jeremiah*. Not having a last name hampered that search, of course, but she found enough information on the other subjects to get a start writing her article.

After a while, she shut the laptop, and since they were told to fend for themselves tonight, went into the kitchen to round up some dinner. Ellie was there when she entered. The caretaker had her head in the industrial refrigerator, butt protruding toward the door. She backed out of it and turned around, noticing Laurie, then carried packages of luncheon meat and cheese to the counter.

Laurie offered a smile. "Hi, there."

Ellie raised an eyebrow and gave her a glassy stare. She was a coarse-looking woman dressed in jeans and a red flannel shirt. Her hands spoke of a rough life. A woman could deny her age, but her hands and neck usually gave it away.

"You're making your own supper tonight," Ellie said in a snippy, dismissive voice.

"I know." Laurie's smile slipped away. "I'm here to see what there is to eat."

"You'll have to wait until I make Leo's sandwich. He's tired."

"That's fine." Laurie turned around so Ellie couldn't see her roll her eyes. The woman didn't need to explain herself. She wasn't in a hurry.

As Laurie made a pot of coffee, the back of her neck prickled oddly. Was Ellie staring at her? Whatever for?

"I'm finished here. Make sure you clean up."

Laurie's gut tightened. Ellie had left the open packages and other sandwich fixings on the counter. "I'd planned to."

"We're taking Leo back to Bozeman tomorrow for more tests." Ellie picked up Leo's tray. "Now that you're here," she said in a loud, demanding voice. "I want our cabin cleaned top to bottom while we're gone."

"But Darby told me to wash bed linens tomorrow. She wants them freshened for the season."

"Darby's not the boss."

"But…" Her complaint faded as Ellie came up to her, eyes narrowed, smirking. She was a short woman but weighed more than Laurie. For some reason, she didn't want to meet her in a back alley.

"Darby doesn't own this ranch." Ellie thrust out her chest. "Before she came crawling back, Leo changed his will. When he's gone, me and Pete and Hank are gonna own this ranch. So, technically, you'll do what I say first."

Laurie was so surprised she couldn't think of a comeback. If it had been Jeremiah or any other man, she'd know how to handle him, but this aggressive little woman was another thing.

Swallowing hard, she nodded. Was she telling the truth about the will?

Then Ellie threw her a look of dismissal and strutted out the back door, failing to see Laurie raise her hand to her forehead in a mock salute. "Yes, ma'am!"

$\sim$

"THERE YOU ARE." Slade suppressed the fluttery feeling in his stomach.

Laurie sat at the dining table with a laptop open in front of her. Blond hair fell into her eyes. She brushed away the strand and glanced up. "Hey."

She followed his progress across the room with her gaze.

"Have you recovered from our adventure?" Her smile lit up his heart. Standing across the table, Slade rested a hand on the back of a chair for support.

"I took a long, soaking bath," she said. "That did the trick."

Visions of Laurie naked in a bubble bath ramped up his desire. He felt his face flush. *Heck.* He didn't need images of a naked Laurie to add to his daydreams.

She leaned back in the chair. "Have you eaten?"

"Yeah. Earlier."

"I made coffee," she said. "It's in the kitchen."

He was glad for a reason to escape. He'd never been so intensely aware of a woman in his whole life. Maybe because he'd grown up with a twin sister, he'd not given girls much thought, but then realized exactly how much trouble they could be after he reached puberty and wanted his first kiss.

What was it about Laurie? He simply wanted to be near her and enjoy her company. Kissing her was another matter altogether.

Coming back with the coffee pot, he freshened her cup. She thanked him, and he sat down across from her. She was in his spot near the head of the table next to Leo's chair.

"Whatcha doing?"

"Research."

"May I ask what?" Slade took a sip of coffee.

"Grizzly bears," she said with a laugh. "And bear spray."

"A little after the fact."

"Ya' think?"

Again, their eyes met. A smile tugged at his lips. He couldn't deny his attraction went beyond the physical. Laurie was one smart lady. "I don't think telling readers about a grizzly bear near the ranch is a very good thing."

"But the bravery of the owner's grandson might make for a good read."

Slade felt himself flush and shook his head. "There wasn't much bravery there. More like desperation and terror."

"It's all in the way I spin it," she said with a wink.

His heart twisted. A reporter was accustomed to spinning stories to suit the purpose of a story. Slade sat back in his chair and thumbed the handle of his coffee mug. He shouldn't disregard Laurie's occupation or forget the reason for her being at the ranch. More importantly, he shouldn't overlook her criticism of his mother in that article from March. Being attracted to Laurie was pointless, as were all the other times he'd been drawn to a good-looking woman.

When he didn't reply, Laurie took a sip of coffee and studied him across the rim of her mug. Slade shifted in his seat. The way she looked at him set off firecrackers in his stomach, no matter his best intentions.

"What do you know about Ellie Montgomery?"

That was a surprising question. "Not much. Mom and Hank seem to depend on her to care for Leo since his operation."

Laurie placed her mug on the tabletop and stroked her cheek as if thinking. "She's mighty bossy."

"I think she's used to having her own way."

"She told me she will own the ranch when Leo dies along with Pete and Hank." Laurie paused as if to assess how he took her statement.

Slade drew a surprised breath and met her gaze. "I've never heard that." He paused and rubbed his chin. "If it's true, it must be because my mom abandoned Leo."

"I can understand that," she said and touched a fingertip to the rim of the mug. "However, as much as my mom screwed with my life, I never totally deserted her."

JAN SCARBROUGH

That was the first time he'd heard Laurie refer to her family. But he wasn't going to fault Darby. She was his mother, after all. "Guilt can be a heavy taskmaster."

"Tell me about it." Laurie bit her lip. "I feel guilty leaving my mom so soon after my grandmother's death."

"Why did you?"

Her eyes narrowed, and she lifted her chin. "Money, why else?"

He didn't know how to respond to that statement, and he realized she knew it.

"Seems foreign for a guy who's had everything he wanted all his life, doesn't it?" Her voice was suddenly hard. "You've never wanted for anything."

"Hey, don't drag me into this." Slade clenched his jaw, feeling his body temperature rise. "I've done nothing to hurt you."

"No, of course not. Your kind never harms a soul." Laurie stood and lowered the screen of her laptop. "You simply don't see the rest of us."

He resented the hell out of that remark. Why did she have such a big chip on her shoulder? "My kind? Who do you think I am?"

"A rich man's son." She picked up her computer and marched into the kitchen. He heard the backdoor slam.

Slade ran a hand through his hair. "What the hell?"

How had their conversation turned sour so suddenly? He didn't need the hassle, that's for sure.

He shook his head. "Women."

CHAPTER NINE

THE NEXT MORNING, Laurie opened the unlocked door and went inside Leo's log cabin. It was an old man's home with the scent of sweet pipe tobacco filling the empty rooms and an atmosphere of dust and disuse inside. She had a common room, a bathroom, and three tiny bedrooms to clean. Reluctance tightened the corners of her mouth. Seeing where Slade slept was just a little too personal.

Slade hadn't come to breakfast, almost as if he avoided her. She didn't blame him. He'd saved her from a bear, and she'd repaid him with snark and anger. Slade couldn't help who his parents were any more than she could.

"What have I done?" she muttered. "He didn't deserve my bad mood."

Pressing her lips together, Laurie sighed, then started with the room she hated the most—the bathroom. It was just too gross to scrub another person's toilet. How had her mother cleaned homes for years?

She made quick work of it and moved into Slade's bedroom next. Sparsely furnished with a dresser, single bed, and straight-back chair, it held a bit of his masculine energy and his musky scent. She folded dirty jeans and hung up wrinkled flannel shirts in the tiny closet where he stored his leather suitcases on the floor. These were intimate tasks for a mother or a wife. Her face grew hot with the heat of her sudden thought and the nagging shame of her last words to him.

She cleaned Leo's room next, filling a plastic bag with used and discarded medications that stuffed his waste basket. There was a photo on his dresser. Laurie's hand trembled when she picked up the frame to dust. A blond woman smiled back at her. She had her arm around the shoulder of a teenage cowgirl with long red hair.

Darby and her mother?

Laurie went very still, her throat thickening with surprise. She studied the picture, taking in the similarities between the woman and the girl. They shared Slade's nose, his cheekbones...and his smile.

Why had Darby's mother killed herself? It didn't make sense. Sarah York had so much to live for—husband, home, daughter, and unconditional love. Leo clearly doted on her. Even today years after her death.

The third bedroom was where bossy Ellie stayed. That room was just as stark as the other two except a multi-colored quilt on the bed gave it a spot of color. A lamp and an upholstered chair with a basket of knitting beside it filled one corner, probably where Ellie relaxed after a long day of minding everyone else's business.

Get a grip. Laurie set her jaw. She'd taken this job. She must either put up with its dangers and demands or quit and go home. The visions of a summer spent babysitting her own mother caused her breath to hitch. *No thank you.* She'd stick it out at the ranch.

Laurie dusted and swept the room. She plumped up a throw pillow on the chair. When she did, she inadvertently kicked the basket and it toppled over. She squatted to shove the yarn and needles back into it.

What the heck? Inside the basket was an old, yellowed photo—the kind people picked up from a drugstore after it was developed before the advent of cell phones and digital photography. Laurie's mouth fell open, and she raised the palm of her hand to cover it.

The picture showed a blond woman sitting on the lap of a long-haired hippie. She was hugging his neck. Was this a younger version of Sarah York, Leo's wife? Nearby a red-haired toddler sat on a blanket. Could the baby pictured be Darby?

Laurie sank to the floor, turned over the photo, and read the names on the back: *Chelsea Clemons. Tim Krebs.*

Tim and Chelsea. Names from her grandmother's diary. She'd come looking for this information and here it was, right in her grasp. But what was Ellie doing with the picture?

"What are you doing in here? Sitting on the floor like that?"

She looked up. Slade stood over her, frowning. She hadn't heard him come in. Her pulse pounded a fast, steady rhythm. Thank god, it hadn't been Ellie.

"Help me up!" Holding up her hand, he grasped it and pulled her to her feet. "I'm actually cleaning the cabin. Ellie's orders. What are you doing here?"

"It's chilly, and I came for my vest."

Their gazes met. Standing stood toe-to-toe, electricity popped between them. "I'm sorry about last night," she blurted out.

"I'm sorry," he said at the same time, then laughed. "We're a fine pair, aren't we?"

"Yes, aren't we?" She joined his laughter. Deep in his eyes, she saw a fire smoldering, and, flattered, she felt her face flush. "Look, what I said was more about me, than you. I haven't had the easiest life, and with my grandmother's death, it's not going to get any easier."

Laurie looked down. He still held her hand. He followed her gaze, giving her hand a squeeze. It was warm. And big. A man's hand.

"Saying *I'm sorry* sounds lame." Slade released her hand and lowered his head. "I wish I could help you somehow."

She sucked in a breath. "You can, actually." She held out the picture in her other hand. "I found it in Ellie's knitting basket. Do you know these people?"

"I've never seen this picture." His brow puckered. "I wonder if that child could be my mother." Then he flipped the photo over and read the back. "Well, damn. Tim Krebs. That's supposed to be the name of my grandfather, my mother's father."

She studied him for a moment. "How do you know?"

Slade turned the picture back over to examine the images. "Mom learned it when she came to the ranch earlier this year. I believe Pete told her. That's when she found out he was her uncle because Tim Krebs is Pete's half-brother."

"What happened to Tim? And who is Chelsea Clemons?"

"Hell, if I know."

She grinned up at him. "Seems like we have a real mystery on our hands."

"There's one way to solve it. Ask Pete," he said. "Let's show him the picture."

"What will Ellie would do when she discovers her picture missing?"

He shook his head. "Who cares?"

"You're right After the way Ellie has treated me, I don't care either."

Slade turned to leave the room.

"Forget something?" He turned back, his gaze questioning as it reconnected with hers. Laurie pointed at his chest. "Your vest."

"Oh, yeah." Clearing his throat, he went into his room and came out wearing a down vest.

As she waited, she smiled to herself at his sheepish behavior. Typical guy not to notice how she'd straightened his room, but maybe he was used to having a maid around given where he came from. No. She wouldn't go there again. Her resentment was her problem. Not his.

Ushering her out of the cabin, Slade lay a hand against her back.

He let it linger there long enough for her to think she felt its warmth through her own winter jacket.

"Thanks for cleaning my room," he said in an emotion-rich voice. "I've been told I'm a slob."

She tilted her head to look up at him. "By your girlfriend?"

"I don't have one, remember?" His eyes lit up, and he chuckled. "By my domineering twin sister."

THEY FOUND Pete repairing the corral fence.

"What's up? You got them saddles finished?" Pete asked and grinned at Laurie, winking at her.

Slade let out a deep breath. "I'm working on them."

The pole fence Pete was fixing was nothing like the pristine white fences at his father's Kentucky horse farm. Next week eighty horses would be milling around in the enclosure during the day. Slade had been told they all went back out to pasture at night, but during the day, the animals were corralled near the barns where they were then used for trail rides.

"Better keep at it. Don't want Hank or Leo to find them not done." Pete chuckled at his own advice.

Laurie glanced fleetingly at Slade, then she stepped closer to the wrangler, holding out the photograph. "Pete, do you know these people?"

Pete stood and put down his nail gun so he could take the picture from Laurie. He rubbed his chin as he studied the photo, front and back, taking his time.

"Never seen this before," he drawled.

"Do you know them?" Slade knew his tone was sharp, but he wished Pete would hurry with his answer.

Laurie's arched an eyebrow at him, urging him to be patient. She turned to Pete. "We thought the child might be Slade's mother."

"It is."

Slade straightened his shoulders, standing taller as he felt a rush of adrenaline. He exchanged glances again with Laurie. "Is Tim Krebs my grandfather?"

"Yup." Pete surveyed him with a no-nonsense look then handed the photo back to Laurie.

"Who is Chelsea Clemons?" Laurie asked.

"That's Darby's mother."

Slade caught the light of excitement in Laurie's eyes. She wet her lips. "But we thought her name was Sarah."

"I don't know why you're asking about this old stuff," he grumbled and picked up his nail gun, letting them know he had to get back to work.

"C'mon, Pete." Slade took a deep breath and held it a second. "Spill it."

He glared at both of them. "She called herself Chelsea Clemons when she was in The People."

"What the hell is The People?" Slade glanced at Laurie. She rubbed her arms as if she was cold.

"Back in the sixties, we was in an underground movement. You know, *Power to the People.* We protested the Vietnam War. When they started blowing up things, I left. Didn't want nothing to do with that crap."

"Is that how you got to the ranch?" Laurie's voice was tense.

"Yup." He turned toward them, putting a hand on his hip. "I told all this to Hank and Darby weeks ago. Might as well let the secret out to you kids too."

"Secret?" Slade shifted his stance, watching the old cowboy. "What secret?"

"This ain't nothing Leo wanted known. He was trying to protect his wife. Folks around here wouldn't take kindly to the truth."

Laurie trembled. "What's the truth, Pete?"

"One bomb killed a policeman," he said. "When Sarah came to the ranch, she'd become a burden to Tim because of Darby. Besides, like Tim, she was running from the law. The ranch was a safe place to hide."

"Wow!" Slade's head jerked back. He felt his heart race. No wonder his mom never talked about her family. "So, Mom didn't know this until recently?"

"No, and Sarah and Leo wouldn't tell her when she was young. If Leo had said something after Sarah's death, maybe things would have been different."

Maybe his mother wouldn't have felt guilty about her mother committing suicide, and then she wouldn't have run away. But that was a lot of *what ifs*. Slade crossed his arms while he watched Leo. "I was told you and Tim were brothers."

"Yup. Half-brothers. Same mom. Different dads. Not much love lost between us. He wasn't a good man. Spent time in jail."

"Where is he now?" Laurie asked.

"Dead. Overdose, they say. That's all I know."

This was too much to digest. He could see Laurie was having trouble with it, visibly shaken.

"Thanks, Pete." He touched Laurie's arm. "We'd better get back to work."

"Yup. Leo don't like no slackers."

Slade walked with Laurie toward the dining hall. At the little wooden bridge over Saga Creek, they stopped and leaned against the railing. Below them, the clear water meandered gently over stones.

"That was interesting." Out of the corner of his eye, he noticed her face was grim. He wanted to help, but she was silent. "You seem troubled."

"I am." She turned toward him and handed him the photo. "You see, I think my grandmother was in that same group."

CHAPTER TEN

TIM TOOK Chelsea to his brother Pete at a ranch in Montana. Tim was pissed with her about her baby. Thankfully, Glen stood up to Tim about Debbie, or we might have been purged because monogamy is not condoned in the collective.

RAKING her hair back from her face, Laurie loaded the industrial size washing machine with sheets. This was her third load. Beside the washer, the dryer whirled, making a grating sound.

She had her story. The names *Chelsea, Tim, Darby, Pete,* and their relationship to Ghost Mountain Ranch were now perfectly clear. With some research into this group called The People, she could put everything together, write the story, and get out of this place.

But she didn't want to.

For one thing, her best source for information remained Pete. He could tell her what the group did before he left it. What was its attraction to young people of the day? And why did they use bombs to prove their point? That crazy idea got her grandfather killed.

Was this why Sarah committed suicide? Guilt? A sane person

would have remorse for causing the death of a policeman and setting bombs that could harm others.

Then there was Slade.

She pulled in a deep breath, then slowly released it. What about Slade? She'd been prepared to dislike him—the son of a wealthy family—while she had nothing. Just a name. And a dream of someday writing an article or a novel, something that people would read. Something that made a difference.

But they had more in common than hippy grandmothers who were sixties radicals. They had the same yearning, the desire to find themselves. To be true to themselves. If she left now, she'd never get to know him.

A spasm of despair twisted through her heart. For the first time in her life, she found a man desirable—physically and emotionally—and she didn't know what to do with that feeling.

She worked silently the rest of the day, doing the job Darby had told her to do before Ellie intervened.

Hours later, when the dinner bell clanged on the dining hall porch, she was more than ready to fold the last sheet, stretch the ache in her lower back, and join the crew for dinner.

THE SMELLS COMING from the dining hall were incredible. Slade's stomach growled with hunger. Why was he like this? It was if nothing satisfied him. He was starved all the time. Grinning to himself, he took the porch steps two at a time. Leo would say because he'd finally put in an honest day's work.

He was late, but no one seemed to notice. Leo sat at the head of the table like a medieval lord. Laurie sat beside him, offering him a platter of sliced bread. She looked up at Slade, smiled briefly, then ducked her head.

Darby and Hank sat in the next two places. Even without touching, they seemed connected in an untold way that ripped Slade's heart. He wasn't upset that his mother had found a new love so soon after his father's death. His mom was still a young woman, and she deserved a life of her own now that she was widowed. He liked and admired Hank. And above all, he wanted that same kind of connectedness Darby and Hank had. He wanted a woman to glance at him with an expression of intimacy. Not simply sexual, but emotional—like his mother and Hank—as if they were soulmates.

"Better grab your plate, boy," Pete said, hassling him as always. The wrangler sat across the table from Darby and beside Ellie, who sat next to his grandfather on his left.

"Hank, I got most of the saddles done." He filled his plate at the sideboard, heaping on the beef stew.

Ellie surveyed his plate as he sat down. "You better take some salad."

Pete frowned and elbowed him when he sat down. "She's always trying to mother us." His words were in a loud whisper as if he wanted her to hear. "Don't do much good."

"You better listen to me, Pete Harden, if you know what's good for you."

He raised an eyebrow. "Hear that? Sounds like my mother too!"

The big front door opened, and with a *woof*, Finn scampered into the room followed by Jeremiah. "Sorry I'm late, folks."

As he filled his plate at the sideboard, Slade was quick to note no one gave him grief for tardiness. Maybe a cowboy with only one name couldn't be intimidated.

Jeremiah sat down beside him. "I went out again this afternoon," he said between bites. "Checked to make sure that grizzly didn't come back. Found his tracks heading into the mountains."

Darby leaned back against her chair. "That's a relief."

"Seems these bears are getting mighty cocky," Leo muttered. "Best make sure we keep our foodstuff and horse feed secure. Keep lids on garbage cans. Probably a good thing to remind guests about bear safety, too."

"And to carry bear spray," Slade prompted.

Darby cleared her throat. "Thank the lord you had it on you."

"I'm thankful too," Laurie said. "Slade saved my life."

Caught in the moment, he stared across the table at her and saw a flush creep across her cheeks. His face felt warm, and he looked down, unable to meet her eyes. The sudden silence was diverted by the scrape of forks on stoneware plates and the rapid panting of Finn.

When he glanced up again, he saw Hank exchange a knowing look with Darby, and his flush deepened.

"Change of topic," Hank stated, surveying the diners. "We have a bit of a problem."

Everyone let Slade's embarrassing moment slide while Hank filled them in on the lack of help for Trail In, the trail drive with eighty horses thirty-six miles through mountain paths from the Madison River valley back to Ghost Mountain Ranch.

"Chris and Jacob can't make it until next week. Thought they'd be here today but got hung up at school. Thing is, we're set to go tomorrow," Hank said. "I'm not sure I can manage with only Pete and Jeremiah."

"I'll go," Slade offered.

Pete snorted. "You don't know nothing about riding a quarter horse, boy, let alone anything about managing a trail drive."

Slade's breath hitched, and he pressed his lips together. The old wrangler was right. He didn't know those things.

"I'll go," Darby said. "I haven't been in years."

Slade thought Hank seemed pleased. "Sounds like a plan," Hank said. "I'd feel better leaving a man at home with Leo and the women."

"And what are we, Hank Slade? Dumb blondes?" Ellie jeered, sweeping a hand toward Laurie.

"Sounds like a sexist remark to me," Laurie agreed, but she had a gleam in her eye that told Slade she wasn't really angry.

Darby cuffed Hank's arm. "You're on shaky ground now."

Hank ran a hand through his hair and spluttered, "Hey, I didn't mean anything."

"Even I know better than to say something stupid like that, and I'm eighty-five-years old."

They all laughed at Leo's comeback. Slade had a feeling Hank would never live his comment down.

An hour later, dishes done, he lingered in the living area, winding down from the day. A soothing fire crackled in the fireplace. Darby, Pete, and Jeremiah had gone to get ready for the early morning ride over the mountains, but Hank sat on edge of the stone hearth, strumming his guitar. Leo's pipe smoke filled the room with cherry tobacco aroma.

Laurie entered and joined Slade on the cracked leather sofa, rubbing shoulders with him and slanting him a look, a smile on her lips. She felt good, being so close, in a way that was comfortably intimate. He clutched the old picture she'd discovered and held it up for her to see. She bent nearer to look at it again, and he could feel her breath on his cheek.

"What's cha got there?" Hank asked.

"Old picture Laurie found." Slade handed it over to him.

Hank gently lay down his guitar and took the photo. "Where did you get this?"

"I found it in Leo's cabin."

He noticed Laurie didn't say *where* in Leo's cabin. Smart. "Pete says it's my mom and grandmother."

That caught Leo's attention. He sat forward. "What?"

Hank got up and gave him the picture. "Old photo. You've seen it."

Leo glanced at it and grunted. He handed it back, dismissing it. "Before my time."

Returning to the hearth, Hank sat down again and fingered the picture. "Darby found this in a locked box of her mother's, along with other pictures and the orange necklace she wears all the time. Thing is, those pictures disappeared right after she found them."

267

That was strange. Slade exchanged glances with Laurie.

"We want to ask Pete more about the radical group he says he was in," Laurie said. "What did they do, actually?"

Hank shrugged. "Why the interest?"

Laurie's gaze shifted from Hank to Slade, then back to Hank. He felt her stiffen. Would she tell Hank about her grandparents?

"Curiosity."

"Not something you're going to write about?" Hank asked. "You know, a good story."

"No, not really." Her voice faded.

"Laurie showed me the picture, and I was interested in my family history." Slade decided to help her out. "For one thing, what was my grandmother's real maiden name?"

"All I ever knew was *Sarah*. Leo, do you know?"

"Harrumph! You people don't need to churn up stuff that's over and done with. Sarah said her name was Sarah and that was good enough for me! Didn't need no last name." Leo tapped his ashes out of his pipe and pushed himself to his feet. "Ellie, time for bed!"

Slade glanced up to find Ellie standing at the kitchen door. How long had she been there silently listening? Her eyes met his, sending a chill down his spine. The look was brief, filled with contempt and anger, then it was gone. She stepped quickly across the room to come to Leo's aid.

"You've gone and got Leo all upset," she snapped. "You should be ashamed of yourselves!" Then, hand on his elbow, she shepherded him across the wooden floor to the front door and outside.

When they were gone, Slade let out a long, pent-up breath. "That was interesting."

"I'm not sure what to make of it myself." Hank turned the photograph over in his hands. "I knew Leo was sensitive about his wife, and I know Darby is."

"Even with the best intentions, the past has a way of haunting us," Laurie said. "We shouldn't cover it up. It's best to explore it and find out the truth."

"Wow! That sounds deep." He was impressed by Laurie. No, she wasn't a dumb blonde.

"Now that we've found out this much, Hank, when you get back with the horses, I want to ask Pete what he remembers." She sounded eager like a reporter after a hot story.

"That's fine. But please keep it between you and Pete," Hank said. He indicated the photo with a tilt of his head. "Do you mind if I return this to Darby?"

Slade looked at Laurie for confirmation. She nodded. "No, go ahead," he said, inhaling sharply. "I wish I knew why my grandmother committed suicide. If we found out, it might make Mom feel better. She always felt it was her fault."

"I know." Hank climbed to his feet, then paused as if remembering. "One more thing you should ask Pete. About a month ago, he mentioned to me, off the cuff like, that maybe Sarah didn't commit suicide. I never said anything to Darby."

Slade's blood pressure spiked. "You're kidding me?"

Hank shook his head. "Nope. And that's all I know. Should have asked him more about it, but, well..." He let his words die as he left the dining room.

The fire popped and snapped. Leo's cherry pipe tobacco aroma hung in the air like a comforting cloud. Slade's pulse pounded and an obsessive *need to know* filled his heart.

Laurie angled her body toward him and lay a hand on his knee. Her lips were parted. "If your grandmother didn't commit suicide," she said in a soft voice, "then who killed her?"

CHAPTER ELEVEN

LAURIE SHUT HER EYES, savoring Slade's nearness, his warmth. She was content in the moment, sitting with Slade, relaxing. In their brief time together, he'd begun to weave his way into her heart.

The realization startled her, causing a deep intake of breath. She sat up.

"What?"

She shaded her eyes from him. The riders were leaving at daylight tomorrow, so it would be two days before they could question Pete. "I think it's time we look up Tim Krebs on the Internet."

"We can do that?" Slade asked. "Hasn't he been dead a long time?"

She rose, breaking their tangible bond. "Sure. We can use my laptop." She scanned his eyes, noticing dark circles beneath them and a softness in his gaze. "I didn't know Tim's last name when I looked before, and I'm not sure anything will come up with the name *Chelsea Clemmons*. Your grandmother seemed very private. You game, or is it too late?"

"Let's do it."

"Be right back."

When she returned with her laptop, they sat together at the dining table and booted it up.

"How do you do this?" he asked, leaning against her shoulder.

"There's a program called *Finder*. It's got all kinds of government records and court documents. It searches many databases. If it finds anything, we'll have to pay for it. There's a monthly fee."

"I've got a credit card."

She glanced at him. "Thanks." She keyed in Tim's name, then paused. "We don't know where he lived."

Slade rubbed his chin. "Good point."

Going with her gut, she keyed in *Chicago*.

"Chicago?"

"Just a guess."

As the databases churned away, warnings popped up on the screen. *Do you really want to know about Tim Krebs?*

"Well, yes," she muttered. "Or we wouldn't be looking."

"This looks thorough," Slade observed.

"If there are any public records about him, this website will find it."

And it did. Tim Krebs was married to a woman named Lisa Ross. He did time for bank robbery from 1973 to 1988. Lisa Ross died in 1990 and so did Tim.

She rubbed her chin. "Pete's information was right. He must have been an unsavory character."

"And I guess he didn't marry my grandmother, but another woman."

"Doesn't look like it, but now we know he did sleep around."

Slade grimaced. "I'm not happy to have him in my family tree."

Laurie sat back. She sympathized with him. However, the facts didn't satisfy her. She wanted more. Why did he rob a bank? Why did he build bombs? "This isn't enough. There's nothing in here about involvement with a radical group."

"Google *The People*."

"Okay." She brought up the search engine and keyed in the

name. Nothing seemed to fit. "I didn't find any specific group by that name when I looked earlier, but I did find out there were militant underground youth movements in the nineteen sixties and seventies mostly protesting civil rights and the Vietnam War."

She switched to Wikipedia. "I bet the group was an off-shoot of *The Weather Underground*." A long page full of information came up complete with over one hundred notes. "Sometimes you can't trust the information on this site, but this entry looks pretty well documented."

He peered over her shoulder. "I studied American history in college but never heard about this group."

She shrugged, feeling a strange kinship with him. "It was before our time, but it affected the lives of our parents."

"How was your grandmother involved?" His voice softened as he sat back.

"I wish I knew." She threw up her hands. Her chest felt tight. "I only have a few entries in my grandmother's diaries to go on. One said my grandfather Glen blew himself up making a bomb. We never talked about him at home. Never went to a grave. It was as if he never existed."

"Sheesh." Slade ran fingers through his hair. "My mom never talked about Sarah either, but she was there with us for as long as I can remember—like a ghost. My dad told me about her once. He said my mom felt guilty about her death. He said to give my mom some slack. Sometimes it was hard to do that when I was a kid."

Ripples of recognition flooded through her. All the useless feelings she'd experienced growing up came back to her as distinct as ever, anger, frustration, shame, guilt. Slade must have felt them too.

"I want to see Sarah's grave," he said in a steady, lower-pitched voice.

She noticed his jawline had tightened. "Do you know where it is?"

"Somewhere behind the cabins. I think I can find it." He stood up, looking down at her with a questioning gaze. "Will you go with me?"

"Sure. Tomorrow after lunch?"

"It's a date."

Feeling herself blush, she looked away, then clicked off the Internet and shut her laptop. "Fine. See you then."

He paused, as if realizing his slip, then cleared his throat. "Will you send me those links? I want to send them to Kelsey."

Laurie glanced up, frowning. "Why?"

"She's my twin." He took a breath and planted his feet in a wide stance. "As much as she's annoying most of the time, I think I should share the info with her. We grew up together with our mother's disfunction concerning Sarah."

UP EARLY, Slade watched his mother, Hank, Pete, and Jeremiah ride out in the frosty morning. Along with a boisterous Finn, they took with them two pack horses carrying what they needed to camp out overnight. In a way, he envied them time on the trail, but felt a rush of pride that Hank had left him to supervise the arrival of seventeen round bales of hay for the horses.

He whistled all morning as he worked, strangely euphoric about last night with Laurie. They'd researched together as a team, and it felt good, unlike the tension of competition between Kelsey and him. He could get used to having Laurie around. The awareness surprised him, causing his heart to race. He had a tendency to overanalyze things. Maybe he shouldn't think about it.

But he couldn't help his jumbled thoughts. By the time he met her on the dining room porch, he trembled with excitement and couldn't suppress a wide grin.

"Ready?"

Her eyes sparkled. "Let's go!"

He inclined his head to indicate the road in front of the dining hall. "This way."

Thirteen guest cabins built mostly in the nineteen thirties, were set apart from each other with their own view of the ranch meadow with Saga Creek running down the middle. Barns, corrals, and most crew cabins were located across the creek. At the last cabin, Slade turned off the main dirt road and took a track climbing steadily through sage and greening grass.

"Pete told me it was up here."

And it was. At the top of the hill, they found a family cemetery surrounded by a jack pole fence. Inside, Sarah's grave was easy to find. It was the newest. Wilted flowers lay beneath the headstone.

Sarah York, Wife of Leo York, and mother of Darby York. 1952–1988

"My god, Sarah was only eighteen when she had your mother."

An overpowering sensation of sorrow blurred his vision. He couldn't react to Laurie's observation, but stared down at the sad little grave.

"You okay?"

"I'm fine, really."

~

BUT HE DIDN'T LOOK fine. He stood beside her, arms hanging at his sides, his expression dull. Because her grandmother was cremated, she didn't have a grave. But Debbie had wanted to take the urn with the cremains home with her. Laurie didn't want them. The thought was too gruesome for words.

"Look. Leo already has his headstone engraved," she pointed out. "He was born in 1934." All the memorial needed was his death date. She shook her head. Not going there.

Slade turned to gaze at her. Sun glinted off his hair. "Thanks for coming up here." His chin trembled. "I didn't expect it to affect me like this."

"I can understand." Her voice was strained.

Meeting his eyes with a wavering smile, she felt drawn toward him, mesmerized by a hyper-awareness of him. His tall frame seemed to block the sun, so the impression of a halo radiated around his head. For a moment, he was god-like in appearance, luring her toward him.

He reached out and touched her shoulders. His fingers were like hot brands burning their way through her jacket. She swayed against him, felt his arms circle behind her to pull her into a tender embrace. The tension between them faded into something different. She felt the heat of his breath against her face. Her own breath quickened. She shuddered in anticipation. Then he cupped her face in his hands, his big manly hands, and tilted her lips up to his.

The kiss, when it came, exploded through her body. It had been so long since she'd been with a man, first year of college, maybe, that she'd forgotten what it was like. The feel of him crashed through her senses, shattering her with a blast of desire.

What am I doing?

She pulled back. Her gaze darted away, breaking eye contact. "Don't do this. We're just friends."

"Are we?" His voice held a wistful tone.

Stepping back, she lifted her chin. "Yes, we're friends. Nothing more."

Her words sounded so final. They were. She couldn't afford to feel anything for this guy. They were from two different worlds.

"I suppose you're right." His smile was bitter. "My mistake."

She gave herself a mental shake. Unfamiliar emotions tore at her. Something had shifted between them, something she couldn't describe, as if a deep chasm had opened up.

And if she approached it, she feared she would fall in.

CHAPTER TWELVE

Friends? He wanted more than friendship but was at a loss how to express his feelings. Pretty damn typical for him.

Laurie avoided him the rest of the day, even working late in the laundry to skip supper. By nine o'clock, the sun had set. Slade shivered as he walked in the darkness from the barn, glad he hadn't gone on Trail Over. Too darn cold for his city tastes to be camping out at night in thirty-degree weather.

Entering the cabin that he shared with his grandfather, he found Leo and Ellie sitting in the small living room. Ellie knitted and Leo puffed on his pipe and read a well-worn paperback by Louis L'Amour.

"It's cold out there," he said by way of greeting, hung up his coat, and sat down in the extra chair.

Leo looked up and grunted. "Montana mountains."

"You should be here in the winter." Ellie sounded superior.

"I suppose." He shrugged and sat back, stretching out his legs. "I'm not sure I'm cut out for the snow."

"You get used to it." Leo lay his paperback on the end table and put his pipe away. "It's a way of life."

"You must love it, Granddad."

Leo grunted again, but Slade thought the sheepish look he gave him was filled with love. Did the old man like to be called *Granddad*?

"Get me to bed, Ellie, old girl."

Ellie folded her knitting and put it into her basket. She stood and helped Leo to his feet. Together they went toward the bathroom where she waited outside, then she escorted him into his bedroom.

No wonder Leo's gruff manner had put Darby off over the years. Under that crotchety exterior, Slade figured Leo was an old softy. His dad had been that way, but Slade had been able to see right through him.

Hunching forward, he rested his elbows on his knees and eyed Ellie's knitting basket on the floor by her chair. His breath hitched. Would she have any more pictures in the basket? He scooted the chair forward and pulled the basket toward him. In a side pocket, he found a sheet of paper that looked like it came from one of his mother's drawing pads. On it was a rough, charcoal sketch of two horses standing in snow—their shaggy coats and tousled manes, their gentle eyes, and sturdy legs. A few lines represented distant mountains.

He would recognize his mother's work anywhere. The simplicity of line was amazing. She could draw a horse with an accuracy that blew him away. It's what made her so popular with her horse-loving clients.

"Good night, Leo." Ellie backed out of Leo's room, pulling his door shut.

Caught! His heart raced as he thrust the paper under his butt and shoved the basket back toward its place. She turned around and saw him with his hand on the basket.

"What the hell are you doing?"

The room was small, and she only needed three steps to scoop up her basket and clutch it to her breast.

He didn't answer and sat back, lifting his chin against her stony glare.

"I know that girl has been snooping in my things. Some stuff is missing too. Now you. You keep out of my room and away from my belongings."

"Yes, ma'am."

"Now give it back."

He lifted a hip and pulled out the drawing, handing it to her. She snatched it from him with a huff and turned on her heel slamming her bedroom door behind her.

Beads of sweat formed on his upper lip. Ellie's furious look shook him to his very core.

The drawing was his mother's if he wasn't mistaken. Why had she given it to Ellie?

Or did she?

❧

MORNING BREAKFAST WAS UNCOMFORTABLE, to say the least. With only four around the big table, they ate in silence. Ellie shot daggers at her, and Slade avoided her gaze. Was he really that upset with her? Laurie supposed so, but she couldn't help it. She treasured her independence, not wanting to be anything like Debbie, not wanting to depend upon a man to the exclusion of anything else. Caring about a man led to falling in love. Love led to heartache. She didn't want that.

"What are your plans today, Laurie, my girl?" Leo asked.

She directed her attention to the old cowboy. She couldn't get angry at the politically incorrect way he addressed her, for there was affection in his smile. "I have five cabins on my list to clean, then I hoped to write the first article Kelsey commissioned."

Leo nodded toward his grandson. "And you?"

"I've got some work down at the barns. Can't wait for the horses to get here." Slade rocked back in his chair and smiled at Leo. "How long does it take for Trail Over?"

"Maybe eight to nine hours." He paused as if remembering. "It's a beautiful sight. All them horses coming through the mountain pass heading straight for the ranch meadow."

"I can't wait to see it." Laurie grinned as she spoke. This was a different way of life. Simple. Down to earth. To think the arrival of eighty horses would be the highlight of her day.

"Just stay away from our cabin when you clean," Ellie said. Then she added a smile as if it was an afterthought to soften her command. "You cleaned it so well the last time, Laurie, I'll be able to keep up with it now."

"Sure thing." Laurie avoided eye contact as she stood. Had Ellie figured out she'd taken the photo? She must have.

Slade caught up with her as she stood on the porch looking over the ranch. There was a chance of rain, and it was uncomfortably cold. She smiled briefly at him, then looked away.

"That was awkward," he said.

His words struck her as criticism, and she stiffened. "What do you mean?"

"Breakfast with Ellie."

Laurie let out a sigh. "I bet she knows I took that photo from her."

"It's more than that." Slade turned to her and acted as if he wanted to reach out and touch her sleeve. "She saw me looking at her knitting basket last night."

Her eyebrows flew up. "You didn't."

"Sure did. I found something else that probably doesn't belong to her."

"What was it?" Laurie's mind raced with possibilities.

"A charcoal sketch that looked like something my mother did."

She rocked back on her heels. "Maybe Darby gave it to her."

Slade lifted a shoulder to shrug and gazed out over the ranch.

"Hank said she lost a bunch of pictures that had been her mother's. Maybe Mom lost the drawing too."

A frown wrinkled her forehead. "You mean Ellie took them?"

"Could have."

"Why would she do that?" She tipped her head. "Unless she's jealous."

"And resents Mom for coming home." He shrugged again. "Another mystery."

"And all we have to do is ask your mother." She strode down the steps.

He followed her as far as the bridge that crossed the small creek. "Hank's office could stand a good cleaning too, and it has Wi-Fi if you want to work someplace other than the dining room."

"And under Ellie's nose?"

"That *is* her domain."

She warmed at Slade's suggestion. Maybe they could have a working relationship if not a romantic one. "Thanks. See you at lunch?"

"Yep. Looking forward to it."

He spun on his heel and headed over the bridge, lifting his hand high in farewell. Why did she suddenly feel an acute, mysterious sense of loss watching him go?

TOO BUSY TO STOP FOR lunch with the crew, Laurie grabbed a sandwich and took it with her laptop to the office. She flicked on the lights and powered up the wall heater. Yes, the place could stand a good cleaning. Dust covered file cabinets and Hank's paper-covered desk. The floor was black with dirt and caked mud.

Her article about grizzly bear safety came together quickly. When finished, she rolled back in Hank's desk chair, took a few deep breaths, satisfied with her effort. Would Kelsey like it? Only one way to find out. Sitting forward, she fired up the Internet and shot an email off to Kelsey with the attachment.

Now she waited for judgment. As a writer, she was used to edits. In fact, her whole life seemed to have been that way. Fix this, Laurie. Fix that. Nothing she did had been good enough for her mother, maybe because her mother's life had been so miserable, especially after her father left them. As a result, she'd never given Debbie much sympathy even though she felt responsible for her.

It had started to sprinkle by the time Laurie shut down her laptop and carried it home. She found her rain slicker, and pulled it on, thankful for the small amount of protection it bought her as she walked back outside. Suddenly, the dinner bell rang, clanging loudly, but it wasn't time to eat. She hurried around the dining hall to see the first of eighty horses trot and canter into the meadow. They followed each other in a zagging line, some single, some in bunches.

Slade stood on the bridge watching, and she ran to join him. "Magnificent," he said with an awed huff.

And it *was* magnificent, horse after horse of all different colors and shades trailed the leaders into the corral. They kept coming. Hooves pounding a steady cadence, cow bell jangling on the lead horse. The energy and beauty of the sight took her own breath away.

"I've never seen anything like it," she murmured.

They stood side-by-side, feeling each other's excitement and vitality. He had her by a few inches in height, and she was forced to look up to him. When she did, a deep yearning shot through her. *No!* She must ignore that feeling. She didn't need a man, especially this one.

Finn, the Karelian bear dog, trotted past, weaving in and out among the horses. Hank, Pete, and Darby followed behind, rounding up strays. They rode across the shallow creek, the horses' hooves making clomping sounds in the rushing water. Jeremiah was last. He paused at the edge of the creek, resting his arm on his saddle horn, and favored her with a steamy gaze.

"Ma'am," he said with a nod.

"Jeremiah." She acknowledged his attention, feeling the pop of electricity emanating from the wrangler as he favored her with a suggestive look.

Then he turned to Slade. "Sorry you missed the ride, Heston, but I'm glad your mother came along. She's a real trooper."

Slade's cheeks flushed. His fists clenched. "That's nice."

Jeremiah winked at Laurie, brought his index finger up to the brim of his hat in a salute, and nudged his horse across the creek.

"I don't like that guy," Slade muttered.

"He's a genuine Western cowboy."

He drew himself up and turned away. "I suppose."

CHAPTER THIRTEEN

S<small>LADE'S STOMACH BURNED</small>, and the pain in his jaw from clenching his teeth was intense. He worked his jaw left and right to ease the pressure. What was the matter with him? He'd never been jealous. All his life, women had chased *him*. He'd never cared enough to do the chasing. His last girlfriend Katherine had been the green-eyed type, and he'd been critical of her snide remarks about other women whom she thought were rivals. The irony wasn't lost on him. Now it was his turn to be in a jealous turmoil, all because of a simple wink and a nod.

Jeremiah whatever his last name was a good-looking man. Slade couldn't deny that. He was strong and competent. Hell, he sat a horse like John Wayne. Slade shouldn't mind all that, but when he saw Jeremiah and Laurie laughing during dinner, his muscles tightened, and he found himself grinding his teeth again.

Everyone sat at the crew dining table that night, congratulating themselves all around on the successful Trail Over.

"Couldn't have got this done without Jeremiah," Hank said during a lull in conversation. "Leo, where did you find this cowboy?"

"Oh, I've known him a while. Used to rodeo with his father."

So, the guy had a past. Good for him. Slade pressed his lips together and stared across the table at Laurie.

"My horse was off in the left hind when we got to the ranch," Pete said, once everyone was finished and pushed back from the table. "Think I'll take a look at him. I put him up in the barn for some stall rest."

"Sounds good," Hank said.

Ellie stood and collected silverware, putting it on a platter. "I could use some kitchen help tonight."

Laurie volunteered quickly. "I'll help."

Slade opened his mouth to speak when Jeremiah said, "Count me in."

Two's company. Three's a crowd. Not for him.

Picking up a mug of coffee, Slade joined Leo and Hank by the fire. While Hank poked the logs to increase the flames, Leo sat down in his favorite chair and pulled out his pipe. Soon the aroma of cherry tobacco mingled with the smell of the roaring fire.

Darby joined Slade on the sofa and placed a motherly hand on his knee. "How's it going?"

"Fine." He took a sip of coffee.

"You seem to be enjoying it here."

"I am." He glanced at his mother. "It's different, but I like it so far."

She looked dreamy-eyed and tired. "I'm glad."

"I haven't seen you drawing as much here as you did in Kentucky."

Darby cocked her head to acknowledge his observation. "Too much going on. I've been too busy." She paused and squeezed his knee. "I'm afraid in the past I used drawing as a means to escape."

"Were you that unhappy with Dad?"

"Not really. It's just that," her voice trailed off, and Slade knew she thought about her mother's death and the guilt that had eaten at her for years.

One more reason to talk to Pete.

"I saw a drawing in our cabin that reminded me of something you'd do." He carefully approached the question he and Laurie wanted answered. "It was a charcoal sketch of two horses with the mountains in the background. Simple, really. A few strokes. Like you do."

"I wondered where that drawing went," she said. "It was in my cabin when I first arrived but disappeared. I guess Leo liked it, but I don't remember showing it to him."

Interesting. But Leo didn't have the drawing. It was in Ellie's knitting basket. How had it ended up there?

He didn't say anything to his mom, instead savored the moment of warmth and closeness with her. They were too few and far between these days since he was grown. No wonder Darby had been so upset about her mother's untimely death. He suspected the loss of a mother any time was hard, but under those circumstances, it had to have been hell for her, especially when she thought it was her fault.

DOING dishes with Jeremiah was nothing like working with Slade. Laurie didn't feel any kind of connection to him. Not like she'd felt to Slade from their first contentious meeting. No sparks sizzled. No heart rapidly pounded. Jeremiah was a take-charge kind of guy and insisted on washing the dishes, sticking his big, rough hands into the soapy water. This was a handsome man, hot in a rugged way with his mustache and long dark hair, but she was not a bit attracted to him.

Yet, thinking of Slade in a romantic way didn't work. She couldn't allow herself to yearn for something out of her reach, so she simply didn't hope.

"Been on KP duty many a time in my life," Jeremiah told her standing at the sink. "I know how to get a dish clean."

"Sounds good." Laurie picked up a dish towel. She dried each plate and stacked them. "So, where are you from, Jeremiah?"

"Here and there," he said with an evasive grunt.

"Sounds as if you've been in the military."

"I did my time in this man's army. Not for me, though."

"I suppose not." She figured the army with its rules and discipline would not be the kind place for a man who liked being his own boss and seemed to live the vagabond life of a true cowboy. "Where did you pick up Finn? He seems to be a good dog."

Jeremiah glanced down at his feet where Finn lay stretched out on his side. "Dog can sleep anywhere," he murmured with a smile. "He's one loyal son of a gun. Saved my life a few times."

That's the most she'd heard him say about his life, but Laurie still felt unsatisfied. He gave her just enough information, but no real details. The reporter inside wanted the whole story.

When all the dishes were dried and stacked, she picked up a load of plates to put them away. The cabinet where they belonged was high above her head, and she stood on tiptoe to reach it.

"Let me help." Jeremiah came up behind her and lifted plates from her hands.

He placed them on the shelf over her head but didn't back away. He crowded her against the cabinet, smothering her with his closeness. She faced him, turning into his hard chest.

"You're a pretty filly." His voice was warm and seductive. His grin cocky. He placed his hands on her shoulders, blocking her path.

Tension hummed in her veins. "Thanks." She tried to slip past.

But he foiled her attempt, gripping her tighter. Then he lowered his head and kissed her lips. She didn't want to kiss him. She thought of Jeremiah as a coworker. But for a crazy moment, she let herself be kissed as an experiment. Had the magic she experienced with Slade been false? Could she so love deprived that any man's attention would satisfy her?

It didn't. His kiss deepened. Revulsion rose in her throat. Sex without commitment or love was no good.

A noise at the door caused her to open her eyes. A movement. Slade! As if sensing her eyes on him, he backed away from the door and was gone.

She turned her head away from Jeremiah's lips and splayed a hand over his chest. "No! This isn't working. Jeremiah. Stop!" She pushed him, but of course, she wasn't strong enough to do much good.

Thankfully, he froze, taking a step backward. He drew himself up and squared his shoulders. "In this day and age, when a woman says *no,* a man best listen. My apologies." He gave a short nod almost like a formal bow. "I thought you wanted it."

"No! What gave you that impression?"

"You're certainly mighty cozy with the owner's grandson."

"Slade?"

"Yep, the greenhorn. I've seen you two together."

She forced herself to remain calm. "I don't know what you mean. There's nothing going on between us."

"Don't give me that crap." The muscles in his shoulders tightened and his jaw clenched. "Seems I'm not rich enough for you, that's all."

Renewed anger flowed through her. "Slade and I are simply co-workers. Just like you and me. Besides, I don't do casual hookups."

Jeremiah shot her a skeptical look. "Nice to know the rules." He picked up a dish towel, dried his hands, whistled to Finn, and strode out of the kitchen.

She stood a moment, trembling, and felt a flush of heat spread through her body. *The nerve of that man!* As she put away the rest of the dishes with shaking hands, it hit her. She cared about Slade. But that was dangerous. She certainly didn't need that kind of complication in her life.

～

EVERYONE WAS GONE from the dining hall when she cut the lights and left the kitchen. She lifted her coat from the coat rack, turned off the lights, and walked out onto the porch. Taking a deep breath, Laurie felt the cold Montana night air sting down into her chest. She stuck her hands into her pockets and stood a moment looking over the ranch. Never tiring of the view of cabins and sage brush and distant mountains, she understood why people didn't want to leave this place.

Pinpricks of light shown in a few cabins across the meadow. Darby and Hank must be home. Pete's was dark, but Jeremiah's cabin was lit. And so were the windows in the barn. Could Pete be down there? Time to ask him what he knew about Darby's father and the life they led in the underground group.

Tightening her fists in the pockets of her coat, Laurie tread down the steps and set off in a fast-paced stride toward the bridge and the barn beyond. By the time she reached the bridge, Slade came out of the night, catching up with her.

"Hold up! Where are you going?"

She turned. He gave her a sad sort of smile. She wanted to reach out and take his hand, but instead, shoved her fists deeper in her pockets. For the first time, she understood the rush of sexual desire.

"What are you doing out here?" she asked.

"I can ask you the same thing."

Did he think she was going to join Jeremiah? The thought slugged her in the gut, and she drew herself up, setting her jaw. "I'm going to the barn to talk to Pete." She wheeled around and began walking. "Come along if you want."

He hurried to join her, breathing hard because of the fast pace she took. "I found out something interesting tonight."

Clearly, he wasn't going to accuse her of anything. "What is it?"

"My mother did do that drawing I found in Ellie's basket. She said it disappeared when she first came to the ranch."

"So why did Ellie have it?"

"Who knows?"

She glanced up at him. "Maybe Pete will know."

The barn smelled of hay and horses and leather. The floors were dirt, the stalls bedded with straw. Only a few horses were stabled there. They were the crew's personal riding horses. If Pete had come to check on his horse, they'd find him here.

"I'll look down in the tack room," Slade said. The light was on in that room as well as the whole barn.

Laurie walked between the stalls. "Pete!"

A mare and foal were in a big box stall. The mare snorted and shoved her baby against the far wall away from Laurie. Another horse seemed restless, circling his stall and pawing at the straw. She remembered Pete rode a spotted horse and found one in the last stall standing against the near rails. Reaching out, she touched the warm neck. The horse's skin quivered at her touch, and it moved to the side of the stall away from her.

That's when Laurie saw a body lying face down in the straw.

"Slade!"

He came running at her scream and took her into his arms. "Laurie, what is it?"

"Oh God!" Trembling, she looked over at the stall. Slade followed her gaze.

"No, it can't be." He slid the door open and went inside the stall, dropping to a knee. "It's Pete," he said.

Lifting a hand to her mouth, Laurie shook uncontrollably. "Is he alive?"

Slade looked up at her, his face ashen. "No, he's dead."

CHAPTER FOURTEEN

LAURIE HUGGED HERSELF, rubbing her arms. She couldn't get warm. Even though the fireplace in the crew dining hall burned brightly, she felt the cold of Pete's death into her very core. Darby sat beside her on the sofa staring into the fire. Her left leg jerked up and down as she tapped her booted heel on the wooden floor.

Leo was asleep, but when she heard the news, Ellie had come from the cabin to join them in the dining hall. Her knitting needles clacked as her busy hands worked with precision.

"Knitting calms me," she said. "I can't believe this has happened."

"No." Darby's voice was flat. "It reminds me of when Leo collapsed in the barn, and EMS came."

"Leo was alive. There was hope for him."

Laurie glanced at Ellie, at her washed-out blond hair and pale, paunchy cheeks. Was the mystery drawing still in that knitting basket that rested at her feet? Probably not. Ellie would have been smart enough to remove it, especially since she knew Slade had seen it.

An hour earlier, Hank had sent the women up to the dining hall while he, Slade, and Jeremiah remained at the barn waiting for the arrival of the sheriff and EMS. For once, Laurie was glad not to be at the center of a story. Finding Pete like she did had upset her. Her insides still quivered at the memory of the wrangler's motionless body and cold hands.

And she couldn't get warm.

The big door swung open, and Hank and Slade tramped into the room.

"Hank!" Darby jumped up and ran to him, collapsing into his embrace.

Laurie stood and stared at Slade. He walked to the fireplace, removed his cowboy hat, and held it loosely in his fingers, warming his backside near the hearth.

"I made a pot of coffee," Ellie said, indicating the sideboard with a tip of her head. "Everything is there for you."

"Sounds good, Ellie. Thank you." Hank pulled Darby with him over to the sideboard, and they filled mugs with hot coffee.

Slade dropped his hat on a side table and rubbed his hands together. His face remained pale and his eyes grim. Laurie touched his coat sleeve, feeling a jolt of connection in her gut. The way he looked at her broke her heart. "What happened to Pete?"

"The sheriff thinks he slipped and fell from the hayloft. Looks as if he'd gone up there to toss down a bale of hay."

"Makes no sense." Hank cradled his coffee mug and turned toward them. "Pete was sure-footed even at his age. He'd been climbing up to haylofts all his life."

Darby brought Slade a mug. "It only takes one mistake."

"Had he been dead long?"

"Not long, they thought," Hank said, "but there's no way to tell for sure."

Nothing could suppress Laurie's feeling of guilt and despair. Numbness swept through her. She sunk down on the sofa. "Enough time for us to do the dishes" she said. "Jeremiah didn't need to help me. He could have gone up to that hayloft for Pete."

"Pete was one independent dude." Hank came over to the hearth, shaking his head slowly. "He never asked anyone for help."

Ellie packed away her knitting and rose. "What did they do with him?"

"They took his body to Bozeman."

"Will they do an autopsy?"

"Probably, even though they think it was an accident." Hank sipped his coffee. "Simply falling from a height is potentially deadly and definitely at sixty-five. The hayloft to the ground is at least ten feet."

"Well, that's that." Ellie sniffed. "I don't look forward to telling Leo."

"He'll take it hard." Hank took a shallow breath. "He's known Pete a long time."

"I'd best be getting back to him." Ellie headed toward the door. "'Night all."

After she was gone, the room grew silent. No one said anything about Pete being Darby's uncle, but Laurie thought about it. Granted, they hadn't had any connection over the years, and only recently Darby had learned the truth about him. Still, the death of any relative was hard.

Her vision blurred as she remembered Mama Bev. She had to find out the truth about her grandmother. Even as she thought it, a lump formed in her throat. Why did generous, loving Bev get involved with a group that built bombs and killed innocent people?

But with Pete gone, Laurie wasn't going to find out the truth.

After Hank and his mother left the dining hall, Slade continued standing with his back to the fireplace. He gazed at Laurie. Hell, she was beautiful with her silky hair falling around her face, and the tip of her nose red because of the cold. Or was it tears?

He loved her beauty about her just as much as he loved her independence and strength. And she was a damn good writer too.

Kelsey had texted him after dinner saying Laurie's article about grizzly bear safety was terrific.

Yet, to see her face frozen in alarm at the barn had wrenched his heart. Guilt slashed his gut. He wished he'd found Pete. He wished he could have spared Laurie the trauma.

"Let me walk you to your cabin," he said.

She hesitated. "Okay."

He surprised her by taking her hand. It was icy. He rubbed her fingers. Then he pulled her to her feet. "You need to warm up."

"I suppose." Her voice sounded lifeless. She squeezed her eyes shut and breathed in slowly. "I'd appreciate your company to my cabin."

Slade kept her hand in his and drew her toward the door. Flicking off the indoor lights, he led her onto the porch. The meadow was dark, and the lights were out in the barn and the cabins across the creek. Only a few security lamps remained lit, casting isolated shadows here and there.

"Since we no longer can ask him anything, I wonder if we should search Pete's cabin tomorrow," she said as they stepped off the porch.

"I don't know what we'd find."

"Maybe something about his past. Maybe he left notes about your grandmother's suicide."

"Or murder." He hated that they'd never know about the most pivotal event in his mother's life—the death of her mother.

The darkness on the side of the dining hall seemed to seep into his soul as they walked around it. Did Laurie feel the despair too? Her grip tightened. When they reached her small cabin, only the porch light burned. She would go into the dark. Alone.

Slade turned her and gently took her shoulders. Holding this woman shouldn't feel so right, but it did. His heart thudded as he searched her eyes. "I think you need company tonight."

She took a step back but remained in his grasp. "We're just friends."

The words cut him to his core, but he lifted his chin. "I know. I just want to keep you company while you sleep. You've been through so much tonight."

He wanted to dip his head and kiss her, but he didn't. He held her gaze. Could she see love in his eyes? It wasn't something he could discuss. He didn't know how. All he could do was offer his comfort on a very horrible night.

"Okay." She dislodged herself and went into the cabin, leaving the lights off.

After taking off her coat, vest, and boots, she crawled into her bed with her clothes on, not saying a word. So, she wasn't going to let him see her undress. Fine. Removing his own coat, he fired the wood stove. "It should be warm in here soon."

When he turned around, Laurie had pulled the blanket over her shoulder and turned on her side facing away from him. She was already fast asleep. He ran his hand through his hair, hesitated for a moment, stooped down, and pulled off his boots. Then he inched into her bed fully clothed. Lying on his back, he heard the rhythm of her breathing as he watched the shadows from the porch light play on the ceiling.

Sometime in the night, Laurie whimpered in her sleep and turned toward him. Her hair tumbled onto his shoulder. With her breath in his ear, he finally fell asleep.

CHAPTER FIFTEEN

L aurie slowly opened her eyes. Dawn had broken and weak sunlight lit the window where she'd failed to draw the curtains last night. Five-forty-five or there about. Sunrise. And Slade Heston was with her in bed.

All her senses suddenly alert, she swallowed hard. Slade's chest rose and fell beneath her cheek. His arm circled her shoulder warm and snug. He smelled of aftershave, a mixture of leather and musk, a very unfamiliar manly smell. Lifting her gaze, she saw the outline of his jaw and its day's growth of beard.

What was she doing in bed with him? They were dressed. Had anything sexual happened?

She didn't think so, and that unexpected release of tension caused her to utter a silent "Thank God."

He shouldn't be here. At the same time, she wanted to remain in his arms and snuggle closer. All her life, after her parents' divorce and what had happened to her mother, she'd avoided relationships with men and their subsequent sexual entanglements. She was unused to being in bed with a man, but for a reason she didn't want to question, she wanted to lie still and let this moment last as long as possible.

She must have stirred slightly. Slade opened his eyes and squinted at her. A flush crept across his cheeks, and he sat up, rubbing the back of his neck.

"Sorry. I must have fallen asleep."

She sat up. "We both did."

He swung his legs over the side of the bed and rose. "I just wanted to keep you warm. I didn't plan on staying the night."

Slade looked so uncomfortable, all disheveled with his hair mussed and his shirt wrinkled. She had to smile at him, but he didn't see it, having looked down as if unable to meet her eyes.

"It's okay." Her chest tightened. "We're friends. We both needed comfort last night after what happened to Pete."

He cleared his throat. "Yes, we're friends."

The sham of that statement rocked Laurie, her heart clogging her throat. *Friends*. She wanted to be more than friends with Slade, but she knew it was impossible. Not with her history. Not with his. She refused to be dependent on a man. And he didn't need a woman like her.

She caught him watching her. Did her indecision play across her face? Did he see the longing in her eyes? She hoped not. Schooling her features, she took a deep breath, and he turned away.

He pulled on his boots and picked up his coat. "I need to clean up before breakfast."

"Me too."

"Want to meet afterward and go to Pete's cabin?"

He looked pleased to have something else to talk about. She was with him, not wanting to think about her emotions. They were too complex. Too unpredictable lately. Finding out what they could about Pete was a much safer topic.

SLADE ENTERED the cabin he shared with his grandfather and Ellie and found Leo sitting in his chair by the table looking out the window. His eyes were grim. A plate of half-eaten eggs was in front of him. He held a coffee mug.

Leo looked up and met his eyes. "Where've you been?"

Taking off his coat, Slade hung it on a peg by the door. He wasn't going to lie. "With Laurie."

His grandfather lifted an eyebrow but didn't say a word.

Slade pulled a deep breath and sat down in the opposite chair. "I'm sorry about Pete."

"I don't believe it." Leo placed the coffee mug on the table and rubbed his hands.

"I know. It's hard to believe he's gone."

He waved a hand as if to dismiss Slade's statement of condolence and shook his head. "No. I don't believe it was an accident."

"What?" Slade's head began to buzz. "The sheriff seemed satisfied it was an accident."

"The sheriff doesn't know Pete."

That's all Leo had to say. He turned away and stared out the window. Dare he ask his grandfather about Sarah's death? About Pete's assertion that her death wasn't an accident? He and Laurie had missed their chance to ask Pete. Would his grandfather know what Pete thought? Was if fair to ask the old man?

The *need to know* yanked at him. If something happened to Leo, Slade would lose his chance. Something inside told him it was now or never.

"Hank told me Pete believed your wife didn't commit suicide," he said with a soft voice. Leo turned to look at him. "Why would he think that?"

"I don't know." His grandfather's voice quivered. "We always thought she did. It's what caused your mother to leave."

"I know." Dead end. Again. He let out a breath of frustration. Maybe they could still find something in Pete's cabin. "Does Pete have any relatives?"

"Your mother." Leo ran a hand through his thinning hair. "But we didn't know it. Not until I got sick, and Pete told her about her father."

"I can't believe Pete kept it a secret all those years."

"Pete and Sarah both. For whatever reason, they never talked about it."

Leo had said he knew Pete, but he didn't know everything about him. Or his wife. It must be hard on his grandfather to think about the secrets that were kept. He'd seen first-hand how devastating secrets could be. His mother was proof.

"I'm going to clean up and get some breakfast. Then Laurie and I will go through Pete's things."

Leo put a hand on his arm and leaned forward. "I thought of something. There are some old paper files up in the attic of the office. I don't know what's in them, but I've kept them for thirty years. You might find something in them."

A jolt shot through Slade's body. He swallowed quickly and nodded. "We'll check them."

"Thank you, son. You're a good boy."

Slade suddenly felt lighter, and his breath came easier. He'd find out about his grandmother's death. He had to. For his mother. And for this old man who wasn't his real grandfather but felt like one.

CHAPTER SIXTEEN

PETE'S CABIN looked like the other cabins on the ranch—plenty of wood on the floor and walls, hand-hewn log furniture, a wood burning stove along with electric heat. Slade held the door open to let Laurie enter ahead of him. She crossed a faded red and yellow wool rug and a floorboard squeaked. Pausing, she looked back at him.

That's when Slade heard noise from the bedroom. His heart pumped. "Who's there?"

Ellie came out of the back room. "It's just me."

"What are you doing here?"

She glared at them. "And why are you two here?"

Laurie shot Slade a quick glance. "I've come to clean Pete's cabin. Slade's with me because I didn't want to come alone."

"And I'm sorting out his clothes." Ellie nodded toward the bedroom. "I thought there might be something worth donating to charity."

Through the door, Slade saw bundles of clothes strewn on the double bed. The old wrangler had been dead only one night, and already the vultures were clawing through his things. It didn't seem proper.

"I'm sure Pete would appreciate the thought," Laurie said. "Do you want me box up the clothes for you? I'm sure you have better things to do."

Ellie surveyed Laurie, her eyes narrow and her lips pressed flat. "Well, yes, I have lunch to put together. I sure will be glad when the summer chef gets here." She drew a quick breath and offered a smile that seemed fake, never reaching her eyes. "Thanks."

"No problem," Slade said.

When Ellie left, Laurie turned to face him. "That was strange."

He nodded, feeling an adrenalin rush. "I bet she was looking for something."

"Just like we are."

Pete's bedroom had been tossed with drawers opened exposing bunches of long underwear and flannel shirts. His desk was also a mess. They found his checkbook and a stack of unpaid bills. Personal photographs were scattered on the desktop: horses, mountain views, scenes of the ranch, and one photograph of Slade's mother as a child standing by another woman—his grandmother.

Laurie pulled open desk drawers. Empty. Ellie had dumped the contents of Pete's desk on the bed. They found nothing to connect Pete to a past life or Darby's mother.

Slade couldn't help feeling defeat. "If there was anything here, Ellie took it."

"But I didn't see anything in her hands."

He nodded. "I know. Maybe we surprised her before she found anything."

"What's up with her anyway?" Laurie raked her hair back from her face. Slade watched her shake the blond strands and felt his heart coil. "I don't trust her."

Sighing, he dipped his head. "But Leo trusts her."

"I suppose. He changed his will to include her."

Slade clenched his jaw and felt a thickening in the back of his throat. "I know. With Pete gone, there's one less to inherit the ranch."

"Geez, I hadn't thought of that." She stared at him with grim eyes and drew a sharp breath. "Let's keep looking."

But they didn't find anything, but then again, they weren't sure what they were searching for.

"Leo told me about old files in the office," Slade said. "Up in the attic. Maybe we can look there. I don't know what we'll find, but it's the only clue we've got."

Laurie let out a sigh. "Okay, but let's put this place back together out of respect for Pete."

Slade had a strong desire to touch her, to let her know he cared. Laurie was compassionate as well as smart and beautiful. Swallowing hard, because of his dry mouth, he clutched his hands into fists by his side.

"Sounds good," he said in a soft voice. "Let's straighten up this place."

LUNCH THAT AFTERNOON was a somber affair. One chair was empty. Laurie glanced around the table feeling the sense of loss. Leo kept reaching out his gnarled hand and patting her sleeve. It was as if he needed physical connection with someone, even a woman he hardly knew.

Jeremiah scowled at her from across the table. She offered him a smile of goodwill. His furrowed eyebrows only drew closer together. He raised his glass in a mocking salute to her.

"Glad to know your rules," he said, then continued with his meal.

She lifted her chin, her gut tightening with anger. "And I'm glad you understand them."

"I suppose we should bury Pete up on the hillside," Leo said, his voice devoid of emotion. He didn't seem aware of the tension between Jeremiah and her. "Not next to Sarah, of course, that's for me. But there's room up there."

Darby let out a heavy sigh. "If that's what you want to do."

"I think it's the right thing to do." Leo's shoulders drooped.

"Darby and I were heading into Bozeman this afternoon to check with the authorities." Hank paused and took a deep breath. "We can make arrangements for Pete."

"Thank you. You might as well find out what needs to be done." Leo gazed down at his hand clasped over Laurie's wrist.

"We'll make it happen," Hank said.

Laurie stroked Leo's hand, hoping he knew she was feeling what he was feeling, sadness for a life gone, a soul departed. Was he also thinking about the end of his own life? When he'd be at rest on the hillside with his wife?

Leo grunted as he stood, pushing back his chair. "Take me back to the cabin, Ellie."

Ellie rushed to help him. She held his arm for support.

"I'll clean up for you," Laurie offered and glanced at Slade.

"I'll help too."

"No." Jeremiah turned to Hank. "With Pete gone, I need help getting a winter's worth of dirt off those horses. We can't expect them to be ready for riders in two weeks if we don't bust our butts now."

"Sounds good. Laurie, sorry to leave cleanup to you."

She shrugged. "That's fine. I can manage."

"We'll have more help next week," Hank said. "That's when the summer staff starts arriving."

So, things were about to change again. The arrival of staff and then paying guests would surely breathe life into this ranch, sitting so close as it did to Ghost Mountain.

Laurie worked over an hour washing dishes and putting everything away. She hadn't been able to talk to Slade before Jeremiah marshaled him off to the barn. Looking back over his shoulder,

Slade had given her a smile. It didn't look or feel like the smile of a simple friend.

Alone with her thoughts, her mind wandered. What was it about the West and this lonesome ranch and the dysfunctional people who'd become strangely important to her? Leo. Darby. Hank.

She mourned Pete. His death hit her harder than she would have imagined a few days ago. It wasn't simply because she'd lost the chance to question him about his brother and Slade's grandmother. She'd liked the old guy. It didn't seem right he was gone.

And then there was Slade. What was up with that? She'd never felt such a stirring in her heart. And she couldn't let those feelings get the best of her.

With cleanup done and no other instructions, she left the kitchen and headed toward the ranch office. She could at least give it a good cleaning, and maybe if she wished hard enough, she could conjure up Slade. After all, he said there might be something to search in the office. No matter what, they still had a job to do.

This time, she tried to block thoughts of Slade from her mind and concentrate on the job, dusting, polishing, and sweeping the floors.

"This place looks great! I hardly recognize it."

Startled by the low male voice behind her, Laurie turned. Slade had paused at the threshold, favoring her with a hooded gaze.

Her heart slammed against her ribs. "It just needed a little elbow grease."

"I finally escaped Jeremiah."

"Good for you."

"He saddled up and took Finn for a ride. Said he needed to clear his head."

"Don't fence me in," Laurie muttered, lifting her head up to smile at him.

"Three hours of grooming mud-caked horses has done me in."

He dropped his cowboy hat onto Hank's desk and rubbed his right arm.

"I'm sorry." She took a step toward him.

The world seemed to spin crazily around them. Her vision clouded as he came toward her. Dipping his head, Slade took her into his arms and kissed her.

She kissed him back like she meant it.

CHAPTER SEVENTEEN

HOLDING this woman shouldn't feel right. He hardly knew her, but she made him feel great. He wanted to stay with her as long as she'd let him. He wanted to say outrageous things to her like *I love you*. But he couldn't force the words from his mouth. He was too busy kissing her, savoring her lips and realizing she was kissing him back.

The thought shocked him, disorienting him. Did she care about him? Or did she do this with other men? He'd seen her and Jeremiah.

His chest burned with jealousy, and he pulled her closer, wrapping her into a huge bear hug against his chest. That didn't ease his pain. He ached and his pulse galloped.

"Enough," Laurie blurted, pushing back. "I can't breathe."

His mind reeling, he dropped his hands and backed away. "I'm sorry."

She stared at him, her perusal intense, assessing. "I don't know what came over me."

"My fault." He lowered his eyes for a split second. He'd never felt like such a jerk.

"I don't trust men." Her words were low as if coming straight from her heart. "My grandfather. My father." She shook her head, not finishing her thought. "But there's something about you."

Good or bad? He couldn't ask but searched her face.

She dragged a shaky breath, fear creeping into her eyes. "I can't do this. I'm going to quit. This whole ranch thing has been a mistake."

Laurie walked toward the door, and he reached for her, never gathering the guts to touch her. "If it's because of me, don't worry. I'll lay off. Leave you alone."

"No." Tears welled in her eyes, but she raised her head with dignity. "It's my fault. My problem. I just can't do this."

Slade watched her walk out the door. His mouth suddenly dry, he focused his attention on the floor. He couldn't believe Laurie was leaving. He'd never see her again. His whole body felt empty. Numb. He sank into Hank's office chair because his legs could no longer support him.

"You're too closed up, Slade," Kelsey had told him. "No one knows what you're thinking. You can't expect to succeed in any relationship if you don't open up to people."

He struggled to find his breath. *Kelsey.* The annoying sister who told him what to do. Scolded him. Treated him like a mother even though they were born only minutes apart.

For an odd reason, he wanted to talk to Kelsey. She couldn't make things right, but Kelsey was familiar. And he needed familiar at the moment.

With a heavy heart, Slade stood and crossed the floor to the landline phone posted on the wall. Using the rotary dial, he dialed his home number. It was after six back in Kentucky. Maybe Kelsey would be home.

"Hello."

"Kelsey?"

"Slade, what's wrong?"

How did she know? Did his voice project his sudden grief and anger with himself? If only he'd kept his hands off Laurie and not caved to impulse.

"Did you hear about Pete?" He tried to deflect Kelsey's curiosity.

"Pete?"

"Yeah, Leo's old wrangler. He's been at the ranch for years."

He heard Kelsey draw a breath. "No, I haven't heard about him."

"He died last night. Fell from a hay loft."

Kelsey gasped. "That's terrible!"

"Yeah. Leo is taking it hard." Slade rubbed his jaw.

"I bet."

Silence between them.

"Slade, what's really wrong?"

He couldn't tell her because he knew what she'd say. *Tell her how you feel. Don't be a chicken.*

"Ah." Slade cleared his throat. "You know Pete was our uncle. Our half-uncle."

"Refresh me."

"When Mom came back from the ranch in March, she told us Pete revealed the name of her father, Tim Krebs. This Krebs was Pete's half-brother. They had the same mother or something."

"Okay. I remember."

"Laurie and I were going to ask him about it. See if he'd tell us more about our grandmother. Like why she committed suicide."

"Laurie?"

Of course, Kelsey would pick up on that.

"She's the girl you hired. The reporter."

"Okay." Kelsey paused. "Why is she interested? I thought she was supposed to be focusing on human interest articles, like that grizzly bear one."

"It's a long story, but she thinks her grandmother knew our grandmother. She's been helping me try to figure it out."

"I see."

Slade could almost hear the wheels turn in Kelsey's mind. "And with Pete gone, we're screwed," he said.

"Was it an accident?"

He cleared his throat. Of course, it was. "That's what the authorities said. Why?"

"Oh, I just wondered." He thought she shrugged. "You know me. I'm a worrier. His death sounds kind of convenient."

"What do you mean?"

"Nothing." She dismissed him. "Just wondered."

And that got him to thinking. Pete's death was a shock to them all, but Leo didn't believe it was an accident. And Kelsey had questions too, and she didn't even know the guy. Maybe he should do a little sleuthing. If his sister was here, she'd be the first one taking action.

She must have read his thoughts. "Hey, I'm heading your way in two days."

"So soon?"

"The breeding shed is shutting down, and we've got Justin to handle things here. He's a good manager."

"Does Mom know?"

"I'll call her." Another pause. "I miss you guys."

Did he miss Kelsey too? It had been liberating not having her around pestering him. But he did miss her. They were twins. There was a special bond between them.

"I miss you too, Sis," he finally said.

CHAPTER EIGHTEEN

LAURIE FLED TO HER CABIN, a tiny refuge from the harsh reality of the ranch. She shut the door and stood with her back against it catching her breath. What was wrong with her? Where was her cocky self-assurance? Why had she succumbed to the charms of a rich man's son?

It wouldn't work, whatever it was flaring between them. It hadn't worked for Mama Bev or her mother. Her family was doomed when it came to men. Her mother had told her often enough about her no-good father. And Bev? Well, she'd been alone as long as Kelsey knew her. Strong. Resourceful. Not needing a man.

That's how she wanted to be. Like Mama Bev. The death of her husband had probably given Bev that strength, just as it had made her mother weak. But she'd never know for sure now that her grandmother was dead and gone.

Tugging her rolling luggage from under the bed, she slung it onto the quilted spread. Unzipping the lid, she opened it. There wasn't much to fill it with. She hadn't brought many clothes with her to the ranch. Maybe she'd known she wouldn't stay long.

Her knees wobbled and gave way. She sank onto the side of the bed and sat there in numb silence.

She hadn't moved for many minutes when someone knocked on her door. Laurie shook herself out of her stupor. Slade? Had he come to tell her…what? She didn't want him to tell her what she'd seen in his eyes. What she guessed was in his heart.

"Laurie? Are you home?"

Darby. Laurie sprang to her feet. "Yes, ma'am."

She opened the door a crack, hoping her boss wouldn't see the suitcase spread out on her bed. It had grown dark during the time she'd sat motionless. The older woman stood on the porch with her red hair reflected by the automated light over the door. Darby had kept her beauty although years of grief and guilt had plagued her. Laurie knew from her interview about her love for horses and painting. Now she understood her love of family and of the sad happiness she'd shared with her first husband. That she'd found her high school sweetheart again was truly heartwarming.

"Are you doing okay?"

Should she tell her Darby was leaving? It didn't seem right, but she needed a ride to the airport tomorrow. "I'm resting a little," she said.

Darby nodded. "I understand. This mountain air is often too thin for my bluegrass blood."

"I know." Laurie swallowed and offered a small smile.

"Well, I thought you might need to open this in private." Darby held out a red, white and blue cardboard envelope. "This priority mail was delivered to you today. I thought it might be something important."

"Yes, thank you." Laurie took the envelope from Darby and turned it over to see the address. *Chicago.*

Darby smiled and backed away from the door. "See you later at dinner, then."

Seeing Slade at dinner was the last thing she wanted. Laurie caught the door frame. "I don't think I'll be at dinner." Darby searched her face. "I'm not hungry."

"Fine. I'll tell Ellie."

"Thanks again."

"No problem."

Laurie softly shut the door. Heart in her throat, she sank once more onto the bed. Was her mother sick? She'd not heard from Debbie since she'd been at the ranch. She glanced at the return address. A law firm. It had to be news about her grandmother's estate. With nervous fingers, she pulled the perforated strip that opened the envelope.

Matthews, Elias and Lee Attorneys at Law

Dear Ms. Chastain:

Your grandmother Beverly Haven left this envelope in our custody with instructions to send it to you upon her death.

Kindest regards,

J.G. Matthews

A letter from her grandmother? She rubbed her forehead and took a few shaky breaths, suddenly feeling cold.

Time slowed to a crawl. She removed a legal-size sealed envelope from the priority outer sleeve and fingered it as if she could tell what was in it using psychic perception. But she couldn't. Fear slithered through her gut. She licked her suddenly dry lips.

Maybe her grandmother had left more money than what they'd found in her checking account. Maybe she wanted her to take care of her mother, as if Laurie wouldn't do that. She'd always watched out for her mom.

No need to put it off. Staring at the white envelope would give her no answers. *I know I can do this.*

Blowing out a deep breath, her cheeks puffing out and her mouth forming an "O," Laurie tore the envelope with her finger making a jagged opening lengthways.

Laurie, if you are reading this, then I am dead and gone. You're left alone to care for your mother now. I know you have always been at odds with her. She's not like you. You don't understand her. That's why I am writing this letter. I want you to understand it's not your mother's fault the way she is. It's mine.

~

I dearly loved your grandfather. I met Glen in high school. My parents thought he was no good. It's just that he'd been brought up differently from me. He wasn't middle class. His parents were old school communists. Activists. But their generation had failed.

Glen had big plans for the future. Change the world plans. It was the late 1960's and blacks were protesting their condition. Kids rioted in the streets. The Vietnam War was raging. Women burned bras. Everything was thrilling: the music, women's liberation, free love, drugs. He helped me leave home when I was eighteen. It was good. We joined a big revolutionary movement. It was up to the youth of America to fight the establishment. We wanted to destroy imperialism, form a classless society, create Utopia. Glen wore old Army fatigue jackets and blue denims. I let my hair grow long and wore free-flowing granny dresses. We wore sunglasses so no one would recognize us.

We joined a collective, shacking up at various houses with members of the group. Monogamy was frowned on, but Glen was faithful to me. To raise money, we got married, and I called my parents. They wired us three hundred dollars but told me never to call again. I didn't see them again for years. I was sad about that, but loyalty was required to the others in the collective, not my bourgeoisie family. The money my parents gave me went to the collective.

I tell you this to try to explain where my head was back then. I was in love. I had purpose. Life was exciting.

And then I got pregnant.

Glen loved Debbie, bless his heart. He said she was the best thing he'd ever done. But children were in the way. They were raised together in the collective. Not necessarily by their real mothers. I volunteered to keep the children as much as I could so that I could watch over Debbie. This worked a couple of years until all mothers with children were purged from the group.

Glen didn't let me go alone. He went with me, but something changed then between us. He became harder. I think he was disappointed. We went to San Francisco where all the action was.

Everyone was going underground, living hand to mouth, moving from house to house. It was easier at that time than now. There were no cell phones. No security cameras. No computers. We took public transportation and didn't own cars.

We found another collective. A small one made of members also purged from the bigger group. Tim ran it and his brother Pete. There were other women. A sixteen-year-old runaway, a high school dropout. They weren't monogamous. They slept around. I know Tim fathered several children. Tim was ruthless, dedicated to urban guerrilla activity. We all thought the country could be brought down only through armed struggle. We were delusional. Full of ourselves. Driven by our purpose.

Debbie grew up in this atmosphere, clinging to her dolls, with no playmates and no early schooling. She stayed in whatever house we were living in, hanging around all day, usually alone. I went to work and left her by herself. It was there she became insecure. Afraid. It was my fault, and I regret it to this day.

Under Tim's leadership, the collective became violent. If necessary, we agreed to kill or die in the effort. That's when Pete went away. The violence wasn't for him. So, Tim and Glen were left with three of us women—me, Chelsea, Lisa—and of course, little Debbie.

Tim didn't like Debbie. He was often cruel to her. Glen and I protected her the best we could. I admit to having second thoughts about staying. But my parents had warned me not to come home, and I was still in love. Those are my only excuses. They aren't good ones.

When a policeman was killed because of our bombing, we knew we were in trouble. Chelsea had had Tim's baby, and he couldn't deal with the child. He wanted to get rid of Chelsea anyway. So, this screwup was a good *excuse to leave. Glen stole an old station wagon and all of us packed into it and headed to Montana. Tim left Chelsea and the baby with his brother Pete. That's the last I saw with them. Lisa liked that, because she had Tim all to herself.*

We landed in Chicago. That's where we were when your grandfather tried making a pipe bomb by himself. It blew up in his face. Debbie and I were left alone.

I then did the hardest thing in my life—I took Debbie and went home. My parents didn't welcome me at first, but when they saw Debbie, they changed their minds. We lived with them while I went to school. It was hard. My parents were angry, but Debbie had a better life. Schooling. Friends. Material wealth. But her personality was already damaged thanks to all those years in the collective.

When you become angry with your mother, please remember this. She's not to blame for her weakness. She's this way because of her early life and my blind love and naiveté.

Take care of yourself, Laurie. You are the daughter I would have loved to have. As it is, I am so proud you are my granddaughter. Don't be afraid to love. Your mother doesn't know how. She doesn't trust men. But don't be like her. Be yourself. You're strong and smart. Your life doesn't need to follow your mother's pattern. Or mine.

I did love your grandfather until I learned I needed to depend upon myself too. I was my own person, and I didn't need to follow him blindly. Of course, it took his death for me to realize it.

Please, don't let my mistakes influence the way you live your life.

I love you.

Mama Bev

LAURIE HAD GONE COMPLETELY STILL. She drew her eyebrows together as she tried to understand what she'd just read. What was Mama Bev saying? Her mother's problems started long before her father came into the picture, and he deserted his family. She was broken as a child.

This life Bev had 'fessed up to sort of made sense. Her grandmother was a person of strong convictions. She loved deeply. Laurie could understand a younger Bev being swept up in a cause, controlled by her passion for a man.

She didn't want to be like that. She wanted no man to control her. But maybe she could find a happy medium.

Her thoughts swirled so quickly she could hardly follow them. Glancing down at the letter, she ran her finger over the type and reading again the information about the collective. Now she knew it didn't matter what she had wanted to ask Pete. From the grave, her grandmother had given her answers.

Please, don't let my mistakes influence the way you live your life.

Her stomach fluttered. Maybe she didn't need to leave the ranch just yet. Maybe she didn't need to run away from her feelings any longer.

She needed to find Slade and tell him.

CHAPTER NINETEEN

KELSEY WOULD BE the first one taking action. The thought spun in Slade's head. He hung up the telephone and took a deep breath. What if Pete's death wasn't an accident? Had they been too quick to take the word of the authorities?

But how would he find out? He shook his head not knowing what he could do. He wasn't a private investigator. He had no tools like the police. Taking up his hat, he set it firmly on his head and left the office. The sun was settling behind a far mountain. Soon it would be dark. He didn't care. Making long strides, he headed toward the barn.

The lights were on. The barn smelled of hay and horse and manure. He walked the aisleway, stopped, and searched the empty stall where Pete was found. What was he looking for? He had no idea.

The accident started in the hay loft. Slade glanced over his head. The loft stretched the length of the barn partially covering the stalls. Bales of hay were stored along the pathway and flakes were dropped into the stall from above, each horse getting the appropriate amount of forage. There wasn't much room to walk when the loft was filled with hay.

Slade touched the ladder and looked up. Wiping his clammy hands on his jeans, he held his breath. Could he do this? Grasping the rung over his head, he placed his boot on the lowest one. *A step at a time.* He used to have no problem climbing on the jungle gym his father installed for Kelsey and him in the back yard. He'd scale the bars to the top and sit there looking over the backyard and the horses in the pasture. Then he had jumped from the hay loft and broke his leg.

It wasn't going to happen now. He needed to do this if only to prove to himself he could.

Reaching the top of the ladder, Slade stepped onto the wooden floor. The roof was tall enough for him to stand upright. No problem with that. But what was he looking for? He scanned the immediate area. Nothing unusual. He walked the path over the stalls. It felt like a tightrope. Refusing to look down, he tried to keep his breathing slow. Deliberate.

The barn door suddenly opened. He flinched at the noise. Finn scampered down the aisleway below, and Jeremiah came in leading a horse. How would he explain himself? He couldn't. He didn't want to try. Slipping behind a stack of hay, he crouched down, pulled off his hat and held his breath.

Whistling, Jeremiah took his sweet time putting his horse away. Slade sat back on his butt and hugged his knees. As he waited what seemed like forever, he glanced up. What the heck? Caught in a wooden splinter above his head was a strand of long, blond hair. He chewed his lip and stared at it.

"Have you seen Slade?"

Laurie. What was she doing here?

"I've checked his cabin," she said. "He wasn't there."

"I'm not his keeper." Jeremiah sounded irritated. "He finished his work an hour ago."

"Thanks." Was Laurie turning to leave?

"Maybe a bear ate him," Jeremiah scoffed.

"That's not funny!"

"No, I guess not. He'd give the bear indigestion."

"You're a jerk, Jeremiah."

The cowboy laughed. "And you, little lady, are a real bitch."

Slade jumped to his feet, ready to defend her. He couldn't be seen behind the hay. He'd have to step around the stack, but Laurie didn't need his help.

"I suppose you consider every woman who turns you down a bitch."

"You got that right. C'mon, Finn. Let's get the hell outta here."

Slade's heartbeat sped up. He rubbed his forehead with the heel of his free hand. Laurie had turned away Jeremiah's advances. What did that mean?

"Jerk," Laurie muttered.

He came around the stack of hay to find Laurie right below him near the stall where they'd found Pete. Looking down made him dizzy, but he fought it.

"Laurie."

She glanced around appearing confused.

"Look up."

She glanced up. Her face reddened when she saw him. "Slade Heston, what are you doing up there?"

"Climb up the ladder. I want to show you something." He offered a grin as he spoke.

When she reached the loft and stood up, Slade caught her upper arms to steady her. They stood together like that, searching each other's eyes. He wanted to pull her into his arms. Why had she come looking for him? Could something have changed? Would she stay?

"Why are you hiding in the hay loft?"

He gestured toward the stack of hay bales. "I'm doing a little sleuthing."

"Why?"

He drew a breath to calm his racing heart. "How do we know Pete's fall was an accident?"

"That's what we were told."

"I know." He moved back to give her room. "I'm no detective, but I thought I'd come up here to see if anything looked off. I found something."

She stiffened. "You did?"

Dropping her arms, he stepped away. "Look at how these hay bales are stacked. I stood up behind them, and you didn't see me."

"Like someone used them for hiding?"

"That's right."

Laurie walked over to the stack and examined them. "It doesn't prove anything."

"I know but look at this." Slade pointed to the lock of blond hair caught in the splinter of wood.

She chewed her lip. "What does that mean?"

"I have no clue," he said. "I thought it strange."

"It's woman's hair because it's so long." She looked back at him, her eyebrows drawn together. "Only Ellie and I have blond hair. And I wasn't up here."

"I know."

"This doesn't prove anything," she said again. "Even if we could test its DNA, it wouldn't prove anything."

He sagged against the wall, feeling hopeless. "But it makes one wonder."

IT DID MAKE HER WONDER. Ellie wasn't her favorite, but that didn't mean she was a murderer.

Laurie rubbed her chin. "Could she and Pete have fought up here?"

"Ellie didn't say anything about a fight. In fact, she acted surprised at his death."

Studying the setup of the hay near this particular stall, it did look different from the other ones above other stalls that were pushed against the wall. And Ellie had no business in the barn. "Could she have pushed Pete?"

"But why?" Slade frowned, looking troubled. "Makes no sense."

"Makes perfect sense if there's now one less person to share in Leo's inheritance."

He sucked in a breath. "That's a perfect reason."

"But we can't prove it." Her words echoed through the quiet barn. They troubled her.

"I know." His frown eased slightly. "I'm not even sure we should tell Hank. We'd sound paranoid."

"Unless we find more evidence."

"Circumstantial evidence, don't you mean? That's all we have. We're not detectives."

He was close enough that she could feel his breath against her cheek and sense his angry frustration. She had searched for him to tell him... what? That she loved him? No way! She wasn't going to admit that. Not yet. But telling him she'd had a change of heart and wasn't leaving was safe enough. Maybe she'd even share the contents of her grandmother's letter. After all, she now had a few answers about the past.

Forcing her gaze away from his eyes, Laurie stared at his calloused hands clutching the cowboy hat.

"Were you looking for me?" His voice was gentle, almost pleading as if he wanted her to be seeking him.

"Yes." All the words she wanted to say caught in her throat. "I want to show you something, but not here. This place gives me the creeps."

CHAPTER TWENTY

You're too closed up, Slade. No one knows what you're thinking. You can't expect to succeed in any relationship if you don't open up to people.

Silently, they walked the path from the barn toward the dining hall. Slade felt as if he was walking through a tunnel, long and dark. Only a few distant security lights illuminated the blackness. Rain must be on its way because the multitude of stars that lit a clear Montana night had disappeared.

Reaching the bridge across Saga Creek, he grabbed Laurie's hand and pulled her close. She came willingly, surprising him. *Love demands risk.* His thoughts exploded in his head. It was now or never. The darkness made it easier. Taking her by the shoulders, he forced her to look at him.

"I want to tell you something, Laurie." His voice was engulfed by the stillness of the night.

"Yes?"

Did she sound eager? He couldn't tell. Leaning forward, he ran his hands over her face, feeling the softness of her skin and the contours of her jaw.

"I don't want you to leave," he whispered.

She reached for him, clutching his shirt. "I don't plan to leave. Not until fall, anyway."

"You don't?" Dare he hope? He swallowed his excitement. "I'm glad."

"Me too." She sounded breathless. "But why don't you want me to leave?"

Was she prodding him? What did she want? In their brief time together, she'd worked her way into his heart. He must tell her. He couldn't chicken out now.

"Because I love you."

Silence hugged them, just as the blackness of the night. The frantic thud of his pulse pounded in his ears. He'd done it. He'd told her how he felt.

She hesitated. She drew a deep breath. In the darkness, she searched his face. Would she laugh at him? Tell him he was a jerk like she'd told Jeremiah? He wouldn't be able to handle that. Not from her. Not after he'd drawn on his courage and taken a risk.

"I love you too, Slade," she said in a soft voice. "I don't know what will come of it, but I couldn't leave without you knowing."

He caught the back of her head and crushed her mouth to his in a prolonged, devouring kiss. She returned his passion just as she'd done earlier. The first drops of rain surrounded them, slow at first and then in a steady downpour, increasing just as desire raged through him. He wanted to respect her and not give in to the desire. He told himself *a kiss is enough.*

"We're getting wet."

"You think?" he murmured against her mouth.

"Let's go to my cabin."

Was this an invitation? He wanted more than a one-night stand. He wanted her to invite him into her life. "Are you sure?"

"As sure as I've ever been," she said and grabbed his hand. "Let's run!"

They fled over the bridge and stumbled and laughed all the way to Laurie's cabin where one table lamp illuminated the darkness and welcomed them.

～

THE MATTRESS SHIFTED as Laurie sat up. The musky scent of a night of lovemaking filled her senses. She felt satiated. Complete.

Slade touched her shoulder. "Don't go."

She glanced back at him and laughed. "Have you forgotten we have work to do?"

"The heck with work."

"Sounds like a rich boy."

His lips pressed tight into a grimace.

"Silly, I'm joking." She kissed him quickly and, before he could reach for her, scooted off the bed and stood up.

His gaze raked her naked body. "I could get used to this."

"I bet you could." Her skin seemed to tingle. Slipping on a sweatshirt, Laurie snatched her grandmother's letter and crawled back into bed. "I want you to read this. My grandmother sent it to me through her lawyer."

His eyes questioned her, but he pushed himself up into a sitting position against the backboard and covered himself with the rumpled sheet.

"I think we should show this to your mother. It explains a lot." Laurie handed him the typed paper.

As he read, she tore her gaze away from his handsome face and focused her attention on the floor. She moistened her lips. What would he think?

"Please, don't let my mistakes influence the way you live your life." His voice was rich and low. "Is this why you decided to stay?"

Unfamiliar emotions clawed at her. She looked back at him and touched the naked planes of his chest. "Yes. Mama Bev's letter explained what we wanted to learn from Pete. Because of the letter,

I came to understand the past has a way of influencing our lives, even if it wasn't our own past."

"Like my mother's."

"She's the little girl in the letter. She needs to know where she came from, just like I did."

"But there's more to it."

This wasn't like her to admit her feelings. Her gut clenched, and for a heartbeat, she felt like a three-year-old child. Scared. Uncertain. She swallowed hard.

"You're right," she said. "I've avoided falling in love, but there's something about you."

He grinned. "It's the magic of the mountains."

She cocked her head. "Could be, but I think I finally understood when you first told me. When you said you loved me, I knew I couldn't deny it any longer."

Slade took her face in his hands. "We have a whole summer to figure this out, don't we?"

"Yes." She was breathless. His breath hitched, and he dipped his head, taking her lips with a feverish kiss.

With a muffled moan of defeat, she sank into his arms, and the workday was forgotten.

The End

KELSEY

CHAPTER ONE

Winnetka, Illinois
July 2017

SHE WAS DEAD. Claire was dead.

That's all Max Lee knew. His wife of one year was dead.

Sweat from the humid Chicago night trickled down his back, chilling him. Why had this happened? His brain scrambled for a logical reason.

A flashing phalanx of police cars surrounded his house. It was on a corner lot, and the harsh, revolving lights on two sides of the house cast beacons of horror into the summer darkness. Crime scene tape stretched around the perimeter of the gray Victorian blocking his access to the front and side doors. He stood on the sidewalk and crossed his arms over his chest. How could he ease the feeling of numbness that seeped through his veins?

"You don't want to see her," one policeman had told him. "It's not a pretty sight."

"No. No. Of course not." His mouth had gone so dry it had been hard to talk.

"Where were you tonight, Mr. Lee?" another cop had asked.

"Working." Dear God, it was ten-thirty. Would the man believe him?

"I suppose you can prove it."

"I was the only one in the office." Beads of sweat peppered his upper lip. How did people on television crime shows prove their innocence? "I suppose there are outside cameras, and maybe a record when I left the parking garage."

"We'll check."

Of course, the police would check. But he didn't kill Claire. He had nothing to do with it, even though he often regretted marrying her. They'd been friends since playpen days. His parents and Claire's were best friends. Their fathers were partners in the same law firm, the firm Max had entered out of law school. Their marriage had been expected, planned for, and celebrated by both families, and he'd not had the guts to break it off.

Thoughts of self-loathing filled his head. Claire had deserved a better husband. One who truly loved her. But she hadn't known the difference. She was in love with him. She was in love with being the good wife and keeping house—the eighty-thousand-dollar house her parents had given them for a wedding present. She'd wanted children.

All that was gone now. His heart felt hollow from sorrow and debilitating guilt. He should have done better by Claire.

"I heard, Max." His father Robert Lee laid a comforting hand on his shoulder. He must have driven over from his home in Highland Park. "This is horrible."

Max reached up and covered his father's hand with his. "Thanks, Dad, for coming."

"Do you know what happened?"

"The police said it was a robbery." He lowered his voice. His breath burst in and out of his lungs. "Claire must have surprised them when she came down the back steps from the master."

"Where were you?"

"At work."

That was one thing his father could understand. He'd spent the years of Max's childhood away from home always at work. Yet, work wasn't a good excuse for Max. He didn't like being a lawyer. He'd gone to the University of Kentucky, thinking he could get away, only to come back home to law school in Chicago.

He couldn't leave the firm now. Not when he was expected to carry on the family tradition. Not with the only child of one of the partners dead. If anything, his guilt would force him to stay. That and a misplaced sense of duty he'd had all his life.

CHAPTER TWO

Ghost Mountain Ranch, Montana
June 2019 - Sunday

SHE HAD her work cut out for her.

Kelsey Heston leaned back in the office chair and stared at the dusty pile of files on the desk. They were stacked around her laptop in a jumbled mess. How did anyone get along without computer automation these days? It's no wonder her grandfather's dude ranch lacked guests and apparently bled money. With organization and the right publicity, she knew she could change things. She'd only been in Montana one night and a day, but she was determined the Ghost Mountain Ranch would be successful by the end of the summer.

It was a good thing she'd come west to help her family.

Yet, it was hard to buckle down to the task at hand. She had a headache, her mother said from altitude sickness. The ranch was at five thousand feet and the distant, snow-topped mountains rose thousands of feet higher.

She stood up and gazed out the window. The ranch was different from her father's horse farm. Yet, the picturesque, mountain-ringed valley, a far cry from the rolling bluegrass hills of home, still took her breath away. Not fancy like the white board fencing and stone barns with large box stalls and padded aisles to protect the horses' hooves that she was used to. Lodge-pole pine log cabins and barns flanked both sides of Saga Creek that cut through the valley, separating two mountain peaks. And during the day, the horses were not turned out into pristine pastures. They were herded into paddocks made of rough-hewn logs to graze on hay rolls unless they carried dudes on mountain trail rides. At night, most of the horses were driven to a mountain meadow and allowed to run free. The change fascinated her.

No wonder her twin brother had fallen in love in such a place.

As if thinking about him conjured him up, Slade Heston shoved open the office door and entered with a chill wind. He wore a tan cowboy hat and a black vest over his red flannel shirt. When he pulled off his hat and held it loosely in his hands, his black hair was shaggy. He looked different. More relaxed but, in a strange way, toughened up with his short beard.

"I was just thinking about you, and here you are." She turned to greet him, not a bit surprised to see him. They were twins, weren't they? This kind of thing often happened between them.

"Laurie and I wanted to talk to you alone." His voice was low and furtive.

"What about?"

"We thought you need to know what's been going on at the ranch, and we want to fill you in about our family history."

What was Slade up to? Was this more than the recent revelation about their grandmother, who apparently had some sort of criminal past, and the fact Leo York had adopted their mother and was not their real grandfather?

Kelsey brushed a strand of hair away from her face. "Sounds like a mystery."

"What we've learned fills in the missing details."

"Well, where is Laurie?"

"She's on her way. I hope you like her, Kelsey."

Kelsey hoped she did too. Right now, the jury was out. She'd hired Laurie Chastain after she'd written an article about her mother's art show to write favorable articles about the dude ranch while she worked the summer season as a housekeeper. So far, Laurie had only produced one article about grizzly bear safety. It was a nice effort, but she hadn't written another. Kelsey supposed Slade had taken up most of her time. Maybe with the arrival of the first guests today would inspire an increase in productivity.

"I want to marry her someday," Slade said when Kelsey didn't reply.

Opening her mouth to protest, she shut it quickly feeling her stomach harden. *You haven't known her that long. You should take things slow.* She wouldn't say that. It was something her mother might say, but even though Kelsey had mothered her brother all their lives, Slade was grown up now. Besides, it was obvious he'd already slept with Laurie. He was living in her one-room cabin.

The door opened, and Laurie entered. Slade dropped his hat on a side table, caught her by her upper arms, and kissed her forehead. She blushed and cast a shy glance at Kelsey.

Turning away to hide her turmoil of mixed feelings, Kelsey gathered up the files she'd piled on the straight-back, visitor's chair and made room for them next to her laptop. "Have a seat."

Laurie took the chair, and Slade stood behind her. Laurie was a pretty blonde, much like herself. But Kelsey was taller and had that slender, curvy model quality she'd always been uncomfortable with. In fact, her good looks had often been the catalyst that drove her to accomplish more, to be more, to do more. Kelsey didn't want to just be a pretty face.

She sat down behind the desk, supporting her arms on the chair rests. "What's going on?"

"How do we start?" Laurie looked up at Slade behind her. She seemed to have a special bond with him, like the one Kelsey cherished.

"With our grandparents," he said. "Tell her about them."

"My grandmother died recently. Her lawyer sent me a long letter last week that my grandmother had written for me several years ago to explain her past. I think she wrote it to help me understand my mother's childhood." Laurie paused and drew a breath. "But it's about your family too. Our grandmothers knew each other."

A bizarre story unfolded about domestic terrorists from the nineteen-seventies. Their mother's mother called herself Chelsea Clemmons, a pseudonym. She was part of a collective that bombed a police station and killed a policeman. During that time, their mother Darby had been born to Chelsea out of wedlock. Darby's father was a radical hippie named Tim Krebs. Laurie's grandparents had also been in the same collective. They'd gone on the run after the bombing, dropping Chelsea and her baby at Ghost Mountain Ranch with Tim's half-brother Pete Harden. Later, Laurie's grandfather had blown himself up while trying to make a bomb, and her grandmother had taken her child, Laurie's mother, home to live with her parents.

Kelsey touched the base of her neck, her mind racing. "So that's how Mom got to the ranch."

"Yes." Slade seemed to have trouble finding the right words. "Then Leo married our grandmother, adopted, and raised our mother."

"Darby knew her mother's name was Sarah," Laurie filled in, "but she never knew about her mother's past or her maiden name."

"And we still don't know who our grandmother was." Slade shifted his weight and gripped the back of the chair. "Where she came from. Why she got caught up in that radical collective."

For thirty years Darby had not returned to the ranch after she'd run away. She'd met and married their father in Kentucky. Kelsey had always known her mother had a troubled past. "I thought she left because she felt guilty her mother committed suicide."

"True," Slade said, "that was a big part of it."

"Tell her what Pete told Hank," Laurie urged.

"Pete said our grandmother might not have committed suicide."

"What?" Hank was her mother's high school sweetheart. They'd found each other again after all these years. He was the main reason she'd chosen to remain in Montana. "So, she had an accident."

Laurie's voice dropped. "Or was murdered."

A flush of adrenalin tingled through Kelsey's body. "Murdered?"

Slade shrugged and took a deep breath. "We'll never know. Pete died before we could ask him."

"You told me about Pete's accident."

Slade's face looked grim. "We think he might have been murdered too—pushed from the hay loft where he broke his neck."

"But we can't prove it," Laurie asserted. "Although we did find a strand of blond hair stuck in a splinter up in the hay loft that seemed suspicious."

"And the only person with blond hair at the ranch at that time besides Laurie was Ellie, Leo's caretaker and the ranch cook. Of course, we have no way of knowing how long the hair was there or even if it is Ellie's."

Kelsey's breath caught. She studied Laurie for a moment. "What motive would Ellie have to kill Pete?"

"A big one," Slade said. "Leo changed his will to give the ranch to Hank, Ellie, and Pete. With Pete gone, there's just she and Hank left to inherit."

"Good grief!" A slight shiver went down her spine. "What does Mom know?"

"I showed Darby my grandmother's letter."

"But we haven't told her what we suspect about her mother. What if she didn't commit suicide?" Slade bit his lower lip. "We don't want to tell her anything until we know for sure."

"And we haven't mentioned our suspicions about Pete," Laurie said.

"Maybe she doesn't need to know." Slade looked worried. "I thought we'd get your opinion."

"Um." Kelsey suddenly felt hot. They were talking about two murders—one now and one in the past. "This is a lot to digest. Maybe we should get more proof about our grandmother."

"Leo told me he stored old records up in the attic." Slade lifted his gaze to the trapdoor in the ceiling that appeared to be an access to the attic. "Laurie and I just haven't had time to find them."

"What could be up there?"

"We don't know," Laurie said with a sigh. "Old files. Hopefully, some sort of a clue."

Kelsey waved her hand over the paperwork on her desk. "You can see I have my work cut out for me here first."

"Whatever you can do will help. I'm afraid we're at a standstill." Laurie looked overwhelmed. "We're not detectives, and we don't think we should accuse Ellie of anything, like you said, without proof."

"I agree about Ellie." Kelsey rubbed her chin. If she helped Slade, maybe she wouldn't feel that ugly pang of jealousy about Laurie. She and Slade might be twins, but they had separate lives. They were adults. They couldn't be tied together forever. "When I get a chance, I'll see what I can find in the attic."

"Thanks, Kelsey."

The cast iron dinner bell at the dining halls clanged loudly, calling everyone to eat.

Laurie stood up. "Lunch time."

Slade gathered his hat and placed it squarely on his head. "Leo doesn't like anyone to be late to meals."

"I'll be right along." Kelsey surveyed the stack of files. She needed time to think. They'd dumped a lot of stuff on her in a short time, and she didn't know how to process it.

Had coming to the Ghost Mountain Ranch been a blunder? Had she walked into a decades old murder mystery with the participants now dead? Or perhaps something more dangerous?

CHAPTER THREE

KELSEY HAD LOVED the two cozy dining halls from the moment of her first meal at the ranch. They were parallel log buildings with a dogtrot kitchen joining them at one end, making the whole structure seem U-shaped. On the right, with windows facing the gravel road, the ranch staff had a gathering spot, a place to unwind and eat. The left dining hall was for the guests. These halls were the only places on the ranch with WIFI, except for the office.

Her stomach growled when she entered the room. Heavenly smells drifted in the air. She hadn't realized how hungry she was. Exposed timbers in the ceiling gave the crew dining hall a rustic, Wild West look. Comfy, worn, leather sofas and chairs faced a fireplace and hearth built from creek stone. A rack of antlers on the wall was the resting spot for a couple of cowboy hats. There was one long dining table in the middle of the room and a sideboard against the wall laden with platters of sandwiches and a tureen of vegetable soup.

Staffed for the summer season, the room was full of energy, loud chatter, and laughter. Dishes clattered and two bearded men served themselves from the sideboard. Many of the staff were young and had answered ads in a dude ranch magazine. This was the first meal where everyone had gathered together.

Kelsey crossed the wide plank floor, acknowledged several hellos, bent down over her grandfather sitting at the head of the table, and kissed his forehead. "Granddad."

He reached up a gnarled hand and patted her cheek. "I'm glad you're here."

"I'm glad too."

So what if he wasn't her real grandfather. Since she'd never known another one, Leo York suited her just fine. She lifted a plate from the sideboard, picked up a ham sandwich and a bowl of soup.

Slade motioned toward her. "Have a seat."

Scooting up to the table between Hank and her brother, Kelsey cast Slade a furtive glance. He lifted an eyebrow in recognition of their recent conversation. If the old wrangler Pete was murdered, had Ellie really done it?

Ellie sat across the table and next to Kelsey's grandfather. She had a generous bust and long blond hair with streaks of gray. She wasn't beautiful, but not bad looking either, in spite of her being what Kelsey might consider *hefty*. Leo certainly seemed to dote on her. Kelsey observed him pat her hand and let her serve him.

The only other people in residence at the time of Pete's death besides her brother and Laurie were her mom and Hank, and a wrangler named Jeremiah. She took a bite of the sandwich and lifted her gaze toward the black-haired wrangler with the handlebar mustache. Jeremiah winked at her, and she almost choked swallowing the bite.

"Don't mess with my sister, Jeremiah." Slade's sudden warning surprised her.

The wrangler answered with a wry smile. "She looks like a woman who can take care of herself, Heston."

"Thanks for the vote of confidence." Kelsey cocked her head, and simply to irritate Slade, she smiled across the table.

Hank quickly cleared his throat, pushed back his chair, and

stood. "We want to welcome everyone to Ghost Mountain Ranch for the season. Let's introduce ourselves. I'm Hank Slade, ranch foreman and head wrangler."

Kelsey followed the introductions, trying to memorize names of the other young people. Across the table next to Jeremiah sat two younger wranglers, the bearded ones Chris and Jacob. They cared for the horses and led riding tours into the mountains. John was an experienced ranch hand hired to help Slade, who had no practical experience working on a ranch at all. Samantha, called Sam, was a floater with many jobs—the nanny if needed, waitress, or a second housekeeper. Tristan was a server and dishwasher, and Shawn was the executive chef, relieving Ellie of all her cooking duties for the summer.

"Our guests arrive this afternoon. Check-in time is three o'clock," Hank said. "Let's make sure everyone feels welcome. This is a guest ranch with emphasis on the word *guest*. The visitors are here to get away from everyday life and have a good time. They're the reason we're here for the summer. It's our job to make them happy."

After lunch, Kelsey walked outside and stood on the covered porch. A fine rain misted the air. Across the creek and beyond the barns, Ghost Mountain loomed over the valley. She shuddered because of the mountain's sinister reputation. Was it haunted as Leo had told her when she first arrived?

The old-timers say it got its name because of an Indian legend. A tribe of the Shoshone called the Sheepeaters lived in the high mountains around here. They say an Indian maid threw herself from the lookout over Saga Creek because her lover did not return from a hunt. Some say they've seen her ghost walking the trail to the overlook.

Or was speculation about Pete's death and the doubt thrown on her grandmother's suicide the cause of her creepy feeling?

Taking a deep breath of the thin, misty air, Kelsey let its chill seep into her being. Her job this summer was critical to the future of her grandfather's dude ranch. She didn't have time for murder mysteries. If she didn't get the guest records automated and make the finances easier to track, after seventy years, this ranch could fail.

Darby joined her. Her mother was slim for her forty-nine years with an abundance of red hair that Kelsey had always loved. She also admired her mother's skills with a paintbrush. Darby was a talented artist, something Kelsey could never be.

"You were mighty quiet after that war of words with Jeremiah," her mom said.

"What's with Slade, anyway? I can take care of myself."

"I know, but he and Jeremiah had a thing recently," Darby paused, "over Laurie."

Kelsey had to smile. "That figures." She could understand how possessive Slade might be over the right woman.

"I get the feeling something else is bothering you, baby. Is it your brother's new girlfriend?" Her mother was super-intuitive when it came to her children.

Kelsey shrugged. "That's part of it, I guess. He told me he wanted to marry her."

"Ah, that's what I thought."

"Don't tell him I told you."

Darby laughed. "My lips are sealed." She pretended to zip her mouth.

"But there's more." Kelsey didn't know how to broach the subject of her grandmother's past, and she wasn't sure she should mention Pete's death since his supposed murder was simply guess-work. She couldn't confide in her mother. Not yet. "I was just thinking about the work ahead of me. You're right, Mom. Grand-dad's files are a mess."

Darby shook her head. "My mother used to keep good records, but after she died, I guess Leo didn't bother."

"I suppose." She didn't want to be too critical. That he hadn't bother was blatantly obvious.

Her mom draped an arm around her shoulder. "Isn't this place beautiful? I never get tired of gazing across the valley and seeing the mountains." Kelsey leaned into her mother's embrace. "Promise me you won't stay cooped up in that office the whole summer. This ranch is too magnificent to miss."

"I promise."

They stood together a long moment. Then Darby gave Kelsey a gentle squeeze. "Got to get to work."

Kelsey chewed her lower lip and watched her mother walk away. Could she keep that promise? Right now, she was unable to clear her mind of the difficult tasks at hand, not just Slade and Laurie's love affair. Their other story had landed on her like a granite boulder.

For the most part, city slickers came to the ranch to get away from urban life, but now she knew for sure her mother's mother had come to Montana to escape the law.

CHAPTER FOUR

THE HOUR-AND-HALF DRIVE from the Bozeman Yellowstone International Airport through Gallatin Canyon took Max Lee into another world of mountains and racing rivers and streams. Yet, his mind remained in Chicago dwelling on the pain and guilt that had overwhelmed his life for two years. It had been tough. Even today, he was coiled tightly, vibrating with anxiety, still trying to do his duty.

"You need a break," his former father-in-law Randall Matthews had said. "I'm afraid I'm going to lose you too."

"I'm okay, sir." He'd tried to cover up his angst, but Randy Jr. had become more perceptive since his daughter's death and saw right through him.

"No, you're not." Randy dropped his head and studied his hands clasped together on the polished mahogany office desk. "We both aren't."

His wife Julie had committed suicide a year ago. She'd never recovered from Claire's death. Now Randy carried an extra burden but continued to come into the office, managing the law firm as if it were his lifeline.

"You're a young man, Max. You should marry again."

"I can't."

"I understand." Randy stood up and turned toward the bank of windows overlooking Lake Michigan. "But you can get away for a while. Take stock of things. Decide what you really want to do with your life."

The senior partner spun around before Max could protest. Raising his hand to silence him, Randy then shoved a manila file folder across the desk toward him.

"I have a job for you to do. Take two weeks. I've booked a stay for you at a dude ranch. It's in Montana."

And that's how Max had found himself following his GPS and turning right off the main highway, down a dirt road, and under a sign reading Ghost Mountain Ranch. The place was a throwback into another century with rustic cabins and outbuildings. The ranch looked deserted except for a lone black and white dog, horses watching him over a pole fence, and a couple of saddled horses tied to an old-fashioned hitching post straight from a Western movie.

He spotted a sign saying *Office* and took the V in the road to the left, parking his rented SUV next to a small log cabin. He knocked and pushed the door open. A shaft of sunlight pierced the dirt caked window, obscuring the fine details of the room.

He could make out a large, battered, wood desk, an old metal file cabinet in the corner next to a window, and a cowhide rug covering part of the floor. The walls were bare except for a few faded photographs of horses and cowboys.

He squinted his eyes to focus on the figure behind the desk. "My name is Max Lee," he said to the blond woman sitting in a captain's chair. "I'm a day late. I'm sorry, but I couldn't get a plane out of O'Hare until today."

The office worker sprang to her feet, rested the palms of her hands on the desktop and stared at him for a long moment. She took a breath and exhaled loudly. "What the hell are you doing here, Max?"

~

HE WENT RIGID. A long silence passed. Old anger surged through Kelsey, still powerful enough to make her mouth tighten. She stood erect, squaring her shoulders.

"I asked you a question."

He lifted his chin, that haughty chin with the slight cleft. "I have a reservation." The door banged shut behind him. "And I might ask you the same thing. What are you doing here? The last time I saw you, Kelsey, you were standing outside your dorm at UK. This is a long way from Kentucky."

Her knees wobbled, and she sank into her chair with the desk protecting her. "If I remember correctly, you had just dumped me."

"That's right."

What had she seen in this guy anyway? He'd been a senior, and she a freshman. Their age difference wasn't their only difference. At the time, she'd wanted one thing—marriage—but he'd had other ideas.

"Did you get what you wanted, or should I say, what your family wanted?" She couldn't keep the bitterness out of her voice.

"I did."

He didn't elaborate. He simply surveyed her across the desk, filling the room with his dazzling energy and raking his blue-eyed gaze over her with a smugness she hated. He was slender with the stamp of elegance on his face. His brown hair was carefully trimmed and his Western clothes crisp and new. He seemed arrogantly at ease.

"I thought you'd be running your father's horse farm by now."

She didn't owe him an explanation. "I am," she said anyway. "But this summer I'm helping out at my grandfather's ranch."

He looked surprised and took a step forward toward the desk. "Leo York is your grandfather?"

"Yes." He didn't need a full explanation.

"That's interesting."

What was her relationship to Leo any business of his? Kelsey gave herself a mental shake and offered an insincere, tight-lipped smile. "I'm afraid you've missed the afternoon ride, but dinner is in thirty minutes. You have time to go to your cabin."

His face became a tight mask, but emotion darkened his eyes. "I don't plan to do any riding. I'm here to do some work without being bothered."

She went into her best hostess mode, sounding like her mother. "Well, we can't have that. You don't come to Montana to sit in your room." Standing, she pulled his reservation card from a file box, noted the location of the cabin, and took her jacket from the coat rack. "If you follow me, I'll show you to your cabin."

Slipping past him, she hit the bracing air outside and pulled a deep breath. No way was she getting into a car with him. She trudged away from the office, up the dirt road, toward cabin thirteen. His car followed slowly.

"I can't believe you're going home after graduation."

"I am. My parents have plans for me. Law school. The firm."

"And the senior partner's daughter?"

"Well, that too."

Kelsey had turned away fighting back tears. Max didn't need to see her cry.

"It's not fair to you, I know. I wanted to tell you earlier."

She had her pride. "That's nice of you."

"It's been good, Kelsey. I've loved our time together."

She couldn't face him. "Chock it up to a college fling. Thanks, Max for being so brave to tell me to my face."

He placed his hand on her shoulder. She wouldn't turn around. He'd see the tears in her eyes. Her red nose. She shook her shoulder free and stepped away.

"Best of luck." But she didn't mean it. She hoped he'd get run over by a garbage truck or something. Something big, heavy, and stinky. Anything to make him hurt as much as he had hurt her.

"I'm sorry, Kelsey."

"I bet." She strode away from him then without ever looking back. This part of her life was over. She'd never be as naïve again. Or as trusting. Or so in love.

How could she handle this new shock? How could she master the anger and unrequited love she'd buried six years ago that had resurfaced in a flash when he'd walked through the door?

Like she'd done before—with courage and resolve.

Hank and her mother had given her a job to do with the ranch records, and Slade and Laurie had dropped a mystery into her lap. That meant she didn't have the time or desire to resurrect a silly puppy love from freshman year.

MAX LET the screen door to his cabin bang shut and dropped his bag on a colorful rug on the floor by the hand-hewn log bed. *Kelsey Heston.* She was the ghost from his past. He took a deep, pained breath and closed his eyes.

He hated himself. No matter how together he acted, his insides weren't calm and collected. *Hell.* He was thrilled to see her again. She hadn't changed, just as beautiful as ever. As he remembered— all through his marriage to Claire.

His wife was dead and gone. He'd lied to her by not telling her about Kelsey. He'd wronged Kelsey too. His chin quivered. There was no point in reliving the past. He had to live with his guilt. Conquer it. Not let it stop him from doing his duty to Randy and the firm.

But a part of him rejoiced he didn't see a ring on her finger. Maybe, just maybe, Kelsey was still available.

CHAPTER FIVE

SHE WAS IN THE WAY, Kelsey knew, but she couldn't help herself. Drawn to Max no matter her best intentions, she stood at the kitchen door, hidden from the guests at the dining room tables. She didn't want him to know his arrival had astounded her, dredged up old memories she'd repressed but not completely buried. He remained as gorgeous as ever. As she remembered him. As she dreamed about him.

Yet, she couldn't forget he'd dumped her. Not with a *Dear John* letter or email. Instead, he'd had the courage to tell her to her face. Maybe that was something. Or maybe that made it worse because he had seen her cry.

You of all people should understand, Kelsey. Your father wants you to run his horse farm. Mine's the same way. He wants me to join his law firm when I am admitted to the bar.

She'd refused to beg him. But made a fool of herself crying. In the end, he'd simply left.

You have a duty to your family like I do. I can't let my love for you intervene.

Love? She hadn't believed him. How could he leave if he loved her? She'd blamed his father. And his stupid family pride. His sense of duty. His ultimate cowardice. She told herself something had been wrong with her that she couldn't keep him. That he'd dumped her and left.

Eventually, she'd pulled herself up by her own bootstraps and gone on with her life. She didn't need him. Didn't need any man. She had a horse farm to run. Her father depended upon her, because he certainly couldn't trust Slade, God love him, to do the job. Kelsey had the mind for numbers and organization. Slade twisted in the wind, unsure of himself and his place in life.

Then her father died last year, and her job became more important.

But through the years, she'd secretly kept up with Max, learning he'd married as his family planned. A friend from freshman year had called her when his wife was killed during a home invasion. Kelsey hadn't done anything about the news. He'd made his choice, hadn't he?

"If you're going to hang around, you might as well earn your keep," Chef Shawn grumbled, breathing down her neck. "Get out there and pick up dirty plates. Tristan can't keep up."

Everyone was expected to pitch in, because the kitchen and its staff were not yet a well-oiled machine. Shawn had produced his first three-course gourmet meal—tossed salad, grilled Moroccan chicken with rice and green beans, and white chocolate raspberry cheesecake—and Tristan dashed back and forth serving the plated desserts and filling water glasses.

Kelsey wasn't about to be accused of slacking. She scurried into the dining hall where guests, fresh off the first day of trail rides, chatted with each other. This dining room had the same kind of stone fireplace, but no cozy chairs or sofa. Five rugged, handmade wooden tables seating eight each filled the floor space. Indian blankets added color to the walls.

Max sat at the table nearest the kitchen with his back to the door. She chose the other side of the table.

"Are you finished?" she asked the first gentleman.

The man nodded, and Kelsey reached to take his plate.

"From the left side!"

She jerked up her head to find Shawn gesturing from the kitchen door and Max watching her across the table. She felt her face flush hot. "My bad."

She rushed around the guest's chair, bumping into it, and jarring the man. "Sorry."

Bending over, she scooped up his plate from the left, and went on to the next diner. When she'd collected five dirty plates, she headed back to the kitchen, avoiding eye contact with Max. Was he grinning? All she needed now was to drop these darn plates.

Jinx. At the kitchen door, Kelsey stubbed her toe, collided with Tristan, and lost her balance. The plates flew from her hands onto the floor making a tremendous crashing sound. Shawn's string of expletives didn't steady her nerves or ease her shame.

"I'm sorry." Kelsey suddenly felt lightheaded. She stooped down to pick up pieces of broken ceramic. Bits of left-over green beans and rice littered the floor.

"Let me help."

"No. I've got this."

Max squatted beside her. He collected shards of plates. The tension in the air between them sizzled like bonfire.

"Don't hurt yourself."

Anger rose inside her because she'd been caught making a fool of herself. "I don't intend to."

Tristan brought a trash can and placed it beside them. He leaned a broom and dustpan against the wall. Kelsey dumped her pieces into the can, then jumped to her feet. She grabbed the broom and swept up the smaller shards as Max climbed to his feet. He discarded his broken plates but didn't move out of her way. She should thank him for his help, but she avoided his eyes and couldn't bring herself to speak.

Chef Shawn did it for her. "Thank you, sir."

"My pleasure." Max acknowledge Shawn with a quiet gallantry

of a man who had nothing to prove. Then he gave her a wry smile and went back to the table.

Kelsey's knuckles whitened around the handle. Truly, her humiliation was complete.

~

KELSEY STOOD on the bridge across Saga Creek and gripped the wooden railing. Pinpricks of light shone from the cabins nestled in the pines on the other side of the creek. In the darkness, she spotted a man striding toward the bridge. *Slade.* Her sixth sense kicked in. Even from the distance, she knew he would recognize her trouble.

His boots hit the wooden planks of the bridge. "What's wrong, Kelsey?"

She didn't turn around. Her chest tightened. "I made a fool of myself in the guest dining room tonight."

"You could never make a fool of yourself."

She sighed, still without looking at him. "Well, I did."

"You want to tell me about it?"

"Not really."

"Okay."

Slade leaned against the railing and looked down at the shallow splashing creek. "I helped Jeremiah with a trail ride today, riding drag, you know, bringing up the rear. I liked the sucking sound of the horses' hooves as the riders waded through the water and avoided the bigger stones."

He was smart enough not to press her. She drew a breath, unable to avoid talking to her twin. "I knew one of our new guests in college."

He paused. "And?"

"Let's just say I made a fool of myself over him back then."

"Is this the guy from freshman year?"

Slade knew a lot about her, things she probably didn't know he knew. She eyed him. "Yes."

"I'll give you some advice."

Offering suggestions was something new for him. She was, after all, the mother figure between the two of them. But Slade had changed in the last few weeks.

"I've learned about myself recently. About love. And since freshman year, you've run from love, Kelsey, just like I did when I thought women only wanted me for my money."

Turning from him, she made a pooh-poohing sound.

"Don't be so ready to scoff," he said. "Loving someone is the greatest thing in the world. Look at Hank and our mom. Don't cut yourself off from the chance of finding happiness. Love is worth the risk."

"Why are you talking about love?" Her chin jerked up and her voice elevated.

"Because you loved the guy from freshman year, and you stopped dating completely after that. Something must have gone on between you."

"Well, it takes two to be in a relationship, and if you remember correctly, the guy dumped *me*." Her breathing was ragged.

He shrugged. "Times change. We change. Maybe you should give the guy a chance. Give yourself a chance. Remember what you told me about opening up to people. Take your own advice, Kelsey."

With that, he turned on his heel and strode off the bridge. OMG! Who would have thought her brother would have the guts to challenge her view of the world?

CHAPTER SIX

MAX SAT on the cabin's covered porch in an old-fashioned rocking chair. The night was chilly, but he was a Chicago native, and he could do cold. Something about the rhythmic rocking back and forth was soothing. Just as the solitude he embraced. However, he was far from content, not being used to the silence of the night and the fresh, spring breeze in the pines behind his cabin. He was more familiar with traffic sounds, police sirens, the frigid Chicago wind, and the constant pressure of his day job.

Plus, the tightness in his chest and the bitter pain of guilt in his throat.

Seeing Kelsey again didn't help his equilibrium. She was a surprise—a troubling surprise. He'd loved her once, but he'd never acted on his feelings for her during his time together with Claire. Yet, his heart knew. Perhaps that's why he couldn't fully embrace Claire as his wife. As a result, he'd wronged both women.

The woman he'd love was in his past. Did he still love her today? He didn't know this new Kelsey. She'd grown up. Changed. Even if a spark still existed, he shouldn't expect anything to come from it. He'd made his choice years ago.

More than that, to find out Kelsey was Leo York's granddaughter was equally disturbing. Leo York was his reason for coming to this isolated canyon, part of the mission handed to him by Randy Jr.

I was ten years old in the sixties when my sister Sarah disappeared. She ran away from home. It broke my parents' hearts. They could never find her, but Dad made provisions for her in his trust anyway. Now my parents are dead, and so are my wife and only child. There's nobody left, Max, but me. If Sarah is still alive, it's my duty to find her. If not, she may have heirs who are entitled to her inheritance.

Randy Matthews only clue was the name Leo York. Years ago, Sarah had written her parents about her marriage to a man by that name, that she was happy, and not to try to contact her.

My parents were angry she'd run away. She was only sixteen. They thought she'd joined one of those radical anti-war groups. They hired a private investigator, but the trail went cold. It was a crazy time. Normal people were afraid. After a while, my parents stopped looking for her. Later, they were sorry they didn't keep searching.

Max rubbed his chin. Sarah would be his wife Claire's aunt. But if Kelsey was Leo's granddaughter, Sarah must have had a child from that marriage to Leo York. Could Sarah still be alive? So many questions he'd promised Randy to find answers for. What if his wife Claire and Darby were first cousins? That would make Kelsey a first cousin once removed to his dead wife.

He couldn't let his fond memories of Kelsey complicate his search.

~

ELLIE QUIETLY PUSHED OPEN the door to Leo's room and peeked inside. The old man was snoring like a thunderstorm. Not dead yet, it seemed. She wished he'd go ahead and kick the bucket. Then she'd own the ranch fair and square, all legal-like. Of course, she'd have to kill Hank first.

Shutting the door softly, she backed away. Since Slade had left

Leo's cabin and gone to live with that bitch Laurie, she had more freedom. The old man listened to her and did whatever she told him to do. He was pliable since he'd hit his head and almost died. Of course, after that damn daughter of his had showed up with her passel of brats, things had gotten trickier.

She scoffed and opened the cabin door. It was chilly outside but not winter cold. She liked it that way. She could think easier with the wind in her face.

She smirked at the blanket of stars overhead. The idiots at the ranch all still thought Pete had accidently fallen to his death. That had worked out better than she'd hoped.

In the distance, she watched Hank make his final nightly rounds. He circled all the cabins, out buildings, and barns on foot before he turned in. If she was lucky, she'd find a way to off him in the night when nobody else was around. Then all she'd have to do was wait for Leo to die. It was too good to be true.

THE CLANGING of a loud bell woke Max from a fitful sleep. He sat up in the bed and rubbed his eyes. Dawn had barely broken in the distance. Slowly, his mind registered the sound. Someone rang the bell to call guests to the dining hall.

Damn. He wasn't hungry, but he wanted coffee. With the pace of a man still deep in the dregs of sleep, Max lumbered out of bed, threw water over his face, and dressed slowly. He opened the door, retreated into the cabin, and took his jacket from the back of a chair. The Montana mountains were cold in June, much too cold for his liking this morning.

The guest dining hall was filled with activity when he arrived. Visitors from all over the United States sat around the long table. He nodded at the couple from Wisconsin and skirted the family with five kids from California. All he wanted was coffee. He poured a cup at the sideboard, added cream, and took his mug to the fireplace with its cozy fire burning.

A weathered cowboy sat at a table nearest the fire. Could it be Leo York? The old man nursed his own mug and cast a pleased gaze toward the guests. A middle-aged woman sat beside him. She was pushed back from the table. A half-finished blanket rested in her lap. She knitted and occasionally glanced up from her task.

"I assume you're Mr. York." Max extended his hand. "I'm Max Lee."

"Nice to meet you, son. Where are you from?"

"Chicago."

He seemed to perk up. "My wife was from Chicago."

"Really? Where, if I might ask?"

He seemed confused. "I don't know. She never said. Ellie, do you know where Sarah was from?"

Ellie reached over and put a hand on Leo's arm. "I didn't know her, Leo. She was dead and gone before I got here."

Answer to question one. Max pulled back an empty chair sat down. "She's dead? I'm so sorry."

Leo didn't answer but stared morosely into his mug.

"You see, honey," Ellie leaned toward Max and said in a confiding voice, "Leo's wife committed suicide years ago at that lookout point on Ghost Mountain. She threw herself off the cliff. It's not something we talk much about. Leo's gotten over it after all these years, but today he seems sort of sad about it."

"What?" Max's gut tightened, and he felt a flush of heat in his face. He focused on Leo, trying to pull himself together. "I can understand that sadness." Max nodded and sipped his coffee. "My wife died tragically too."

From the kitchen door where he'd spied Kelsey yesterday, a cowboy and cowgirl entered. The man was Hank, who ran the place. He'd introduced himself at dinner last night. The woman crossed the floor to greet Leo with a kiss on his forehead, her red hair falling into her eyes. She pushed the strands away.

"Good morning, Dad." She nodded toward the caretaker. "Ellie."

"Ms. Darby," Ellie acknowledged.

Dad. Question two answered and case closed. This must be Kelsey's mother. Sarah's daughter.

Leo reached up and grasped his daughter's hand. "'Morning, sweetheart."

Darby turned to Max. "You must be our newest guest. Kelsey said you arrived late yesterday afternoon."

He stood up to shake Darby's hand. "Yes, ma'am. Max Lee from Chicago."

"Well, Max, we'll need to get you on the back of a horse this morning. It's going to be a beautiful day in the Gallatin Canyon."

"Ah, I'm not here to ride," he responded, shaking his head.

"Nonsense! We don't take no for an answer here." She grinned at him, and Max saw traces of Randall Senior's wife in her smile. "We've never lost a novice yet. Our trail horses are perfectly safe."

Max took a fortifying breath. "I'm really here to do some work. I hadn't planned on riding."

"Just for today," she urged. "Will put you on our safest horse and ride up the valley. It's perfectly flat. We might get rain tomorrow, so today's the day."

"Don't be afraid, boy," Leo spoke up. "My daughter will take good care of you."

Max smiled and nodded. He could agree to go and not follow through. He needed to learn more about this family, so he could tell Randy.

But not from the back of a damn horse.

CHAPTER SEVEN

Max had not counted on the persistence of Darby. After breakfast, she rounded him up and herded him to the corral. Saddled horses stood at a long hitching post, their tails swishing as the rising sun warmed their backs. Each one was branded with a double mountain marking for Ghost Mountain Ranch.

Rides were arranged each morning depending upon what the guests wanted to do. A handful of eager riders dressed in cowboy gear piled into a pickup truck and the cab of a long horse trailer filled with saddled animals. Led by two wranglers, this group was headed on a daylong ride near Yellowstone. They carried their lunches with them and a canteen of water.

The family of five remained. One by one the parents and kids climbed steps to a flat mounting block. Hank led a horse up to each rider and helped each child mount, then their parents. Each horse was led away from the block and stirrups adjusted. Max heard them say this ride would take most of the morning and was headed to Sunset Point, a rock escarpment across the main highway at the entrance to the ranch.

Soon Max found himself sitting alone on a log as the corral cleared out. Hopefully, he could slip away. He stood up just as

Darby led a spotted horse out from the barn. The horse was fitted with a Western saddle, saddlebag, rain slicker, and bridle.

"Glad to see you're ready to go," she said with a mischievous smile. Was she kidding him?

"I'd rather not." His tone was glum.

"Nonsense." She led the horse to the mounting block and covered its legs and rump with a hiss of fly spray.

"I've never ridden a horse."

"That's okay. All you have to do is sit quietly on his back and let him have his head."

"What does that mean?"

"Don't pull on his reins. Shamrock knows what to do. He'll follow my horse so all you do is sit there and enjoy the scenery."

Right. Randy Jr. didn't warn him he would need to ride a horse to get up close and personal to the object of his investigation. But maybe this was the best way, his chance to learn something about Darby and her past, and to make sure she was Sarah's daughter and Randy's niece.

Darby waved him toward the mounting block. "C'mon now."

Pressing his lips together, Max climbed the steps. He stood there with a heaviness in his gut.

Darby led the spotted horse forward and grinned up at him. "Go on."

Like he'd watched the others do, he straddled the western saddle, and she led the horse away from the mounting block a few steps. Max grabbed the horn for support, thankful he had something to hang on to.

"Always hold your reins," she instructed, handing them to him.

"But don't pull them." Was his voice shaking?

"Not unless you want to stop."

He saw the twinkle in her eyes. "You must enjoy torturing your guests."

Darby grinned. She lengthened his stirrups and guided the toe of his shoe into each one. "I'm simply trying to give you the full ranch experience, but if you really don't want to go...." She paused and looked over her shoulder. "Oh, here's my daughter. She's going with us."

Looking through the horse's ears, he noticed Kelsey approaching the corral. She was dressed in boots and jeans, a flannel shirt, and a standard black cowboy hat. He straightened his spine. This might prove interesting. "No, I'll go."

Kelsey caught sight of him and slowed her steps. She raised her chin and met his gaze. Her cheeks flushed pink. Yes, this would be very interesting.

~

KELSEY HAD NOT WANTED to trail ride this morning, but her mother's tenacity had won out. Standing silently, looking up at Max, she felt her muscles tense. Did Darby know about her past involvement with Max? She didn't think so. She'd never introduced him or brought him around the house. Her mom was simply trying to accommodate her ranch guest and had included her in the undertaking.

"This is my daughter Kelsey," Darby said to Max.

His face grim, he nodded. "We've met."

"That's right. You met yesterday. Kelsey knows how to ride. I thought she could ride drag for us since the other wranglers are busy." Darby turned on her heel and retreated to the barn.

Kelsey didn't know what to say, and she didn't know how to tamp down that cramp in her stomach. Was it nerves? She had hoped to marry this man until his father stole him away. More to the point, until he'd not stood up to his family and allowed them to dictate his life.

She stared into his steady brown eyes. "I'm sorry about this."

"Why be sorry?" His frown eased slightly.

"Because you probably didn't count on your past showing up on your vacation."

369

"I'm not here on vacation." Looking down from the back of the spotted quarter horse, he returned her gaze. "I'm here to work."

"Okay." What was he up to? The Max she'd known always had a purpose for everything. It made sense he wasn't here on vacation. Max had never had time for a holiday. Serious and first born, he was much like herself. Maybe that's why he'd ended it. The duty thing ran deep for both of them.

Her mother led two horses from the barn—one a golden-colored buckskin gelding with a black mane and tail and the other a pretty chestnut mare. Darby draped the buckskin's reins over the hitching post and led the mare to the mounting block.

"Here you go, Kelsey."

Kelsey mounted quickly. It hadn't been that long since she'd been on the back of a horse, but she soon realized the barrel-chested cowpony with a western saddle would take some getting used to. The horse didn't feel like the sleek retired Thoroughbreds she rode in Kentucky. Yet, sitting astride a horse again felt damn good. Relishing the warming sun on her back, Kelsey put a quiet hand on the mare's neck.

They left the corral area with her mother leading the way followed by Max. Kelsey brought up the rear as they walked quietly past the cabins and took the narrow trail through the stream-fed valley along Saga Creek. She quickly got the hang of riding with the heavier saddle.

The sky was robin's egg blue with fluffy white clouds. Mountains on the horizon were topped with snow, and the wind blew a fresh, earthy scent of summer sage through the lush meadow of wildflowers decked out in colors of glossy red, yellow, and white. The only flowers Kelsey recognized were the purple bluebonnet lupines. Tall pines, spruce, and aspen trees peppered the edge of the valley on the hillsides and rock escarpments.

"Where are we headed, Mrs. York?"

Darby shifted in her saddle and looked over her shoulder. Her horse kept a steady pace without her guidance. "It's Mrs. Heston, actually."

"Oh, sorry. I didn't know."

"York is my maiden name, Mr. Lee."

"I see."

"But please call me Darby."

"And I'm Max."

Darby straightened in her saddle. "We're headed a couple miles up the valley. It's an easy ride. We'll turn around and return the same way."

They rode in silence for a while, the horses plodding along. Even a hardened city guy like Max should be able to enjoy the scenery. A red-tailed hawk flushed from a tree. The bird rose in a sweeping spiral to the east.

Was that really Max riding in front of her, sitting upright with perfect posture as if he was born in the saddle? She'd been a stupid kid when she was in love with him. But now that he was here in the flesh, she didn't know how to take him any more than she knew how to understand her confusing reaction to him.

"How long have you lived on the ranch, Darby?"

Her mother paused a moment perhaps in thought. "I grew up here but left at eighteen and lived in Kentucky for many years," she said. "I've only been back home a few months."

"I see."

"My father got sick."

Why did Mom feel the need to explain? Kelsey wouldn't have. Their lives were none of Max's business. She swatted at an annoying gnat that seemed to accompany her mare.

Then suddenly, a large, slow-moving moose with a huge rack of antlers crossed the path a hundred yards ahead. Darby lifted her hand, and they halted. The big animal drank from the creek, then clomped across it, disappearing into the trees on the hillside.

Darby nudged her horse forward. "You don't want to mess with those big guys."

"That was magnificent." Max sounded in awe.

"Bet you don't see that often in Chicago." Kelsey couldn't help keeping the snark from her voice.

"Not very often."

She tightened her jaw. Certainly, Max heard her tone, but acted as if he chose to ignore it. But did he? She couldn't see his face. Was he really laughing at her like he'd done last night?

CHAPTER EIGHT

MAX COCKED his head remembering the Kelsey from college. She would have never talked to him with such sarcasm and disrespect. His throat thickened. He'd hurt her. The years between his leaving and now had changed her, and he felt sorry for that.

The trail ride wasn't bad except for the gnats attacking his bare arms, and the sting of the horse's swishing tail. The gentle motion of the horse didn't frighten him after a few minutes. In fact, his horse had its nose up against the lead horse's butt. Shamrock wasn't going anywhere fast.

Several minutes later, the handheld radio strapped to Darby's saddle crackled. Darby raised her hand to call another halt. Max pulled back on the reins as he'd been instructed, but old Shamrock had already stopped.

"Jeremiah to Darby."

Darby unhooked her radio and raised it to her ear. "Darby to Jeremiah. Go ahead."

The radio crackled again. The volume was so loud Max could hear what was being said.

"Hank's fallen from his horse. I think his leg is broken."

"Dear God! Where are you?"

"Coming down from Sunset Point. I need someone to take him to Bozeman."

"Big Sky is closer. I'll be right there."

"Okay. Clear."

Darby wheeled her horse around. Her face had paled and there was panic in her eyes. "Hank never falls from a horse. Something else must be wrong."

"He'll be okay, Mom."

"I don't know that." Darby shook her head. She unhooked a can of bear spray from her belt and handed it to Kelsey. "Take this in case you need it. Just follow the trail. You can easily get Max back to the ranch."

With that Darby spurred her horse into a gallop and left the two of them alone. The silence between them was intense. Only the wind in the nearby pines and the cawing of a family of crows broke the stillness.

A look of revulsion passed over Kelsey as she studied the can of bear spray in her hand. "What do I do with this?" She hooked it onto her belt, then cleared her throat. "Well, I guess we'd better get back. Maybe we can help."

She guided her horse around him and headed toward the ranch. Luckily, Shamrock followed without any help from him. They rode without speaking. Max had a wonderful view of her straight back and her luscious backside. Kelsey was a beautiful, sexy woman with long limbs and long blond hair. A dangerous yearning thrummed through his body, and his breathing suddenly seemed too loud.

Several more minutes passed, then Shamrock did the unthinkable. He stopped, dropped his head, and started to munch grass.

Max's chest tightened. "Kelsey!"

She looked over her shoulder and laughed.

"What do I do?" He cursed under his breath.

She rode back to him. "Jerk his head up. That horse knows better than that."

"Your mother said to give him his head, keep the reins loose."

Kelsey reached over, grabbed the reins, and tugged Shamrock's head up. Her saddle leather creaked as she leaned toward him and positioned the reins in his hands. "Keep a hold of him, not too loose and not too slack. He doesn't respect you."

Her nearness started Max's heart hammering, and he flushed with mortification. "Thanks."

"Don't mention it." She smacked his horse's rump with the palm of her hand.

Shamrock jumped forward a step. Unprepared Max wobbled in the saddle. He grabbed the saddle horn and managed to stay upright.

Kelsey caught up to him, riding beside him, and her knee bumped against his. Once again deep longing shot through him. He was out of his comfort zone. Her nearness didn't help. She, more than the damn horse, threw him off balance. It hadn't been that way in college. He'd been in control. Somehow their roles had flipped, and he wasn't sure that was a good thing.

"So, what's your real purpose for being here, Max?"

Kelsey's voice was curt, critical, direct to the point. Max inhaled a long, deep breath and bit back a terse reply. He glanced quickly at her profile, noticing her jaw clamped shut. Kelsey had always been smart. She'd already guessed there was more to his visit than a simple vacation. What would it hurt to come clean?

"I'm actually here to learn more about your family."

She was startled. "What in heavens name for?"

"My boss asked me to confirm sketchy information he'd been given."

"Are you some sort of detective?"

"No, only a humble lawyer."

"There's nothing humble about you, Max Lee."

Now he had to laugh. "Normally, you're right, but I must admit I'm not too comfortable on the back of this horse."

"Wait until the soreness kicks in. Your leg and thigh muscles won't know what hit them." She seemed pleased by her response.

Max caught a faint smile on her lips that quickly vanished as she turned toward him. "Seriously, what business does this boss have with my family?"

"He's searching for his sister, and he was told she was married to Leo York."

Kelsey halted and gaped at him. "That would be my grand-mother. We never knew anything about her family. She refused to talk about her background, my mother said."

Max stopped Shamrock so close he almost touched Kelsey again. With sunshine glinting off her hair, he drank in her loveli-ness and felt that old attraction hit him full force.

"Her name was Sarah Matthews," he said gently.

"Matthews," she tested the name.

"She was born in Highland Park, Illinois, and ran away from home when she was sixteen. The only contact she had with her family after that was a one-line letter saying she was married to Leo York and happy."

Kelsey's eyes clouded. "I suppose she was happy for a while, but eventually something went wrong. No one knows why she committed suicide."

CHAPTER NINE

THE LOOK in Max's eyes was suspicious. "Suicide? I can't believe she'd do that."

Kelsey gripped her reins with her fist, and her mare tossed her head in protest. "That's right. That's what the authorities told Leo at the time." Nudging the horse, she rode on. She needed to gather her thoughts.

Things were moving too fast. Besides Max's revelation, there was the information Slade and Laurie had learned about Sarah's criminal past and Darby's real father, an ex-con named Tim Krebs. She bet Max didn't know anything about that history.

Another long stretch of silence ensued, but this one wasn't as tense as before. Something had changed between them.

She glanced at Max. "What's your boss' name?"

"Randall Matthews, Jr." Max's voice was deep and firm. "He was Claire's father."

"Was she your wife?" Seeing the pain in his eyes, she'd simply guessed.

He hesitated, nodded, then looked ahead. "Randy will take Sarah's suicide hard."

"Why is that?"

"His own wife committed suicide after Claire was killed."

But what if Sarah didn't kill herself? Slade and Laurie had dropped that mystery into her lap, and now more than ever, she wanted to investigate it.

"Please don't tell my mother about...who is he really? Your father-in-law?"

"Yes, but he's also senior partner in my law firm and technically my employer."

That old duty thing reared its head. Becoming a lawyer was Max's responsibility according to his family. Marrying the boss' daughter was too.

"Well, there are things you need to know before you talk to my mother. I'd appreciate you don't spring this news on Darby right away. Will you stop by my cabin after dinner?"

"That's the most pleasant thing I've heard all day."

Max's eyes twinkled, and somewhere deep inside, she was petrified.

THE BARNS and corrals eventually came into view. Kelsey was afraid to ride faster, because Max didn't know how to trot or canter. So, she bit her lip and patiently rode on at a walk. There was activity near the hitching post area, but she couldn't make it out at the distance.

As they drew nearer, she noticed a ranch truck leave the parking area. Several people milled around, then the guests who'd been on the ride with Hank and Jeremiah wandered away, leaving Slade with the horses.

"How's Hank?" Kelsey called out, bringing her horse to a halt.

"In pain. It took a lot for him to ride down the mountain after his saddle slipped," Slade said.

"Slipped?" She lifted her right leg over the cantle which was higher than she was used to with an English saddle and dropped to the ground.

"Yeah. Hank used Jeremiah's horse to come down the mountain and Jeremiah rode bareback on Hank's, somehow hanging on to Hank's saddle with one hand. It was a sight to see them ride in."

"I bet."

"Mom has taken Hank to the regional hospital in Big Sky. They should be able to set a broken leg since it's a ski resort town." Slade took Kelsey's horse. Six other horses stood at the hitching post waiting to be unsaddled and turned out.

Now or never. Kelsey drew a deep breath. She had to help Max dismount. She turned around and walked over to Max, who rested his arms on the saddle horn and looked down at her with eyes filled with desire.

Did he realize he gave himself away so blatantly?

"Are you ready to get down from there?"

"You've got that right."

She placed one hand on the horse's shoulder and the other on the leather skirt of the saddle. She stood near Max's blue jean clad leg and thigh, watching him watch her. She felt his heat. Her hormones reawakened. She was vulnerable. Max was back in her life for however long he stayed at the ranch, and she needed to be very careful.

"You want to dismount on your left side." She gave him a close-lipped smile. "What you need to do is swing your right leg over the saddle. Remember the back part is high. Then rest your belly in the seat of the saddle, take your left foot out of the stirrup, kick it free, and drop."

"Sounds easy enough."

But it wasn't. Max's leg got stuck on the cantle when he tried to swing it over. Kelsey helped get it across by putting her hands on his thigh. Then suddenly he pushed back, landing on his right foot with the left still stuck in the stirrup. He tried to gain his balance on one foot, hopping, until he toppled backwards, falling against Kelsey, and they both hit the dirt.

He rolled over, easing his weight off her, but he was still on top in an all-too-familiar position from years ago. He braced his hands on the ground near her shoulders and pushed up to gaze into her eyes. "I could kiss you right now."

"You better not!"

Kelsey shoved his chest and squirmed beneath him. This wouldn't do! He had no business giving into stray sexual feelings, and she didn't need those feelings either. It had taken her years to get over the heartache of their break-up. She had no interest in revisiting that pain.

Max grinned and scrambled to his feet. He extended his hand, but she pushed off with her palms placed firmly on the ground and climbed to her feet by herself. She hoped her angry glare gave him the message she wanted to send. *Back off, buster. I don't need you or your help.*

"You two all right?" Slade snatched up the spotted horse's reins.

"Perfect," Kelsey snapped.

Max simply dusted off the dirt from his jeans and grinned like the devil.

Suddenly, Jeremiah stormed out of the barn. His black and white dog ran at his heels barking. "What the hell, Heston?"

"What?" Still holding the horse, Slade turned to face the angry wrangler.

"Hank's cinch hobble has been sliced and so has one of his latigo leathers. That's why his saddle slipped, you idiot."

"Wait a minute. I didn't have anything to do with that."

Kelsey had no idea what Jeremiah was talking about. She figured it had something to do with the Western saddle. English saddles didn't have parts by those names.

"It's your job to check the equipment before you put it on the horse."

Slade looked troubled. "But I didn't notice any problem."

"It's your job to notice, rich boy." Jeremiah shoved his chest, forcing Slade back against the horse who sidestepped out of the way.

Slade righted himself and fists flying came after Jeremiah. The wrangler connected with his knuckles, sending Slade sailing off his feet.

"Slade!" Kelsey dropped to her brother's side. His nose was bleeding.

Max intervened, stepping in front of them, blocking Jeremiah to face his wrath. "Maybe you're blaming the kid to cover up your own negligence. You're in charge here. I think you should have noticed it."

"Stay out of this, dude." Jeremiah grabbed Max's shirt near his neck and drew back his fist.

In a swift movement, Max seized the wrangler's fist with his left hand, broke his grip, and jerked his head to the side. Then he shoved Jeremiah's right shoulder away and landed a punch to the man's jaw with his right fist, taking him down.

"Next time don't tangle with someone who's had eight years of self-defense training," he said and walked away.

DARBY BROUGHT Hank home before dinner. Kelsey was at the office when her mother stopped the truck outside.

"I wanted to let you know we're back," she said. Her mom looked tired her eyebrows pulled tight with worry.

"Is he okay?"

"Not really." Darby removed her cowboy hat and smoothed her hair that she wore pulled back from her face. "He has a severe sprain with ligament damage to his left leg. The doctor said it would have been better to have broken it."

"Ouch! I bet it's painful."

"And swollen." Darby glanced out the window. "They put him in a walking boot, but he's not a happy camper at the moment. He must keep his leg elevated and ice it several times a day."

That certainly wouldn't go over well for a guy as active as Hank. "Tell him we're thinking about him, Mom."

"Will do." She opened the office door. "I'd better get him home before he lets loose with a string of expletives."

"And, Mom! Tell him to talk to Jeremiah. He thinks part of his saddle was tampered with. Jeremiah accused Slade, but you know Slade wouldn't have had a clue about anything like that."

"Damn! I knew there was a reason Hank fell from his horse." Darby let out a sigh of relief. "He's too good of a cowboy to fall like that but too good not to have checked his tack."

"What if he didn't saddle his own horse? Could Jeremiah have damaged his leathers?"

"Hank knows him. I don't." Darby shook her head. "He hired him. I'll talk to Hank."

Kelsey watched her mother leave and shut the door. She sank into her chair.

Did they really know the people they'd hired to run the ranch?

CHAPTER TEN

After dinner Max strode to Kelsey's cabin. It looked much like his own with rustic décor like a Western movie. Kelsey's twin Slade and Laurie were already there sitting on Kelsey's queen-sized bed. They whispered with their heads together. Max clasped his hands behind his back. Seeing young love on such a blatant display quickened his heartbeat.

He remembered Slade from years ago. Kelsey and he had run into him at a fraternity party after a basketball game. His only memory of Slade was of him playing a chug game with his frat brothers. He'd grown up. They all had. Life had changed them.

"Thanks for your help today." Slade looked sheepish.

"No problem," Max said. "You were blindsided."

"Still." Slade didn't finish his sentence and looked away. Max figured he was embarrassed about not standing up for himself.

Laurie glanced at Slade, then back at Max. "Kelsey says you have something to tell us."

He nodded and took a seat at the writing desk. "My boss is Randall Matthews, Jr. He sent me to the ranch in hopes of discovering his sister Sarah."

"My grandmother?" Slade looked surprised.

"Yes."

Then Laurie told her piece of the story helping him put puzzle pieces of the past together. Her grandmother had known Sarah. She fumbled with a Priority Mail envelope and pulled out a letter her grandmother had written to her.

"My grandmother left this letter with a lawyer for me to read if she died." Laurie handed Max the cover letter and the longer one from her grandmother.

He smiled. "Ironically, this letter came from my firm and was written by Randy Jr. I'm sure he didn't know what your grandmother wrote to you or his questions may have been answered."

Max dropped his gaze to the grandmother's letter.

When a policeman was killed because of our bombing, we knew we were in trouble. Chelsea had had Tim's baby, and he couldn't deal with the child. He wanted to get rid of Chelsea anyway. So, this screwup was a good excuse to leave. Glen stole an old station wagon and all of us piled into it and headed to Montana. Tim left Chelsea and the baby with his brother Pete.

Max lifted his head. Kelsey lounged against the door jamb with her arms crossed. He had an unexpected vision of burying his fingers in her hair, tipping her head back, and kissing her. A surprising bolt of desire ripped through him, and he shifted in the straight-backed chair with a woven cane seat. He bit his tongue to regain his concentration on the subject at hand and continued to read.

It was the late 1960s and Blacks were protesting their condition. Kids rioted in the streets. The Vietnam War was raging. Women burned bras. Everything was thrilling: the music, women's liberation, free love, drugs. He helped me leave home when I was eighteen. It was good. We joined a big revolutionary movement. It was up to the youth of America to fight the establishment. We wanted to destroy imperialism, form a classless society, create Utopia. Glen wore old Army fatigue jackets and blue denims. I let my hair grow long and wore free-flowing granny dresses. We wore sunglasses so no one would recognize us.

When he finished reading, Max looked up again. "This explains what happened to Sarah, and why her family couldn't find her. She didn't want to be found. She was a domestic terrorist."

"It was a different time," Laurie said. "No social media or street cameras. Easier to disappear."

"The family didn't forget Sarah," Max said. "She and any heirs are named in a trust. Kelsey, your mother stands to inherit a fortune."

"I don't think it matters to our mother." Kelsey's voice was firm.

"All she wants is to know the reason her mother committed suicide." Slade finished his twin's thought.

"But we've recently come to think Sarah might have been murdered," Laurie said softly.

"And it's damn frustrating we may never know the truth." Slade's tone deepened, and he flexed his fingers.

"It seems to me you have uncovered plenty of information recently. Let's hope we will find more. I'm sure Randy Jr. will want to know what happened. I'll be glad to help during my two weeks here."

Kelsey straightened, shoving her shoulders back. "Two weeks? I thought since you had the information you came for, you'd leave."

Max cocked his head, unable to hold back a smile. "My boss has already paid for this vacation. Besides, I find the ranch and its inhabitants very intriguing."

"I bet." Kelsey scowled.

Slade stood up and grabbed Laurie's hand. "Time for us to go home," he said with a grin. "We're in the way here."

Max handed Laurie her letter, and the couple excused themselves. Kelsey held the door open and turned back to him. "Do you know your way back to your cabin?"

"I can find it."

"Good."

He came to his feet, towering over her, and gazed into her eyes. "Don't be afraid of me, Kelsey."

"Afraid? No way! I'm simply annoyed that you showed up here, and you seem to think you can pick up where you left off years ago."

He cupped her face with his hands. She was so soft. So desirable. Did he want to pick up where they left off? "I hope I haven't given you that impression. But perhaps, it's what you wish."

She shook off his hands. "You *said* you wanted to kiss me."

Shrugging, Max smiled. "True. You got me there."

"So, don't deny you want to pick up where we left off."

"Yes, I deny it." Suddenly, he didn't want to go backwards to the guy he was then. "I want to start fresh, if you'll have me."

Kelsey pivoted toward the door and pointed the way out. "I think you better leave. I have work to do tomorrow. Today's trail ride interrupted it and put me behind."

"You'll change your mind. We have two weeks to get reacquainted, remember?"

"Actually, only ten days." She gave his back a shove and slammed the door behind him.

～

THE ARROGANCE of that man was beyond belief. Did he think she was so needy weak she'd simply fall into bed with him?

Kelsey shoved her hands into the pockets of her jacket. The morning air was brisk, to say the least, but there was a good, clean feeling about it. A feeling of renewal and purpose.

She opened the back door of the kitchen and stepped inside. It was a well-designed, shiny industrial kitchen, perfect for feeding many summer guests. Shawn was busy at the gas stove. Tristan and the floater Samantha rushed in and out of the guest dining room. Kelsey wrapped up a bear claw pastry in a paper napkin and shoved it in her coat pocket and poured coffee into a mug. Knowing she could find cream in the staff dining hall, she skirted Sam and slipped into the other room.

"Good morning, Ellie." The older woman stood with her back to the door and seemed to be adding sugar and cream to a coffee mug. She turned, bringing the mug up to her lips, and stared at Kelsey without a word. "How's my grandfather doing this morning?" Kelsey asked.

Ellie lowered her mug and wiped her mouth with her sleeve. "He's doing a bit poorly this morning. I've left him to his breakfast, but I doubt he eats it."

Something about Ellie didn't feel right. Was Kelsey only suspicious because Laurie and Slade had their doubts about her? Or was it the cold hostility in the woman's blue eyes?

"Maybe I'll drop by later to see how he's doing," Kelsey said as she poured cream into her mug.

"Yes, do that. Leo will be pleased."

"Well, I've got to get to work." Kelsey turned to leave.

"What are you doing in the office? That was one of my jobs before Leo got sick."

Kelsey turned back to Ellie and cupped her hot mug in her hands for warmth. "Right now, I'm compiling a database of names and addresses of previous guests. I'm only able to go back five years so far. I hope to get ten years of data ultimately, but Leo's handwriting is hard to read, and his records are sketchy."

Ellie nodded in agreement. "I had trouble reading Leo's writing too. Have you worked on the bank books? Hank took that over from me in January."

Kelsey narrowed her gaze and couldn't help frowning. "No, I haven't gotten that far yet."

Her answer seemed to satisfy Ellie, who abruptly turned away. "Fine. Have a good day."

Kelsey watched her return to the kitchen. Why did she ask about the accounting books? That didn't have the right ring to it either. Maybe she'd take a look at them a whole lot sooner than she'd planned.

One more mystery to file under Ellie's name.

CHAPTER ELEVEN

KELSEY WORKED ALL MORNING, purposefully skipping lunch when the bell rang at noon. She had too much inputting to do, and like she told Ellie, Leo's scrawl was hard to read. Ellie's tight cursive was easier, but there were only two years of her records. Surely, if Kelsey could document all the names and addresses in a database, they could market to former guests during the off-season.

No way did she want to face the fact she was also avoiding her ex-boyfriend.

The door suddenly opened, and Max entered. Kelsey looked up from her laptop. For a moment, he stood silent and unmoving.

"Good afternoon." His voice was warm, but he didn't approach the desk.

She swallowed, her heart beating a little too fast. "Hello."

"You were right about being sore. My leg muscles are screaming."

Kelsey took note of the strong lines of his jaw, the proud tilt of his head. Did it cost him something to admit a weakness?

"You'll get over it."

"I understand why cowboys are bowlegged." He chuckled and came across the room. "Mind if I sit down?"

"No. Go ahead."

He sat back in the chair, relaxed, legs outstretched. "You gave me a lot to think about last night."

"It's a complicated story." Kelsey shut her laptop. "When I was young, I only had my mom, dad, and Slade. I never dreamed my mother would have such a complex family tree."

"Like something from a novel."

"More like a good mystery."

"Or a romance." He chuckled with the same low laughter that had once charmed her.

She frowned. "I wouldn't go that far."

"Then maybe a tragedy."

"That's more like it."

They sat wordlessly for a moment. She didn't know what to say to him. How to react.

His eyes were penetrating as if he wanted more. "Is there anything I can help you with?"

Help? She didn't need help, not with the database. Kelsey sat back in her chair, put her arms on the arm rest, and chewed her lip. "Slade says there could be more files in the attic. You can help me look for them."

"Okay. How do we get there?"

"I think there's a ladder?" She directed her eyes to the ceiling where a short rope dropped down from what looked like a trap door.

He followed her gaze, then pushed the chair back and rose. "That should be easy enough." Max tugged on the rope and a ladder unfolded. "Is there a light in the attic?"

"I don't know."

"What about a flashlight then?"

Kelsey pulled open the desk drawers and found a flashlight in the bottom one. She carried it to Max, who stood at the base of the ladder.

"Thanks." He surveyed her with a look that seemed to pierce

right into her soul, then grinned. "You'll have to spot me as I climb. I wouldn't like to fall again."

"I bet."

She held the ladder as he ascended, trying not to drool over the vision of the hip pockets of his jeans.

He disappeared into the hole, then stomped around on the attic floor above her head. "Did you find anything?"

"Bits of broken furniture." He paused. "I found four file boxes. Is that what you want?"

"I guess. Slade said there were old files in the attic."

"Okay. Here comes the first box. It's awkward and dusty, but not too heavy."

Max lowered the first box from the hole. Kelsey climbed two rungs up the ladder to take the carton from him and drop it to the floor. They repeated the action three more times, then he came down the ladder slowly.

"What do you think are in these?" He helped her stack the boxes in the corner.

"Old reservations, I think. I don't know if they'll help me compile the database, but we'll see."

His brown hair was tousled slightly. He ran his hand over his head. Kelsey's breath caught in her throat. She couldn't believe he stood there, so near she could reach out and touch him—so near she could run *her* fingers through his hair. For a year after their breakup, she'd ached for him, but then she'd stopped. Grew cynical. Scoffed at romantic love. At men. But now Max was here, no longer a dream, and she resisted the urge to slip back into the way she had been before she knew better.

Once again, they stared at each other, then Max turned away. "Mind if I use your landline? My cell phone won't work."

"No cell reception in the mountains."

He glanced at her again. "I want to call Randy to tell him what I've found."

"Sure." Kelsey studied the floor a moment, then she found safety by sitting behind the desk again.

She watched as Max used the old-fashioned rotary phone on the wall to dial the number. Pretending to work on the computer, she listened to him talk to the man who was her mother's uncle.

At one point, he brought down the phone and looked across the room. "Randy is anxious to come out here. Do you have room for him to stay?"

"He wants to come here?" Her voice was shaky, disbelieving.

"Yes, as soon as he can get a flight out."

"We usually book for a week—Sunday to Saturday." She opened her laptop and brought up the current reservations.

"He can stay with me."

She wrinkled her nose. "Actually, we're far from full. There's an open cabin next to yours." Kelsey lifted her head and connected with his gaze. "Tell him to come on."

What would her mother think? She and Slade better find time to tell her before this new relative dropped from the sky.

Max hung up the phone and turned back toward her. "You've made Randy's day. He's so excited. I'm sure this gives him something to live for."

"Yes, well, I suppose that's a good thing."

He put his palms on the desk and leaned forward. "Yes, it's a good thing. Coming here, seeing you again, has been a damn good thing too."

CHAPTER TWELVE

KELSEY KNEW Hank was champing at the bit to get back to work. Because he was incapacitated, Darby had commandeered the new four-wheel drive utility task vehicle Slade had purchased for his grandfather and brought Hank to the staff dining room for dinner. Now he sat on the end of the sofa with his left leg elevated nursing his sorrows with a bottle of beer. Ellie sat on the other corner of the sofa nearest Leo. As always, she seemed engrossed in her knitting.

The staff had left the dining hall an hour earlier. While the wranglers ran the horses to the night pasture and the kitchen staff finished up, Samantha led the children in games outside. Kelsey paced behind the sofa where her mom sat with Hank and Ellie. Where was everyone? They'd agreed to tell Darby and Leo about Sarah. She bit her lip, her mouth dry. How would her mother react to the news?

"It sure is hell gettin' old." Leo turned up his own icy bottle and guzzled a mouthful. He sat in his easy chair with his pipe and tobacco close at hand.

"Tell me about it." Hank chugged the rest of his beer, then

lowered it and fiddled with the empty bottle, rolling the neck between his fingers.

"Don't you boys get drunk now," Ellie warned. "I don't want to have to carry Leo to bed."

"You don't have to worry none about me, woman."

Leo sounded gruff, but Kelsey had learned he was an old softy.

"I'm going to get you old sidewinders some coffee. Ellie's right. Two bottles of beer should be your limit." Darby got up and went to the sideboard. She was pouring coffee into mugs when the door burst open, and Slade and Laurie entered along with Max.

Kelsey couldn't help herself. She was glad to see Max. She didn't want to feel pleased about his arrival, about the way he gazed at her with approval and a cocky grin on his lips that seemed to remind her of his earlier promise. Did she want to get to know him again?

Her mother brought coffee over to Leo and Hank then looked expectantly at the quartet. "What's up?"

"We need to talk to you, Mom," Slade said.

Darby paused. "Okay." She tilted her head to the side. "Do you want to talk to me privately? Or here?"

Kelsey wet her lips, looking around the group sitting near the fireplace. "No. Our grandfather needs to hear this too."

Laurie poked Slade in the side. "I don't think Ellie needs to hear."

Slade tipped his chin up and looked the caretaker straight in the eye. "Laurie's right. Ellie, do you mind excusing yourself? We'll see Leo gets home."

Ellie climbed to her feet in a huff. She packed up her knitting, glared at the room as if to say she knew when she wasn't wanted, then left wordlessly through the kitchen door. Was that a calculating look in her eyes? Or was Kelsey imaging it because of Slade and Laurie's suspicions?

"Okay." Darby's breath hitched. "What's going on? You've got my curiosity up. Is this as earthshattering as Laurie's letter?"

Slade pulled three chairs into the circle surrounding the fireplace. He sat on the stone hearth and rested his elbows on his knees. "Have a seat, Mom. You may find it is earthshattering."

When everyone was seated and uncomfortable, staring at each other, Kelsey gave herself a mental shake. The best way to explain was fast. "Mom, this is Max Lee."

"I know. We met."

"What you don't know is he's come all the way from Chicago hoping to meet you."

Darby furrowed her eyebrows. She turned her attention to the guest. "Whatever for?"

Max ran his hand through his hair and hesitated for a moment. "My boss Randall Matthews sent me here to find out about Sarah Matthews, his sister."

Darby's mouth dropped open. Her gaze darted toward her father. Leo's eyes had widened, and he gasped.

"My mother?"

"Yes, ma'am."

"Dear God," Leo rasped. "She never told me her last name even though I asked a million times."

Darby rubbed a hand over her eyes. "How do you know she's my mother?"

Max cleared his throat. "The last correspondence her parents had from her, she said she was happily married to Leo York and not to come looking for her."

Tears welled in Leo's eyes. "Dear God," he said again.

Kelsey watched her mother go to Leo, kneel, and put her arms around him. She laid her head on his shoulder.

"Sarah ran away from her home near Chicago at sixteen. Her brother Randy was only ten at the time," Max explained.

As the story unfolded, her mother sank to the floor by Leo's chair. Laurie handed him the letter from her grandmother, the one Darby and Max had already read. Everyone sat silently as the family patriarch scanned it.

Moments later, he lowered the letter. "This explains many

things."

"And now we know the rest of the story." Darby's eyes had reddened with tears. "Thank you, Max, for telling us."

Kelsey met Slade's gaze. He seemed to be thinking what she was thinking. *We don't know everything. Why did Sarah commit suicide? Or was she murdered?*

"Randy is the only one of his family left alive. He wants to meet you, Darby, and the rest of your family." Max inhaled deeply. "As heir to the Matthews fortune, you stand to inherit your mother's portion of the trust."

~

WHAT THE HELL? Ellie stood with her ear to the kitchen door where she could hear what was going on in the dining room. The bitch had been married to a rich man, and now she and her brats would inherit more money. When Hank married her, he'd be as rich as she was. Didn't seem fair. Didn't seem right.

Maybe Hank wouldn't want the ranch when he was married. Maybe the whole crew of them would go back to Kentucky and leave her and Leo the hell alone. Ellie turned from the door and stalked through the kitchen, not saying a word to the nosy staff. She was glad that boy had told her to leave. She had too much nervous energy to sit there calmly like everything was hunky-dory.

Her plan to off Hank hadn't worked so well. She should have known the bastard was too good a horseman. But now he was gimpy. Maybe she'd figure out another way to get rid of him. Maybe she could implicate Jeremiah again, or she could just bide her time. She'd done a good job waiting for the right time to off her father. In the end, that bastard got what he deserved.

Going outside and into the night, she let the kitchen door bang shut as if to say good riddance. No matter what, she knew her days of fetching for this family would soon be over. Sooner, she hoped, rather than later.

CHAPTER THIRTEEN

I WANT TO START FRESH, if you'll have me.

The next day, Kelsey resisted once more the urge to see Max. Scars from her past might not be visible, but she carried them in her heart. Max had hurt her once. Never again, she vowed. To prevent any future foolishness on her part, it was easier to stay away from him.

Besides she didn't know what he meant by wanting to start fresh. She doubted if he knew either.

By noon she'd finished her database of old reservations. It wasn't much, maybe ten years' worth of information. That's all the records she could find except for whatever was in the four file boxes and searching through them seemed like a disheartening task.

Have you worked on the bank books?

Ellie's interest piqued hers. She'd put off paying bills because she'd been concentrating on creating a database of the former guests. Now she needed to tackle the envelopes she'd shoved into a desk drawer and pay invoices.

Trouble was Ghost Mountain Ranch didn't have any computer accounting records. Kelsey could only find a huge manual spreadsheet that looked as difficult to figure out as Leo's handwriting. And there were no cancelled checks because banks no longer mailed them. She had nothing to compare the spreadsheet to.

Chewing her bottom lip, she sat down in the chair behind the desk. Looking into the spreadsheet probably wouldn't matter if she didn't have a bad feeling about Ellie. And if Ellie hadn't asked point blank.

As happened yesterday afternoon, the door opened and in walked Max. Her throat swelled closed. Once again, he filled the room with his vitality, squaring his broad shoulders and grinning at her. His eyes flashed when she didn't speak. She couldn't. It was like facing her past, and all her old emotions came rushing in. The man instinctively made her feel uncomfortable.

Or was it the love she'd never quite conquered?

THE TENSION in the room was palpable. Max regretted it, but Kelsey's open hostility only made him more determined to get along if nothing else.

"Hi, Kelsey. How's your morning been?"

"Fine."

Her vulnerable mouth invited him. He longed to kiss her lips. Hold her in his arms. Love her.

But he couldn't. He'd had his chance years ago. Telling her he wanted to start fresh had been a mistake. Because of Claire. Because of his past with Kelsey. His duty to his family remained, and it was disheartening to think he could easily forget it.

Forcing a cheerful smile, he approached the desk. She smelled of flowers and springtime. "I want to invite you to ride with me to Bozeman this afternoon." His voice was suddenly husky. "Randy arrives around six."

To his surprise, she nodded. "Fine. If you first take me by the bank before it closes. I need to make arrangements to get access to the online checking account."

~

RANDALL MATTHEWS ARRIVED at Bozeman Yellowstone International Airport on the United flight from Chicago-O'Hare. He pulled a small carryon and didn't stop at the luggage carrousel but came straight out to Max's rented SUV in the short-term lot. To Kelsey's surprise, he had red hair tinged with gray like her mom.

She stepped out of the car to shake his hand. "Mr. Matthews?"

Instead of a handshake, he pulled her into a massive embrace, pinning her arms to her side. Kelsey looked wide-eyed over his shoulder at Max, who grinned.

"I'm Randy," he said. "You must be Kelsey. That makes you my grand-niece. Max has told me all about you."

Kelsey caught Max's attention again, then lifted an eyebrow. He pulled his lips together in a sheepish expression and cocked his head. Randy released her, and she stepped back.

"You have red hair like my mom."

"And you're a blonde like my sister Sarah. I can see the family resemblance."

Her father had never been close to his family of wealthy bourbon tycoons. His father's parents were dead, and they'd rarely got together with her dad's brothers. To find family now, family who wanted to be together, was a new experience.

"You're traveling light." Max threw Randy's carryon into the back of the car and opened the front door for him.

"I had to make arrangements fast and was lucky to get the last seat on the plane. Tourist season, I was told."

"It is that. Most guest ranches are booked solid." Kelsey climbed into the back behind the driver's seat, glad to be able to study Randy's profile as Max drove.

Randy wanted to know everything about her. She told him about growing up on a horse farm in Kentucky, about running the place after her father's death, and about her mother finally coming back to her Montana roots. She left out the part about loving Max. That was years ago when she was a gullible college kid. And this man was the father of Max's deceased wife. They shared a history. A business. A tragedy.

More than an hour later, they pulled into the long drive down the valley to the ranch. "We're at nearly five thousand feet. If you get a headache, or feel as if you have the flu, it's altitude sickness," Kelsey warned. "Let us know, and we'll get you something for it."

Randy didn't seem concerned. Fading sunshine illuminated the crags and crevasses of the surrounding mountains making the shadows in the valley deeper, darker. He sat forward, pressing against his seat belt and took in the sights of the ranch.

"If you look to your right, Randy, you'll see Ghost Mountain," Kelsey said, trying to shake the sinister sensation she felt when she looked at its pine-covered rock face.

Randy turned toward the window. "Is that where Sarah died?"

Kelsey swallowed hard. "Yes." Her words were faint.

Max glanced at Randy, then over his shoulder at her. "They say she committed suicide."

"That's what you said." There was a hitch in Randy's voice.

Kelsey could tell Randy struggled with the information. "But some of us don't want to believe it."

"Some of us?"

"My brother and me. Laurie, his girlfriend."

Max stopped in the parking spot between his cabin and Randy's. Kelsey was glad for the change of topic. They had no proof—only speculation from an old wrangler who was dead.

"Max will show you to your cabin. The door isn't locked." Kelsey climbed out of the SUV and checked her watch. "Dinner has already been served but come on into the staff dining room when you're ready. My mom and Leo are waiting. We'll have supper for you."

"Thank you, Kelsey. It's been so nice meeting you."

"Same here. See you in a few."

Kelsey turned to leave but caught Max looking at her, his eyes challenging. She lifted her chin a little, staring back at him. She didn't want the powerful pull he seemed to wield on her body, her heart. She didn't want to be drawn to him, his magnetism. She didn't want to risk loving him again. She just wouldn't take that chance.

CHAPTER FOURTEEN

MAX ESCORTED Randy to his cabin door. The man had celebrated too much that night and was a bit wobbly on his feet. The night had been emotional for everyone. Randy had thanked Leo for taking care of his sister, for believing in her and loving her. That brought tears to Darby and Randy's eyes.

After tucking Randy safely in bed, Max walked to Kelsey's cabin, drawing her outside to sit with him on the porch steps.

"The introductions seemed to go well tonight." Since Kelsey seemed pensive, he broke the silence, longing to put his arm around her and pull her close. With much to regret, he was reluctant to act on his feelings.

"Yes."

Nothing more. She continued closed off to him, not speaking, and his attempts to open her up always went awry. He couldn't blame her. Not with their history.

He studied the stars, millions of them, pinpricks of light in the vastness of space. The moon, past its first quarter, seemed to hang in the big sky. "Why does the night sky seem so massive on clear nights like this?"

"They don't call Montana Big Sky Country for nothing."

"It fits."

Max argued with himself. He wanted Kelsey, but his old habits were hard to stop. His loyalty to his family, his career, all played a part in his reticence. How could he speak up when he knew he couldn't—shouldn't—act on his feelings?

~

KELSEY NURSED A SINKING feeling in her stomach. Her grandmother had run away, and so had her mother. What if she was like them? She glanced at Max, at his upturned face with its day's growth of beard. The night sky seemed to envelop them in a way she'd never felt.

I don't get you, Mom. You have so many people who love you—Daddy, Slade, and me. If I was loved by so many people, I'd get over what happened long ago, the things I couldn't control.

She'd once berated her mother for not dealing with her past, avoiding confrontation. Was she in the same boat? Max was back in her life, for however long she didn't know. He was a widower. He was free. In the past, she couldn't control his leaving, but she could control *her* attitude—her actions now.

But did she want him? Her former love had been the infatuation of a schoolgirl. Could there be a different kind of love between them today?

I want to start fresh, if you'll have me.

She rubbed her bottom lip. What did Max mean by starting fresh? It had come out of left field. Should she take it seriously? And what did he want—a lover or a wife? More importantly, what did she want? A husband? A friend? She wrestled with the conflict in silence.

Max lowered his head, glancing sideways at her. "Randy wants to see his sister's grave tomorrow."

Kelsey caught his gaze. "That's fine. I'll go with you. I haven't seen it either."

"What about your mother? Do you think she'd join us?"

"I don't think so. Those emotions are still too raw for her."

Max nodded and climbed to his feet. "I understand."

He offered his hand and pulled her up. Standing so near, she peered up at him. She fought the desire to retreat into her cabin. To run and hide. He kept her hand in his and squeezed it, looking as if he wanted to kiss her.

But he didn't.

"Let's go after breakfast." His voice was tender.

"Sounds good." Kelsey pulled her hand away and turned toward the cabin door.

"Good night."

Her lips parted, but she couldn't speak. Instead, she nodded, then stepped inside and shut the door.

CHAPTER FIFTEEN

THE NEXT MORNING WAS A SUNNY, but crisp day. Wind in the lodge-pole pines whipped Kelsey's hair into her face, and she pushed it back, tucking a strand behind her ear. The day was simply gorgeous. No clouds. The blue sky seemed to go on forever over the log cabins and pole fences of the ranch.

She met Max and Randy at Max's cabin. "Slade told me where to go. It's not far."

She led the way down the main ranch road past eight guest cabins separated by space for parking cars. At the last cabin, she took a track climbing steadily through green grass, scraggly sage, and blue, purple, and yellow wildflowers to the top of a small hill. The family cemetery was surrounded by a jack pole fence, the kind of western fence used on rocky terrain where post holes couldn't be set. At intervals, it had crisscrossed poles for support with long poles attached. Inside, her grandmother's grave was easy to find. A new bouquet of store-bought daisies lay beneath the headstone.

Sarah York, Wife of Leo York, and mother of Darby York. 1952–1988

"Oh, dear God." Randy dropped to his knees. Tears welled quickly in his eyes, and he sobbed.

Kelsey had never seen a man weep and so overcome by grief

that he cried out loud. Stunned, she swayed on her heels, her chest tightening. Taking a few steps away, she tried to give him his privacy. Then suddenly, memories of her father came flashing back.

Don't cry, Kelsey. Get back in the saddle. You're not hurt. Falling makes you tough. It's how you learn to ride.

She turned her back on the graveyard and looked over the ranch, the cabins, and barns below the hill. Smoke curled from the kitchen chimney. On the other side of the buildings, Ghost Mountain loomed, casting its shadow over the whole valley. A stiff breeze picked up. Kelsey shivered.

"I'm sure he's crying for all he's lost in his life," Max said, coming to stand beside her. He gave her a sidelong glance. "His sister, his wife, his daughter."

Did Max grieve for his wife too? The thought hadn't crossed her mind. She looked up and considered him quietly as the wind whipped around them.

"I guess you know how he feels." She turned toward the view of the ranch. "You lost your wife too."

"Yes, I suppose." His response seemed evasive. He avoided looking her in the eye, left her side, and walked back to Randy.

Kelsey stared at his back. What did he mean by that relatively cavalier remark? Didn't Max grieve for his wife. Hadn't he loved her?

Kelsey followed. Randy sat back on his heels, still surveying the headstone. He wiped his eyes with the back of a hand.

"I'll pay to have her maiden name added to the marker," he said. "She deserves her rightful identity."

"I'm sure Leo will appreciate that, Randy."

"It's the least I can do." He struggled to his feet. "It's good to get some closure."

Closure? That was something Kelsey had never gotten with Max. Was this trip his way to finish off an old love affair?

Kelsey drew in a deep breath. "Sorry, guys, I need to get to work."

"I understand," Randy said. "Do you mind if I stay here a while?"

"I think it would be safe if Max stays with you. I don't think there's any scary wildlife around, but Slade and Laurie were attacked by a grizzly earlier this month when they hiked up Ghost Mountain."

"In that case." Randy hesitated.

"Just make noise coming down the hillside. You'll be fine."

Kelsey retreated, fast walking back to her office sanctuary. She wanted to plug in numbers into an electronic spreadsheet she'd created, then compare them with the canceled checks from the ranch's online banking account. She also wanted to avoid the conflict erupting in her head. Keeping busy was the best remedy.

However, her respite was short-lived. Max soon pushed open the office door and peeked inside. "Mind if I come in?"

"No." She sat away from the computer. His presence filled her with trepidation.

"Randy decided with the possibility of wild animals around, he'd rather come back to his cabin. He may leave today or tomorrow morning." He approached the desk. "And I thought I'd help you sort through your boxes."

Kelsey let out a sigh. She pulled herself together and shut down her laptop. "Okay.

"You don't mind, do you?" His voice faded into silence.

She scoured his dark head held high, the curve of his cheekbone, the slight cleft in his chin, his hooded eyes hiding his thoughts. Fear knotted in her stomach—fear of her own emotions, her failure to stand up for herself no matter her best intentions, her panicked desire to love him again.

"No, why would I mind?"

"I got the impression you were avoiding me on the hill."

"Well." She looked away. *Get back in the saddle. You're not hurt. Falling makes you tough.* Her father's words drummed in her head. Biting her lower lip, she turned and studied his face. "I imagine you have much in common with Randy. He misses his daughter and you miss your wife."

Max averted his gaze. He suddenly looked pale. "Of course, I miss Claire. We were childhood friends."

"I see." Her voice was terse.

He took a deep, pained breath, and closed his eyes. "No, you don't see. I'm afraid I didn't love her like I should have loved her. That, I truly regret."

"Okay." What was she supposed to think? To say?

He opened his eyes but stared at his feet. "I hate myself for not being able to love her like she deserved as my wife."

"Why is that?"

"She was my friend. You know I was expected to marry her."

Kelsey sat back in her chair. "I know that very well."

"What you don't know is how hard it was for me. I was miserable." His voice cracked. "But Claire never knew. She was happy."

Her chin jutted up. And she was supposed to understand that? She'd been the one dumped. Hurt. Max raised his head and made strong eye contact, saying with his gaze he understood her anger.

"Forgive me," he said. "I felt I didn't have a choice."

What did he want from her? Could she easily absolve him? "Well, it's over and done with. We all have our demons."

Max nodded, seeming to collect himself. He offered an uncomfortable grin. "We have work to do." He lifted a dusty box into the chair across from the desk. "Tell me what you're looking for."

"Old reservations." She paused glad he'd changed the subject. "Also, Slade and Laurie are hoping we might be able to find some sort of clue to Sarah's death."

"In the reservations?"

"I guess."

Max took off the top of the box marked four. Kelsey stood near him, studying a heap of papers. He removed a handful, individual reservations from 2009 to 1999, and slowly flipped through them.

"What a mess," Max said, "I don't envy you your task."

The next box, marked three, contained ten more years of scattered reservations in no particular order.

"I have recorded the current registrations for the last ten years to 2009." Kelsey chewed her lower lip. "It looks as if Leo dumped the old paperwork into a box of ten-year increments."

"That means box one should contain records from when Sarah was alive."

Dread shot through her stomach. "You're right."

Max rearranged the boxes, stacking them in correct order on the floor, then he brought box one up to the chair. Slowly, dramatically, he lifted the lid. Box one was filled with green hardcover journals with numbered ruled pages. The books went back to 1975.

Kelsey picked up one ledger and sat down behind the desk, gaining some breathing space between them. "Sarah must have kept these books. The handwriting is legible. Everything is recorded by date of arrival and departure."

"She died in 1988 according to the headstone." Max picked out one ledger and shifted the box to the floor. "This is the book for 1988."

Kelsey's mouth grew dry. She stared across the desk as Max flipped through each page.

"Oh, my God," he said.

Her breathing stopped a second. She licked her lips. "What is it?"

"What was the name of Darby's real father?"

"Pete, the guy who died, told us it was Tim Krebs."

"What was the date of your grandmother's death?"

"I don't know for sure. Sometime in July 1988."

"Look at this!" Max turned the ledger around and thrust it toward her.

She blinked, adjusting her eyes to the small, rounded handwriting. Tim Krebs' name was entered for July 10 to July 16, 1988. It was circled three times in red ink.

Breath caught in her throat. What could that mean?

CHAPTER SIXTEEN

LATER THAT EVENING, Max lounged against the door jamb of Kelsey's one-bedroom cabin. Laurie and Slade sat on the bed. Kelsey held the green ledger open for them to see the name of Tim Krebs.

"What can this mean?" Slade asked the same question Kelsey had asked earlier.

"I wish Pete was here." Kelsey gave Laurie the ledger and sat down in the high-back, chair next to the writing desk. "He could straighten this out."

Laurie ran her fingertip over the red and black ink. "Pete knew his half-brother had been at the ranch at the time of Sarah's death. He knew Krebs' relationship with Sarah and Darby."

Max pushed himself away from the door. "He also knew the kind of man his brother was." He leaned a hip against the edge of the desk beside Kelsey. She was so near he could smell her fresh, floral scent.

"But our mother was told Sarah hiked the mountain alone to commit suicide," Slade said.

"Pete didn't think she committed suicide." Laurie clutched Slade's arm. "That's what he told Hank."

"Dear God." Kelsey released a long sigh. "Would Tim have been there when Sarah died? What if Tim went with her?"

Max's throat closed. Their combined efforts were leading to a troubling conclusion. "What if Tim pushed her?"

"She died on a Friday night according to Mom," Slade said. "She had been out camping all night with Hank and came home to find the police here and her mother dead."

"July 15 was a Friday night," Laurie pointed out. "I looked it up on Google."

The silence was heavy. No one said a word, but they stared at each other, mouths agape.

Laurie blinked and shook her head slightly. "We'll never know, will we?"

"I don't see how," Kelsey agreed.

"We'll never be able to prove anything legally," Max said, "but we have enough evidence for a logical supposition."

"A lot of good that will do," Laurie pooh-poohed.

Kelsey pushed her chair back and rose. "It can give our mother some much needed closure."

"I agree." Max slanted a look at her. "But let's not tell her yet. Randy is returning to Chicago tomorrow. Let me ask him to look into Tim Krebs. Maybe he can find more information about him before we tell Darby."

"Laurie and I researched him on the Internet," Slade said. "We didn't find much, did we?"

"No." Laurie shook her head. "Only the basics. Tim Krebs was married to a woman named Lisa Ross. He did time for bank robbery from 1973 to 1988. Lisa Ross died in 1990 and so did Tim."

Max made a mental note of the facts. "Randy's a lawyer. He has sources and, more than that, motivation to find out what really happened to his sister."

Kelsey touched his arm. "Do you really think Randy can find something?"

A half-smile curved Max's mouth. A throbbing ache caused his heart to pulsate wildly. Kelsey was so beautiful. So very dear. He placed his hand over hers on his sleeve.

"It doesn't hurt to try, does it?"

*H*E *HAD LOVED her but had let her go.*

Max's head spun with the hard fact of his mistake as he drove Randy to the airport in Bozeman. It didn't take long to fill him in on Tim Krebs and his relationship with Sarah. Randy had brightened once he realized the information gave him a new purpose. If he could find out more about this man, perhaps he would have answers about his sister and her death.

Max spent most of the trip in silence, hardly seeing the beauty of the canyon and rushing river beside the road. He wrestled with what he should do about Kelsey—what he wanted to do. Part of him wanted to go on with his life and tell Kelsey he loved her, but the other part wallowed in guilt from the past—of Claire's death and his part in deceiving her about his true feelings.

He pulled the SUV up to the airport drop-off and climbed out of the driver's side. Pulling Randy's carry-on bag from the back, he met Randy on the curb with it. Max shook his hand. "I'm glad you came, Randy. I'm glad you got your answers."

"When I get home, I have my work cut out for me. First, the family trust, and then I need to find out more about this Krebs fellow." He clapped Max's shoulder.

"I'll be home at the end of next week." Randy was his boss after all. "Thanks for sending me out here. I've enjoyed my vacation."

"I noticed." Randy grinned and took the handle of the carry-on from Max. "Don't let this girl get away, buddy. You've done your duty by your family and my family. Now take care of yourself."

Max didn't know what to say.

Randy took a few steps away, then turned back looking over his shoulder. "Life's too short not to take advantage of every opportunity."

"S'long, Randy."

The older man raised his hand in farewell and walked into the terminal.

Max watched him disappear into the crowd. He jammed fingers through his hair. What about that? Was Randy giving him his freedom?

He slipped back into the SUV, knowing he'd have more to chew on during the drive home.

CHAPTER SEVENTEEN

THE RHYTHM of dude ranch life set in with all of the week's guest gone by three o'clock Saturday afternoon. The wranglers drove the herd to the overnight pasture where the horses would stay until Monday morning, freshening up for the next week of trail rides. Laurie and Sam cleaned cabins and made beds with fresh sheets. Slade was busy wiping off saddles and checking other tack while Hank sat in the ranch utility vehicle and supervised John repairing fences.

In the office, Kelsey let her guest database project go for the moment. After ten years the addresses in the file boxes might not be as accurate as they needed to be. Besides, she wanted to work on the bank accounts. Leo had never paid for anything electronically. Bills were paid by check, so having access to the canceled checks online was a big help.

She discovered Hank's signature on the cancelled checks for the first five months of the year. Everything in the spreadsheet lined up with the online checks. Then she paid the pressing bills—hay, kitchen supplies, farrier, veterinarian, two-week salary for Jeremiah and Ellie. Paychecks for the new staff would be paid at the end of June. Next, she started with January 2018, comparing the check numbers in the spreadsheet with the cancelled checks online, the amounts, and the payees.

That's when she found a discrepancy. Her blood ran cold.

The January 19th check number 8011 in the spreadsheet was made out to the Landside Hay Company. The same check online was made out to Ellie Montgomery for the whopping sum of two thousand dollars, the same amount in the spreadsheet.

She sat away from the laptop. Her heart pounded. Could this be right? Ellie had free rein with the ranch's books for two years. Leo had trusted her. Was his trust misplaced? Or could this be a one-time incident?

Engrossed in her new problem, Kelsey didn't hear the office door open.

"Sorry to bother you. You seem to be concentrating."

She looked up to see Max across the desk, a lock of his brown hair drooping romantically on his forehead and a smile on his face that went up to his eyes. She was unprepared to find him so near. For an instant, her gaze held his. She found it hard to breathe. He seemed to suck up all the oxygen in the room. She forced herself to glance away, telling herself not to care about him.

"I've been busy paying bills." She didn't have enough evidence to tell him what she'd found. Not yet, anyway.

"I thought you could use a break." The rich timbre of his voice had a calming effect on her frayed nerves. "Would you like to go to dinner in Big Sky tonight? I've included Slade and Laurie in my invitation and made reservations at a saloon and restaurant called The Saddleback."

This wasn't a date if Slade and Laurie were going along. She fought not to lick her suddenly dry lips.

"Come on." His smile was definitely playful. "It will give us a break from Chef Shawn's food."

"I find nothing wrong with Shawn's food."

"Change of pace, then. I only have one more week."

"Six days actually."

One more week, and then he'd be gone. Was that good? Or bad? She logged off the Internet banking account and shut down her laptop, then averted her gaze and made a big deal of putting her paper files and spreadsheet binder into the top desk drawer. She didn't like being pressured, but what could it hurt?

She rose from the chair, her fingers on the edge of the desk. "Okay, Mr. Lee. I'll go with you, but I'm not going Dutch. This is your treat. I figure a fancy lawyer can foot the whole bill."

ELLIE STOOD on Leo's porch and watched Darby's kids and that writer Laurie pile into the rented SUV of the guest who stayed over —the lawyer guy who'd brought Sarah's brother to the ranch. They were laughing, having a good time. Not a care in the world. *No.* Not like her.

Those kids didn't see her, not really, not the real person she was. To them she was nothing. Just the old broad who took care of Leo.

But she'd seen them looking at her, speculating. What did they think they knew? They knew nothing. They had no clue.

As the car drove past Leo's cabin, she lifted her hand in farewell, but they didn't return her wave. She wasn't one of them, but she could have been. She could have been, if circumstances had been different. It ripped at her gut. She'd been invisible most of her life except when her drunken father caught her in bed at night. She'd never been able to fight him off. The bastard was too strong, but not strong enough in the end. It had felt good to give him what he deserved, the bastard. His alcohol and drug combination just didn't pan out for the old fucker that time. He was too strung out to know what she'd dropped into his glass. She sure didn't feel bad about it.

She and her husband Chet had been good together at first. They'd pulled several jobs together. Small scams. Nothing big. But after ten years, he'd left her for another woman. In the end, he was no better than her father. He got his comeuppance too when the cops found out about the bad checks he'd passed. Funny how things work out.

After Chet left her, she didn't have the guts to go out on her own. Not until she'd realized how unfair her life had been, and she'd vowed to change things. Funny how murder empowers you. Once you cross that line the first time, you can do anything you want. Now she knew what she wanted, and she was going to get it. And no one would stop her.

Ellie stepped off the porch. Old Man York was asleep. Couldn't keep his eyes open these days. No guests were on the property. The ranch was quiet with the staff having time off. At the office she tried the doorknob and, of course, the door opened. No one locked anything around here. No one expected bad things to happen in this fantasy world—this make-believe ranch catering to city dudes.

Kelsey's laptop was on the desk. What was with kids these days? Everyone had a device of some sort. Ellie didn't have a cell phone or a laptop. She liked it that way. Off the grid made it easier to disappear. But that meant she knew nothing about electronic devices. She opened the top of the computer and the screen lit up asking for a password. *Damn!* She slammed the top down.

She didn't need a stupid computer anyway. There was a paper record around here someplace. Opening the top desk drawer, she rifled through the paperwork until she found the manual spread-sheet. That was more like it. Much too easy. She took the binder out of the drawer and shut it.

The January 2018 accounts had a red mark next to the hay bill. Kelsey was snooping. She'd suspected that by the way the bitch had looked at her. Ellie picked up the spreadsheet binder and took it with her.

The weather was going to be cold enough tonight to light the wood stove.

CHAPTER EIGHTEEN

K<small>ELSEY WAS</small> surprised by the good time the four of them had. They'd eaten steaks and drank wine and craft beer. They'd laughed and chatted about music and movies and the latest electronic devices, then the talk grew serious. Laurie and Slade told Max about finding Pete dead in the barn and the implications for Leo's will. With Pete gone, only Ellie and Hank were left to inherit the ranch.

That night Kelsey finally saw what a good fit Laurie was for Slade. They made a cute couple. She was glad they'd found each other.

Back at the ranch, Max pulled the SUV into his parking spot. Laurie's cabin was behind the dining halls and since Max's cabin was the first one past the dining rooms, her cabin was near. She and Slade scrabbled out of the car, saying thanks for the fine evening. Kelsey suppressed a smile seeing how they practically ran hand-and-hand behind the dining halls.

Max noticed too. "One guess about what they have planned tonight?" he said with a chuckle.

She felt a bit melancholy. Slade was her twin. He'd always attracted girls. She could have had her share of boyfriends too if she'd wanted them. But after Max, well, other men didn't measure up. Or turn her on.

"Let me walk you back to your cabin." Max's voice was suddenly soft in the darkness as if he sensed her sadness. "I need to clear my head after all that wine."

She didn't answer. The pit of her stomach burned as Max came around to open her door. He handed her out of the car and kept her hand during their walk past the dining halls, past Leo's dark cabin, and to her own.

On the porch, he pulled her around to face him, holding her upper arms and gripping her jacket sleeves. His eyes glittered in the darkness, and his mouth was drawn taut as he surveyed her face. She felt the heat and vitality of the man. The chemistry she'd felt between them all night exploded. Lifting her head, she caught the resolve on his face.

"I honored my marriage vows while I was married. It's been two years since Claire died. Even Randy says I've done my duty to the family. It's time to move on." His voice shook with the passion of his desire. "Remember what I said? I want to start fresh with you."

What do I want?

She'd advised her mother to let go of the past. There were things she couldn't control; therefore, she had to make the best of the situation as it was today. In his own way, her father Colton had told her the same thing.

Get back in the saddle. You're not hurt.

Honestly, was she still hurt by Max's leaving? At one point, years ago, he'd hurt her. But not today. She'd put aside her feelings for him and forged her own way without him. She was okay with herself. With her life. With who she'd become.

But tonight, seeing the yearning in his eyes, she knew she wanted him to start fresh too…with her.

Standing on tiptoe, she wrapped her arms around his neck. He let out a breath. Had he been holding it? Then he pressed her too him, hugging her tight, his arms around her shoulders. They stood together unmoving, trembling with anticipation. She nuzzled his neck, and he buried his face in her hair.

Kelsey pulled back, dropping her arms to place her palms on his chest. "I, um, I better go inside."

But she couldn't move. Her feet seemed glued to the wooden slats of the porch.

"I think we'd better go inside too," Max whispered.

Rising up on her tiptoes again, she kissed him long and hard. He returned her kiss, and memories of long ago flooded back. Would starting over finish what they'd begun? Would she have closure and be ready to move on?

Kelsey was barely aware when Max reached for the doorknob. She didn't have time to catch her breath when he drew her into her cabin and kicked the door shut behind them.

CHAPTER NINETEEN

THE BREAKFAST BELL clanged at seven o'clock. Kelsey groaned and opened her eyes. Max lay on his back beside her snoring slightly. A feeling of heaviness enveloped her. She shut her eyes, squeezing them tight. Why had she gone to bed with him? What good would come out of it?

Turning over on her side away from him, Kelsey opened her eyes again and stared at the cabin wall. She relived the night after he'd drawn her inside. It had been beautiful, loving, wild, passionate—all the things that happened when you loved someone and made love.

But had it really happened like that? His wife had died two years ago. She hadn't been intimate with anyone in years either. Could it have been pure, physical lust—not love?

Did she still love him? Who knew? She sure didn't.

Letting out a sigh, she sat up, her legs dangling off the side of the bed. The outside was already bright, a beautiful but probably nippy day. A Montana mountain day.

Max touched her between her shoulder blades, then ran a fingertip down her spine. She shivered.

"Good morning."

She glanced over her shoulder to see his disheveled brown hair falling in his sleepy eyes. "Good morning to you."

"I could get used to this."

"Yes," she said, but did she mean it? They were two different people now with two different lives. Kelsey didn't see how a real relationship could come of a one-night stand.

Placing her bare feet on the cold floor, she stood up, well aware she was naked, vulnerable. Facing him, she examined his hairy chest and well-defined muscular body, not quite bodybuilder ripped, but he certainly kept in shape. A sheet covered him up to the waist. She sank her teeth into her lower lip, then offered a tentative smile.

He watched her, and her body seemed to tingle where his gaze touched it. She stayed still without moving, letting him look at her as she took him in. Then she shook herself out of the trance.

"I need to get ready. Guests come today, and I have more accounting work to do."

She walked quickly into the bathroom, aware of his eyes following her. Shutting the door, she let out a long breath, her heart beating wildly.

MAX ACCOMPANIED her to the back door of the kitchen. He brushed her lips with his and went on to his cabin to clean up. Kelsey hurried inside, wrapped up a bagel, and poured herself a cup of coffee. The second dining room was loud with the chatter of staff and clatter of dishes. She kissed her grandfather's cheek before crossing over to the sideboard where the cream was kept.

Ellie's good morning smile was more of a smirk, her eyes sharp pinpoints.

"Aren't you going to eat breakfast?" Darby asked.

Kelsey held up her napkin-wrapped bagel and poured cream into her mug. "I've got work to do this morning."

Laurie scooted her chair back. "I'll walk out with you. I need to put the linens into one more cabin." She carried her plate and utensils into the kitchen, then joined Kelsey at the door.

They left the dining hall together. "What was that look Ellie gave you? It certainly looked like the evil eye."

"She probably knows Max stayed over at my cabin last night."

Laurie grabbed Kelsey's arm. "He didn't!"

"He did." Kelsey felt the weight of Laurie's gaze upon her. "It was a long night."

Laurie laughed. "But was it a good night?"

Kelsey hesitated. Had it been a good night? She found herself ambivalent about their time together, about her response to Max. "I suppose. I enjoyed it at the time," she finally admitted with a smile.

"But you're unsure." Laurie was perceptive enough to understand. They walked on.

"I don't know if I want to get involved with him. There doesn't seem to be much permanence with Max."

"But he was married. That means he's not afraid of commitment. His wife died, so he's free to marry again if he wants."

Kelsey took the two steps up to the office porch. She looked down on Laurie. "*If* he wants to." *And if I want to.* "It could have been the wine, the fellowship, a simple one-night stand."

"Well, it could be all that. We don't know much about Max, do we?" Laurie's forehead wrinkled. "I'd better not tell Slade," she said with a sigh. "It might awaken his overprotective brotherly instincts."

"We wouldn't want to stir that up," Kelsey replied, grinning.

She waved farewell to Laurie and went inside the office, her mind on their conversation. Sitting down behind the desk, Kelsey set down her coffee mug and bagel. She didn't touch her laptop but gazed at it with unfocused eyes, her thoughts spinning. She didn't know what she wanted, but of course, what happened between them would hinge on Max. More importantly, it also depended upon her duty to her father and his life's work, his Kentucky thoroughbred breeding farm. She would never move to Chicago and leave her dad's farm, even if Slade was keen on taking it over. Which he wasn't.

Ironic, wasn't it? Kelsey now had the same problem Max had years ago. He had felt obligated to his family. He'd left her because of it. Now she was facing the same dilemma.

The thing was, she loved the family farm too much to leave it. So, sleeping with Max didn't make much sense. Her duty was to her family and her father's legacy. That was more important than one night making love to an ex-boyfriend.

That decided, Kelsey opened the top drawer and looked for the spreadsheet so she could continue to review the 2018 expenditures. She didn't find the binder on top of the checkbook, envelopes, and bills. Had she misplaced the spreadsheet? She searched two other drawers but found nothing.

With dread beating in her heart, Kelsey leaned back in the chair and twined her fingers together.

Where was it?

Her breathing became difficult. She stared across the room and a raw certainty struck her. The spreadsheet was missing.

And Ellie had taken it.

CHAPTER TWENTY

MAYBE THE SMUG smile Ellie had given her in the dining hall was because she knew she had the spreadsheet, not because she'd seen Max leave her cabin this morning.

Kelsey sat forward, rested her elbows on the desktop, and placed her face in her hands. She breathed in slowly, trying to think, trying to regain her composure.

She had no proof Ellie took it. And she now had no evidence Ellie recorded the hay company's name in the spreadsheet but made out the check to herself. However, she did have access to the cancelled checks online. She sat up and logged into the online banking account. Maybe the discrepancy she found yesterday was a one-time thing.

But it wasn't.

After thirty minutes of research, she found fifteen other checks made out to Ellie totaling more than twelve thousand dollars.

Ellie had embezzled the ranch. Sweet, dependable Ellie was a crook.

The knowledge sat heavily in her stomach.

"GRANDDAD?" Kelsey cracked his cabin door and stuck her head inside.

"C'mon in." Leo sat near the window in a shabby armchair reading a tattered Louis L'amour paperback. One of Ellie's colorful, knitted lap blankets covered his legs. He removed his spectacles and smiled up at her.

Her grandfather, actually her step-grandfather, was gnarled and crotchety with thin strands of gray hair sticking out over his ears and bald patches on top. But Kelsey couldn't help loving him. He was a generous fellow, having made a home for her mother and grandmother. For that she was thankful.

She sat down in the companion chair, noticing a basket of knitting by its side. "Where's Ellie?"

"Gone to get me a sandwich. Didn't eat much breakfast. Couldn't stomach it then."

She nodded, leaned forward with her elbows on her knees, and wove her fingers together. "Is the book good?"

"Better be. I've read it four times."

"If I bought you a tablet, you could read electronic books. The print is bigger and it's backlit so you can see it better."

"Don't need no new-fangled gadget."

"Oh, okay." She sat back, still clasping her hands, and dropped the subject. That attitude must be why nothing was automated on the ranch, even though the technology had been available for years. And also, why it had been easy for Ellie to embezzle from the ranch bank account. Goodness knew what else she had done.

"You got something on your mind?" Leo was direct.

"Well," she hesitated. "Not really."

He pulled a frowned. "Don't lie to me, girl. You're just like your mother in that respect."

"What do you mean?"

"I could always tell when she was lying."

She crossed her arms. *Caught.* "Okay, I was wondering how well you know Ellie."

"She's been a good employee for two years." He frowned. "Why?"

"I know you depend on her, but I'm not sure she's as honest as she seems."

Leo shifted in his chair and cocked his head to the side. "You know something, child. Out with it."

Kelsey drew in a deep breath. What should she tell him? She had no proof. "Um, I think she took the ranch spreadsheet binder from the office."

"You're doing the books this summer, aren't you?"

"Yes, sir."

"Why would she take the spreadsheet?"

"I think she may be stealing from you."

The silence was long and painful. Finally, Leo cleared his throat. "Go into her room and look for it. You won't find it, but if it will satisfy you, have a look."

Kelsey quickly stood up and went into the second bedroom. The shelf above the closet was bare, and the floor only contained boots and shoes. Her hands trembling, she pulled open each drawer, but found only women's clothing. She looked under the bed. *Nothing.*

"What the hell are you doing in my bedroom?"

Rising from the floor, Kelsey steeled her nerves without moving, then she slowly turned. Ellie glared at her from the doorway, her eyes seeming to bulge from their sockets. Her cheeks were red, her fists clenched.

"I think you know." Kelsey entered Ellie's personal space, her body tense. "You took the ranch spreadsheet."

Ellie's laughter had an edge to it. "Did you find it in my room?"

Kelsey hated to admit the truth. "No."

"Then how do you know I took it? You probably misplaced it. Young people aren't very dependable."

Kelsey couldn't answer her. Her heart pounded, and she wanted to grab the short, dumpy woman by the shoulders and shake the truth from her. Instead, she shouldered past her and stopped in front of her grandfather.

"Sorry to trouble you. I guess I was wrong."

Leo nodded several times. "I'm glad we got that settled."

Kelsey's head jerked up. "Yes, it's settled for now." She let the sarcasm drip from her remark. "See you at dinner."

Stooping down, she kissed Leo's forehead, then fled the stuffy cabin.

CHAPTER TWENTY-ONE

WHEN SHE RETURNED to the office, a family with two horse-crazy little girls from Kentucky had arrived early. They were from Louisville and were excited to learn Kelsey lived on a real horse farm near Lexington.

"What are you doing way out here," the mother asked as they walked out of the office onto the porch after signing in.

Kelsey noticed Max chatting with the father. "Working this summer" she replied. "I'll go home when the season ends."

She pointed them in the direction of their cabin and told the little girls they could go down to the barn to see the baby colt if a parent went along. As they piled into their SUV, Kelsey glanced at Max. Ignoring the fluttering in her chest, she went back inside the office. He followed.

Unable to think of anything to say, Kelsey stood motionless inside the door. He reached for her, cupping her cheek, and tenderly kissed her. His lips were warm and moist. Visions of their night together frolicked in her head.

"Good morning, again," he murmured against her mouth.

She took a step backward in a desperate attempt to create space between them and gain the appearance of control. "It's afternoon."

"Time flies," he said, "when I'm with you."

She glimpsed humor and yearning in his eyes, a peculiar combination. She shook her head in a gesture of annoyance, then turned away and collapsed in the chair behind the desk.

He took the chair across from her. "I heard you say you plan to leave after the summer season."

"And you're leaving Saturday."

"I have a job to get back to."

"And I have a horse farm to run."

He waved his hand in a dismissive gesture. "Airplanes make the trip to Kentucky every day."

"I don't do long distance." Her voice was firm. Would he understand the message?

"That's fair." He lifted his head, making eye contact, then sat silently a moment.

Kelsey crossed her arms over her chest, protecting herself. She wasn't in the mood. "It remains to be seen if last night was a mistake." She kept her voice controlled.

He sat forward, suddenly growing thoughtful. "I hope you don't think so."

"I don't want to talk about it." She looked away from him, biting her lip. "There are other things going on."

"Kelsey, what's wrong?" His attitude changed suddenly. He sounded concerned.

She connected with his gaze once more and exhaled. "Ellie has been embezzling the ranch, but I can't prove it."

As she told him her story, Kelsey realized Max took her seriously. That was a relief to know she *wasn't* crazy. He believed her, unlike Leo. But without the spreadsheet, Max also realized they had no evidence.

"Is there anything about Ellie in her personnel file?"

"I hadn't thought to look." Kelsey opened the middle drawer that contained files of employees. She extracted the one saying Ellie

Montgomery, placed it on the desktop, and opened it. Of course, it was empty. Had it been tampered with too?

He climbed to his feet. "May I use your landline?"

"Sure. Go ahead."

Max called Randy, who had already made it home to Chicago, and asked him to look into a woman named Ellie Montgomery. They needed any information fast. Randy said he'd see what he could find out.

"I'm worried, Max," Kelsey said when he hung up. Her mouth was dry. She cleared her throat. "What if we're assuming the worst? Overanalyzing what we think we know about Ellie? We could be wrong."

"Or what if we are proactive by following the clues to their logical conclusions?"

"But what if they aren't logical? What if Ellie is what she seems —a dependable, caring employee?"

"Who stands to inherit part of this ranch someday."

THE HESTON GIRL knew too much. Thankfully, Leo didn't believe her, but Ellie feared her time was running out. Her troubles had started when that red-headed bitch returned to the ranch in March. Then her nosy kids showed up.

Ellie took a deep breath, her knitting needles flying in her hands —knit a row, purl a row. She glanced at Leo, who was snoring loudly in his easy chair, the side of his mouth drooping open.

No. Her problems actually started when Leo hired that damn Hank. She'd not bargained for Leo calling his old buddy to come home and take over the ranch. Slitting the leather on Leo's saddle had backfired. The old man fell off the horse all right, just like Hank, but he'd lived—like Hank. The blood clot in Leo's brain almost did the old man in though. He'd spent time in the hospital.

Yet, he'd recovered and here he sat, sidelined, needing care, but still snoring away as pretty as you please.

Tonight, she'd noticed a change toward her in the staff dining hall. The mood had been strained. In the other dining room, she could hear this week's new guests laughing and talking—getting to know each other over one of Shawn's gourmet dinners. But the staff table had been oddly quiet. Those Heston kids and that interfering Laurie ducked their heads, avoiding eye contact, but had peeked up from their plates to stare at her. That lawyer guy, who'd shown up at the ranch last week, ate with the ranch crew as if he belonged. Something was going on between him and Kelsey. She didn't like it. That man was trouble too.

Ellie's nostrils flared. Her heart pounded, and she felt a rush of heat spread through her body. She had to act just like Chet and her daddy taught her. She couldn't wait much longer.

CHAPTER TWENTY-TWO

KELSEY WAS WELL-AWARE of Max sitting near her feet as she pushed the rocking chair back and forth. He and Slade sat together on the top step of Max's front porch where the two couples had gathered. The night was chilly with a multitude of stars overhead. For a split second, Kelsey hated the thought of Max leaving on Saturday. No matter how indifferent she acted, she would miss him.

"We need to tell Mom and Hank what we suspect," Slade said after a long moment of quiet. "At least, they can fire her ass."

Laurie, wrapped in a red wool blanket against the nighttime cold, sat in the second rocker. "But who will watch after Leo?"

"That will have to be addressed. I'm sure Darby and Hank will figure it out." Max looked up at Kelsey. She saw fire dance in his eyes as if he wanted her.

A shudder swept through her. She drummed her fingers on the arm of the chair and manufactured a smile for him trying to be pleasant despite the chasm she'd tried to create between them. He returned her smile, meeting her gaze, and she lowered her head suddenly self-conscious.

Laughter and music from one of the nearby cabins broke the

stillness of the night. As the wind died, the four sat silently engaged in their own thoughts. Kelsey turned her focus to Ghost Mountain, a looming shadow in the distance. Was supernatural evil stalking the ranch at the base of that mountain? Or was the malevolence simply human?

A noise caught Kelsey's attention. Two headlights from the ranch's utility vehicle bobbed up and down approaching along the well-traveled dirt road from the dining halls.

"Hank is making his nightly rounds," Slade observed.

"Maybe we should tell him about the missing spreadsheet, and he can break it to Mom." Kelsey didn't like keeping secrets.

"Good idea." Slade climbed to his feet and rested his hand on the wooden porch support waiting for Hank.

The UTV approached in a slow, jerky manner, weaving to the edge of the road and then back into the center. Kelsey saw Hank wipe his temple with the back of his hand.

Slade came down the steps. "Hey, Hank, can we talk to you a minute?"

Hank didn't glance Slade's way. He seemed dazed, oblivious to everything around him, and drove right past Max's cabin.

"Is he drunk?" Kelsey heard alarm in Laurie's voice.

Max rushed down the steps, following Slade. "Something's wrong."

Suddenly, the UTV lurched to the right, skidded, and headed directly toward the security light.

Kelsey stood up, her heart in her throat. "Hank! Watch out!"

The utility vehicle crashed into the pole, the motor still running, and came to a halt. Hank slumped over the steering wheel.

The next few minutes were a nightmare. Hank was unconscious, his breathing shallow and his skin pasty. He smelled of alcohol. Slade and Max discussed the safety of moving him but decided to go ahead. They didn't think he'd struck his head, and they might need to resuscitate him. Lifting Hank from the UTV, Max and Slade rested him on the flat road.

Laurie draped her blanket over his prone body. "He seems drunk."

Max knelt, lifted Hank's wrist, and put two fingers near the older man's thumb. "His heartbeat is slow. He has all the symptoms of an opioid overdose."

"Dear God!" Kelsey couldn't believe it. "How do you know?"

"I've seen this before." Max got to his feet. "I have something that might help."

Before Kelsey could ask what that something might be, Max darted toward his cabin. Laurie joined Kelsey, and side-by-side, they hooked arms, holding each other, and waited for Max to return.

Kelsey's heartbeat seemed sluggish. A horrendous dread settled in her stomach. What if Hank died? Her mother would never be the same.

"I feel so helpless," Laurie whispered. She was shaking.

"I'm not hanging around. I'm going for help." Slade jumped into the utility vehicle. With care, he backed up, then veered to the right, bounced over the grass and sage, and turned back onto the road, heading toward the office where the landline telephone was kept.

Max sprinted back, passing Slade on the road. He held something in his hand. With the security light illuminating the drama below, he knelt beside Hank and lifted his head.

"Max, what is that?"

"Narcan." Max squirted the drug into Hank's nostril. "If I'm right, this will bring him around."

Almost immediately, Hank gasped for breath and opened his eyes. He coughed several times, then turned his head to the side and vomited.

DARBY EXITED a treatment room at the medical center in Big Sky. With tears welling in her eyes, she walked over to where Kelsey and

Max sat and took his hand. "Hank had hydrocodone in his system. You saved his life. Thank you, Max."

"I'm glad I had Narcan available."

"How did you happen have it?" Darby asked.

"I'm from Chicago, remember?" His smile seemed reticent. "I carry it with me, because I never know when I might need it in the city."

"Well, I'm thankful you were here."

Kelsey rose and hugged her mother. "Did Hank say what happened?"

"The last thing he remembers is Ellie giving him a mug of hot coffee with whisky in it. You know how he likes it, especially on a cold night."

Kelsey met Max's gaze. "Ellie," they said in unison.

"Then he felt dizzy and drowsy." Darby shook her head. "He doesn't remember anything else."

"Will he be able to come home tonight?" Kelsey asked.

"The doctor is keeping him for observation. You go back to the ranch. I'll stay and call if he gets to go home tomorrow."

Kelsey was quiet as Max walked her to the rental SUV. He opened the passenger door, and she climbed in. He joined her on the driver's side. Moments of silence passed between them. Max didn't move. Hazarding a glance his way, she sank her teeth into her lower lip. Her thoughts spun out of control.

"What are we going to do about Ellie?"

"I don't know. I'd like to have proof." Max rubbed his forehead. "We need to find that coffee mug."

"And see if we can find something else in it besides coffee."

"And whisky." Max turned on the engine, backed away from the parking spot, and gunned the SUV.

Sunrise crept over the mountaintops, revealing the valley below with soft, murky light. Entering the ranch property, they stopped at the V in the ranch access road because Jeremiah and other wranglers herded the horses into the grounds from the night pasture. Max waited for them to pass, then drove to his cabin and parked beside it. Slade had left the utility vehicle near the cabin last night after escorting the ambulance from the ranch entrance.

Max hopped out and strode to the UTV. Kelsey ran to catch up. The coffee mug lay on its side on the floorboard, all the liquid spilled. He lifted up the empty mug and showed it to Kelsey.

"A lot of good this will do us." She felt despondent. "It's empty!"

"I'm not so sure. Look at the white residue inside."

"It could be sugar."

Max shook his head. "I don't think so. This is how Ellie poisoned Hank. She probably took one or more hydrocodone tablets, crushed them, and slipped the powder into his coffee."

"Why add the whiskey? To make is stronger?"

"To cover up any taste is my guess. Besides, once a tablet is crushed, it becomes more potent—more deadly."

Kelsey's pulse picked up as she replayed the events of the past night in her head. "I'm worried about Leo." Her voice lowered. "Ellie might try the same thing on him."

"Despite her façade of deference and compassion, she's a threat." Max stepped nearer and stroked Kelsey's cheek with the back of his fingers. "That's why I'd better take this mug to the authorities and tell them what we suspect."

She nodded, agreeing, but in her heart, she didn't want him to leave, not even for a few hours.

"I'll be back soon." He placed a gentle kiss on her lips. "You go sit with Leo until I return."

Nodding again, she backed away. His words were meant to comfort her. How did he know she didn't want him to leave? Did he read her mind? They seemed to have a rare connection, something that she had with no one else except maybe her twin. An otherworldly bond based on history and—dare she admit it—love?

CHAPTER TWENTY-THREE

THE RANCH WAS EERILY quiet in the morning light. Five-thirty was too early to rouse Leo. She'd been up all night, and Kelsey was exhausted. She stopped by her cabin to change clothes, wash her face, and brush her teeth. She'd only lain down on the bed for a moment's rest when she jerked awake. The clock next to her bed read nine o'clock. She'd fallen fast asleep hours ago and had even slept through the clanging dinner bell.

At this time of the day, breakfast would be finished, and the first trail rides of the week underway. Laurie and Sam would be cleaning cabins, and Chef Shawn and Tristan working in the kitchen preparing lunch and dinner. If Slade was around, he'd be far away at the barn.

Uneasiness prickled her scalp. Too much time had passed, and she'd failed to protect Leo. His cabin was a few yards away. He always went back there after breakfast. Scrambling to her feet, she put on her boots, and hurried to the cabin. There, she quietly opened the front entrance. "Leo, are you home? Are you napping?"

She waited a heartbeat, then went inside. No one was in the living room, but his bedroom door was cracked. She heard a scuffling noise—grunts and heavy breathing.

"Leo?" She tiptoed across the room and touched the door. It swung open.

Ellie leaned over her grandfather's bed. She had a pillow in her hands.

Kelsey darted toward the bed and shoved Ellie's shoulder, pushing her aside. "What are you doing?" Stooping over Leo, Kelsey examined him. His eyes were shut. His breath came in short, quick gasps.

A bloodcurdling scream emerged from Ellie's throat. Kelsey turned. A shudder crawled up her spine.

Ellie stalked toward Kelsey brandishing a utility knife probably from the kitchen—small, but sharp enough to cut flesh.

Kelsey raised her hands defensively. "We know you killed Pete," Kelsey said with a bravado she didn't feel. "We know you tried to kill Hank. Now Leo! What is wrong with you?"

"If you had proof, I'd already be arrested." Ellie's words were a low growl. Her face had transformed from the compliant, helpful caretaker into that of a snarling beast.

"Max has gone to Bozeman to get that proof. He's gone to find out what you put into Hank's coffee."

"Has he now?" The dark threat of Ellie's tone left Kelsey with a profound sense of dread. "Well, when he comes back, he won't find his little sweetheart waiting for him. We're going to take a long walk."

"You won't get away with this."

She snickered with contempt. "I have so far."

"I know you've embezzled from the ranch. I have proof."

"Your proof is in that wood stove in the living room." Ellie jerked her head toward the door.

Kelsey drew a shaky breath, her heart ramming her chest. "What are you going to do?"

"You'll see. Turn around." Kelsey hesitated. "I said, turn around!"

Like Kelsey had seen on so many television cop shows, Ellie spun her around, shoved her face against the wall, seized her arms, and drew them behind her back. Then in a swift move, she clapped handcuffs over her wrists. Where had she gotten handcuffs? And where had she gotten the strength to compel Kelsey into submission? She was like a brutal prison guard. The whole scenario seemed surreal.

"Now we're taking that little walk."

Ellie pushed Kelsey out of the bedroom toward the open cabin door, then marched her prisoner down the stairs. One hand gripped the handcuffs and the other with the knife pressed against Kelsey's back, Ellie pricked her shirt and skin just enough to validate her intent.

Ellie cracked the cabin door and peered both ways. Seeing no one, she shoved Kelsey over the threshold and down the stairs. In lockstep, she propelled her along the road to the bridge over Saga Creek, forcing her toward the barns and Ghost Mountain behind them.

Where was Slade? Would he see them walking in this strange fashion? Would he rescue her?

"If you scream, we won't finish our little walk." Ellie forced the blade harder against Kelsey's back. "You'll die right here. I'll drag your body into the woods for the bears to find. By the time your bones are found, I'll make sure everyone thinks your "boyfriend" killed you because you turned him down."

Kelsey grimaced in pain. Had the knife drawn blood? Surely, if she ran, she could outpace a fat old woman.

As if Ellie read her mind, she tightened her grip on the handcuffs and jerked hard, almost pulling Kelsey's arms out of her shoulder sockets. "I may be fat, but you can't outrun me, girl."

"Why are you doing this?" Kelsey gasped in agony. The pain in her arms and shoulders was excruciating. She allowed herself to be herded up the trail into the mountains.

"It's my time to get what is due me." Ellie's voice sounded wild, uncharacteristically feral. Her words made no sense.

"From the looks of it, you were trying to hasten your inheritance." Kelsey's words came out in short huffs. Kill Pete. Then Hank. Finally, my grandfather."

"Shut up! The old man ain't your grandfather."

"He's close enough. What do you care whether he is my real grandfather or not?"

Kelsey stumbled on a tree root almost going down. Ellie's yanked on her wrists, sending waves of pain up to her shoulders.

"Shut up! I'm done talking to you."

They walked in silence, up the winding trail, the sound of their booted feet loud in the stillness around them. Had the wildlife fled from the scene, also afraid? Her breath labored, Kelsey grew hot, sweat dropping from her forehead onto her face, slipping between her breasts and under her arms. The pace was fast. Each second of the trek was an agony from the thin air and exertion and pain in her back and arms.

Kelsey had never been on this trail, but Slade and Laurie had described to her how the overlook, where her grandmother died, jutted out over the rocks below. She inhaled sharply. That was where Ellie was taking her! *The lookout Oh, God, did Ellie intend to throw her off the same cliff where her grandmother had died?*

"What makes you think you'll get away with this?" Kelsey hissed.

"Tim Krebs did." Ellie's answer was blunt, almost gleeful.

"Tim Krebs killed my grandmother?" Kelsey couldn't believe her words. "How do you know?"

"The old bastard told my mother."

Questions spun in her head. How did Ellie's mother know Tim Krebs? That man was supposed to be her mother's father. Why had he been at the ranch at the time of her grandmother's death? To kill her?

"You're saying Sarah York didn't commit suicide?"

"That's what I'm saying," Ellie growled. "And that's how I know it can be done."

"I don't understand. Why would he do that?"

"You're as stupid as she was. Why do you think?"

She gave Kelsey a shove. Kelsey fell to her knees, feeling the point of the knife prick her back. How could she save herself? Struggling to regain her feet, she then plodded on as fear swelled in her belly.

CHAPTER TWENTY-FOUR

MAX TOOK the turnoff to Ghost Mountain Ranch too fast and skidded on the gravel and dirt road. He fought off a wave of paralyzing fear threatening to shut down his ability to think. He should never have left Kelsey alone. If Ellie was capable of murdering Pete and attempting to poison Hank, she would have no compunction about killing anyone else who got in her way. He should have warned Slade to keep an eye on her instead of putting that responsibility on Kelsey.

Thank God, he'd stopped in Big Sky at the Gallatin County Sheriff Office instead of going all the way to Bozeman. Otherwise, he'd be nowhere near the ranch. The officer had listened to his story and taken the coffee mug. Results would not be available for a week.

A week might be too late.

He pulled up in front of the office and slammed the truck into park. He leaned over the steering wheel and stared at a man limping down the road past the dining halls. Was that Leo?

Max pulled up beside him and lowered the driver's window. "Leo, where are you going?" The old man was disheveled and in his pajamas. His feet were bare.

"She took Kelsey." His gravelly voice was hard to hear. "I need that new-fangled golf cart to go after her."

"Who took Kelsey?" Max caught his breath. He already knew the answer.

"That damn Ellie!" Leo didn't stop his laborious walk. "She put a pillow over my face. If Kelsey hadn't come in when she did...." His words faded.

If that woman hurt one hair on Kelsey's head, he'd strangler her. "Where did they go?"

"Kelsey tried to warn me about Ellie." Leo paused and turned stricken eyes on Max. "But I didn't listen."

Max cut him off. "Where did they go?"

Leo jerked his head. "Up Ghost Mountain. On the trail behind the barns."

"Call the sheriff, Leo. I'm going to get her."

MAX EXHALED A JAGGED BREATH, his pulse drumming in erratic rhythm as he drove the utility vehicle up the mountain trail. He only hoped the UTV wasn't damaged from the wreck last night. So far, it was operating well enough, the four-wheel-drive clawing over rocks and tree roots. A tree branch whipped him in the face, and he brushed it away. He didn't know where he was going but sensed the day would end badly if he didn't find Kelsey in time.

As he ascended, the trail narrowed, hardly allowing for the UTV to pass. He came to a log that had fallen across the path. It had been sawed in two, probably by a ranch hand during normal trail maintenance, but he couldn't squeeze the four-wheeler through. Turning off the engine, he climbed out and followed the path on foot. Within fifteen minutes, he heard voices. He crouched behind a boulder.

"You and your family must suffer."

A chill crawled across his sweaty skin. *Ellie!*

"For what? We haven't done anything to you. We welcomed you into the family. Leo trusted you. What could we have possibly done to you?" He could hear the fear in Kelsey's voice.

Thank God. She was still alive.

"Your mother had all the fucking good luck. Good stepdaddy, rich husband. Now she's getting money from a family she never knew. Well, she should have known my family. That would have changed things for her. Don't matter now. She'll cry when she finds out you committed suicide, just like her precious mother."

Max recoiled at Ellie's ramblings, horrified by her words.

"People won't believe I committed suicide with my hands handcuffed behind my back. Besides, killing me won't bring you peace."

"Close enough." Ellie laughed. "I'll be long gone before anyone finds you."

He peered around the boulder. Ellie stood with her back to him. He waved his hand to attract Kelsey's attention.

"Slade and Laurie know what you've done." Kelsey's voice broke. She jerked her head to indicate she'd spotted him. "You won't get away with this."

"Who says I won't. You won't be here to know, will you? Now get moving around that fence."

The exposed stony summit had been cordoned off after Sarah's fall. Leo erected a low, jack pole fence a few feet from the edge of the cliff to prevent another accident. The barrier was built in sections six feet in length. Each section consisted of two logs that made up an X to support two thinner cross timbers that provided an obstruction to anyone approaching the dangerous section of the trail. As customary in mountainous regions, the Xs were not cemented into the ground; instead, they rested on the rocky outcropping. After thirty years of neglect, the once strong fence now looked as if a gentle breeze would knock it over.

Kelsey did not move, her face ashen and her body trembling. With her arms pinioned behind her back, she knew she was a dead woman, if Ellie got her around the fence. "No. If you are going to kill me, you'll have to work to do it."

Ellie swung the knife in front of Kelsey's face. "I said move!"

"No!"

Max gasped as the knife narrowly missed Kelsey's cheek.

Now or never.

"Stop!"

Ellie turned, her eyes filled with shock. Max lunged and hit her full force in the stomach. The impact knocked the knife from her hand. Ellie, arms flailing, toppled backwards into the fence. The weathered wooden poles crumbled under their combined weight. She landed on her back near the edge of the cliff with Max on top of her. The knife lay in the gravel beside them. Max rolled off her and they both scrabbled for the knife. He gained his feet first and advanced towards her, knife in hand. Ellie rapidly skittered backwards, apparently unaware of her proximity to the edge of the cliff.

Max's eyes widen. He reached for her.

"No! No! no!" She pushed herself back one more time. Her scream tortured the air as her last motion slid her off the smooth boulder and she thudded onto the rocks below.

Max dropped the knife at his feet and peered over the edge. He saw Ellie's bloodied body fifty feet below.

"Max!" Kelsey rushed toward him. Max turned towards her.

She was unable to throw her arms around him. He did the next best thing and caught her to his chest. He locked her tight against him, holding her close, her head tucked under his chin, their breathing becoming less ragged as moments passed.

Max gazed out over Kelsey's head beyond the lookout, trying not to think what he'd find if he looked down the mountain. Instead, he let the scenery soothe him. They were surrounded by incredible views of mountain ranges in every direction. The ranch buildings looked like wooden toys, spread out in the valley below them at the foot of Ghost Mountain.

And Kelsey was safe in his arms.

CHAPTER TWENTY-FIVE

HOURS LATER, Kelsey sat on the sofa in the staff dining hall in front of the blazing fire. Slade had built it big to drive away the chill from her body. The scent of Leo's cherry pipe tobacco wafted over her, comforting her. Her grandfather sat in his easy chair and puffed silently on his pipe, tapping it occasionally, putting a match to it when it snuffed out.

Normally, the steady heartbeat of her family, she felt at odds right now with the plucky image she always tried to create. She had not felt brave today; she had not known what to do, not been able to escape from Ellie. Massaging her fingertips over the red marks on her wrist to lessen the pain, she couldn't quite come to grips with the conflicting emotions arising from her narrow escape. She was alive, but Ellie was dead and Max, although he had saved her, had been the direct cause of Ellie's death. How did they live with that? She wanted to weep, as she replayed the memories of the day in her mind.

Somehow, she and Max had made it down the mountain that morning. At the UTV, Max had backed the vehicle down the trail until he could turn it around, and they'd clambered aboard. A few hundred yards down the path and around a bend, they had come upon Slade and Laurie rushing up to meet them. Both men headed back up the mountain to see if they could do anything for Ellie. Kelsey sat with her aching arms behind her back, trying to keep her balance as Laurie drove the four-wheeler the final distance to the valley below.

The Gallatin County Sheriff, along with a mountain rescue unit and ambulance, arrived soon after Leo placed a call from the ranch office. By then, Jeremiah had returned from the trail ride, and while the other wranglers saw to the horses, he removed her handcuffs with a hacksaw and bolt cutters. Before the sheriff interviewed Leo and Kelsey, she called her mother at the hospital and was able to tell her the truth. Sarah York did not commit suicide as everyone always suspected. Tim Krebs had shoved her off the lookout, much as Ellie had fallen to her death that day.

Kelsey supposed it had to be some comfort for her mother to know she had nothing to do with Sarah's death. After thirty years, that ghost of guilt could be assuaged. It had lived too long in her mother's soul, coloring her life, keeping her away from the men she held most dear. That the murderer was Darby's real father, well, that had to hurt in some way, but her mother had never known the man. If what Laurie and her grandmother's letter said was true, he wasn't a good person. *No.* He was evil. There was a big difference.

Kelsey had been standing on the dining room porch when the rescue team brought the recovered body down the mountain. Glad she had been too far away to see any gory details, she'd fled into the dining room where she now sat.

She wanted Max, wanted him near her, holding her, telling her everything would be all right. He'd been so heroic. He'd rescued her from a terrifying death. But because his actions had killed Ellie, hours ago Max had gone to Big Sky with the sheriff. And so, she waited, staring at the crackling flames, feeling the heat upon her face, trying to forget the horrors of the day.

"Kelsey!" Darby rushed into the dining hall. "Are you all right?"

Kelsey came to her feet and let her mother give her a mighty hug. "Yes, Mom."

Darby turned to Leo. "And you, you old scalawag, I hear you tried to save Kelsey yourself."

"Humph." Leo dismissed Darby's words with a wave of his hand, not standing up. "Kelsey is the one who saved me."

Darby dropped to her knees and embraced him. "I'm glad you're safe."

Hank followed Darby into the hall, hobbling slowly. He looked pale and weak. Kelsey squeezed his hand. "I'm glad you're okay."

Hank touched her arm. "Can't kill an old cowboy like me that easily." He gave a shallow laugh. "But I think I need to sit a spell."

Kelsey led him to her seat on the sofa, then sat beside him. With a shake of his head, he silently examined her bruised wrist and patted her knee. She knew what he was trying to say, and she was thankful, too, he'd survived.

Laurie came in from the kitchen carrying a tray of mugs and a pot of coffee. She sat it down on the hearth.

Slade followed with a big chocolate cake, forks, and plates. "Chef saved this for us from the guest dinner."

"Sounds good." Darby helped them served the coffee and cake, then everyone sat quietly and ate, the mood in the room subdued.

Really, it should be. After all, a woman had died today. No matter what Ellie had done and tried to do, she was a human being.

What had driven her to her anger? What had caused her cruelty? She'd been jealous. But why? Was she a psychopath, lacking a conscience?

The dining hall door opened. Kelsey caught a glimpse of Max out of the corner of her eye. Hopping up, she set down her plate, and ran to him. She gazed up at him and touched the plastic butterfly bandage on his cheek.

"I've been cleared of wrongdoing," he said, his voice low and rough. He cupped her cheek. "Are you okay?"

She nodded and rising on her toes, she kissed him. Salty tears welled in her eyes, and the emotion she'd held in trickled out.

"Don't cry, love," he whispered. "Everything is okay."

Max put his arm around her shoulder and drew her toward the fire. He repeated his good news to her family, declined coffee and cake, and stood a moment, seeming reluctant to say more or let her go.

Kelsey pressed nearer to him wanting to mesh her body with his and disappear into it, but she remained silent waiting for him to speak.

"I have other news." Max paused. "The sheriff discovered Ellie Montgomery had been arrested for a few petty crimes. Nothing big, but a background check would have discovered her record."

Kelsey stiffened. One more thing she needed to initiate for her grandfather's ranch. That and double signatures on checks. The ranch didn't need any more embezzlement or crooked employees.

"But my most important news comes from Randy Matthews. I talked to him while I was in Big Sky." Max left Kelsey standing and knelt before Darby, who now sat on the sofa beside Hank. He drew a big breath. "This won't sit well with you, ma'am, but Randy discovered Ellie was your half-sister."

The shock reverberated around the room with gasps and protests. Kelsey felt cold. That would explain Ellie's jealousy and why she wanted to harm her mother.

"What?" Darby's face paled, and Hank took her hand.

"Tim Krebs married a woman named Lisa Ross in 1972." Max rose and returned to Kelsey's side.

"We found out that much when Laurie looked up his name on the internet," Slade said.

"But did you find out they had a daughter named Eleanor Ross in 1972? She changed her name to Montgomery when she married."

Slade shook his head. "No, we missed that one."

Darby looked incredulous, still trying to take in the facts. "Then Ellie was my half-sister?"

"Yes. My grandmother's letter explained monogamy wasn't practiced in those radical communes," Laurie said. "Tim fathered several children. He was with Lisa when you and your mother were dropped at the ranch."

"What's the old saying?" Slade asked with a chuckle. "Sex, drugs, and rock and roll?"

Tears slipped slowly down Darby's cheeks. "Then why would he kill my mother?"

"Your mom died in 1988," Slade explained.

"The same year Tim Krebs got out of jail and visited the ranch," Laurie finished for him.

Kelsey shivered, a feeling of ice snaking through her body. Max put his arm once more around her shoulder and crushed her to him. "Ellie bragged about Tim killing your mother," she told Darby. "I think he wanted something from her, probably money, but your mother wouldn't give it to him. Maybe he thought if he threatened to tell Leo the truth about Sarah, he could blackmail her."

"It's my fault," Leo sputtered, laying down his pipe, as his own tears fell. "Sweet Sarah and Darby came to me in 1970. She didn't want me to know the truth. She kept her past private, but I knew she'd been hurt. I'm the reason Sarah went up that mountain with that man. To stop him from telling me and Darby the truth. That bastard ruined my life and Darby's."

Kelsey's heart twisted. She couldn't let Leo come to that horrible conclusion. "No, Granddad. Our mother had a good life with our father who loved her. She has Slade and me. Now she has Hank. And all of us are here with you tonight. Your family. And we love you!"

CHAPTER TWENTY-SIX

IT WAS OVER. Evil at Ghost Mountain Ranch had been silenced. Kelsey's relief was intense and satisfying.

She strolled outside to the porch watching Darby and Hank drive away in the UTV. The little vehicle had gotten a lot of action today. Slade and Laurie helped Leo back to his cabin. With Ellie gone, the family would need to find another caretaker for him—an honest one without a hidden agenda. In the meantime, Slade would stay with his grandfather at night until someone suitable came along.

Kelsey watched the guests gathered around the fire pit roasting marshmallows and chatting, she hoped, unaware of the true events that had precipitated the emergency response that afternoon. Several of the wranglers' personal horses wandered between cabins nibbling the spring grass. Overhead millions of stars sparkled in the big Montana sky.

As beautiful as the ranch was with its streams racing with winter runoff and its majestic white-capped mountains framing the distance, Kelsey knew she didn't belong here. Her home was Kentucky. She loved the white fences and rolling bluegrass fields spotted with round, thoroughbred mares and springtime foals.

JAN SCARBROUGH

She'd go home after Hank and her mother's wedding in August. She'd carry out her father's wishes and run the breeding operation he created.

Where did that leave her and Max? She'd already told him she didn't do long distance. She meant it with all her heart. As much as she loved him, she wouldn't lose her father's dream for Max. He'd sacrificed their love once by deserting her for his family in Chicago. He'd had his chance. She would sacrifice that love again with great regret, but sacrifice it, she would.

As if thinking about him caused him to appear, Max suddenly stood beside her, arms at his sides, his gaze taking in the bonfire and laughing guests.

"Penny for your thoughts." His words were soft and gentle.

Wrapping her arms around herself, she took a calming breath. "You don't want to hear them."

"Let me guess." He turned to her, caught her chin and tipped it up, then looked her straight in the eye. "You're going back to Kentucky. You're going to manage the horse farm."

She dislodged his hand from her chin and looked away. "I told you that."

"No compromise?"

"None."

He ran his hand through his hair and hesitated for a moment. "What if I compromise?"

"What do you mean?" She straightened her shoulders.

"What if I quit my job and moved to Kentucky?"

"And why would you do that?"

"So you'll marry me."

Kelsey felt the tension drain from her body. "You're serious?"

"Dead serious."

Her throat went dry. "Are you asking?"

"I'm asking." Max got down on one knee and took her hand. The warmth of his grasp and the strength of his fingers surged into her chilled, wearied body. "I love you, Kelsey. I've loved you for

460

years. I don't have a ring at the moment, but we can pick one out together."

Is this what she wanted? Wasn't she okay by herself? She'd created a life. She had been happy with that life. Now Max was back to ruin everything.

But would he destroy her life again? He'd come after her, climbing Ghost Mountain and saving her. She felt safe with him. More alive. Happier. She didn't have to change for him. She could be herself *and* be his wife. She could love him as she'd always wanted to love him.

"Get up, silly." Kelsey felt his powerful gaze on her as he rose. Her pulse quickened. "I'll marry you, but in Kentucky. I want a church wedding and a white dress with a long lace train. I want to leave the church in a horse drawn carriage. I want dancing and champagne."

"Anything your heart desires."

"Good." She pressed her face against his chest, feeling his heartbeat. His arms surrounded her. "Because I've waited for you to come to your senses for a very long time."

The End

OTHER BOOKS BY JAN SCARBROUGH

Contemporary Romance—Bluegrass Homecoming

- Prequel (ebook)
- Secrets (ebook / paperback with the Prequel)
- Nom de Plume (ebook)

Contemporary Romance—Bluegrass Reunion

- Kentucky Blue Bloods (ebook / paperback)
- Kentucky Bride / Kentucky Heat (ebook)
- Kentucky Cowboy (ebook)
- Kentucky Flame (ebook / paperback)
- Kentucky Groom (ebook)
- Kentucky Rain (ebook)
- Kentucky Woman (ebook / paperback)

Contemporary Romance—a romance of the Bluegrass

- Betting On Love (ebook)

Contemporary Romance—Montana Ranchers

- Brody: The Montana McKennas (ebook / paperback)

- Mercer: The Montana McKennas (ebook / paperback)
- Liz: The Montana McKennas (ebook / paperback)

~

Contemporary Romance—Winchesters of Legend

- A Groovy Christmas—1968 & 1969 (ebook)
- The Reunion Game (ebook)
- Santa's Kiss (ebook)
- Heart to Heart (ebook / paperback)
- Coming Home—a Winchesters of Legend Boxed Set (ebook)

~

Medieval Romance

- Freely Given (FREE ebook)
- My Lord Raven (ebook / paperback)

~

Gothic Romance

- Tangled Memories (ebook / paperback)
- Timeless (ebook)

ABOUT THE AUTHOR

Jan Scarbrough is the author of two popular Bluegrass series, writing heartwarming contemporary romances about home and family, single moms and children, and if the plot allows, about another passion—horses. Living in the horse country of Kentucky makes it easy for Jan to add small town, Southern charm to her books and the excitement of a Bluegrass horse race or a competitive horse show.

Leaving her contemporary voice behind, Jan has written paranormal gothic romances: Tangled Memories, a Romance Writers of America (RWA) Golden Heart finalist, and Timeless. Her medieval romance, My Lord Raven is a story of honor and betrayal.

A member of Novelist, Inc., Jan self-publishes her books with the help of her husband. She has published 25 romances.

Jan lives in Louisville, Kentucky, with two rescued dogs, one rescued cat, and a husband she rescued 20 years ago.

When she isn't writing, she loves to ride American Saddlebred horses, drive grandchildren to activities, and volunteer with Alley Cat Advocates.

THANK YOU!

For purchasing this book from
Saddle Horse Press